Stitches in Air

a novel about Mozart's Mother

Stitches in Air

a novel about Mozart's Mother

Liane Ellison Norman

SMOKE AND
MIRRORS PRESS

PITTSBURGH
2001

First Edition

Smoke and Mirrors Press
1139 Wightman Street
Pittsburgh, Pennsylvania 15217

Printed in the United States of America

ISBN 0-9709590-0-1 (HC)
ISBN 0-9709590-1-X (PB)

Library of Congress Control Number: 2001117283

10 9 8 7 6 5 4 3 2 1

An Introductory Note

In the beginning I had no thought of writing a novel. I thought I would write about Wolfgang Amadeus Mozart-*the* Mozart. It didn't take long to find that there was already a vast literature on the subject. But as I read Emily Anderson's translation and collection of the Mozart letters, I noticed references by Leopold Mozart to "my wife" and by Wolfgang Mozart to "Mama." I found some few letters to her, even fewer from her. Like most people, I had never thought about Mozart's mother. I was even startled to realize that, yes, he must have had one. Perhaps I would write her biography. I began to investigate.

I soon discovered that there isn't enough information about Mozart's mother for a biography. There are parish records of her birth, marriage, the births and deaths of her children, her own death. There are the aforementioned letters, and I found a couple of short articles about her plus a little genealogical information. In most Mozart biography, Anna Pertl Mozart is referred to dismissively, if at all, as a shadowy woman, good natured but inferior in intellect, of vulgar temperament, an erratic speller. These attributions, I decided, are less descriptive of her than of biographers.

I asked myself, what if I were Mozart's mother? And tried, with my late twentieth-century American Quaker imagination, to answer that question about an eighteenth-century Salzburg Catholic. The "Afterword" at the end of this novel lays out, in broad terms, what is fact and what is fiction.

Acknowledgments

I am in debt to many people.

Librarians, said the then-Director of the Pennsylvania Council on the Humanities, Craig Eisendrath, are "genetically wired for helpfulness." As I worked on this book, they proved his point over and over again. Thanks are due librarians at the Bancroft and Music libraries at the University of California at Berkeley; Kathryn Logan, Kirby Dilworth, Heather Brodhead, Katherine Snovak, James Bobick and John Forbis from the Carnegie Library of Pittsburgh. At the University of Pittsburgh Bill Forsythe of Hillman Library, Jonathan Erlen of the Falk Medical Library and librarians of the Frick Fine Arts Library were helpful, as were Leonard C. Bruno of the Library of Congress and librarians at the Mozarteum in Salzburg. My research and work with the late Bob Croneberger, Director, and Sara Oates of the Community Relations office of the Carnegie Library of Pittsburgh have helped me to understand and articulate what a radical force for democracy public libraries are.

A helpful clerk in a map store in Berkeley, California ingeniously found map-like drawings of seventeenth-century Salzburg and Vienna, which, in conjunction with modern maps and visits, helped to establish the lay of the land in those cities. Several physicians helped me find out about diseases in Salzburg: thanks to Herbert Needleman and James Snyder, both friends as well as doctors, and to Dr. Peter Linden. I am grateful to Chef Fritz Blank, food historian and proprietor of the Deux Cheminées in Philadelphia, for the knowledge of what the Mozarts likely ate for dinner; to the Wig Shop in Williamsburg for information on the construction of Nannerl's hairdo; and to my bibliophile friend Nicholas Lane for information on eighteenth-century anti-semitism and travel. Austen and Jane Flanders were generous with information on eighteenth-century England and French terms, as was my old friend Ruey Morelli with Italian, while Joel Tarr, Phillip Hallen, Eric Mood and Steve Fendes helped me with plumbing, waste disposal and pontoon bridges. Invaluable historical help came from Seymour Drescher, Peter Stearns, Merry Wiesner, Mary Linderman, the late Diana Forsythe, Karen Hudson-Brown, William L. Monical, Mary Lewis and Don Franklin. Mozart scholars Neal Zaslaw, Cliff Eisen and Maynard Solomon were helpful; Elaine Nienow generously sent me a copy of Nannerl Mozart's notebook. Sisters of Mercy Pat McCann and Maria Green, Sister Roberta Campbell and her sister nuns at St. Benedict's Convent north of Pittsburgh, Sister Demetria King of the Benedictine Sisters of Latrobe, Pennsylvania, and Father Bede Peay were unstintingly helpful as I sought to understand convent life at Nonnberg, where I imagined that Mozart's mother spent some of her youth. Leonora Cayard, Dirk Lehman and Richard Korb kindly helped with translation from German into English.

A different and essential kind of help came from friends who have expressed confidence in and affection for me during the years of research and writing. When I began this work, Margo and Bob Wing were singularly generous as I worked at the summer house my in-laws, the late Marian and Charles Norman, wisely built long ago in Inverness, California. My dear friend, Muriel Bennett, often rescued me from loneliness. The late W. H. Ferry, known affectionately as Ping, sent me every clipping about Mozart he encountered in his vast reading; his wife, Carol Bernstein Ferry, has never failed to express her support, as has Annette Kolodny. Many friends have patiently, demandingly and forgivingly read and commented on all, or part of, drafts of the manuscript. They are Emily Davidson, Joan Friedberg, Patricia Furey, Mark Harris, Nancy Hedderick, James Kissane, Todd May, Andrew Norman, Heidi Norman, Marie Norman, Marianne Novy, Daniel Peters, Rob Ruck, Molly Rush, Michael Sand, Darlene Sanders, Elizabeth Segel, Jeanne Shaffer, Beatrice and the late Joseph Frazier Wall. Members of my book club, a rare and wonderful group of women, read astutely and made useful suggestions: thanks to Maggie Patterson, Anne Faigen, Megan Hall and Karen Guthrie. Each of my sisters - Laurel Ellison, Linda Jessup and her husband David Jessup, and Linnea Brecunier - kindly read the manuscript at various stages, reassured me with praise and made wise suggestions. All of these generous and beloved people have kept me from making a million errors: the other million are my own responsibility.

When I needed to convert a narrative that read like history into fiction, Kate Maloy gave me sound advice. Emily Davidson edited with an eagle eye for detail and a fine sense of clear and effective prose. Todd Sanders has masterminded production of this book with a fine artistic sense, coupled with design, computer and organizational skills.

I believe that I am unusually blessed in friends and family, who have expressed confidence in me as the author of *Stitches in Air.* At the same time they challenged me to reach more deeply into what I knew. My mother, Laurel Everett, gave me the experience of *having* a mother; while Andrew, Marie and Emily have given me the experience of *being* a mother. My beloved grandchildren, Katie Rose Davidson, Reece Ellison and Kai Lucas Norman, and Maya Linnea Weiss, startle me with evidence of the genius in every child. I thank them, with love, from the bottom of my heart.

My aunt, the late Constance Ellison, left the bequest that made this book a reality.

My husband, Robert Toll Norman, is the hero of this project. From the beginning, he has believed in it and in me to accomplish it. When we traveled together to Salzburg and Vienna, he enthusiastically mapped out tours, found Mozart dwellings, took pictures and put up with my dislike of travel more graciously than was warranted. He has read endless drafts with patience and insight. More than that, he has been my dearest friend, my companion, the clearest constant in my life. This book is dedicated to him.

For Bob

It was the custom in St. Gilgen for the village women to go together into the apricot orchard in November, when all the world was dull and lifeless. In the year of Our Lord 1720, Eva Rosina Pertl, already great with child, took her one-year-old daughter Gertrud on her hip and went with her friends and neighbors to cut a branch from a tree that looked as if it had never borne fruit. She carried it home and put it in a pewter pot filled with water by the stove in the great, windowed room, from which she could see the church, the village, and best of all, the Wolfgangsee, thick with ice.

On Christmas Eve, as Eva Rosina labored to give birth, the apricot branch burst into fragrant bloom. Her husband, Wolf Nicolaus, brought the flowering branch to his wife's bedside when he was at last allowed to see her and his second tiny daughter. "It augers well, my dear," said Wolf Nicolaus as he stroked the fine hair on the child's head. "Surely the child will flower."

PART I

I

1724

ANNA SAT ON THE HARPSICHORD STOOL, her short legs swinging. Her mother had lifted the lid of the instrument for her, so that it stood raised on its tapered stick like the upbeating wing of a heron or hawk. "Now," said Anna with satisfaction, "I will sing." Her clear soprano soared and circled, accompanied by the rude continuo of her hands on the keys.

Across the room, five year-old Gertrud was absorbed in her father's book with the woodcuts of saints, her face earnest. She had completed the small task of stitching her mother had set her, and was thinking about St. Wilgefortis, the mother of God, who was not pictured except in Gertrud's imagination. She was arrayed in glittering robes, crowned in gold, her hair mixed in with flowering vines in which stars bloomed. She would be, Gertrud figured out, the grandmother of the Lord Jesus. Gertrud's eyes focused again on the men and women who suffered because of their goodness. They quickened her imagination the way music stirred Anna's.

Even at four Anna knew that music was the ordering force of the universe. Whenever her mother or father lifted the harpsichord's lid, treasure spilled out. She knew what lay under the harpsichord's lid. Her father held her up to look inside the instrument, showing her the ivory jacks that jumped to pluck the strings when you touched the keys. The jacks moved so fast - like the sprites of the woods and meadows - that you could hardly see them. Under the strings was a lacy design cut out of gilded paper and stuck onto the wood. When she sat at the harpsichord, the air grew brighter, colors more vibrant. She could hear whole orchestras in every note she played. Her songs told all the stories she had ever heard, of witches and saints and dragons, princes and queens, the fairy people and wicked ogres. When Anna touched the keys, she could conjure violins and violas, oboes and horns that spoke as familiarly as the forest creatures.

Anna's mother, Eva Rosina, left her mending and sat down beside the child, showing her how to finger a rapid passage, her slender hands darting over the harpsichord keys like dragonflies at the water's edge. Eva Rosina and her husband, Wolfgang Nicolaus, had been teaching Anna for over a year now, surprised and delighted by her quickness, the assurance of her hands on the keys, the precision and feeling with which their younger daughter mastered the exercises she was given: the little sonatas, minuets and songs. Eva Rosina was glad to take time from her household tasks to sit with the child and help to shape her native gifts, which it seemed to the mother were unusual in one so young.

Eva Rosina knew very well that her daughters, who had no fortune, must grow up to be good housewives. Even so, she was determined that the girls would also have music to gladden their daily lives. Gertrud, though pliant, showed little interest, but Anna stood at the harpsichord on her toes, grasping the edge of the keyboard as her mother tried to teach the older girl. "Let me! Me too!" she insisted, until Eva Rosina took Anna onto her lap to watch what Gertrud learned.

Gertrud was obedient and eager to please her mother, who said that every woman should be proficient in music, but it did not reach out to her, as it did to her smaller sister, to grapple her soul. "Let Anna play, Mama," Gertrud said, sliding down from the stool. So it was Anna who learned the simple songs and dances. When her father played on his violin, Anna asked to play it too, though it was too big for her. She sang lustily in a voice both clear and true, the songs that her parents sang and others of her own contriving. When she raised her voice, Anna felt the world expand around her, she and the harpsichord at its center.

Anna knew how proud her father was of the harpsichord. "Your mother brought it to me when I married her," Wolf Nicolaus told his younger daughter, his long fingers spreading out over the keys. "It was her father's - your grandfather's."

Anna studied the beautiful instrument with its rippling grain and satiny finish. Around its name - Papa said it was "Silbermann" - there were painted flowers and gilded swirls. The harpsichord had the place of honor in the large front room. One of Anna's tasks, which she fulfilled with solemn zeal every morning, was to dust the parts of the harpsichord she could reach from the milking stool her mother let her use. She admired the way the light that poured in through the large windows shone on the wood.

When creditors worried Wolf Nicolaus - which was often, because he was a public man and was expected to keep up appearances, though he was paid starveling wages - he said to Eva Rosina, "I could part with anything to pay my debts except the Silbermann. And, of course, you and the girls." He always laughed heartily, but Anna was uneasy at the thought that someone might want her or Gertrud or the harpsichord in payment of a debt.

Eva Rosina too loved the harpsichord. It was like a part of her, something that had survived the deaths of her father, a court musician, and her first husband. It was distinctly hers and spoke out in accompaniment of her own voice when she played and sang.

But of all the Pertls in St. Gilgen, it was Anna who most craved the resonant harmonies of harpsichord, violins, lutes and recorders. She hungered for the play of many voices, weaving together like those of the village children at hide-and-seek or those of the women gossiping together as they yearly boiled their clothes and spread them in the sun to dry. Nearly every day she awoke to her father's singing as he washed himself at the basin before he rode off on his great roan to see to the affairs of the district. In the afternoons and evenings, for as long as the candle burned, one of her parents played the harpsichord, which they always opened with ceremony. Each night the girls slept cradled in lullabies.

Visitors from St. Gilgen and from all over the District of Hüttenstein, where Wolf Nicolaus served as Deputy Prefect, were welcome to make and hear music in the Pertl household. Often musicians traveled all the way from Salzburg, some two hours over bad roads, to make music with the Pertls. Not so long ago, just as the mountain air had begun to sharpen to a winter's edge, a carriage full of Salzburgers had driven over the hills to the District Court House for an afternoon of music. The men dismounted, stiff from the ride, and brushed the dust of the road from their clothes. One of them took off his wig and shook it out.

How Anna had laughed to see a man take the hair from his head. The sunshine lit up the dust in the air like tiny, dancing fires. A fresh loaf and slices of a newly cured ham were set out, a dish of butter with a design pressed into it, preserved fruits and nuts and the new wine from the recent harvest. A light snow, fallen days before, had not melted from the fields, though the trees - at first embroidered white - were now bare. When there was a moment's quiet, Anna could hear the small lipping sounds of the lake on the edge of which the Pertl house sat.

Often Wolf Nicolaus and his friends played their own compositions. But on that early winter day, they played a sonata by one Franz von Biber. "Listen, child," said the man who had taken off his hair, as the musicians tuned up their instruments. "Here is some music written by the *kapellmeister* many years since, the man who directed all the music for the Archbishop's court. Listen and you will hear some animals."

Anna sat as near as she might. Sure enough, there were the small companions of Anna's life, the cock announcing the day, the hen scratching the village roads, the frog singing of a summer's evening and the nightingale trilling in the woods. They sprang forth from the strings and spoke in music. Anna was amazed. It was as if a branched bolt of lightning streaked down the night sky, touched her and lighted her bones so that everyone could see her, inside and out. You could make music that sounded like the world; you could put it down in spots on paper, and other people could play it just the way you had heard it in your head, even if you were dead by then! She would, she determined, be like Herr Biber, a great composer, perhaps a *kapellmeister* to the Archbishop in the capital city of Salzburg. She would conduct a large orchestra. Everyone would hear her and say, "Listen! That is Anna Pertl's voice."

Anna remembered her intention as she sat by her mother, playing and singing, feeling as if all the wild creatures of the forest had crept close to her as she made music. She was startled by a loud noise, someone pounding on the door of the District Court House.

Gertrud, who had fallen asleep over the book of saints, awoke with a start.

"Go down and see what it is, Anna," said her mother, standing up to tidy away the sheets of music. "I must see to supper." The sun was low in the sky.

Anna ran down the stairs and opened the door. There stood Jakob, the youngest son of Hermann Fuerbach, the most substantial farmer and landholder in the district. The boy's blue eyes were wide. "Anna," he panted. "Your mother . . . . Your father . . . . Fetch Frau Pertl."

Anna could not understand. Down the stairs behind her came her mother and Gertrud.

Anna heard her mother's cry, "No!" Turning in from the lane toward her house came a procession of farmers carrying something on a slab of wood. An arm hung down. It wore her father's black sleeve with the ruff of lace her mother had made. The fingers touched the hard November road as if it were a keyboard.

Gertrud darted around her mother. "Papa!" she shrieked.

The men carrying the door looked at the ground, never glancing at Anna, her mother or Gertrud, who moved numbly out of the way. As the men carried their burden up the stairs, they grunted and groaned softly at the steepness of the ascent. They put the door, which Anna could now see held her father, down on the kitchen table. His eyes were wide open. His mouth was open, as if he were angry or afraid. Anna knew that her father could not possibly be afraid. He must be angry. She tried to think what she had done wrong.

"Wolf!" his wife cried. She cradled his strange face in her arms. "What happened?" she whispered, her face bleached as white as linen.

Hermannn Fuerbach stepped forward, a great strong man with wide shoulders. He towered over the others. He was a natural leader, a man of substance, who held some of the dead man's debts. He rubbed his large, chapped hands together slowly. "Sorry to bring 'im like this, Frau Pertl. Found 'im on the road back o' my east field. Thrown. Horse down. Leg broke. Cut 'is throat. Horse I mean. Wife'll be over."

Everyone came, the women first. They helped Eva Rosina bathe her husband and wrap him in clean linen. They put coins on his eyes, brought food, talked softly, wept, urged the new widow to sit. But Eva Rosina could not sit still. She was a frenzy of activity, her lips pressed tightly together.

Anna did not understand that her father was gone forever. The gathering of friends and neighbors seemed an adventure to her and made her feel important. She stood by the harpsichord and caressed its smooth wood, seeking reassurance. Eva Rosina did what was needful, cleaning, speaking to her neighbors and the priest, holding herself tightly against her second widowhood. Gertrud, pale and numb, was her mother's shadow.

The Archbishop of Salzburg, Franz Anton, the Prince of Harrach, sent his men to St. Gilgen. Anna thought it was a splendid thing for these men to come so far on her father's account. She held her head high as she watched all the people of the district fill and overfill the little church. She heard the priest say what a valued servant her father was to the Archbishop and more than that, to all of them throughout the whole district of Hüttenstein, how he had helped people in need, administered justice with an even hand, lived a life of rectitude and honor.

But the Archbishop's men did not enter the church to hear Wolfgang Nicolaus praised. They went into the District Court House during the Mass and the burial. Anna, holding her mother's cold hand, watched as cold earth fell on the box in which her father had been nailed shut. When the bereaved family returned to the District Court House, which Wolf Nicolaus had built with his own funds, it was to find the Archbishop's men carrying out all their chests and pots, the featherbeds and linens, the piles of music and all of Wolfgang Nicolaus' many books. "To pay the debts," one of the men said to the widow, when she protested. The strangers cast the clothes out onto the floor and carried the heavy wardrobe down the stairs. Eva Rosina watched all this, her face and hands clenched.

The last thing the Archbishop's men took was the harpsichord. The great birdwing lid had been left open since Anna had run downstairs to answer the door and found the farmers with her father's lifeless body. Two men closed the lid and lifted the glowing instrument off its legs.

Eva Rosina, at last, wept. "Wolf said his debts should never be paid this way," she sobbed. "I meant it for you someday, Anna."

Anna felt her voice rise up in her. She ran at the men like a terrier. "Stop it!" she screamed. "Leave it!" She stamped her foot so hard she felt the concussion at the top of her head. "Stop!" She looked to her mother for comfort, but could find none.

"Shush, Anna," whispered Gertrud. "You must not make them angry."

Anna, puzzled, fell silent.

The Archbishop's men called out to one another and made rough jokes as they carried the Pertl's household possessions out of the house. A crowd had gathered to watch as mourners left the church. Eva Rosina and her daughters could hear the rise of their indignation with each piece of property that was carried out the door and loaded onto the cart drawn up below. A sullen roar went up from the crowd downstairs as the beautiful harpsichord was loaded atop the other furnishings, lashed to the load as if it were no more than a table or chair. Anna ran to the window to see the men tie her mother's horse, the goat and the cow onto the back of the cart. The people watching muttered angrily, their voices coming to Anna through the windows into the chilled room. Some shook their fists. Anna could see the Archbishop's men confer with nervous looks at the crowd of villagers. One of them darted back up the stairs. He fetched the legs on which the harpsichord had stood, his face very red.

"No!" Anna cried, forgetting Gertrud's admonition. She must do what she could to rescue the harpsichord. "No! No! No!"

No one seemed to hear her. Without glancing at her, the man left the room with the harpsichord legs. Eva Rosina and Gertrud stood like stones. Anna felt, at that moment, that she had no more power than a speck of dust.

2

1724

WHAT WAS EVA ROSINA TO DO? Though Wolf Nicolaus had been a great favorite of the Archbishop, his patronage did not extend to his Vice Prefect's widow and orphans. It took several petitions in Eva Rosina's uncertain hand-for she had little book learning-before he granted her a small widow's stipend of eight florins a month. A woman and two small girls could not live on such a pittance.

Among all the debts that burdened the widow there was one that offered hope. Not long before the untimely death of the Vice Prefect, the priest of a nearby town had asked him to permit the execution of a woman accused of witchcraft. According to the priest and several of his parishioners, this woman had caused the deaths of herds and flocks and several infants. Three village women swore that she had extra teats to suckle her familiars, the cats she kept, and the ravens that perched on her roof.

Eva Rosina remembered her husband's perturbation. "They say I must decide, Eva. There's no doubt she has a wicked tongue. She has few friends."

"A wicked tongue is not a crime, Wolf, and who's to say where ravens may rest? As for cats, if she hadn't any, they would say she suckled rats," Eva Rosina had replied, slamming the pewter plates onto their shelf.

Wolf Nicolaus had ridden out many times to this village, was gone long and always returned in an evil temper. "It is settled," he said at last to his wife. "I did as well as I could." He sighed deeply. "She will be put in the stocks and given twenty-five strokes. And Eva," he continued, his voice heavy, "the priest is to remind her husband to beat her every month for five years."

"It was the best you could do, Wolf," said Eva Rosina, blowing out her breath through tight lips. Her sleep was troubled for many nights.

Now she thought of Nonnberg, the Benedictine convent in Salzburg. The Nonnberg Cellarer owed the Widow Pertl some gratitude, for it was her sister whom Wolf Nicolaus had saved from execution as a witch.

The Abbess at Nonnberg would know of Wolfgang Nicolaus Pertl's kindness, but Eva Rosina also remembered that the Abbess, a noblewoman, had known Wolf Nicolaus as a young musician. Nonnberg was renowned for its cultivation of the arts, especially music. Further, needlework done there was a marvel; its lace was said to rival snowflakes for fineness, and both its lace and embroidery were sought after by princes and prelates to honor God.

This little city of ladies, Eva Rosina thought, might charitably provide her daughters a virtuous education, while she must earn her own bread. She thought Gertrud and Anna would do well to learn the fine needlework of the Nonnberg nuns. Gertrud's ultimate vocation seemed already clear: in seven years, she might enter the convent as a novice, though she would have little if any dowry. By that time, however, Eva Rosina hoped she might have become a favorite of the nuns. As for Anna, Eva Rosina urged the early sweetness of her voice and her musical promise with the Abbess, who was persuaded to take the girls in for charity's sake.

After a long, jolting drive in a farmer's wagon, Eva Rosina and her daughters reached Nonnberg. Night had fallen and a freezing rain had soaked the little company of exiles to the skin. The farmer left them to climb the steep, dark stairs and to feel their way along the path and under the dark stone arch to the gate house. Eva Rosina took her frightened daughters to the vestibule where, in the light of a smoking candle, a small window opened to her knocking. The face of the aged Porteress appeared behind the grating. Anna, standing tiptoe, could see a mole on the side of her nose, where three white hairs threw small shadows against her pale skin. "Gruss Gott," said the nun gruffly.

To Anna, the familiar greeting sounded like a curse. She was terrified. Stories about ogres and witches swarmed in her head. She clutched at Gertrud's hand. I want to go home, she thought. Why doesn't Mama take us home?

"I am Frau Pertl," said their mother, her voice hard and unfamiliar. Anna could not imagine that voice ever lifting in song.

Anna heard rustling and clanking and, finally, the widow and her daughters were admitted to a dim entry hall to be met by a wizened Benedictine. Her long thin face thrust forward out of the white linen wimple. The black of her habit melted into the shadows Her beads clicked when she moved. Slowly she leaned down to inspect the girls, taking first Gertrud's and then Anna's chin in her hard, leathery claw and tipping their faces up so far that Anna feared her head might come off. The old woman made a strange, strangling noise in her throat. "Ach," she sighed. "They are expected."

Anna thought that she would drown in her terror of the dark hall, where fearful shapes danced in time to the candle's flame.

"This is best," said Eva Rosina. Her voice was dry and tight. "You will be well looked after." The widow was frozen in her misery. She had all she could do to master the understanding that she had been left alone in the world with youngsters she was too poor to keep. She could not bear to think what her leaving was like for them.

"Mama," Anna whispered. "Could you sing me a song?"

Gertrud gave her sister a little shove. "Anna," she whispered, "be quiet."

Eva Rosina knelt and put her arms around Anna. "Sweetheart," she said, her voice still unfamiliar. "I cannot sing just now." She fought off tears. "I cannot take care of you, Anna." It was a terrible thing to say to one's child. "I must work. Go with sister," she said. Anna was confused. Her mother had always worked and Anna stood with her sister, Gertrud, but now her mother pushed her toward the strange nun.

The hand that grasped Anna and pulled her from her mother was the rough claw that had tipped up her face. "Mama!" Anna whimpered. "Mama!" she roared.

As the girls were led away, Anna twisted back, trying to see her mother, but her mother had turned away and gone back into the night. The old nun pushed Gertrud and Anna along, none too gently, her hands on the backs of their necks. She made soft groaning sounds as she walked. The deep shadows rivaled the night into which their mother had disappeared. The girls had no idea where they were going. Nothing was familiar.

Gertrud was nearly fainting. Over and over she said to herself, "Hail Mary full of grace, hail Mary full of grace."

Anna twisted away and fell to the ground sobbing and shrieking. "Mama!" she cried. "Mama! Mama!" Her voice echoed from the stony walls.

The hunched nun pulled her back up with her pitiless hands. "Be still, child. You'll wake the dead."

"Anna," Gertrud pleaded fearfully. "Be quiet. Please, be quiet." She knew she should do something to help her sister, but she could not tell what it was. She was afraid that she too might fall down in a fit of sobbing if she allowed herself even a single tear.

But Anna wanted to wake the dead. She wanted her voice to reach out beyond the dark place that surrounded her, to pull her father and mother back to her. When she sang, back in St. Gilgen, her father and mother had come and exclaimed with delight. When she had screamed and cried, she had sometimes been punished. Now nothing happened.

The nun took the girls through the convent's dark hallways and told them to undress and go to bed in small adjoining closets without candles. Gertrud lay awake for a long time, her body rigid with fear and longing and then fell through darkness. A tall and graceful woman, crowned in gold and starry vines, radiating light from her face and every fold of her glittering robes, caught the child in her arms and cradled her so that she might sleep. It was the comfortable St. Wilgefortis, the mother of God, who had given birth to the creator of the world.

Anna, knowing she must be silent, exhausted herself with smothered weeping. She slept at last and dreamed of St. Gilgen by the Wolfgangsee, whose surface reflected the thickly-forested mountains and whose floor was cobbled with smooth speckled brown stones that were slippery to her bare feet when she waded. She and Gertrud were not allowed to swim: only boys could swim. Anna stood in front of her house, clear in the mountain light, and knew exactly how the lake looked in all its moods. She could see the tiny golden flowers that drove snowdrifts away in the springtime, nibbling at the icy crusts. She could feel the wind that combed the grass. Birds sang on every branch of every tree, and from inside her house came the sound of the harpsichord and of voices, her mother's, her father's and her own, singing a canon. The world and all its creatures made music.

She dreamed she rode out with her father, who cautioned her not to make a sound as the horse carried them through the shady forest. Sunshine fell through the dark leaves like shining coins. The horse's feet made no noise because the forest floor was carpeted with fallen leaves. Her father pointed his arm straight to the long nose of a fox frozen in the shadows. Again he pointed to the stillness of a doe and her fawn in the speckled light. "The animals are safe when they are silent," he told her. In the protection of his strong arm and chest, feeling the shifting of the horse under her, nothing bad could ever happen, she thought.

They stopped at farms so that the Deputy Prefect could make his inquiries, gather rents and resolve disputes. He pointed out which farmhouses had the largest piles of dung. These were prosperous farms with many animals. "They will marry their daughters well," he said. Anna thought that if she was to marry well, her father should get a much larger pile of dung than two horses, one cow and a goat could make.

From high on her father's horse, Anna stared at the children playing in the dirt with goats and kittens. Older children came out of the houses or to the edge of the field to stare back. Anna and her father were always offered something to eat; creamy cheese, warm bread, fresh milk, beer, downy apricots or smooth plums. One farmer's wife did not offer them food; she did not even look up at the visitors. Her babe had tumbled into the fire and died of its burns. Anna clung to her father's hand as they went into the house, where the old grandmother in the smoky room was wrapping the little body in a coarse cloth. The fire in the clay stove in the corner was open to the room.

Later in Anna's dream, the Wolfgangsee became an enchanted, frozen lake, blue and clear though snow lay around it in deep drifts. Anna walked out on the thick ice so far that no one could see her. She looked down to see a large trout which, even through the ice, she caught in her hands. Her mother had told her the story of the fisherman's discontented wife and the magical fish. "I will put you back in the lake if you will give me just one wish," Anna said to the trout. "I want to go home. I want Mama. I don't need another house, just the one I had." And then the sky was aboil with great racing clouds. "You are greedy," said the fish, which seized Anna and dragged her down, down into the cold water under the ice. She could not call out. Her voice was stopped with water and weeds. No one came to comfort her. She wanted to cry out, but no sound came.

From that night on, Anna could not speak.

The nuns did not notice at first. They thought Anna was no more than shy. "You'll soon find your way about," said Sister Sybilla, the Cellarer, when the girls, who had been allowed to sleep late that first morning, found their way to the kitchen. Sister Sybilla was a vigorous woman. She directed the work of lay sisters, who peeled vegetables and scrubbed the floors while Sister Sybilla bustled about the larders accounting for supplies. "Two new bolts of woolen," she intoned. "Have the cobbler in for Rosika's shoes." To one of the lay sisters she said, "You missed that spot. Do it again. Josefa, give a stir to that soup. I smell it burning."

Though Anna ate the bread and drank the milk set before her, she felt empty. She knew her voice was gone. All the voices were gone, her father's, her mother's, the sounds of the lake, the birds. Music was gone. What good was a voice if no one listened?

"She is a defiant one," insisted Sister Erentraud, after several weeks had passed. She walked in the frozen garden with Sister Emma after supper, when talking was allowed. "We all heard the way she carried on the night she came to Nonnberg. I have no doubt she is a wicked and willful child, in need of correction. We had best keep a sharp eye on her." Sister Erentraud had once been a comely girl but she had a dark and disapproving look that furrowed her brow and thinned her lips. She wanted desperately to be good, but felt that her blood was curdled and her heart a stone.

"Oh, I think neither wicked nor willful," good-natured Sister Emma replied. She had been assigned to teach the children needlework, but thought it wise first to give them time to get used to their new surroundings. "More like, the child's a half-wit. She deserves our kindness on that account, as wits, be they half- or whole-, come ready-mixed in our heads and can be none of our doing."

Gertrud overheard the two nuns talking where she sat huddled on a wooden bench, her legs drawn up under her skirt, her chin resting on her knees, her cloak pulled tight around her. She sat there, chilled and aching for her mother, but keeping her own counsel. She was used to being quiet and obedient and understood that it did no good to carry on.

"Their mother was hard pressed, no doubt, left as she was with nothing," said Sister Emma, her merry face drawn into sympathetic lines. "She told the Abbess the younger one could sing and play the harpsichord. She was herself, the mother, a fine musician and no doubt hoped the little one might someday learn as well."

Sister Erentraud snorted. "Sing, can she? She can't so much as say her name. She has that foolish look about her, mouth all agape and eyes staring.

She'll come to naught. Maybe she can be taught to scrub the floors and tiles and carry out the ashes." She paused to move her hands further into her sleeves, where each was warmed by the other arm. "She cannot be allowed near our beautiful objects." The nuns at Nonnberg guarded with care many treasures of art and antiquity, some that went back to the time of the Romans.

All Gertrud could feel was her own loneliness and loss. She said her prayers more dutifully than ever in her life, imploring rescue from as many saints as she could name. She repeated in her heart what she heard the nuns sing. "God, come to my assistance. Lord, make haste to help me." The choir nuns began the divine office with these words seven times a day and once during the night. Gertrud prayed them fervently. St. Wilgefortis, who had held her that first night, appeared to her again.

The glowing saint reached out her arms for Gertrud. "Never fear," she said. "I have rocked God himself and the Virgin Mary in my arms and also her son and your mother and her mother before her." The light that came from St. Wilgefortis pierced Gertrud, who saw that she looked exactly like Eva Rosina, her own mother. "I will embrace your suffering, my child, and you will take your friends where you find them," Saint Wilgefortis said. "You must obey the good sisters in everything. You must care for Anna." A jeweled dragon came out of the darkness and St. Wilgefortis sat on its back and flew into the sky.

Gertrud, who had always been conscientious, became more so. She felt wronged when she heard the nuns disparage her sister, but if she spoke up for Anna, who did nothing to help herself, the nuns might be angry. How could she take care of her sister? What was the matter anyway, that Anna would not speak as she used to? Anna had always had more than her share of her parents' attention, because she so often made trouble. Now the nuns did not think so much of her, Gertrud, the careful child, as of her obstinate sister, who could be good if only she would. More and more, Gertrud took refuge in St. Wilgefortis' cradling arms.

Anna had been a high-spirited, voluble little girl, often punished for her reckless tongue. All day long her voice had burst from her in speech and song. Now she could say nothing, nor sing a note. She had all she could do to keep breathing. She woke reluctantly each day. She heard no familiar cock nor chorus of birdsong, for even the birds outside the convent seemed to keep the discipline of silence.

Everything seemed cold and silent to Anna. She was used to putting her feet out of bed on a scrubbed wooden floor. The flagstones of the convent were like ice on her feet. There was no color left anywhere. The small windows of her sleeping cell had thick circles of glass in them, which let in a muted light. She could not see out.

She could not tell what time it was. At home in St. Gilgen, she had wakened to the light as it came through the windows. Later, light entered on the opposite side of the house. "The sun has run across the sky," her mother had told her. She had known it was time for dinner by the rich smells of the meals her mother made. All day her mother had sung, unless she went off to help a woman in her time of trouble, and then Anna could sing herself. Now time passed according to the hours of the divine office and she was summoned by a bell to prayer, to meals, to sleep, to waking. She could not remember which corridor or heavy door went where. The doors must be pulled open by great iron rings set too high for her to grasp. She did not want to understand these new things, to be able to open the doors. If she did, then how could she ever go back to St. Gilgen?

At meals, Gertrud and Anna ate thick porridge and soup and heavy bread. The odor of cooking cabbage mixed with the smell of mildew on damp stone. The nuns moved like shadows, going and coming in silence, beads clicking, their faces cut off by their linen wimples. To Anna, they were all alike. She could not think of her mother, who had vanished into the dark night, without pain so severe it felt like a blow. It was better not to think of her at all. She tried to remember her father singing, with his head thrown back. When she thought of the music he had made, of her mother's lilting voice, of the harpsichord opened and its jacks springing to pluck the strings, a void opened in her soul. She was clenched, desolate and mute.

3

1724-1726

ON A MILD DECEMBER DAY, not long after Gertrud's and Anna's mother had left them at the ancient convent, the girls walked out of doors and stood up on the wooden bench that lay beside the stone wall to look across the broad fields to the high, snowy mountains. They could not see the mighty fortress, Hohen Salzburg, though they knew it rose above the convent, a fortress built long ago to protect the rich salt mines of Salzburg and to shelter any archbishop threatened by enemies.

They looked down on the bustling city, through which the great river Salzach ran. The river separated the larger, busier district on the near side from the far side, where the laborers - tanners, shoemakers and dyers - lived and worked. Eva Rosina, who had been licensed as a midwife in her late husband's district, now had license from the city of Salzburg to perform that office for the women who lived meagerly on the far side of the river.

Below the two girls lay a multitude of red tiled roofs and church spires.

"Look Anna," cried Gertrud in awe. "Look at all the churches!" She took her sister's hand. "In St. Gilgen, we had only one church for everyone. Here I think every single person has a church! The Salzburg people must be very holy."

Not long before their father's death, Wolf Nicolaus had taken Gertrud and Anna across the road from their house to the village church. He had showed them their names and the dates of their births recorded in the parish book. Now it came back to Anna how he had pointed with his long finger.

"Here it is, little one. Twenty-fifth December, the day of our Lord's birth, 1720. And here it is written, 'Anna Maria Walburga, legitimate daughter of the industrious Wolfgangus Nicolaus Pertl, Deputy Prefect of this place, and of Eva Rosina Altman his wife.' See, some is written in Latin and some in our own tongue."

He had shown them the many names recording the baptism of souls. There was Gertrud's name, set down the year before Anna's.

Anna could still feel her astonishment. There she was, written down in a book, Anna Maria Walburga Pertl. Anyone could read out her name. It would never vanish. She begged her father to let her stay and look at it some more and, left alone, traced the words with her small finger, trying to say them aloud as her father had.

When she ran back home again, it was to prance around her mother in excitement. "Mama, Mama! My name is in a book! Everyone will know me!"

In all the churches that lay below her in Salzburg, Anna knew, there was no book with her name inscribed for everyone to read. Salzburg seemed to her immense and ugly. You would get lost in all those dark alleyways. There was nowhere to catch little green frogs in your hands. Perhaps the harpsichord, taken roughly from her house, had been taken to one of those buildings below, but who could tell which one?

"Mama is down there somewhere," said Gertrud wistfully.

Anna tried with all her might but could see nothing of her mother. From Nonnberg, the people in Salzburg looked as small as St. Gilgen's field mice scurrying in the grasses, going about a business that took them into holes in the ground. If you were very, very quiet, you could hear the tiny hidden creatures biting on the roots of grasses and flowers. They made a ticking sound but you could hear it only by keeping absolutely still. The only thing she could hear from Salzburg were the church bells, but she had the feeling that no matter how quietly you sat, you would not be able to hear the small sounds of mice and voles.

Gertrud led Anna to the little graveyard where they looked at the stones. Who might lie there? Anna had no idea. She knew the churchyard in St. Gilgen; her father lay in a deep hole there, and she had been told to throw dirt on him. His rich singing voice, which sometimes she heard in her dreams, was buried in the ground.

Sister Erentraud, who had been named for Nonnberg's first abbess when she had made her profession, came looking for Anna and Gertrud. She felt her bad temper rise up of its own accord. "Bad girls!" she scolded, "Where have you been?"

Anna thought Sister Erentraud looked like the turtle she had once seen near the Wolfgangsee. She snapped her thin lips together when she talked just the way the turtle did when it darted its head at flies. Sister Erentraud had the same slow-blinking, scaly eyelids as well.

"You are wanted inside for instruction, and here I find you lolling about," scolded Sister Erentraud.

Gertrud was abashed. "I did not know," she mumbled. "We wanted to see . . . ."

"Speak up, girl. I can't hear you." Sister Erentraud cleared her throat and spat out her words. "You are not allowed to come and go as you please here like rude country folk. At Nonnberg, we have discipline. Now go along inside to Sister Emma."

Anna took a last wild look around, as if she might never see the sky again. Heaven had always seemed wide in St. Gilgen. But here at Nonnberg it had shrunk. Slowly she followed her sister. She did not like Salzburg, but it was better to look down at it than to be inside.

Good-natured Sister Emma had charge of the famous needlework done by the nuns, both the plain work of clothing and linens for daily use and the elaborate altar cloths, copes, stoles and hangings needed to honor God. She was to continue what Eva Rosina had begun, to teach the girls what every woman needed to know - how to ply the needle. They must learn to make and mend clothing, sheets, shrouds and other necessaries. She would also teach them how to embroider and make lace. "You must pay close attention," she said to Anna. "When you go into the world, you may need to earn your living with your needle."

"And you," she said to Gertrud, "even if you stay here, you must do your share of the sewing. One may praise God in many ways. St. Benedict told us that when we live by the labor of our hands, then we are true sisters. Of course," she chuckled, "St. Benedict spoke of brothers, not sisters. But we who follow his rule, know he meant to speak of us as well." She took the girls to see the great chests in which the oldest and most beautiful works of lace and embroidery were kept. "We must preserve the finest of the old and make new," she told them.

Anna breathed in the familiar smell that came up from the chest. It was lavender to keep the moths away. She and Gertrud had gone out with their mother to harvest lavender and then had packed the fragrant purple flowers into little bags tied up with light cord. Anna knew that lavender kept the crawling and flying things out of linens.

Sister Emma set them to work on simple seams and hems. "Here, Anna," she said, wetting the thread between her lips. "You squint to find the eye, like this, and then guide the thread through, like this, so that it finds the little opening. Our Lord taught us that a man with all his riches could no more go to heaven than a beast burdened with his load could pass through this little slit. Sometimes even a thread seems too wide to fit through. But if you hold your breath, your hand does not shake and you may see through the needle's eye, as if to Heaven. There! And now, your needle takes little bites of the stuff. Here, see how the needle comes up and then goes right down again. It can prick your finger behind, just a little, so you know where the point is."

Gertrud's fingers were like the rest of her, obedient and clever. Again and again, the radiant Saint Wilgefortis came to her and told her to attend to her duties, to do as she was told and thus to gain favor with the nuns. Gertrud took up her needle exactly as instructed, threaded it without trouble and sat to her work.

Anna stabbed her thread at the needle till the end frayed and would not pass through the eye. Her hand would not take instruction. She pricked her finger, which bled onto the linen. She squirmed and dozed and thought of catching the tiny, glistening frogs at the edge of the Wolfgangsee, holding them carefully in the cage of her hands, and feeling their soft pulse against her fingers.

Anna was wakened gently by Sister Emma. "Poor little one," she crooned, "left alone in a strange place." She held the child against her bosom and thought, for a fleeting instant, that it was hard not to have children of her own.

Anna did not want to wake up. It felt good to nestle against the heavy cloth that made up the nun's habit.

"When it comes to making bobbin lace," Sister Emma reported to the other nuns, "Gertrud is a quick study. She follows the prickings carefully, as I have taught her. Her fingers are nimble and her work is neat."

Everyone nodded. Gertrud had quickly become a great favorite, for she was eager to please.

"Anna, despite her lack of wit," Sister Emma went on, "is learning too. But I cannot persuade her to follow the prickings," as the patterns for making lace were called. "She sets to work slowly at first, and then in haste. She makes clumsy and outlandish patterns." Sister Emma laughed lightly, her face dimpling. "She is a stubborn child. She puts all sorts of odd pictures in her lace, and I let her go her own way. It's as if the things she can't say with her tongue, she can say with her fingers. And then, when the linen gets soiled and tangled, I pull it all out and she sets to again. I would swear," she mused, "that the shapes she makes speak to her. I can almost see her listening."

"You indulge her," commented Sister Erentraud sourly. Other habited heads nodded their agreement. But needlework was Sister Emma's domain. No one could challenge it.

It was as Sister Emma suspected. Anna felt that the odd figures left standing against the air when the lace came off its pins on the pillow spoke and sang to her, and she could hear them far better than the nuns, when they broke their silence. "Stitches in air," Sister Emma told her, "from the Italian, *punto in aria*." When Anna made her own lace in her own way, no one expected her to be clever and she was free to listen to the music inside her. She could hear an inner voice that darted and soared from one pitch to another.

"You should have a care, though," Sister Sybilla cautioned. "What the girl does could be held in the world as witches' knots, and then we might all be taken and burned for your trouble." Her management of the stores and supplies and the money that came in and left the Abbey took her out into the world to buy what was needful, and she heard people talk. Fear of witches ran like a pestilence through villages and towns. Had not her own sister nearly been put to death on the strength of such suspicions?

But Sister Emma would not take Anna to task for disobeying her instructions. Some intuition told her to let the child do as she would. "We must make allowances for children, Sister," she said. She made it a point to admire Anna's rough work, discerning the stories she told with her fingers before ripping out the dirty thread to wash and rewind on the smooth wooden and ivory bobbins.

Anna was not sorry to see her work undone, for it was only in the making that she could hear the music buried in the safety of her soul. She understood that Sister Emma was kind and sometimes Anna laid a few flowering weeds plucked from the herb garden on the table in the nun's workroom. Sister Emma recognized the tribute and beamed her cheerful smile on the child, glad to see this small spark of friendship.

More than two years passed and still Anna did not speak. St. Wilgefortis, who had become Gertrud's constant companion, reminded the child to be a mother to her small sister. Sometimes Gertrud's soul rebelled. It was too much, at only seven, to have her six year-old sister in care. But in return for obedience to St. Wilgefortis, Gertrud gained her protection. Sometimes, when Anna came stealing in across the cold flagstones of a night to creep into Gertrud's bed Gertrud thought the comfortable saint held both of them.

All of Anna's senses grew dull. She heard others speak as if from a great distance. Whatever she touched felt far off as well. She followed Gertrud about like a little dog, trotting along beside her, but she absorbed few of the lessons Gertrud learned so swiftly. She did as Gertrud told her, helping with the assigned tasks. Together they cleaned and scrubbed the pots with ashes, carried small armloads of firewood into the kitchen, took the smoked cheeses wrapped in cloths to the cool shelves of the larder. They gathered into baskets the harvest of apples, plums and late berries, plucked heavy bunches of grapes for wine. Sometimes the children rode in a cart with others of the nuns outside of town to the huge garden plot kept by the Abbey, where most of their food was grown. They worked hard, though Sister Agnes did not task them as severely as she did her sister nuns, who worked until sweat soaked the linen of their wimples and dirt stained their blue aprons. Anna heard distantly the words read at mealtimes and the talk among the nuns after supper, when silence was lifted and conversation permitted before vespers.

But Anna's silence did not lift.

"Could it be," queried Sister Hildegard, "that hers is holy silence?"

"Nonsense," snapped Sister Erentraud. "Stubbornness, defiance, nothing more!"

Gertrud, well aware that she was destined for God's service, made the nuns her friends, as St. Wilgefortis advised her. The nuns marveled at what Gertrud told them of the visitations of this saint.

Sister Immaculata, the Prioress, was wary. "Our task, as you know sisters, has ever been to preserve and guard the great works of art that have been entrusted to us. Enthusiasm can lead to error." She was a tall, ungainly woman with a redhead's coloring and green eyes.

"Surely," said Sister Hildegard, "you do not doubt Gertrud. She is too young for deception. Perhaps she was sent to us, to awaken us. I believe she brings us great gifts from God, Immaculata." Sister Hildegard was as round and soft as Sister Immaculata was angular and stern.

"Well then," said Sister Immaculata dryly. "But keep your wits about you, Hildegard."

"I believe that Gertrud is greatly gifted," said Sister Hildegard to Abbess Eugenia, a beautiful noblewoman who had been long in her position. "I think one might call her," she said hesitantly, "a mystic." She rushed to counter the gesture of doubt she saw in the Abbess's hands. "The child has a kind of receptivity to the divine. At first I thought it was only that she wanted her mother, these visions she has, and conversations too. But I have been convinced that it is Saint Wilgefortis herself, the very mother of God, who comes to her."

Abbess Eugenia moved her head, its elaborate coif regally on her long neck, in a way that reminded Sister Hildegard of one of the river swans. "We must do nothing to discourage her," the Abbess replied, "but you must teach her to know that our special province at Nonnberg has always been the preservation of the liturgy and its great works of art."

"Anna," said Gertrud, who feared her sister's silence, which had gone on now, what? two years? longer? "You must learn the psalms. If one of the sisters makes a mistake in the psalms, she is punished severely, and Sister Hildegard says that children must be whipped if they make mistakes. Today I saw Sister Helene lying flat down on the Oratory floor for one error. She sought out the punishment herself for a fault in the psalms and Abbess Eugenia said she must stay there through the whole day. I will teach you." She took Anna's hand. "Vigils begin this way. 'Lord, open my lips and my mouth shall proclaim your praise.' "

Anna shook her head. She had grown used to her silence. She pretended to pray when Gertrud told her to. She knelt and pressed her hands together in the proper fashion. But she had taken against God, who had arranged everything to go awry and who had the power to claim Gertrud's attention and adoration, which she believed should be hers alone.

What danger might her voice bring her? She could no longer remember how her father looked, but she remembered his words, "The animals are safe when they are silent." How often had her unruly tongue displeased him? She remembered she had been making music when the terrible news of his death had come.

Gertrud tried to explain to her sullen, wordless sister. "God is good, Anna. Sister Wilgefortis tells me about God."

Anna folded her arms across her chest, mutinous in her resistance.

4

1727

SISTER ERENTRAUD WAS DISTRACTED by a biting louse on her side. She could not get at it through the heavy folds of her habit. It drove her nearly wild. It had bitten her through Matins and Prime. Now that she had to teach this idiot at the clavier, she wanted to scream. Why should she be assigned the hopeless cases? Why should Sister Gisella always be spared the dull girls? "Here, play this," she said, thrusting a page black with closely written notes in front of Anna, who had now reached her seventh year.

Anna looked at the page dense with ink. She could play the notes. She knew them. She knew how they should sound. But she did not want Sister Erentraud, who railed at her, taunted her, to know that she knew.

"You are a simpleton," scolded Sister Erentraud, "a worthless creature, sent to try my patience. If it were not for you, I might forget the devil lives."

Anna held everything that happened to her at a distance. That way, nothing could touch her. As if Sister Erentraud spoke from another room, Anna heard the venom in her voice. While she watched the nun stab at her side with her elbow, Anna was far away, listening for the melodies and rhythms that still stirred within her.

Sister Erentraud saw that the child had closed her eyes. How dare this wretched child ignore her? "Sleep, will you?" she raged, "You stupid girl. Witches will come by night and cut out your useless tongue! If you will be so obstinate," she railed, "you will play nothing more than scales. Come. You are to go to the cellar, where you will learn to mend your ways by playing this scale one hundred times." She demonstrated a scale, one octave only, played slowly, first with one hand, then the other.

Carrying a candle, she pulled the resisting Anna by the hand through the corridors, stacked and piled with sculpture and paintings and down into the dim catacombs to a dusty room. "Now," said Sister Erentraud, her fists turned backward on her hips, "Do what I showed you."

The candle flickered around the room, full of old stored furniture covered in cobwebs. An old harpsichord sat on a trunk. Anna tried a few keys, which were out of tune and thick with grit. Some of them stuck. The miserable instrument had been discarded as beyond repair and was kept where it was never cleaned. Anna wiped her hands on her dress. Behind all the lumber of broken wardrobes and chests she heard the rustling of mice.

It seemed forever to Anna that she sat there. When Sister Erentraud returned, the candle had guttered out and Anna had gone to sleep, leaning her arms and head on the folded music rack of the dusty old instrument.

"You simple-minded idiot!" hissed the nun. "You have disobeyed me. Look, you have hardly touched the keys at all. They are covered in dust still. How can I teach you anything?" She jerked Anna sharply by the arm and hauled her back up the stairs, where she was made to stand in disgrace, facing the corner in the corridor, where all could see her shame.

How cold the Wolfgangsee was, Anna remembered. When she waded in, her feet hurt at first, then lost all feeling. But it was best to stay in the water longer, because her feet pained most when she came out and began to warm up again. She tried to remember St. Gilgen and the house that sat beside the Wolfgansee. It had all grown dim. She tried to recover the outrage she had felt when the men had carried away the harpsichord, but that had dulled too. She had been silent for a long time now and had almost forgotten why. Sometimes her silence was glorious with sound, as if larks still filled the air with their warbling; sometimes she felt only the small power of her defiance.

When the Widow Pertl had made her arrangements with the Abbess Eugenia at Nonnberg, she had extracted the promise that Anna would be assigned the best music teacher, Sister Gisella, the Chantress. This woman was revered even beyond the convent because, in restoring the old manuscripts and musical scores and in governing the music of Nonnberg, she kept the tradition that had made the convent a center of music. This was no small achievement in Salzburg, a town with a musical pulse, where instrument makers, musicians and bell founders had flourished since the ancient times, where the first opera in the German tongue had emerged. The people of Salzburg and visitors from every corner of the world came to Nonnberg's vaulted stone outer chapel to hear services sung by the choir nuns, their voices floating through the transom that opened between the inner and outer chapels, as if from Heaven. It was mostly the old works they sang, carefully preserved by Sister Gisella.

Sometimes, though, the nuns sang works written in the old style by Sister Gisella herself, though the townsfolk did not know it, for such a thing would be unnatural. Women, lacking reason and judgment, could never compose their own works.

Sister Gisella, happy to be cloistered among women who kept the secret that she composed, selected the hymns and set them to music of her own. She directed the choir nuns to lift their voices in the divine office and the Mass, one choir facing the other with the Abbess sitting on her throne at the head. Sister Gisella supervised the restoration of ancient manuscripts by the nuns and kept the library for the Abbey. She cared for the convent's treasured musical instruments, most of which had been kept in good repair even through the thirty terrible years of religious war that, a hundred years before, had ravaged the countryside and ruined whole towns, though never Salzburg.

Despite the promise to the Widow Pertl that Sister Gisella would teach Anna, the nuns agreed that Sister Gisella was far too important and busy to teach a mute to sing. "Anna must learn the graces befitting a woman who must needs marry a man of the world," decreed Abbess Eugenia in chapter, "for she is a comely child, though dull-witted, and can be trained to household tasks, as no man looks for wits in a wife."

Sister Sybilla objected. Wolfgang Nicolaus Pertl had once interceded on her sister's behalf and now this same sister had once again been hailed before the elders of her village. After days of strenuous questioning and torture, she had confessed to allowing the devil to have his way with her in return for money. Sister Sybilla was beside herself, for this time there was no Wolfgang Nicolaus Pertl to intercede. "But it was promised that Sister Gisella would teach her," she wailed. She had the distinct sense that if a promise to the Widow Pertl were broken, her sister's peril would be even greater than it already was.

Sister Rosika, the infirmarian, was a tall, spare woman with a brusque voice that might suit a man. She was known to be as gentle as an angel, but she tolerated no nonsense. "We discussed this, Sybilla. We did not know when we took the child that she was mute," she said. "A promise extracted in ignorance cannot bind us."

"I think," offered Sister Emma gravely, "that she will speak when she is ready. Her lace has changed. She is very apt with the bobbins now and her lace has become a credit to us in this short time. Her mother counsels us to patience. Perhaps," she offered tentatively, "Gisella should teach her."

Sister Gisella, aware of Sister Erentraud's slender self-regard, said nothing.

Sister Erentraud stood up. "I *thank* you for your good *opinion*, Sister," she snorted. She stalked out, knowing full well she would be disciplined. She had often been warned to govern her temper and would no doubt be rebuked before the community. She feared having to take her meals alone, not being allowed to lead either psalm or refrain. As she sought to walk off her anger around and around the orchard, she dwelt on how her father had beaten her when she had wanted to go to Italy to study music in Milan in the convent of Santa Radegonda. A coarse man, owner of two arsenic mines, he had plenty of money to send her to Italy for study. But he had raged at her and locked her in her room for weeks. Finally, Erentraud, nearly deranged with loneliness, gave in and learned the tinkling music that would show off her fine arms to advantage of an evening. When she turned down one suitor after another, her father took her to Nonnberg and paid a lavish dowry to be rid of her.

When she was fair, Sister Erentraud knew that Sister Gisella was the master musician and she the journeyman. Sister Erentraud's task was to teach the unpromising town girls, whose parents wanted them to acquire the graces and adornments to marry well. She should no longer mind; she had, after all, renounced the world. But Anna brought out the worst in her. She kept a slender switch at the ready when the child came on unwilling feet for her wasted instruction.

"How could your mother pretend you could sing, you foolish, deceitful child?" Sister Erentraud spat. "You are fit for nothing but carrying ashes from the fire."

No one knew about Anna's torment at the hands of Sister Erentraud. It seemed to Anna it would never end. When the choir sang the Masses composed by Sister Gisella, Anna could still hear her own voice singing deep in the marrow of her bones. "I can sing," Anna thought stubbornly, though inside she grew colder, smaller, harder, less sure. At night, asleep in her tiny cell, she dreamed she composed, playing storms of sound on a magnificent harpsichord whose lid was wide open, singing in a frenzy of sound. She awoke to desolation. She tiptoed across the cold flagstones of her little room, out into the dark corridor into the next small cell, where she crawled into Gertrud's bed. There, she and her sister curled together for warmth.

But once Anna got in bed with her, Gertrud often could not sleep. She worried about her sister. What should she do to help her?

When Sister Hildegard saw that Gertrud was preoccupied and wore dark circles under her eyes, she asked, "Are you ill, my child?"

"No," said Gertrud. She did not know how to explain her perplexity.

The nuns conferred. "There's something on the child's mind," said Sister Emma. "Something gnaws at her. She's distracted. Just yesterday she put in a sleeve wrongside out."

Sister Veronika, the kitchener, nodded. She had large, crooked teeth and spoke behind her hand to hide them. "She took nearly an hour on one pot today, and left a good deal of soot behind. The younger one is no use at all. She just rubs her hand around and around in the same place and pays no attention."

"What did I tell you?" said Sister Erentraud. "It was a mistake to take them. They have been naught but trouble from the first."

Several days before Christmas, Sister Erentraud, longing for the world's festivities, beat Anna's hands for her obstinacy until the fingers swelled like the sausages her mother had used to make.

Anna stumbled back to her sleeping cell, while Sister Erentraud fled to the chapel to seek forgiveness for yet another in her litany of sins. She was conscious that her name, a great gift from the monastery, should remind her to be better than she was. But demons seemed, at times, to govern her nature. She wondered if her namesake Erentraud, the founding abbess of Nonnberg, had ever yielded to such wicked impulse.

Gertrud was sent to find her sister. She saw Anna's swollen hands stretched out on the pillow and woke her. "Who did this, Anna?" she demanded. "Who did this to you?"

Anna said nothing. She did not wish to leave her dream, in which she played the great harpsichord, whose brilliant sounds swept her up like a leaf in a tempest.

Gertrud dared not take her sister's injured hands. She summoned all her strength to pray for guidance. What is it my sister wants? Who has hurt her? Why can she not tell me? Help me, please.

It was as if the wise, strong tones of St. Wilgefortis answered her. "It is her voice, Gertrud. She must find her voice."

"Anna?" Gertrud inquired, slowly and clearly. "Can you sing?" It seemed a fool's question, but St. Wilgefortis made her ask it. She wanted Anna to hear her and to answer. She looked hard into Anna's eyes, as if she could see into hidden recesses. She studied Anna's face, the twin of her own.

Anna heard Gertrud's question through her muddle of pain and despair. Could she sing? She did not know, but she nodded. The movement of her head was so little that Gertrud could only venture a guess that she had seen the response.

"You can, Anna, can't you?"

Again Anna barely nodded. It seemed a great effort.

Gertrud straightway put on her clean pinafore. "You must tidy up a little, Anna. You must look your best." She combed through her sister's tangled hair, plaiting it neatly. She fetched water from the basin and bathed Anna's face. Then she took Anna by the wrist, fearing to hurt her poor hand, and led her through the dark hallways to Sister Gisella's workroom, next to the library.

Anna felt Gertrud's touch, cool and gentle on her wrist. It soothed her burning hand. She could feel Gertrud tremble as she faced Sister Gisella, a short nun with the attentive but colorless face, a woman whose habit was always slightly awry.

Gertrud took a great breath and spoke. "My sister can sing," she announced, softly but deliberately.

Sister Gisella sat close by the harpsichord, repairing a violin. She raised one shaggy eyebrow and put the instrument down.

Anna was startled to hear with perfect clarity the sound of the polished wood, curving along the gentle swell of the belly, glowing the color of wine in candlelight, as it touched the table. The bridge was like lace cut into the striations of ivory-colored wood. The strings ran through the minute grooves in the bridge, along the dull satin of the neck to the fantastic scroll whose carving made a lady's head, her ringlets touched with light.

"I think not," said Sister Gisella. "I had hoped to teach her, but I understand she is dumb, and who knows, deaf and a half-wit as well." She smiled with apology. "I am sorry to speak so bluntly to you, but truth is truth."

"No," insisted Gertrud. Her clear voice rose and cracked and Anna could tell she was both angry and frightened. "She can sing." She held up her sister's hand by one wrist. "Look. Someone has hurt her. This is not right." Sister Gisella's face darkened. Her brows drew together.

Anna moved closer to Gertrud, who summoned her strength. Gertrud was not used to talking back. "When we came here," she said, "they told my mother that Anna could learn with you. I know she can sing." She was not at all sure this was true, but St. Wilgefortis stood close by her on the other side from Anna, telling her what to say.

Anna felt her voice return to her like a blow between her shoulder blades. It was as if a tree had burst into blossom inside her and all the branches were set quivering as a million birds alighted on the tiniest twigs, where they sang and sang. Anna could see that Sister Gisella's face, which had appeared flat and colorless only a moment before, was rosy. She could see the mingled brown and white hairs of the nun's eyebrows, the way they curled and tangled together above the clear gray eyes flecked with gold. Anna could hardly breathe, so powerful and immediate was Sister Gisella's reality.

Sister Gisella cocked her head like an inquiring bird. Her voice was gentle. Anna heard it directly, from her mouth, rather than echoed back from a distance, as she had heard nothing save her sister's voice until then.

"Can you sing?" Sister Gisella asked her, her intricate eyebrow shooting up again.

"Yes," Anna whispered.

"Then let me hear," said the nun.

Anna gulped the air and opened her mouth, having no idea what would come out. Her voice, feeble and rusty at first, issued forth in a lullaby, one her mother had used to sing to her at bedtime. It was as if all the utterances she had not made for so long were stored up, and the heavy latch to those stores had been lifted by some sure hand. Anna sang as if her life depended on it, improvising from the simple lullaby a crude aria.

When she stopped, Gertrud clapped her hands. "See?" she said.

"Yes," said Sister Gisella. "I do see."

It was the end of Anna's three-year silence. The nuns regarded the return of her voice as a miracle, a gift to be laid at the feet of the Christ Child, the anniversary of whose nativity was upon them. "The miracle was Gertrud," Anna told her mother, who had come to join her daughters before the Christmas vespers that would bring half of Salzburg to pack into the outer chapel. Anna was to sing with the choir nuns. There was a small solo precisely fitted to her fresh soprano.

Gertrud shrugged. It was hard to explain to anyone but the nuns how Saint Wilgefortis had led her.

"I used to tell you," said Eva Rosina, smoothing back Anna's curly hair, "how it was on Christmas Eve seven years ago." Her face was light with relief, for she had not understood nor known what to do about her child's long silence.

"That November, when I was great with child - that was you, Anna - I walked out with the other women of St. Gilgen to the orchard at the edge of town. I carried you in my arms," she said to Gertrud, "because you were just learning to walk. All the trees, apricot and apple, pear and quince, seemed dead. You would never think they could bear flower or fruit. But we did it every year, gathered a branch for each household from the apricot trees. It was an act of faith. I carried home a bough and stood it in water near the kitchen stove. And on Christmas Eve that apricot branch burst into bloom. You," she said, "were born on the morning after, on Christmas Day."

Anna smiled to think of the pure white flowers blooming in midwinter. She would think of the apricot, blooming on Christmas Eve, as she sang for her mother and Gertrud.

5

1729

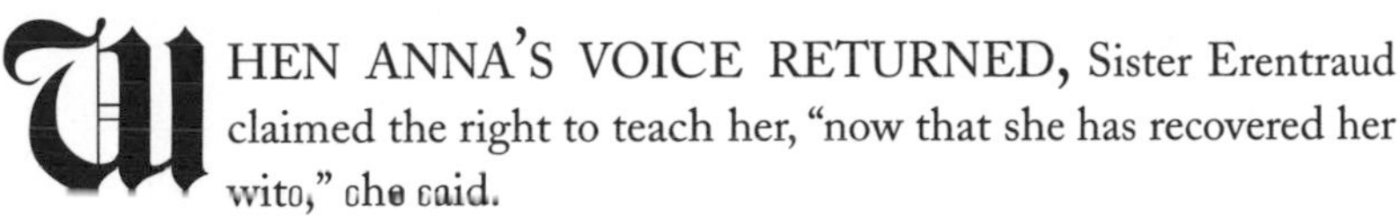

WHEN ANNA'S VOICE RETURNED, Sister Erentraud claimed the right to teach her, "now that she has recovered her wits," she said.

But the Abbess said no. In the presence of the whole community, she reproached Sister Erentraud for her harshness toward Anna and her lack of humility. Sister Erentraud was excommunicated from table for a month and made to lay prostrate at the feet of her sisters in the Oratory.

Nine year-old Anna now played on tuned instruments with clean keys in light rooms. She was surrounded now by sound and color. Each night, long before the return of light, she heard the quiet knock, a whispered "Venite" and the answering "Exsultemus," as one sister woke the others for Matins at midnight. She heard the brushing of thick cloth and the slight tap of shoes down the flagstones toward the chapel. Sometimes, she heard the nuns return, though oftener she slept too deeply, too dreamlessly. She awoke promptly. The birds, which had seemed to Anna silent in Nonnberg's precincts, now answered the cock's crow with their waking raptures outside her window. She washed and dressed quickly in time to join in Prime

Anna could see by looking at Gertrud, still her mirror and now a leggy girl of ten, that she herself flourished. She was filled with strength and purpose. "I want to make music," she told Sister Gisella. "When I am grown up, I mean."

"Well," Sister Gisella said a little doubtfully, "I do not know the world any more. You may not have an easy time of it." Sister Gisella had never in her life taught a student as gifted or eager as Anna Pertl. Genius, mused the nun, was never thought to exist in a woman, but it was genius she watched unfurl miraculously, like a flower in the spring. It sent a steady pleasure through Sister Gisella, as if her pulse had grown stronger, to teach such a one. Each morning she awakened with anticipation, knowing that she might leave her mark indelibly on the world through Anna. And yet, she reminded herself, the world is not like Nonnberg.

"Sister Erentraud says no woman can earn her bread by music," Anna said.

"Mmmm," said Sister Gisella, considering. "Sister Erentraud could not. She was not allowed. Her father made her give it up and I think she will never cease to be angry. She picks at it like a sore, pulling off the scab so that it hurts her again and again."

"Well, I am going to earn my bread by music," Anna declared confidently. "I will sing in the Archbishop's court. My grandfather did. And my father, too when he was young. We always had music in St. Gilgen," Anna chattered on. Now that she had found her voice, she was voluble. When Sister Gisella was not keeping silence, she liked nothing better than to converse with the child. "Perhaps," said Anna, "I will be *kapellmeister* someday - not right at first, of course - or maybe court composer." She rolled her aching shoulder blades back until they almost touched. She had been working at the harpsichord for several hours, hardly looking up. "Sister Gisella, Gertrud read to me from the scriptures, from St. Paul. It said that a woman must obey her husband and be silent." Anna frowned. "Is that true?"

Sister Gisella's face, laughing a moment before, sank inwards. "It's true. It's what many – most – say," she admitted. "The Archbishop decrees it repeatedly, that women should be silent in church. All the patriarchs say the same thing." She rolled her eyes heavenward. "Did you know," she asked, "that at one time the bishops bricked up the women's abbeys so that no one should have converse with the women who lived there? Nor hear any music the women made? I have thought much about this," she said slowly. "Perhaps I was born too soon. There was no place in the world for me to be a musician."

"It was the music I heard in the church that brought me here," Sister Gisella confided to Anna. "Imagine, I thought, if I could find a way to praise God by making music! My father did not mind whether he paid a dowry to Nonnberg or to a suitor. It was all the same to him."

"As for Gertrud and St. Paul, whatever clerics and the Pope may say, I have never heard God himself forbid a woman to use her voice."

"But scripture?" Anna insisted.

"Written down by men," Sister Gisella laughed, "and that is no doubt heresy, Anna. But the clergy, too. What are they but men who tell us what God intends? Think, Anna, of all the women who sing their children to sleep! They raise their voices in the fields and at their looms and spindles. They have voices," she said, raising her shaggy eyebrow for emphasis, "and those voices must be gifts from God. From where else would they come?"

"Your voice, my dear, is from God, no doubt about that. It is a great gift, to be cared for and used, for to reject a gift is ingratitude. I dare to call it genius, Anna. To neglect it would affront your Maker. Never forget that."

Sister Gisella was a learned woman, who had read much and deeply. "It is said," she mused, "that ancient women sang poetry in the common tongue so that all could understand. There was Hrothswitha, who lived so long ago that no one knows when. It is said that her very name means 'she who makes a loud sound.' She wrote plays and verse and many people heard her work and loved her for it. And think of the noble lady Hildegard, who founded and governed at Bingen. You have heard of her, Anna?"

Anna shook her head. She cherished Sister Gisella's stories. These stories were her possessions, which she took out of her memory when silence ruled the convent, turning them this way and that in her mind, then storing them carefully in her heart.

"Well, Hildegard was a remarkable person. She lived, what? Six centuries back? Long, long ago, it was. Hildegard listed all the plants and herbs and named their uses in healing so that others would have her knowledge. She described how blood goes about inside the body. She found out that taking sugar can cause a particular sickness. She studied contagion and made wise rules for its prevention. Though she herself pledged to chastity and bore no children, she understood all there is to know about childbearing." Sister Gisella's face lit up when she spoke of the ancient Hildegard.

"She was a great mystic, Anna. She had visions. She spoke with God directly, just as you and I speak to one another. She traveled the wide world, and wherever she went she taught what she knew. People listened to her. Just think, Anna," Sister Gisella chuckled, "once she even chastised the Pope! She said to him, 'You neglect justice.' Can you imagine?"

"But best of all, she composed many works, some to be sung in church in honor of saints and their feast days. She was without fear, for they say a voice from Heaven instructed her."

After that conversation, the Lady Hildegard of Bingen became Anna's ideal, second after Sister Gisella. Anna pictured Hildegard, dressed in robes as fine as those the Abbess of Nonnberg wore, traveling far and wide on a noble white horse and concocting her medicines with a wide blue apron to save her dress. She saw her conduct her own compositions, her long white arms stretching up, the sleeves falling back to her shoulders. And in the choir stalls, the singers all held sheets of music with notes she had written.

Sister Gisella had gathered news of other composers who were women as well. "I have heard of one Margharita Grimani. It is said she wrote oratorios for the Emperor's court in Vienna and that she also wrote an opera - imagine! - to celebrate his name day. And these other as well: Isabella Leonardo, Francesca Caccini and Barbara Strozzi, all lived - and not so long ago, either - in the Italian cities." She numbered the names on her fingers. "Elisabeth-Claude Jacquet de la Guerre in Paris, who died not so long ago, as I've been told. No doubt there are others. I hear news from visitors when they come, but I don't hear all there is. Some, it is said, compose, some sing, some perform on instruments. The way people think may be changing. But," she sighed, "many who tell me about these things censure them. They say it is not a woman's place and it seems to me there is more vehemence now than ever."

"You must keep in mind," Sister Gisella warned, "Hildegard of Bingen - and her followers too - were punished for their temerity. They were all denied the sacraments on her account until just before her death. The Bishop used to come, bringing his retinue, and stay for months. Of course, the ladies of Bingen were bound by hospitality, but they were eaten nearly out of house and home, which was the Bishop's plan. The ladies grew thin from their generosity. But listen to this, Anna. Hildegard bade her ladies grow more hops and kept the visitors merry with beer. And then a miracle happened."

"What?" asked Anna.

"The hens all lay double, at sunup and sundown. The cabbages grew twice as many in one place. When the bread rose, it ran over the crocks and made three times as many loaves. And the cows gave nothing but cream. Their bags almost burst, they were so full, and the cheeses in the larder tripled. "

'My Lord,' said the Lady Abbess Hildegard to the Bishop, 'you have brought us good fortune. Please you to stay for many years.' And so the Bishop went sulking away at last, taking all his men with him."

The sun had risen until it was overhead. It was almost time for Anna to go to her other duties.

Sister Gisella was in a high humor. "Can you imagine what they said as they rode back to their homes, Anna! 'How can it be, my Lord, that these ladies, who lack the immortal soul, receive such favors from God?' 'Can they bewitch the plants and the livestock?' 'They lack genius, to be sure, but they set a good table!' 'As you said, my Lord, they are hardly human at all. Perhaps they understand the cows and hens well, being close to them in nature.' The Pope himself," she said, "once forbade women music as an offense against modesty, distracting them - us - from our proper occupation!"

Anna would not hear Sister Gisella's warning nor anyone's, aflame as she was with her ambitions. Anna repeated to herself the names of these musicians, like the beads of the rosary. One day, she thought, her name - Maria Anna Walburga Pertl, written down in the baptismal register in St. Gilgen - would be among them. One day, when she was grown, she would leave Nonnberg for the court, and there she would compose whatever music was wanted.

That afternoon Gertrud and Anna knelt side by side in the late sun, which fell like a benediction on their backs, their knees sinking into the soil, rich and black and warmed by the day's heat. "It smells good," said Anna, luxuriating in the odors of ripe fruit, moist earth and the cooking that floated up the slope from the refectory. It was one of Anna's favorite tasks, to pull the stubborn weeds from among the herbs grown for both kitchen and infirmary, to harvest the dense globes of cabbage with a long knife, stripping away the tattered coarse leaves and exposing the pearly layers. She pretended that this harvest was the miracle that kept the ladies of Bingen from starving while it sent the Bishop home marveling. She told Gertrud the story of the Lady Abbess, Hildegard of Bingen and the miracles that had overcome the wicked intentions of the Bishop.

Gertrud sat back on her heels. "But do you think the Bishop really intended to harm the ladies of Bingen?" she wondered.

"Well," said Anna stoutly. "They wanted the ladies to stop doing things, you know, real things, like knowing about - I don't know - blood going about inside and writing music and . . . ."

"But surely the Bishop knew best," worried Gertrud.

Anna knew that Gertrud was different, a better person than she. Gertrud could read anything. Sister Gisella trusted her with the fragile old volumes from her library. Though Gertrud admired the decoration and showed Anna the vivid figures painted in blue and red and touched with real gold, Gertrud especially liked to read what the mystics had written. She had learned enough Latin that she could make sense of the texts.

Gertrud was allowed to dust the old paintings and statues that had been tended through the ages by the sisters of Nonnberg. Because of her visions, her intimacy with St. Wilgefortis, Gertrud was accepted by the nuns as a prodigy, gifted by God with understandings beyond the usual ken of so young a girl. The nuns regarded her with awe, but treated her as one of themselves, even though she was too young to enter as a novice. Sister Rosika had yielded when Gertrud begged to tend the sick and help in the infirmary. The ailing nuns liked her sunny face, her soft hands and the alacrity of her care.

Anna had always known in her heart that Gertrud would one day take her vows and stay at Nonnberg. Someday, she thought, Gertrud will be Abbess and all will honor her. But on this day in the garden she did not like Gertrud to be too good, too earnest. Anna hefted a cabbage in her hand. "Did you see that Sister Magdelena fell asleep at dinner today," she said to Gertrud. "Her nose was almost in her plate. She snorts when she eats and also when she sleeps."

Gertrud laughed. "She gets confused, poor old dear. Some of the sisters say she was once the greatest beauty in Salzburg and every man wanted to marry her. I wonder why it was she came to Nonnberg." Gertrud brushed her fine hair back, leaving a streak of dirt on her smooth forehead.

Anna put down the cabbage and sat back on her heels. "Will I ever see you, when you make your profession?" she asked.

"Of course," said Gertrud. She brushed one dirty hand off with the other and reached out to grasp Anna's, equally dirty. "You can come to visit. Maybe you can even sing with the choir, since they know you and you have been inside."

Anna was silent for a moment and then stabbed her cabbage knife deep into the loose dirt. "But you will have to wear the habit and the wimple," she fretted, "and you won't have beautiful dresses."

Gertrud rubbed the top of her cheek, leaving another streak of dirt. "Sister Emma says I shouldn't think about fine dresses," she admitted, "but sometimes I do anyway."

"Well," said Anna. "You would look lovely in taffeta and velvet now! Your face is covered with dirt."

"Yours too," giggled Gertrud.

Anna was glad her sister was not too holy for fun. It was good, there in warm and chiming fall air that always came just before the first frost. When they had finished cutting cabbages, Anna and Gertrud set to gathering the last of the apples and plums. That morning Sister Sybilla had said, "The fruit is full of sugar now. There may be a frost tonight. We daren't wait another day."

Gertrud and Anna picked carefully, putting the fruit already pecked by birds in one basket and setting the perfect fruit so lightly in the other that no bruises would mar what must see the convent through the hard winter. The damaged fruit would be boiled up with honey for preserves.

"I will live in Salzburg," Anna said, stretching out her slender arms for the simple pleasure of feeling how easily her body moved. "I will wear whatever dresses I like. I will be the court composer, Gertrud." She preened a little. Some of the nuns had told her she was a beauty and would find a rich husband. But what did she want a husband for? She was enough by herself.

Gertrud frowned, her fair hair blown and tugged loose about her dirt-streaked face. "But of course you'll get married Anna. And then you will have to take care of your husband and help with his work, and there will be apprentices and servants to tend to. And then children."

"Hmm," said Anna, reaching for an apple brilliantly streaked with red and green. It fit smoothly into her hand, needing just the smallest twist to leave its stem behind. "About that I don't know, but I am going to be a composer." She spoke with confidence.

Gertrud studied Anna, her head cocked to the side, her springing hair lit up from behind. "You can do it, Anna," she said slowly. "You can be different from others. If you pray, God will listen."

"I will, Gertrud," pledged Anna. "I will pray. I will make music, too."

The girls carried their harvest in to Sister Sybilla, who would direct the bruising and salting down of cabbage for sauerkraut. She would supervise the preservation of the best fruit, dried so it would last the ladies of Nonnberg until the next summer, and the boiling of the rest in the large black kettle with the sweet smelling honey taken from the abbey's combs. Back and forth Gertrud and Anna went, from garden and orchard to kitchen, carrying the baskets full of the harvest. Their arms ached from their heavy burdens. From across the orchard came Sister Mathilde and Sister Clementine, carrying their baskets and nodding pleasantly to the younger girls as they passed.

"Oh Gertrud," Anna exclaimed as they carried the last load of apples between them. "Look." An unfledged bird lay up against a tree in the orchard, its awkward bones covered with glistening flesh. Its eye had been picked out by ants. "The storm last night must have tossed it out of the nest," cried Anna.

"It is the wrong time for a bird to hatch," frowned Gertrud, squatting beside the ungainly little corpse. "It should have hatched in the spring. It would have frozen to death anyway."

"Poor little thing. It will never get to sing now," said Anna.

6

1729-1730

SISTER ROSIKA HIKED UP HER SKIRTS AND RAN up the long stone stairs that led to Nonnberg. She arrived at chapter with her wimple awry, her beads swinging. She took a moment to compose herself, but her face was still red with running and she breathed heavily.

"The pox," she gasped. "It has come to Salzburg!"

All measure of prayerful deliberation fled the chapter room.

Sister Magdelena began to weep. "We will all die this time," she wailed. "We are done for." The old woman dreaded to meet her Maker, fearing her soul's accounts were not in order.

"We will pray, Sister," said Abbess Eugenia. Turning to Sister Rosika, she said, "Tell us. How is it in the town, then?"

"The fear . . . . bad as the disease," panted Sister Rosika. She should not have burst in so suddenly with such news. Sister Magdelena was already hysterical and the fear would spread through the convent like a fire through hay.

"Many have fled through the city's gates, leaving their kin to suffer alone. By a decree from the Council, only those found to have clear skin are permitted to enter the city. Some force their ailing neighbors to stay inside their houses, nailing their doors shut. They stick up signs warning of the disease. Some flee by night with their relatives when they sicken. It is said they take them to abandoned barns or huts outside the town walls and leave them there to die without comfort or absolution."

"We must provide what help we can," said the Abbess, "both comfort and nursing. Sister Rosika, take as many as will go with you. Do not delay. Sybilla, see to it that our supplies are adequate for ourselves and for Rosika to take with her to town. Sister Magdelena, you may help Sister Veronika in the kitchen. Our ladies will need warm food and your cooking will help them in their task."

Abbess Eugenia stretched her long neck and turned her head to either side. She knew the flighty Magdelena would exert herself if she were kept busy.

"I will go with you," said Sister Erentraud quietly to Sister Rosika. "I can be of assistance in nursing."

Everyone was surprised. "You, Erentraud?" asked the Abbess.

Sister Rosika said, firmly. "Thank you, Sister. Your help will be welcome." Sister Erentraud bowed her head. She would be glad to be of use elsewhere, so that she would not see Anna in the corridors, the oratory, the refectory, the garden. It rankled to see how the child thrived under the care of Sister Gisella.

The word of the pox spread through the convent as if it were the contagion itself borne on the wind. Gertrud and Anna heard while employed at their pillows, making lace to meet a special commission from the Archbishop for liturgical fittings. "Gertrud," whispered Anna. "Mama is down there in Salzburg."

Gertrud let her bobbins go for a moment. "I think she told me she had the pox once when she was young, Anna. She has that little dimple on her face. I think that was the pox." She took up her bobbins again. "But Anna, think of people running away and leaving the sick to die alone! How can they do that?"

Anna could understand perfectly. "They are frightened," she said. "I would run away."

"No, you wouldn't," said Gertrud. "You would never leave someone who needed you, no matter what."

The nuns took every precaution. Anna helped them sprinkle vinegar in all the rooms. Anything that came from outside the convent was held over the smoke of a fire made of green wood. Sister Magdelena wore a bloodstone around her neck for protection.

Sister Mathilde looked feverish as she came to the chapter room. "My bones ache," she complained. "My cousin's wife gave me a tonic, just to be safe. I have taken it three times already."

"What is it, Mathilde?" asked Sister Rosika patiently.

"You take sheep's dung in a round cake and steep it for an hour in white wine and swallow the liquor once every day. My cousin's wife says it never fails to cure," said Sister Mathilde. Her plain, fair face was flushed. Later that day, she took to bed in the infirmary, ordered there by Sister Rosika. Two days later she died in agony.

Sister Veronika insisted on taking two or three of the crusts that had formed on Mathilde's body to bury in the farthest part of the orchard. "This has been known to keep off the pox," she whispered to Anna, who was helping her scrub the soot off pots.

Sister Rosika and Sister Erentraud began to gather a group of nuns to nurse the sick and dying of Salzburg.

"I will go," Gertrud volunteered.

"No," Anna cried. "You will get sick and die."

"Anna," said Gertrud firmly. "I can help the sisters in town. They need me."

"Some call *me* stubborn," Anna retorted. "You are as bad."

Eva Rosina, fearing for her daughters, climbed up the long stairway to Nonnberg as often as she could. She brought stories of the people she tended in Salzburg. The city, she said, was as silent these days as a tomb.

"The people go about looking at the ground, as if a greeting would infect them, when they have to go out at all. Oh Anna, I was just with one poor woman, a tanner's wife," said Eva Rosina. "She was burning up with fever and all covered with oozing sores. She had a long and difficult trial, and then her babe was born dead. Perhaps it was just as well, for after all that suffering, the poor woman herself died. I heard her last confession. I made her take a morsel of bread and a sup of water and," she whispered, "gave her absolution. It was not my place, but who else would come, as she was poor and her husband had fled from her to save his own life?" Eva Rosina rubbed her forehead with the back of her hand. "She thanked me for it, poor thing, and I lied and told her I had the authorization so that she could die in peace."

Gertrud left with the nursing sisters early every morning and returned late by yellow lantern light. Because Sister Rosika's experience led her to insist that cleanliness would protect those who worked with the sick and dying, she allowed those who had spent their day nursing to bring pitchers of water, kept warm on the back of the kitchen stove, to their rooms. Once Gertrud came in, she washed. Restless and wide awake, she wanted to tell Anna, who had slept but fitfully in her older sister's bed, about the terrible things she saw.

"Everyone is afraid," she whispered. "The sickness comes from nowhere. People cannot tell what sins they have committed. The good ones go as well as the wicked. The ones with money call a physician. Then they get worse. Sister Rosika says the doctors are foolish. They close all the shutters and nail up blankets over them to keep out the draft. They order the fire built up and feather comforters put on. And then they draw the bed curtains, even though the sick one is on fire with fever! The doctors won't let them change the bedding. Oh Anna. It stinks! The linens get all covered with sweat and pus and blood. The smell by itself is enough to infect you."

Anna put her arms around her sister. Gertrud seemed thinner to Anna, who felt that if she could be close enough, Gertrud could take her strength.

"Sister Rosika has seen other outbreaks of smallpox," said Gertrud. "She says that when the smallpox comes, it is better to be too poor to hire a doctor. She keeps the sick people cool and clean and then they sometimes get well. She says poor people are stronger, too, because they don't eat so much rich food nor sit about all day. Sister Rosika knows everything."

"What do you do to help?" Anna asked.

"Just little things. I take off the dirty linens and put on clean ones." She shuddered. "I hate to touch them. I wash the dirty things and spread them to dry. I take the chamber pots to the river. I open the windows to let the air in. Sometimes I feed people broth. Sister Rosika says I do help."

"And Anna, you'd be surprised. Sister Erentraud is such a splendid nurse. She is patient and kind. She keeps peoples' spirits up, even when they are their sickest. Sometimes she sings to them in a quiet voice. She is calm and comforting."

One night Anna woke up, dreaming that a fire burned through the abbey. The flames consumed the stalls in the oratory, the great carved altar, the precious art works, the clothes on the beds. Gertrud, next to her in the narrow bed, was hot as a stove.

"Anna," she groaned, "my head hurts." It was not like Gertrud to complain. "I have sharp pains here and in my back." She pushed the cover back and touched her loins with the tips of her fingers. "Like knives."

Anna got up and ran barefoot on the cold floor to get Sister Rosika, who was nowhere to be found. Following Matins, she had gone to the farthest reaches of the orchard to walk alone for awhile, to pray for strength and quietude of spirit. But Anna found Sister Erentraud coming from Matins. She was preparing to leave for her work of mercy in Salzburg, though it was still the middle of the night.

Anna hesitated. Sister Erentraud did not like her any more than she ever had. How could she ask her for help? But how could she not? Gertrud was in pain.

"Sister," she said timidly. "Gertrud is ill. Could you come to her?"

Sister Erentraud had surprised herself by the joy that filled her heart as she went every day down the stairs to Salzburg to tend the sick and dying. She felt strong and light. And now this child, who had tormented her so, needed her help.

"Of course I will come," she said. She walked quickly to Gertrud's room, felt her forehead, covered the child with a light sheet and threw open the windows. "Stay with her, Anna. I will ask that you be excused from other duties. I will bring you a basin of cool water and some clean cloths. Bathe her body to keep her cool." She put a hand on Anna's shoulder for a moment.

"Thank you," said Anna. "Sister?"

"Yes?" said Sister Erentraud.

Anna hesitated. She could think of nothing else to say. "Thank you," she repeated.

All day and through the night, Anna sat with Gertrud, wringing out cloths and sponging her sister gently. Even so, Gertrud's fever rose. She grew delirious, talking wildly in a hoarse voice and thrashing about in her bed. Anna was terrified.

Eva Rosina had been told of her daughter's illness. She came from Salzburg whenever she could be spared from her duties. The Abbess allowed her to come into the abbey so that she could take her turn at her child's side. When Gertrud fell into a stupor, Anna feared she had died. "Gertrud!" she cried out, and her mother, who dozed in her chair, startled and came to Gertrud's side.

"She's still alive," said Eva Rosina. But her heart sank. She had seen too many cases of the pox.

After a few days, as Anna slept in the chair by Gertrud's side, holding her hand, Gertrud said, "Anna?" and smiled feebly. She took a small broth from Anna's hands, though she had some difficulty swallowing even so thin a gruel. She seemed stronger and sat up against a pillow. Anna's heart bounded up. Neither Eva Rosina nor Sister Rosika were as hopeful, but Anna did not notice.

"My throat hurts," Gertrud complained.

Sister Rosika looked inside her mouth. "Pox sores," she said under her breath. It was not a good sign.

Gertrud tried to talk to Anna, but her voice was rough and then gone. Sores broke out all over her fair body. Her fever returned. She wept to swallow even her own spit, which ran from between her lips and crusted on her chin. Her face swelled up so that Anna scarcely knew her. When Anna touched her, Gertrud gestured feebly. "Can't see," she muttered.

Anna was almost glad that Gertrud's blindness kept her from seeing the sores that were so close they ran into one another, bleeding together so that her whole body was black.

A terrible stench rose from Gertrud in spite of the air from outside and the clean linens on her bed. Anna thought she could not bear the smell, but she could not leave her sister's side. Finally, as she sat with Gertrud, holding her blackened hand as carefully as she could, Gertrud began to bleed from her nose and mouth. She screamed through the pain of her swollen throat and blistered lips.

Sister Erentraud came and went, and the other nuns too, despite their fear of disease. They prayed for Gertrud to St. Wilgefortis, the mother of God and Gertrud's patroness. They lit candles for the sick child in her room and in the chapel as well. Anna hardly glanced at the flickering lights or at the small plain crucifix that hung on the wall.

When Gertrud died Anna felt something like relief. She could not endure that her sister should suffer such torment for another moment. But once

Gertrud's tortured body had been blessed and buried - as hastily as was seemly - Anna could not be comforted. She sank into unspeakable sorrow and affliction. On countless occasions she reached for Gertrud in the night or turned to share some pleasure or pain with her in the daytime, only to suffer such grief as if her sister's death had occurred but hours before. She would not look in the glass, feeling that the best part of herself was gone, that only dross remained.

She could not speak her trouble to the nuns. She imagined that they blamed her for their loss. She feared to blaspheme and lose their love by asking them why God would take his young handmaiden from the earth, when she, Anna, who was not so good, remained.

"It is God's will," said the nuns to one another.

Anna's soul rebelled against the will of a God who would first leave young girls fatherless and then take away a child of such virtue as Gertrud. She felt dark inside, her voice once again extinguished.

Sister Erentraud now longed to help Anna, whom she had at one time so resented. She spoke with Sister Emma. "We could lose this one too," she said. "She has not spoken nor sung for a month. I am afraid she will be mute again."

Sister Emma nodded. "She sits at her pillow as if frozen, poor little thing, so young for such trouble. She needs a task that will bring her back to us."

Sister Erentraud spoke to Sister Gisella. "Why do you not ask her to compose something, maybe even a Mass for the dead?" she inquired.

Sister Gisella looked inquiringly at Sister Erentraud. "You have ever been ill-disposed to her," she observed. "Now you ask her to compose?"

Sister Erentraud studied the floor, then raised her eyes to Sister Gisella. "I had lost hope in God's mercy," she said quietly. "Anna had what I had not, the prospect of music, your love and prompting. I hated her because I could not *be* her. Now she has lost what she loved and I do not hate her anymore. It is a burden lifted."

Sister Gisella grasped Erentraud's hand. "Thank you," Sister Gisella said, her eyes misting. "I had mistaken you . . . ." Sister Gisella called Anna to her. "Anna," she said sternly. "You owe your sister a piece of music, a Kyrie, perhaps, which the choir nuns will sing in her honor. You are a big girl now, of ten. Gertrud would not want you to languish in silence. Come, I will show you. Let us begin with 'Lord, have mercy upon us,' sung three times, and then 'Christ, have mercy upon us . . . .'"

It was as if Anna's wick had been trimmed and lit. A small light began to burn in her soul. "No," she said. "Not just a kyrie. A whole mass, a requiem."

"Oh!" Sister Gisella exclaimed. "That would be a very big undertaking, my child."

"I know," said Anna stubbornly. "But I want to."

"There are many parts to a requiem," warned Sister Gisella.

"I know, Sister," said Anna, determined.

"Then you must start with *Requiem aeternam dona eis, Domine,*" explained Sister Gisella. " 'Lord, grant them eternal rest.' "

Anna began to work on her requiem that very day. It was a child's work, imitating what she had heard sung in the oratory, rough and ungainly, but full of love for her sister and yearning to find peace for herself. Dies Irae, she thought, the day of wrath. Why, that day has already come for Gertrud and for me, too, when God sent such torments to her poor body. And that day is still in me, the wrath I feel toward God. She wrote down the notes, hearing them resound in her head and remembering for a moment the way storms had swept the Wolfgangsee, the slapping waves on the shore, the crashing thunder and bolts of lightening, the roil of clouds, and the wind that drove the rain. The storm cleared. Sanctus, she wrote, and Benedictus, Holy, holy, holy and Blessed is He that cometh, and then Agnus Dei. She imagined Gertrud wandering in the green pastures of St. Gilgen among the spring lambs. Lux aeterna, Sister Gisella explained, meant that God's light should shine on Gertrud forever and ever, world without end.

"There," said Anna after a month of unremitting application to her task. Her hands were covered in ink and there was ink on her face. Her hair was untidy and her apron smeared, but there was a pile of manuscript pages on the table, smudged and blotted.

Sister Gisella allowed the child to conduct her own work, showing Anna how it was done and admiring the firmness with which Anna led the nuns in their singing. When the choir nuns sang Anna's requiem, in remembrance of the child they too had lost, Anna's mother was granted special admittance to the oratory.

One day when Anna woke nearly six months after Gertrud's death, she thought before anything else of the composition that lay on the desk in the workroom. She had only just started it, a languorous melody that would begin in a minor key and then move to a brisk allegro. At the noon meal

Sister Gottefried read from the venerable Christine of Pisan. "All wives of artisans should be very painstaking and diligent if they wish to have the necessities of life. They should encourage their husbands or their workmen to get to work early in the morning and work until late, for mark our words, there is no trade so good that if you neglect your work you will not have difficulty putting bread on the table . . . ."

Gertrud once said something like that, Anna thought. Then, startled, she realized it was the first time she had thought of Gertrud that day.

7

1742

OU HAVE A VISITOR IN THE PARLOR, ANNA," said Sister Veronika. She hid her large teeth behind her hand and whispered, "A fine-looking young man, handsomely turned out, too."

Anna, now a comely young woman of twenty-two years, frowned. "Who?" she asked, washing her hands with water from a pitcher. She dried them off and pressed them into the small of her back, arching to relieve the ache that came from bending over the wooden table to chop onions, ginger and parsley for a stew of partridges.

"Someone from the court, I think," said Sister Veronika. "Here, pin these sleeves up for me, will you?"

Anna felt a ringing in her ears. From the court! It could only be the *Kapellmeister* himself! Suddenly it seemed important to do everything deliberately, so that she might savor the anticipation. Carefully she folded back the rough fabric of Sister Veronika's sleeves, memorizing the feel of the habit, the same material as her own dress.

Sister Veronika, her strong arms now free, took the cover from a large wooden bowl and lifted out an ebullient mound of dough, her rough, red fingers sinking into it. She scraped out the small pieces that stuck to the wooden tray and began kneading. "Go," she said, "Do not keep him waiting."

Anna pushed up some of the fine hair that always came loose with her exertions, tucking the strands behind her ears and into the braid coiled at the back of her neck. Her hands smelled of onions and ginger. She took off her voluminous apron and settled her bodice, which had worked up a little. She walked slowly to the parlor, trying to slow her breathing.

There, waiting for her, was a slender young man, about her own age - very young and wearing very ordinary lace for a *kapellmeister*, Anna thought. His light brown hair was pulled back from his finely molded face. He wore a blue coat with gold buttons, snuff-colored breeches, and a striped vest. He stood and bowed as she entered. Anna noticed his good shoes of polished leather with neat buckles. "I am Anna Pertl," she said.

"Fraulein," he said, with another bow. "It is good of you to see me." He waited politely until she sat on a wooden chair before he resumed his seat.

Anna noticed that his left eyebrow was raised at the outer edge, giving him a quizzical look. She admired the elegance of his wrists, the ample cuffs of his coat, the braid that bordered his buttonholes. She sat at the edge of her chair, aware that her dress was shabby, the sleeves and hem let down so that the faded creases showed. Her clothes had no adornment at all. She might as well be a postulant or a novice.

"I, um, believe it was you . . . the *Exsultate, jubilate* . . . it had only the initials, AP." Leopold Mozart, whom Anna believed to be the *Kapellmeister*, spoke in a pleasant tenor. What a lovely little woman this Anna Pertl was! He had not known that "AP" was a woman at first. He should have guessed: who else would Sister Gisella have known? Now he noticed Anna's blue eyes, set like spring iris under fine brows, her skin still flushed, though he had no way of knowing she had worked in the hot kitchen. Her curly blond hair, plaited and pinned up in back had come loose around her face to form a nimbus. In that plain old dress she glowed more splendidly than all the ladies in silks and jewels at court.

Several days earlier, Leopold had spoken with Sister Gisella, who knew many of the musicians at court and had persuaded one of them to slip Anna's *Exsultate, jubilate* into a stack of music to be looked over by the Archbishop's *Kapellmeister*, the director of the court musical establishment.

The *Kapellmeister,* Ernest Eberlin had inquired diligently: whose work was it? No one knew, but someone finally admitted that Sister Gisella from the Abbey at Nonnberg had sent it on behalf of a friend. "Find out who he is," Eberlin had said to his fourth violinist, Leopold Mozart, who was used to running errands for his employer.

Leopold too was taken with AP's composition, a sort of plainsong embellished with a soaring melody. Surely it was not composed by Sister

Gisella herself. "Who is the composer, Sister?" he had asked. "I have a message for him from the *Kapellmeister*."

"Is it good then?" Sister Gisella had asked eagerly. "What judgment does Herr Eberlin make, Herr Mozart?"

"That it is indeed good work," said Leopold. He had found himself squinting to see through the grill behind which Sister Gisella spoke. He wished to see this holy woman as one person, rather than as disconnected squares of face. "Herr Eberlin wants to know who composed it. I think he will give this man work when he can be found."

"No man at all," came the reedy voice from behind the grill. "Rather, a young woman who has lived with us these many years. One Anna Pertl. Her mother is a midwife in Salzburg, a widow who gave her daughters into our keeping as children."

Leopold was startled. A woman?

"She is gifted with genius," said Sister Gisella. Her view of this man was as interrupted as his of her. "She has composed many pieces for our use. I have taught her everything I know. Now it is time for her to go into the world. She is a young woman of two and twenty years, a fine singer, but better - an accomplished composer. I sent her composition to Herr Eberlin to find out how it would be judged beyond these walls." She was aware that her hands, under her scapular, were cold as they held one another tightly to control their trembling.

"I will have to tell Herr Eberlin," said Leopold had said slowly. "He likes the composition, but he has strong views about women. He will not like to find this out. He may judge that witchcraft enchanted his senses and confused his reason."

"Ah," said Sister Gisella, drawing a long breath. "But you have my word, the child has been well raised among good women devoted to God. Anna is virtuous in every respect. I have instructed her myself almost from the time her father died. He himself was a fine musician, as Herr Eberlin will remember. Everyone in Salzburg knew of Wolfgang Nicolaus Pertl's gifts, and those of his wife as well. You must take my word that Anna is observant in every way, faithful in prayer, skilled and devoted to her woman's duties. She composed this piece herself, calling on no dark powers to aid her."

"I see," said Leopold, rubbing his chin with his forefinger, "but it is no easy thing to oppose one's employer, for the *Kapellmeister* but holds the views of the Prince Archbishop, who governs you, as well."

"My dear young man," said Sister Gisella with asperity. "Prince he may be and delegated by the Church, but we here at Nonnberg are governed by our Abbess, the Lady Eugenia von Hoffmann."

"I beg your pardon," said Leopold, surprised to find the nun on the far side of the grill so prickly.

Leopold had gone back to the *Kapellmeister* with the unwelcome news that the composer of the *Exsultate, jubilate* was a woman, while Sister Gisella had rushed to Anna, who, sitting over her lace, had fallen to dreaming, her head on her hand. "He likes it," said Sister Gisella. "The *Kapellmeister* sent his man to say he likes the *Exsultate, jubilate*!"

Anna jumped up, the bobbins clattering and tangling as they fell from her lap, and strode up and down the room, which was all at once too small, too gray, too still. Her dress felt tight. Her shoes pinched. There would be work straightening the bobbins, but she would attend to that later.

Sister Gisella warned, "You must not get your heart set on anything, Anna, for Herr Eberlin has read and taken in St. Paul and all those who came after. He thinks no woman can compose."

"But he saw what I did!" Anna rejoiced. "And he liked it! Now, when I go out . . . ."

"Which must be soon, my child," said Sister Gisella. "It is time - past time - for you to leave us, to go back to the world. We have been selfish, keeping you among us when you are not meant for this life. You are a woman now, and winsome. I think perhaps you must find a good husband and give him children."

Anna had stayed outside the convent from time to time during illnesses, recovering at her mother's modest apartment next to the Town Hall. Following Gertrud's death, Eva Rosina allowed no one else to attend to Anna in sickness. These periods, however, were brief "Can I have music outside?" Anna asked. "Can I compose?"

Sister Gisella was contrite. She had encouraged the girl. "Listen to me," she said. "Listen. I do not know if you can have music." She spoke slowly, as if she pulled heavy buckets up from a deep well. "Some women have made a life for themselves with music. I have told you their names and stories so far as I know them. But pay attention, Anna. It is hard, very hard, and it may not be possible."

Sister Gisella paused, balked because she herself could not really understand what she was saying. It made no sense to her to say, this is the work of a male, this of a female, when you had proof under your very nose that music was present in each case. What was it that got in the way?

"Anna," said Sister Gisella, taking her protégé by the shoulders. "Listen to me. You have no one to sponsor you, no one to be godfather to your music. There is no one to urge your case with those who have position. You may have to settle for something else altogether." She thought, I must confess my transgression at the chapter of faults. I have indulged my own fancies with this child, caught her up in my passion to her detriment. I have meant her to do what I could not, used her for my own purposes. She should have been schooled for kitchen work - and her lace is very fine by now - and perhaps a little, polite music, nothing more.

"Sister," interrupted Anna, who could not hear her mentor's warnings. "I must go out of doors for awhile. I cannot stay in just now."

"Go then," said Sister Gisella.

Anna had gone singing and laughing, weeping a little, then singing and laughing again, to the far end of the orchard, feeling the strength of her slim young body as she strode along, swinging her arms. I can do anything, she had thought, hugging herself, anything I like! I am ready to live in the world!

It had been several days since Sister Gisella had brought that news that so rejoiced and unsettled Anna and she had hardly touched the ground since, refusing to hear her mentor's warnings. Now she sat in the parlor, her heart pounding in her rusty dress, as plain as a serving maid's, visited by the *Kapellmeister* himself, who had seen and liked her humble composition. Who would have thought he would be so handsome or so young! Her cheeks were flushed and her breath come too fast.

Leopold found his tongue too big for his mouth. He was sent with a message, but he could think only of this young woman's beauty, which caused him to be aware of the rush of his blood through his veins. He did not wish to tell her what Eberlin had bade him say, but he had been sent for that purpose alone and had no freedom in the matter. "Pardon me," he apologized. "I have not introduced myself. I am Leopold Mozart, newly appointed fourth violinist in the *kapell* orchestra and," he laughed, "errand boy for the *Kapellmeister* - not," he hastened to add, his face flushing, "not that I am anything but proud . . . no, no . . . I mean, it is a pleasure . . . ." He saw Anna's face fall and wondered why.

Anna had been so sure it was the *Kapellmeister* himself who had come to speak with her. "You are not . . . ? Herr Eberlin did not . . . ?" This Leopold Mozart, well disposed as he was, did not hold a high position.

Leopold was covered with confusion. "No," he said. "My mistake. I am sorry. It is my honor," he stammered, "no, that is not what I mean. I mean that Herr Eberlin, the *Kapellmeister*, says I must say that, I mean it is not my view, but I have no choice. Herr Eberlin holds that a woman cannot compose."

"But I can!" Anna exclaimed. "I did. He saw what I did!"

Leopold felt himself torn. How could he disappoint this enchanting creature? But how could he contravene his orders? "Sister Gisella told me you sing?" he inquired.

"Oh yes," Anna said, "yes, of course. I have had the best tuition. Sister Gisella says she has taught me everything."

"Will you be leaving the Abbey?" asked Leopold.

"Yes," said Anna. "Very soon. I will live with my mother."

"Yes, good," said Leopold. "Then perhaps you can sing for Herr Eberlin. He needs sopranos - are you soprano? And then maybe I can help . . . ."

"Yes," Anna said. "Yes, I will sing for Herr Eberlin." The bell for dinner rang far off in the Refectory. "I must go in to dinner now. Thank you, Herr Mozart. Please tell Herr Eberlin I can sing." Singing was not composing, of course, but it would be a start.

And so it was set in motion that Anna would leave Nonnberg to live with her mother. Sister Emma arranged commissions for Anna's lacework with several noble houses, and Sister Erentraud was glad to give Anna some of her music pupils. "They will not have to climb all those stairs up from the town to the convent if you can go to them," she explained. Sister Gisella presented to Anna her own treasured copy of *Gradus ad Parnassum*, the treatise on composition by Johann Josef Fux. "This man - some call him the 'Emperor of Music' - has guarded polyphony, Anna, as we sisters of Nonnberg have cared for all the arts when barbarians have threatened. He has protected counterpoint. He is a good man, Anna. See here, he has written, 'My object is to help young persons who want to learn. I knew and still know many who have fine talents and are more anxious to study; however, lacking means and a teacher, they cannot realize their ambition, but remain, as it were, forever desperately athirst.'"

Anna took the little volume, caressing it, unable to speak. She looked at the beloved faces around her. Sister Gisella had sustained her more than bread. Sister Emma had stayed with her through her darkest times. Sister Erentraud had hated her at first, then helped her when Gertrud suffered and died. The others had given her their skills and affection. Nonnberg had been her home for eighteen years. Anna knew no other. These women were her mothers. But down the long flight of stone steps - one hundred and forty-four, said Sister Sybilla, who climbed them often enough to know - lay her destiny, the court that needed sopranos and the good looking Herr Leopold Mozart who would assist her.

PART 2

8

1742–1745

ANNA RAN QUICKLY DOWN THE STONE STAIRWAY from Nonnberg full of confidence. Carrying her small clutch of possessions in a bundle, she strode into the market square. She had often visited her mother in Salzburg, but now she would live, earn her bread and make music in this great noisy city. Everywhere there was scaffolding where buildings were being put up and repaired. Workmen called to one another, laughing and cursing, hammering, chipping stone with their mallets and chisels. From every direction carriages and wagons clattered on the cobbles. She had never seen so many people as had congregated to buy cheese and butter, fruits and cabbages, yard goods and needles, shoe buckles, saddles and gloves. Eagerly she made her way through the narrow alleys toward her mother's *pensione*.

Anna saw people of every shape and size, some wearing the finest of silks and velvets, encrusted with braid and embroidery, some dressed plainly in wool and still others wearing homespun, coarse and stained. She saw familiar German faces, both red and pale, but also swarthy visages. She was amazed to see a man with a skin so black it shone blue. Around her floated scraps of conversation, mostly German, but there were other tongues she could not understand. Odd phrases of music floated from open windows in the buildings that bordered the streets, mixing with all the perfumes from shops, stalls and invisible kitchens. There were so many lives in the city, such a warp and weft of commerce, dealings and gossip!

She entered the Judengasse, the dark alley where Jews lived, with some trepidation, passing a bearded figure wearing a round hat and a long black coat with a badge that the nuns had told her Jews must wear. She had heard of the Jews, who had been banished from Salzburg in perpetuity centuries earlier. First, said Sister Rosika, the Jews had stolen communion wafers, taken them to the synagogue and stabbed them, so that the blood of Our Lord burst forth, then burned the broken wafers. Some had been punished, burned at the stake, the rest sent away. When later they were allowed to return, they stole a precious likeness of the Virgin Mary, and after that, no Archbishop would permit them to live in Salzburg. Still, said Sister Emma, because Jews could charm money from trees, some few Hebrew merchants or dealers in coins were allowed to stay in Salzburg at the Archbishop's pleasure, though subject to a heavy tax. Jews were accursed people, said Sister Sybilla, not people at all really. Though they would not eat pork, they kept sows to suckle their offspring. There was a wooden statue showing this very outrage in the Town Hall.

Anna's pleasure and excitement contended with fear. Propelled forward by her prospects, she drew back from the unknown dangers of the world. She was tempted to turn and run back up the Nonnberg steps in search of the familiar order. Here was a city full of possibility, and yet she was a stranger, unpracticed in its ways. She made herself go on until she reached Getreidegasse, a wider, busier street, where she climbed the stairs to her mother's apartment in the building next to the Town Hall.

The *pensione* she shared with her mother was darker, tidier and more plainly furnished than Anna remembered. She realized that she had never once thought of her mother's life, which had been so bright, fair and spacious in St. Gilgen, and was now so much reduced. Her mother's brother, a commercial man of fierce religious rectitude just down the river in Mülln, had helped Eva Rosina in small ways, but hard work and limited income had taken their toll. Her mother looked, Anna thought, as worn as an old shoe, a little turned up at the edges, both brittle from use and softened by wear. When it came to daily life, neither mother nor daughter knew the other nor the other's ways.

Herr Mozart was as good as his word. He sought her out and arranged an audition with *Kapellmeister* Eberlin, who was grudging in approval. "The voice is pleasing," admitted the *Kapellmeister*, turning to Mozart. He was a little man with a dry voice, the marks of the pox graven into his face. He wore a heavily powdered wig and yellowed lace.

Anna was tongue-tied. Herr Mozart had called him a kind man of superior talents, but she could not forget that he had liked her composition when he thought it was by a man yet found it lacking when he knew a woman had composed it.

Leopold had not the standing to make demands, but he pressed his superior. "Is not Fraulein Pertl's voice true and pure?"

"Yes," conceded Eberlin, "The voice is good, and the ear, um, yes."

"And you have need of a strong soprano," Leopold urged.

"Yes," said the *Kapellmeister*, "soprano, yes. She can sing, Mozart, but only from time to time. The choir boys will do for the most part. And counter tenors. Never pay a woman money. They get notions. Then, nothing but trouble and disruption. See to it she comes promptly at the assigned hour." He flapped his hand. "Woman is a flighty thing. Never forget it, Mozart."

As if I were not right here, Anna thought indignantly, to speak to directly! Herr Mozart glanced at her, lifting an eyebrow in complicity. Anna held her tongue, grateful for the eyebrow. This Leopold Mozart, who seemed well-disposed toward her, might serve as her advocate. Perhaps with his help and over time, the *Kapellmeister* would be won over to see that she could compose as well. Singing was her best hope.

Leopold saw her out of Eberlin's sanctuary in the court precincts.

"He did not once look at me," Anna laughed shakily, "nor address his remarks to me."

"I noticed," sympathized Leopold. "But he is a remarkable man, Fraulein - may I call you Anna? You cannot imagine how swiftly he composes. He is, I admit it, old-fashioned, decidedly old-fashioned in his views, and he must also serve his master, the Archbishop."

Anna sighed. At Nonnberg she had known what to do. Here in Salzburg, she was a fish out of water and must take what advice she could. She sighed again. If the fourth violinist could call her Anna, she could be as familiar. "Leopold," she said shyly, putting out her hand to him, "thank you."

Leopold had not thought he would marry. His mother, a stern fixture of the Catholic faction in Augsburg, had intended him for the celibate life of priesthood. Every time his eye espied female beauty, his mother loomed reproachfully. He dreaded to cross her again, as he had when he left the city of his birth. "I will call on you, Anna," Leopold promised, defying the specter of his mother. Already his heart was caught up in the snares of Anna's beauty.

Leopold kept his promise, coming to Anna when her mother was also at home, and then, as the weeks became months, more frequently, often contriving to meet her as she came and went from court, a student's house or a household which commissioned her lace. He often walked with her, inquiring about her music, telling her about his work.

Anna had plenty to do. Thanks partly to Sister Erentraud, partly to Leopold's efforts, it was not long before she was in demand to teach the keyboard and singing to young ladies in burghers' families. As her lace was admired, her commissions multiplied. Her small income, added to her mother's, kept them both in modest comfort, their simple board augmented by the nuns at Nonnberg, who sent with her fruit and cheese, eggs and sometimes a hen for stewing when she took her news up to her old friends.

Anna and her mother went about decently. Both were clever with their needles and were able to make and mend what they needed. They were able to buy more wood for the stove than Eva Rosina had afforded alone. "Finally," she said, "I am able to stay warm in the winter," for though she received firewood along with her pay from the city, it had never been enough. Anna liked her freedom, the opportunity to walk vigorously through the streets, to provide for herself, to assist her mother. Though she worked hard, she found time to compose small liturgical works - a Gloria, a Kyrie, a Benedictus, a hymn or two, some settings for the psalms - which she took to Sister Gisella, whose choir nuns often performed what her protégé devised.

From the beginning, Anna saw in Leopold her chance to thrive as a musician. He had made himself indispensable to the *Kapellmeister* and, because of his excellent education and quick wit, consorted with influential men at court. Shyly, hesitantly, Anna showed Leopold her compositions.

The young man fell under Anna's spell. Though strong, Anna appeared delicate, supple, narrow of waist and nicely curved. She had a fine rosy skin, a slender neck, fair curling hair, and deep blue eyes well-set under arched brows. Her full lips curved with good humor, and her Hapsburg nose suggested to him that she would move as easily among the nobility as he himself intended to do. But he understood that to win her, he must love her music as well as her beauty. Together they spent many an hour discussing this canticle and that hymn, this phrase and that cadence. "I have given your Gloria and the Benedictus to Eberlin," he confessed. "I made bold to put my name on them, for he would not look at them if he thought they were yours."

Anna was of two minds about this ruse. On the one hand, she wanted her music performed, no matter who had the credit. On the other, she wanted for herself whatever notice her work might bring. As it was, Leopold received plentiful praise. "It is the best you have done," said Eberlin in her hearing, "and the little Fraulein Pertl handled the soprano part very nicely, indeed." The Archbishop himself applauded his fourth violinist and complimented him with a present of several shillings. "Fine work, Mozart," said the Prince Archbishop. "I judge that you will go far."

Leopold gave the money to Anna. "It is yours," he said, delighted that he could secure her gratitude.

In fair weather, Anna and Leopold walked along the river, both upstream and down. They crossed the bridge and walked up the steep southern road to the town gate. "I remember so little about St. Gilgen," Anna lamented, for her birthplace lay some two or three hours by horseback along the same road. "I would like to go back. I remember that my father took me to the church to see my name in the parish record book, and I remember the brown pebbles in the lake and the ducks. I remember . . . ." She did not know whether the images she sometimes saw were real or made up.

"Someday," Leopold declared boldly, "I will take you there." He would do whatever she wished. What he wanted was to seize her, cover her with kisses, ask her to marry him on the spot. He had spoken to Eberlin in general terms about marriage, but his superior made it clear that Leopold should not consider changing his condition for some time. Leopold knew he must govern his affections.

Anna laughed. "I would like that," she said. Her nerve ends tingled when his sleeve brushed hers. "Have you always lived here?" she inquired.

"No, no," said Leopold, "I come from Augsburg. My father was a master bookbinder from a line of architects and stone masons. I left just after he died."

"Why?" Anna asked.

Leopold looked out over Salzburg and remembered how he had come to live in this city of enlightened thought. He had left his mother to grieve her husband's loss and her son's defection, raging angrily about both. She blamed him for his father's death and predicted that the faithless Leopold would soon have her death on his conscience as well. "My father wished me to join him in bookbinding, for I was the eldest, but my mother would have me be a priest, and she prevailed. I learned what a priest must know at the Gymnasium and the Lyceum - the ancient philosophers, the church fathers, languages. But I wanted the sciences as well. I wanted to know about the steam engines that drained water from the shafts of the mines. I wanted to know about the Fuggers - Jews, you know, who know where to put money so it will yield still more wealth. It is Fuggers who made the mines possible. I wanted to know about medicine, about the humors in the body, how farm land is drained, how the planets move in the heavens," he shook his head impatiently, like a proud horse, "base metals, how they can be changed to precious ones, how levers can lift great weights. I would rather have been apprenticed in the bookbindery than consort with the priests, who were so full of superstition and narrow judgment. What saved me was music. I sang, played the violin, composed."

"Augsburg is a beautiful city, a free imperial city. All manner of people live there - Calvinists, Lutherans, even Jews. And both Catholics and Lutherans may sit on the Council, though neither likes the other. My mother cannot abide anyone but Catholics and prefers those highly placed. She would have me be a prince of the church, even though we were not nobility."

Anna could hear the anger in Leopold's voice.

"I had reached my seventeenth year," he went on, "when my father died suddenly of an apoplexy."

"Oh," Anna exhaled. "I was only four when my father died. I thought the world had ended. I lost my voice." She did not know how to explain what had befallen her with the death of her father.

"And I found mine," said Leopold somewhat grimly. "I took my sorrow to Father Sembler, who had been so kind to me at the Lyceum. He was just then preparing to remove to the university in Salzburg, where, he said, all the newest thinking was professed. Would I accompany him, pursue my studies in Salzburg?" Leopold passed his hand across his eyes. "Strange to say, I felt like a prisoner pardoned. I knew then that I had an aversion to being a priest and that I should have no choice if I stayed in Augsburg." He shuddered, "Even so, it was hard to leave."

His mother had stormed and shrieked: he was now the head of the family; he was forbidden to leave her in their grief and loss; what of his duty to her, who had given him birth in pain and suffering? His younger brothers, apprenticed to their father's bookbinding trade, looked on and said nothing. The uncles came in thundering, appealed to the memory of Georg Mozart, master bookbinder, and ordered their nephew to mind his mother.

But they only strengthened Leopold's resistance. "I had read those who say that liberty is a great good, and I believed them - believe them still," he told Anna. "I persuaded an ironmonger to carry me with a full load to Salzburg, where I arrived with nothing at all in my purse, and I begged my entrance fee of Father Sembler's friends."

Father Sembler had been Leopold's salvation. Because he was considered a distinguished philosopher, everyone of any importance wanted him for dinner, and the priest, who often arrived with Leopold in tow, persuaded his hosts that to employ the young man in miscellaneous secretarial tasks would be a mark of distinction. Leopold made himself useful and learned to carry servitude like rank. He kept his linens mended and snowy white, his shoes cobbled and shined, his fingernails trimmed and clean. He did not like to wear a wig, which, he said, attracted vermin and made his head too warm, but he kept his hair clean and well-tied back. He ate daintily at table, using a fork with grace. He appeared to be a man to take into account.

"I did well, received a public commendation at the end of the first year," Leopold laughed. He held out his hand to Anna and together, as no one was anywhere nearby to see and gossip, they walked hand-in-hand, back down toward the river and their haunts on the other side of town.

What happened next, Anna wondered. How did he come by music? But Leopold was not yet sure enough of her affection to tell her of the revolution in his heart.

"Where have you been so late?" Eva Rosina fussed, when Anna came in, flushed from her long walk.

"Walking with Leopold Mozart," Anna admitted.

Eva Rosina smiled. She thought that Anna would do well to marry an artisan like Leopold, one who held a position at court. To be sure, such a one could not expect riches, but he seemed to Eva Rosina a steady young man, intelligent, well-educated, with a sensible head on his shoulders. Anna brought no dowry but her beauty to any union. Eva Rosina only hoped

Anna would not burden Leopold with her nonsense about composing. If so able and promising a man as the late Wolf Nicolaus could not earn his bread by music, how could his daughter hope for more?

9

1745-1747

OHHH!" ANNA EXCLAIMED, "THAT IS SALT?" Leopold chuckled. He liked to be able to explain things to Anna, who, because of her long years at Nonnberg, found the world so new and interesting. By torchlight the salt rock under the earth was brilliantly colored-yellow, red, blue and white.

"I shall think of its real color whenever I make sauerkraut," said Anna, "or salt meat for winter or season a stew. I had not imagined!"

"They dig it out in great chunks," said Leopold. A train of small boys grunted and moved past Anna and Leopold, laboring under their burden of dirt, rocks and raw salt. Anna had a quick glimpse of their thin, grimed faces, set and blank. "They will take it to the pit I showed you, filled with fresh water. The rocks and dirt will fall to the bottom and the clean brine will go through pipes to where it will be boiled in iron pans to make the whitest salt in the world. It goes to every city in Europe."

"Mama says that if you put salt on the wood, the fire will burn all colors," Anna said, "but she has never tried it for herself, not wishing to waste what she has paid for."

It was rare for Leopold to have a holiday from court, but the Archbishop was traveling away from town and had left much of his establishment behind. Leopold had seized on the occasion to show Anna some of the wonders just outside of Salzburg. Now they must hurry back to town for Wenzel and Marianna Gilowsky had planned an afternoon's entertainment, during which compositions by both Anna and Leopold were to be played. No one was to know, of course, that Anna had composed the trio sonata for the occasion. Leopold would take whatever credit there was: it was better if word did not get out that Anna composed, since both the Archbishop and the *Kapellmeister* would frown on it. The disapproval of either might prevent Anna from singing at court and might even affect Leopold's advancement, for he wore his heart on his sleeve where Fraulein Pertl was concerned.

Wenzel Gilowsky, the court surgeon, was one of Leopold's closest friends, and his wife, Marianna, had quickly developed an affection for Anna, which she reciprocated. The Gilowskys were generous with hospitality, and Leopold was often invited for an afternoon of cards or music, or to shoot air guns at gaily painted targets for money. Eva Rosina often called for Wenzel when she could not deliver a babe who presented sideways or breech. "He is that rare surgeon," she told Anna, "who will use the new instruments to turn and grasp the child, but always as a last resort and with gentle care. I have seen infants torn to shreds by less cautious doctors using forceps."

Though a physician had accompanied the Archbishop on his journey, Wenzel was not the one who had been required to go. "While the cat's away," he said gaily to Leopold, "the mice will play music. You must come, my dear Leopold, bearing your finest compositions. Anna too, and of course her mother is welcome as well. I will invite all the best conversation in Salzburg."

Anna dressed carefully in her newly-stitched light wool, a becoming gray, trimmed with lace fichu and flounces of her own making. She was conscious that she looked well in it, that the boning she had sewn into the bodice showed off her straight back and narrow waist. She imagined taking a bow when her trio sonata was performed, but knew that, instead, she would applaud Leopold.

"No wonder Leopold is besotted!" exclaimed Marianna, greeting Anna at the door. Marianna, flushed and dewy, had hair almost as red as the sunset. It framed her face in a thousand quivering curls. Her rounded form was neat and stylishly turned out in thin ivory wool with rose-colored trim. "You must meet our special friend, Anna." She lowered her voice. "She is a Jewess. I count on you to be kind to her." She took Anna's arm and drew her to a tall woman wearing an elegant black dress of foreign cut and a splendidly embroidered shawl. "Margarethe Arnstein," said Marianna, "may I present my dear friend Anna Pertl, whom you will love as I do."

The pressure on Anna's arm told her to sit beside this exotic woman, whose heavily lidded, dark eyes had, Anna thought, a tragic cast to them, and whose dark cloud of hair was caught back in a coil studded with pearls. Anna caught her breath as she saw that the black stuff of the Fraulein Arnstein's dress was not really black, but such an intricate texture of deep colors as she had never seen before. "I beg your pardon," said Anna, realizing that this woman might easily misconstrue her gasp, for the few Jews to set foot in Salzburg rarely entered a Christian household. "I was taken by surprise. The stuff in your dress . . . ."

"It is remarkable, is it not?" said Margarethe, glancing at Anna from hooded eyes. "My father brought it from Persia. The shawl also."

"He travels about then?" Anna asked.

"Yes," said Margarethe. She looked about the salon, which had filled with people, and found him, indicating him with a nod of her head. He was a fleshy man, not dressed like a Jew at all, but like any other wealthy Salzburg merchant. Neither, noted Anna, wore the badge that marked their race. "He is a dealer in precious jewels and coin, sojourning in Salzburg to assist your Prince Archbishop in the matter of a loan."

"You travel where he does?" asked Anna.

"Yes," said Margarethe. "I am not married and my mother is deceased. I accompany him as his hostess and assistant."

"I think it must be wonderful to see other places," mused Anna. "Sometimes Herr Mozart - the one standing over there, by the harpsichord in the blue coat - introduces me to travelers." She was surprised to find that Fraulein Arnstein, though of the Hebrew race, was a presentable and intelligent young woman.

"I saw you come in together. You make a handsome couple. He carries himself well," said Margarethe. She flushed. "Not," she breathed quickly, "that it is my place to pass judgment . . . ."

"No, no," said Anna, putting her hand on Margarethe's arm, "please, you are among friends here. Otherwise Wenzel and Marianna would not have invited you."

Margarethe nodded. "Thank you," she said quietly. "Sometimes we are not wanted. Yes, I do like to travel. For the most part, anyway. You never know, of course, what you will find. There are awkward situations." She flushed.

"Look," Anna said, "they are bringing out the instruments. Let us move closer." Before her composition there were others, including a dance suite by Leopold, which received much applause and enthusiastic comment. There was also an "*Instrumental-Kalender*," a piece depicting the seasons, composed by a friend of Wenzel's from Esterhaz at Eisenstadt. When Leopold rose to begin her trio sonata, Anna felt her stomach roil. As Leopold raised his bow and his eyebrow, glancing at the other violinist, the cellist and harpsichordist, she gripped one hand with another. But the opening slow movement, with its alternating ostinato patterns, set the two violins into conversation, Leopold's making a statement, the other violin answering. She had written passages requiring considerable virtuosity. The presto sent both treble voices scampering like squirrels, up and down trees, followed by their plumy tails; then the adagio, in which the two violins and the cello spoke in a three-way canon, and then the contrapuntal allegro.

"Bravo! Bravo, maestro!" called out the guests at the conclusion, applauding vigorously. "It is your best yet, Leopold," said Wenzel. "Indeed it is," echoed the prosperous merchant, Lorenz Hagenauer.

When he bowed, Leopold looked directly at Anna, raised his eyebrow and put his hand over his heart. Anna took a deep breath, her face hot. The fingernails of one hand had bitten into the palm of the other. She rubbed them together, realizing that Margarethe was staring at her cramped and wounded hands. Anna laughed shakily. "Did you like it?"

"I did," said Margarethe. "And, judging from the harm you have done yourself, you were *gripped* by it."

And then, without intending to, Anna found herself confiding to this woman, this alien. "It is mine," said Anna, almost too softly to be heard. "But we agreed, Herr Mozart and I, to pass it off as his. The Archbishop and his *Kapellmeister* would object if they knew."

"I liked it so much. I am so pleased that it is yours, Fraulein!" exclaimed Margarethe. She went on quietly, "It is unfair. I too must keep secrets. But Fraulein Pertl, you have a great gift. You must use it, even if you must pretend otherwise."

As the guests partook of the splendid repast set before them, the talk turned to the young Hapsburg Empress Maria Theresa. "Because she is so green and a woman," said Sigmund Haffner, recently returned from Vienna, "the Prussian king threatens to take Silesia, despite his pledges to her late father. There is fear that she cannot stand up to the Prussian Frederick. Nevertheless, everyone talks of her reforms."

Silvester Barisani spoke in his quick Italian way, carving the air with his precise hands. "If she embroils Salzburg in a war," he said, "I want nothing to do with her reforms."

"Is it true, as they say, that the Empress hates the Church?" asked the wife of the Court Chancellor.

"No, no," answered Herr Haffner. "She is a good religious woman. Of that all are agreed. But she wishes to make some reforms in the direction of toleration. They say in Vienna that the freer flow of commerce and invention needs Calvinists, Lutherans and Jews." He bowed in the direction of Solomon Arnstein, Margarethe's father.

"But," said Margarethe, emboldened by the kindness of her hostess and Anna, "the Empress rails at Jews, taxes them heavily, and holds the reins so tight they nearly choke. She has tried to expel them - us - from Bohemia," she said, her voice tremulous.

"Margarethe!" said her father, warning in his voice.

Anna had never before thought how hard the lot was of the Jews. This new acquaintance, Margarethe, spoke from the pain of exclusion, and her father instantly blanched white with the fear of repercussions. "Then the Empress is unjust," Anna ventured. She was not used to speaking up in company, judging it better to keep her opinions to herself. But Margarethe now knew of and liked Anna's trio sonata, and for that Anna owed her some loyalty.

The talk turned to witches. Ernst Antretter had heard from an emissary to the court. "They say two men were seized and put to death in Karpfen."

"It wasn't so long ago that they burned those fourteen women in Szegedin," murmured his affianced, Elizabeth. "Remember what a pother was afoot even here in Salzburg, accusations of all kinds flying thick and fast. No one felt safe."

The company uneasily recalled the days, not so long since, when so many had perished in suspicion and torment, and neighbor was set against neighbor. Jakob Mannhardt recollected, "My mother still remembers the two old crones - Hedwig, I don't remember her surname, and old widow Brunner - burned in St. Peter's churchyard, charged with bringing down the rain of hail that spoiled the crops. My mother knew the widow woman. She speaks of it to this day, chewing it over and over, how the old woman was penniless, lame, unclean. A nasty piece of work, she says, but hardly able to call out the weather!"

"I wish they would not hunt people and torture them," Anna said. "I am sure I would say anything, even untruths, if people set about to hurt me."

Talk of witches and torture made everyone edgy and before long the guests took their way home. Anna was surprised that she had spoken out with unaccustomed boldness. Perhaps it was having confessed her secret to Margarethe Arnstein, perhaps it was the applause her work had won. As she and Leopold walked toward the apartment she shared with her mother, she reflected that she felt at ease with him and his friends. She particularly hoped that she would see Fraulein Arnstein more often.

"Your trio sonata pleased everyone," said Leopold. "It is very fine. But difficult."

Anna flushed with pleasure. She valued his praise more than anyone's.

After a long pause, Leopold continued, "I have not told you, Anna, how it was I gave up my studies at the University. I have not told anyone till now. It was only a year after the public commendation of my work. I heard a piece of organ music, a part of the *Apparatus musico-organisticus* by Georg Muffat. It combined the beauties of the Italian with the more learned German style and I was struck dumb. Oh, I thought my heart would . . . ." he gestured with his long fingers, as if he could pluck the right words from the air, " . . . . break. Yet not break. Be made whole. I cannot explain it, Anna. Words are not enough. I knew that I must give up learning for music."

"Something like that happened to me," said Anna, "when I was just a little child, maybe three or four years old. It was when my father and his friends played . . . ."

Leopold interrupted her. "I took to missing instruction in natural sciences so that I could play on the violin and attempt to compose. I was called in by the Dean. I still remember how angry he was. 'I have stood by you,' " said Leopold, imitating the high, dry anger of the Dean, " 'but you are delinquent and cannot continue as a student at the University.' I bowed my head as if I felt remorse, but what I felt was - joy, Anna! - despite the disgrace. Father Sembler, thank God, was sympathetic. He helped me find a position with the Cathedral Canon, the Count of Thurn, Valsassina and Taxis." Seeing no recognition in Anna's eyes, Leopold explained. "The count owns nearly all of the conveyance, Anna, the coaches and carriages that carry travelers and mail wherever German is spoken, even beyond. I was hired to serve the count as a musician, but also to conduct his correspondence and keep his affairs in order. My mother heard what I had done - gossip travels even to Augsburg - and wrote, berating me. She said she washed her hands of me." It was deeply painful for Leopold to tell Anna these things.

Leopold's brother had also remonstrated in a letter from Augsburg. He too had an education, Johann Christian wrote furiously, but he would not betray his father's trade to be an organgrinder for a man who carried other peoples' bums and letters. Pained as Leopold was by the scolding and contempt of his family, Leopold believed he must be free to do as his heart dictated. It was a new time, and sons were no longer vassals to their fathers - or mothers.

Leopold told Anna how he had dedicated a set of trios to his employer. They were written in the Italian manner and he had not only composed them, but engraved them in copper with his own hand. Despite his mother's anger, Leopold thought that had his father still lived, he would have admired his son's handiwork, and - who knows? - might have counseled him to take the path he felt his feet so clearly set on. He went to work on the composition of a cantata for the Passion season. He also began to make notes for a treatise which would explain all the art that was needed to play the violin. Such instruction was needed, for there were few young men who learned correctly. As the teacher of several young boys in the Thurn and Taxis household, Leopold found himself hard pressed to undo the careless habits of the poorly instructed. He would give their teachers a basis to avoid faulty tuition.

"I have," said Leopold, "taken care to make the acquaintance of the best people in Salzburg, and now I am fourth violinist in the court and believe it is time to take a wife."

Anna was startled. Leopold marry? She felt a moment's regret that she would lose so good a friend.

"*You*, Anna. I want to marry *you*," said Leopold. "And I believe that Eberlin would permit it now." Indeed, before he had broached the subject to Anna, Leopold had made sure of his superior's consent.

Anna was surprised. She had not thought of marrying. Her life went on very well as it was. She was able to make sufficient money and, most important, she was able to compose. Through Leopold she had been introduced into good society. But then, why should she not marry? Leopold was handsome, cheerful, careful of her determination to compose, and very likely to prosper. Everyone admired him for his energy, his learning, the figure he cut at court and around town. "Yes," she said. "Yes, I will marry you. But," she said, "you know I must have music."

10

1747-1748

"ALL THE LAWS OF NATURE AND RELIGION tell us that on the man's shoulders rest responsibility for the care of wife and children. It is his task to represent his family in civic matters,' " read Leopold to Anna. Books on the government of the household were much in style. " 'But the wife,' " he went on, smiling at Anna, " 'is mistress of all else.' "

" 'Scripture tells us,' " he read, " 'that a good wife is priceless beyond precious jewels.' "

"A good wife?" Anna queried.

"Mmmm," said Leopold, " 'She is God-fearing, modest and kindly . . .' hmm, 'created so by Nature . . . . looks after all the affairs of the household, cares for the property, looks after the children and servants, makes sure that food is in reserve, that soap and candles are made and stored . . . sees to the making and care of clothing and helps her husband in all his undertakings.' " Leopold raised his eyebrow in his customary skeptical way. "But," he said, "you will be glad to hear that the husband must rule with consideration for the faults and weaknesses his wife brings with her, for who among us is without flaw?' "

Anna snorted. "And when," she asked, "does the good wife compose?"

"That, I think," Leopold answered, smiling broadly at the foolishness of which some men were guilty, "must be counted among her faults and weaknesses." He grew serious. "Nowhere, sweetheart, do these authors take genius into account." He had long ago conceded inwardly that genius - the

God-given flame of invention - danced within Anna, illuminating whatever composition she undertook. He composed much and swiftly, but what he did had neither the lift nor depth of hers, which, passed off as his, garnered more praise than his best efforts.

Leopold burned to possess - be possessed by - genius. This need drove him as fiercely as a drunkard's thirst.

To mark their betrothal, Anna gave to him her one most precious possession - the *Gradus ad Parnassum* by Josef Fux, the book Sister Gisella had given to her when she left Nonnberg. This gift was meant to seal their mutual understanding that both were composers and that he would protect her calling as she would serve his. Leopold took it with pleasure, seeing her present as a sign of her confidence in his gifts. He inscribed on the flyleaf, "*1746 Ex Libris Leopoldi Mozart.*"

A shadow fell upon the season of their marriage: a rumor from Unterzell that a professed nun, Sister Cecilia, was accused of bringing afflictions upon her convent. Her trial for witchcraft was on every tongue, even in Salzburg. Leopold was furious. "Such foolishness will drag us all backwards into superstitious times," he fretted.

"Shhh," said Anna. She was sick with pity and apprehension. "Someone will hear you." She darted a look behind her as they walked through the marketplace.

"Such a thing could never happen here," he said.

"It could," Anna countered. "My father acted to save just such a woman from execution in a village near St. Gilgen."

"When I was a child," Leopold admitted, "my mother often threatened that the witch of nearby Dillingen would fly by night and snatch me if I failed to behave. But that was a story meant for children. Men are reasonable now."

"Hah!" snorted Anna. "What about Unterzell? Where are the reasonable men there?" She had heard stories all her life about women charged with witchcraft, and they chilled her to the bone.

Having applied to and received permission to marry from the Council of Augsburg, Leopold had other matters on his mind. "I have been thinking about our marriage vows," he said. "I think there is no lack of reason in vows taken when two people marry, with God as their witness."

"I should hope not!" she exclaimed.

"But," he said earnestly, "vows in general are to be avoided. For example," he said, "if a man makes a vow to God, there can be no real contract, for who can tell whether God consents to be a party to it. But in this case, the contract will be between you and me, Anna, and no one can object."

But Leopold thought that Anna might well object to the wedding sermon. "God created woman from the rib of man to be a helpmeet unto him. And therefore, a wife follows her husband everywhere like a snail. She carries his household upon her back. For he is her God," intoned the priest. Leopold was relieved when Anna meekly plighted her troth as they stood up together to be wed in the Cathedral.

"Snail, indeed!" Anna huffed, as she, her new husband and her mother hurried the short way to the new apartment Leopold had taken on the third floor of the merchant Lorenz Haganauer's house. "I would like to see a snail enter into a contract! A snail at least carries its own house upon its back. It does not require its wife to do it."

Leopold laughed. "I half expected you to speak up," he said, "for requiring that your husband be your God."

"With whom I could hardly exchange vows, my dear!" Anna joined Leopold in laughter.

Eva Rosina spoke up with asperity. "When in Rome," she scolded her daughter, "you must do as the Romans do." Eva Rosina would live with them in their new quarters.

Anna was pleased with their living arrangements. It was an old apartment, but clean, spacious and respectable. Ample light came through the large, deep-set windows. The apartment faced Getreidegasse on one side, the busy street lined with shops. Anna could look down on the farmers and millers bringing their produce to town. The tavern, Zu den Aliirten, and the water pump stood within view. On the other side, the market, the Benedictine University square and the glorious new collegiate church were but a hop and a skip away.

Anna made sure that Leopold went more beautifully adorned with lace than other men of his station. Her housekeeping was admired by other women, for she had learned from the best of teachers - a whole abbeyful of nuns - how to preserve foods, make medicines, shape dresses to the figure that would wear them and keep all in shining order.

But soon after their wedding Anna began to feel very green. Her breasts hurt and she could hold nothing down.

"Ahh!" said Eva Rosina with satisfaction. "Your husband can hold his head high. No one can doubt he is a man, now you are with child."

Anna raised her head from the basin into which she had vomited her breakfast. Though weak, she was irritated by her mother's words. Had Leopold ever held his head low? "I had not thought to have a child so soon," she said. "I had other . . . plans."

Eva Rosina scoured the table. "Anna," she said, "I wanted music for you. It is the best adornment to any life. But how can you expect to do what your father, rest his soul, could never do? You would make your husband's life a hell, were you to set yourself up against him," she said.

"But it would not be against him," Anna protested. Leopold admired her work, enough that he was willing to put his name to it. "Some women have composed. Sister Gisella named them, and she did not know all by any means."

Eva Rosina had been changed by her trials. She missed making music herself and was very glad to go into households where others made music. But Anna did not understand how chancy life was, how one's fortunes could change in an instant. She straightened up, her hands on her hips, her face stern. "Be aware, Anna, that if men find you frivolous, thoughtless, or lacking in good character, your husband will suffer for it. Who knows? You might be taken for a witch." She crossed herself. "Be sensible, Anna. You brought nothing to your marriage. You must heed the Archbishop who pays your husband's salary. It is he who puts bread on your table."

Anna was too sick for rejoinders. In any case, Eva Rosina spoke nothing but the common wisdom.

Anna retched through the days. The thought of dinner, even a choice piece of fowl, sent her for a basin. Even so, she had much to do to equip and settle her new home. Gretl, the servant girl, dreamy and forgetful, had need of instruction. She could spend the day dusting a windowsill. She had to be taught to keep the stoves cleaned and the fires built. She took the slops and night soil to the river of a morning, but always tardily. Anna showed her how to clean the dishes and keep the floors swept, how to make candles and soap, to do the small laundry. When the large yearly wash should come round, she would be a help with the heavy lifting and wringing. Anna went with Gretl to market, taught her to cook and to put lavender in the linens and cupboards to keep away flying vermin. One chest, Anna cautioned Gretl, was Anna's alone to care for. She did not tell Gretl that under the best linens, at the bottom, were her compositions. Anna herself did all the mending, made most of the clothes, knit all the stockings and always had a piece of lace underway.

The news that Anna Mozart was with child traveled quickly, from Leopold to his landlord, Hagenauer, to his wife, Theresa, and from thence speedily from mouth to mouth. Suddenly it seemed to Anna that no one spoke of anything but childbearing in the marketplace and at the water tap.

The chill air settled Anna's stomach as she stood with acquaintances at the pump. The cold rose from the cobblestones through her stout shoes and heavy stockings, but she welcomed the thin winter sunshine.

"In Hallein they say the maidens who get with child in the fall bring forth monsters, rats, tortoises and such," said Adelheide Althaus, a widow whose thin face was framed in dewlaps. "They resemble the fathers but their claws tear the mothers inside." Frau Althaus gloried in strange happenings and savage tales.

"Never mind her," whispered stout Henriette Wiesner to Anna, rolling her eyes. "I will say a special prayer for you to Our Lady."

Solid and respectable Theresa Hagenauer saw herself as her tenant's protectress and put an arm around Anna's shoulder. "You would do well to speak with St. Margaret," she advised, her sharp face softening. "I will have a word with her myself on your account."

Lise Bruner hugged her cloak more tightly around her. Her children chased one another with cheerful cries. "What you want to do, Anna, is avoid food that makes you fart," she said knowingly, "but take plenty of bread with your soup, more than enough, or you'll have the babe coming out betimes, creeping in search of something to eat." The others nodded at this good advice.

Babette Möll, who lived in the apartment that adjoined the Mozart's, offered Anna the charm that had kept her safe through two pregnancies.

Anna reported these conversations to her mother. "Fiddle-faddle," snapped Eva Rosina, "though prayer never goes amiss."

Not wishing to trouble her husband, but dreading the ordeal before her, Anna confessed to the priest, "I am fearful, Father, of the hazards that lie ahead." She did not tell him that she feared most that household tasks and ill health would dispossess her of music.

"It is your calling on this earth, my child," counseled the priest in a thin voice. "You must commend your soul to God, showing your obedience to his will. If death should come to you in the performance of your duty to your husband, why else have you been created?"

Anna was bled regularly because Leopold was insistent, but she did not feel any stronger for it. Eberlin would not let her sing at court, now that she was a wife and soon a mother. She longed for music. Unlike food, it would not turn her stomach.

One afternoon, when Anna sat playing one of the several claviers Leopold kept in the front room, her husband came in from court. He frowned. "Anna, is this wise? To tempt God when you are with child?"

Anna retorted irritably, "I hardly think God will object if one of his poor creatures fingers a clavier."

Leopold groaned. "I cannot tell what is right, Anna. Reason tells me there can be no harm, but can everyone be wrong?"

"If everyone is right," Anna retorted, "why did God lodge within me this hunger - this need - for music? I cannot understand how a little music will endanger this child." She rested her hand on her belly, which had begun to swell, and felt under her fingers the faintest stirring. "Leopold!" she exclaimed, "come here and feel! I think the babe has quickened!" It had been only the slightest motion, no more than a flutter, but it felt to her as if the earth had moved.

Leopold put his hand on the thick, gathered wool of her skirt, frowning in concentration. He could feel nothing.

Anna knew she had felt her child. At once it made powerful claims on her. At that moment she knew that the babe was grappled to her as music was. "But Leopold, if I make music, may not the child wish to do the same? Not just my music," she added quickly. "Yours too. Leopold," she pleaded, "you of all people know me. I would do nothing to harm this little soul. How could I?"

Leopold had not felt the child move, yet he knew a mannekin had been entrusted to his wife's body. It pleased him to think that his son might take from its mother her genius, a son who might bring honor to his father and to Salzburg. He had long thought there was no harm in her music, but there was the danger that his wife - the mother of this coming child - might be thought an oddity. Still, he thought with some relief, everyone knew that a woman who was with child might exhibit untoward crotchets and cravings. Whereas one woman might think on a rabbit stew, his wife thought on composition. "Blessed be the fruit of thy womb," he said stiffly with a resigned sigh.

Anna too sighed and left the clavier. She sat to her lace, which would adorn the christening dress already cut out and stitched. The fruit of her womb? Silent, she thought of all the fruit at Nonnberg: apples, plums, pears, apricots: snowy blossoms in spring, then tiny hard buds, then rich, ripe pendants, each with its bloom of smooth or velvet skin, bursting with juice. But where the fruit fell and lay neglected against the damp of the earth for even a short time, brown, pulpy rot spread and firm fruit dissolved back into the earth. The nuns gathered the slightly spoiled fruit to cut up for preserves, but some they left on the ground. What of the fruit of her soul? If not plucked, might it not fall and rot? Poor Leopold. She knew men pressed their views on him, as women did on her.

Theresa advised her which women she should invite to attend her lying-in, those whose invitation would not stir resentments and enmities against her or her husband. These were not just friends, but women whose husbands' positions must be taken into account, whose brothers' and fathers' standings must be carefully reckoned. There had been occasions when a woman, angry at her exclusion, had cursed a laboring woman or even brought charges of witchcraft.

"Nothing is simple!" Anna exclaimed to Margarethe Arnstein, whom she visited from time to time. "You would think we had invited the Archbishop to dine!"

Both women laughed to think of the Prince Archbishop climbing the dark stairs to the Mozart's small apartment, going down the steps to Anna's cramped little kitchen and sitting at her scarred table.

In the heat of late summer, when Anna was near her time, Leopold rushed into the kitchen. Anna turned ponderously from the kettle, the wooden spoon at her lips.

"Anna Bayerin!" he gasped. "She is to be executed in the churchyard of St. Peter's a week from Thursday. She is said to be possessed."

Anna knew old Frau Bayerin, who was perhaps not so old as she looked. She was sometimes seen about the streets wearing a man's breeches. Her hair hung down in an unruly tangle. She made Anna uneasy. "Possessed?" she asked, feeling faint. She sat on the steps from the entry hall to the kitchen. "She is said to have done unspeakable acts, witchcraft," said Leopold. "They say she enchanted a pig that suckles her at night, that she cursed God and uttered calumnies against the Archbishop." He took her hand. "You should not hear such things so close to your time, Anna, but better you should hear from me."

"Mama says Frau Bayerin's lot is hard," mused Anna. Poor wretch, alone in the dungeon at the castle, no doubt tortured, in pain, disgraced, knowing that death was not far off. "I have seen her children, all of them with deformities. The lip and mouth of the oldest, split from birth. One with a withered foot and the youngest is blind."

"It is all her doing, so they say," said Leopold. "Oh, why cannot men be *reasonable*?" Leopold had left his hometown of Augsburg, incurred the anger of his mother and brothers, to pursue the enlightened thinking of men like Leibnitz, Wolff and Muratori, who held that medieval customs and superstitions must give way to reason.

Eva Rosina came in, out of breath from the stairs. "You have heard," she panted. She paced in the kitchen as well as she could in the space left by the stove, the table and its stools. "I delivered all her children," she said vehemently. "She is possessed by nothing but shocks to her mind and body. She has always risen daily before light and labored at the washtub for Frau Gutkind, whose husband engages in such chicanery and who pays her pfennigs. Herr Bayerin drinks up every penny he earns."

Anna had rarely seen her mother so exercised.

" . . . . and he never gives her rest, even when she still bleeds from a child she has buried. She wears more bruises than clothes. How could she not be peculiar?"

Leopold said, "It is said she raves about plots. Everyone - her husband, certain priests, the Archbishop himself - wishes to do away with her."

Eva Rosina exclaimed, "She is unhinged by ill treatment. And she will have to pay the cost of the ropes with which they have bound her and stretched her to make her confess. She must pay - ahead of time - for the executioner. Her husband says he will not pay a pfennig on her account. They say she laughed in her tormentors' faces and asked them how they would get blood from a turnip."

"Ha," said Leopold scornfully, "they say they want only truth of her, but what truth will come from stretching the poor woman till she is out of joint?" He shook his head. "These superstitions degrade all Germans in the eyes of the world."

Like everyone in Salzburg, Anna and Marianna Gilowsky talked about the coming execution the next day as they walked along the river. "They do no better in Vienna," mused Marianna. "Wenzel says the Empress has set up a commission to apprehend the women who sell their own bodies to live. Widows and spinsters are to be watched and those taken in prostitution punished harshly." She brushed her red hair back from her pale, freckled face. "Imagine, Anna! Then, when they are taken, their hair is cut off, and they are put in chains and made to sweep the streets and push trash barrows."

"Why could the Empress not let them work as apprentices to learn a trade?" Anna wondered. "Then they could work in a shop or go out as servants." Her belly twisted and she gasped. Had her time come? Should she turn back? But it felt so good to be out of the house and walking, even in the heat. "What," she wondered, "if I had not married? I earned small money on my own, but that could change in an instant. What then would I have to sell but my body?" She gestured at her bulk and laughed.

"You would never sell yourself," said Marianna.

"Well, think," said Anna. "What if Wenzel died - God forbid such a thing should happen," she crossed herself quickly. "How would you live? Would the Archbishop give you a pension? Would your father take you back? You are gently bred, Marianna, and forgive me, but you know less about earning your bread than I do. How would you put food on the table?" Wenzel, of course, was of noble birth, but he *could* though surely he never *would* - leave his estate away from his wife.

Marianna nodded thoughtfully. "You are right, Anna. I might run mad and do terrible things."

Anna went home and composed a hymn to St. Margaret, who had lived back in the mists of time and had become the patron saint of women in childbirth. Anna's simple hymn was a prayer that St. Margaret would succor her in her own trouble. But fearing Leopold's disapproval, Anna laid her work away in her chest, under the linens and lavender.

On the day of Frau Bayerin's execution, Anna lumbered up the gray stone stairs to the chapel at Nonnberg to ask the ancient wooden statue of the Jungfrau Maria, who held the infant Jesus on her hip, to bring her through her time of trial. She bade farewell to the nuns, fearing she might not survive the ordeal that lay ahead - many did not. She went away, feeling the same twisting she had felt on her walk with Marianna. Her apprehension about delivering the child was countered by readiness to be rid of the burden that upset her balance and swelled her feet. It is time, she thought.

II

1748

ANNA AWOKE IN THE DARKNESS, her belly tight as a fist. Her shift and the bedclothes were soaked. She felt unwell, dazed and confused. She heaved her body to the edge of the bed where it clenched and unclenched, making her cry out.

Leopold woke. "What is it?" he muttered.

Anna gasped. Pain swept through her body like fire, feeding on everything in its way.

Leopold lit the lamp. He reached out to touch Anna, who was hot and wet. He went in his nightshirt to waken his mother-in-law. "The time has come," he whispered.

Eva Rosina was washed, dressed and combed in a trice and at her daughter's side.

"She is well advanced," she said to Leopold. "Call the women Anna named to you. Then wait downstairs." Tenderly she cleaned her daughter and changed the bed. "Here," she said, helping Anna to sit up and wrapping a piece of linen towel around the bedpost. "Pull on this when the pain seizes you, but hold back from pushing just yet."

It was the mother of Anna's childhood, beautiful, young and graceful in the wavering candlelight, as if she had returned from Anna's dreams.

"All is well, child," said Eva Rosina. "All will be well." Her hands were cool and sure when she examined Anna's most private parts. "You are strong. Summon up your courage now, for you have a trial before you."

She moved about surely, transforming Anna's bedroom, ordinarily shared with Leopold, into a place no man dared breach. She drew a heavy curtain over the window, closed the doors and blocked up the keyholes so that no light could enter. Eva Rosina had told Anna to purchase many candles beyond those in her own store, the cost of which led Leopold to complain of expense. The candlelight harried the darkness into the corners, throwing a weave of shadows onto the walls as the attendant women moved about, doing what was needful, speaking quietly, touching her with reassurance, rubbing her back and helping her to walk around as the hours passed. They brought her a comforter when she was cold, told her of their trials, prayed with her for courage, bathed her face and smoothed back her hair. As she tired with the effort, Theresa and Marianna prepared a special posset of ale and wine mulled with sugar and spices to keep Anna's spirits up. She was strengthened by her friends, but it was her mother who helped her most. Calm and assured, knowing just what to do, she quieted Anna when spasms wracked her and her resolve flagged.

Then, suddenly, she split apart. She was pulled inside out, as if something outside herself had seized her. All the forces in the heavens and on the earth bore down upon her to press a tiny scrap of a son into her mother's hands. Eva Rosina held the infant up, still joined to his mother by the twisted blue cord. He was no bigger than a kitten, Anna thought, red, hairless and wizened. She was baptized with wonder. Gloria sang in her blood, in excelsis Deo.

Eva Rosina cut and tied the navel string and washed the little boy and wrapped him in soft linen that hung beside the kitchen stove to warm. Then Anna held him, her heart gripped by his tiny fingers. He squeaked like a nest of mice. She felt the milder contractions of the afterbirth but paid them no heed. Coming out of blood and muck, she thought, this child was as perfect as the bud of a flower. All the women gathered to admire the infant, who passed from one experienced pair of arms to another.

"You forget," said Theresa, usually so stern and businesslike, "each time, you forget how small they are."

"A miracle," smiled Marianna, brushing back the copper hair that had drifted forward. She was great with child herself.

Elizabeth Baumgartner, the girl affianced to Leopold's dear friend, Ernst Antretter, had never before witnessed a birth. It filled her with dread and exaltation. She stroked the fine down of hair on the child's head. "Look how strong he is!" she exclaimed with delight. "He holds his head up already! And look, he grasps my finger!"

Eva Rosina cleaned Anna's swollen and stretched private parts with soothing herbs steeped in water, and changed the sodden bed linens once again, allowing Anna to sit up holding her child. Eva Rosina insisted always on cleanliness. Few midwives changed a woman's clothing nor the bedclothes, fearing to provoke more blood, but Eva Rosina was sure that clean clothes helped in healing. For all the women she had delivered, she had lost fewer than most: others might complain of her novel methods, but never her results. She helped Anna into a fresh, unbloodied shift and into the smooth bed, opened the windows, blew out the candles and unstopped the keyholes. Her work done, she went below where Leopold waited to tell him the good news of his firstborn son.

On tiptoe, Leopold entered his room. He felt an intruder in his own sleeping chamber, the very air and look of which seemed changed. His wife was a stranger to him, her hair escaped from its braid straggling damply against her neck, her weak smile no longer his alone. The shapeless infant - his heir - rooted like a piglet in Anna's shift. "Let him have the breast, Anna," said Eva Rosina.

"No! No!" Leopold exclaimed in horror. "It must never be said that Leopold Mozart's wife is a creature, like a cow or a pig. We will pay for a nurse to come in and suckle." Though he disliked expense, he wanted to cut a good figure among his friends and associates. His wife would do as well-born women did. He was worn with waiting and thought perhaps men had the harder part of childbirth, shut out of the chamber to wait and worry.

"But look, Leopold," countered Anna. "Look at him. He wants to suck."

Leopold edged closer and touched the velvet skin of his son. A thrill ran up his finger, but he was firm. "No, Anna. Lorenz told me that Theresa knows an excellent nurse to suckle, and the babe can take pap, as I did." Leopold recoiled from all this animal business of giving birth. He did not like to think of his wife's place of secret joy as stretching and bleeding to admit this child. It all seemed to him divorced from reason.

Anna was sure her mother, full of wisdom and experience, must be right that she should suckle her son. But her fatigue was too great for contention and Leopold was her husband. In the little over nine months they had been married, she had discovered how masterful he was.

She let herself sink back into the soft featherbed. She was exhausted, but she could not sleep. Exsultate, jubilate, sanctus, benedictus: had she pen and paper, she could write such music as had never been heard. She heard the merest caress of violins, swelling and an oboe obligato, a tender and wistful sound, giving onto a chorale of joy and benediction. She was weak, but felt she should run out of doors, to shout out the glad tidings. She knew full well that her friends, who had left her to sweep off their neglected steps and make their own dinners, would spread the pleasant news abroad. She propped her head on her elbow to watch the little boy sleep, curled into himself like the fiddlehead of a fern, his small fist pressed against his cheek. Anna could not understand how, in the few minutes of his little life, he had conquered her entirely. She was not the same person she had been the day before.

The next morning, Leopold took the child to the Cathedral to be baptized Johann Leopold Joachim. The little christening gown, which had seemed to Anna too small to fit any living creature when she made and trimmed it with her own lace, was too big. As he pushed out his tiny arms and legs, she recognized the same movements she had felt when he lived in her womb. She hated to let the child out of her sight long enough for the priest to touch his forehead with the blessed water. "Wrap him up warmly," she instructed. "Use my shawl, that one on the chair."

Because Eva Rosina had unusual views, Anna was permitted to walk around indoors, even during the first week of her lying-in. She was sore and bruised, but thanks to her mother's skill, untorn. Several times she took her son out to the loggia that overlooked the courtyard, showing him the vibrant blue of the autumn sky. Raising her face to the warm sun, she sang the hymn she had written to St. Margaret, letting her voice rise softly into the warm air.

Anna's lying-in lasted a full month, as if she had been a noblewoman. Daily Eva Rosina bathed her daughter's privities with healing decoctions and made comforting poultices to draw away the pain. For the first week, Anna's friends were in and out, bringing her the news from outside along with the dishes they had made for Leopold's dinner, admiring Joachim, who lay in the crook of Anna's arm, giving her advice and encouragement. Anna refused to swaddle her child, for Eva Rosina thought it better that he could kick and squirm more freely.

Adelheide Althaus, deprived of the monstrous birth she had predicted in the marketplace, climbed up the stairs to scold. "Not swaddle!" she croaked, her lips pursed and puckered. "He'll grow up crooked in body and soul. The bones are soft, too soft. The child will grow awry," she warned insistently.

Both Theresa and Marianna, who came often, hushed her.

Anna was not worried. She was content to spoil Joachim, holding him when he cried and often when he did not. She thought he studied her face intently, his little mouth gaping and gumming. "Look," Anna cried, "He sees me. Look how he follows my finger!"

"No, no," said Theresa. "No babe that young can see."

Anna knew better. Alone with Joachim, she stuck out her tongue and his little tongue returned the gesture. She was sure he tried to smile when she smiled. She memorized the child, studying each part for its perfection. His fingers grasped hers and his toes gripped the air when she touched the soles of his feet. He turned his mouth against her bursting breasts, which he could not have, and nuzzled the cloth.

A week after Joachim's birth, Anna feasted the women who had helped her in her trial, though Leopold grudged the expense. Together they all rejoiced in the healthy babe that God had given to Anna. Anna heard their stories of children born and children lost with new sympathy. She had become a part of that great tapestry of birth and death.

When the feasting was done, other guests arrived to bless Joachim, who seemed strong and likely to live. Margarethe Arnstein came, somewhat timidly, never sure of her welcome in a Christian household. Both Anna and Leopold were happy to see her, and she stayed, holding Joachim and talking with his parents until the golden fall light gave way to evening shadows.

At the end of the month, Anna went veiled to church with her mother and her friends, where they gave thanks for Anna's safe deliverance. Anna was strong by this time and sang the psalm with full voice. "O praise the Lord, for his mercy is confirmed upon us." After her churching, Anna was allowed to be out and around town once more.

With Anna, Leopold inventoried all the boy's tiny parts, as enchanted as Anna was by this son and heir. But even so he complained of the costs. "The candles, the nurse, the extra time for the servant girl, all the visitors, the wine, the feasting, three offerings for the priest and his clerk. It is very much, Anna. Still, I would not wish to be found wanting in any particular." Gently he stroked the child's cheek with his long finger.

"Well, my mother does not require payment, and you and I were welcomed into the world in the same kind," Anna reminded him.

"True," he admitted, "but we have to give your mother board and room. Sometimes, my dear, I wonder how we will live from one month to the next." Leopold liked to live well, to keep up appearances, but he was tormented by the fear of poverty and chafed at the interruptions of visitors who came to bring blessings to his son. "There is always someone turning up. I have my work to do, but they come and go and rob me of time."

He wrote the news of his first born to his mother, as he had written the news of his marriage, and he was bitter to receive no answer from her nor any present. His mother sat in Augsburg, endlessly aggrieved by her eldest son's defection, and he nursed his grievance in Salzburg. Leopold had a brief glimpse of his mother's loss: what if this little son should grow up and leave him? But it flitted away to be replaced by the conviction that he was right and she wrong.

Barely six weeks after Joachim's birth, Anna attended Marianna, who brought a blue-tinged child into the world. He lived only a few days and Marianna sank into despair. Her friends had all they could do to reach and hold fast to her spirit. Anna took little Joachim and sat with Marianna daily. "Do you dislike to see my child?" she asked. "Does he remind you of your loss?"

"I like to have you come, Anna. And I like having Joachim here. But it is true," she wept, "sometimes I cannot bear it that you have a child and I have none," said Marianna in a low voice. "I know it is selfish of me . . . ."

Anna placed little Joachim in her arms. "You may have my son too," she said. "He cannot have too many who love him."

Marianna's husband, Wenzel, was also distraught, but he had patients who required his services. He was glad of Anna's company for his wife and Anna gave her friend as much time as she could spare.

Nevertheless, Anna soon carried her little son up the stairs to Nonnberg for the blessing of her friends.

Sister Gisella held him tenderly. "Look at these fingers," she marveled. "He will play on the fiddles and keyboard with ease." The nun carried the child to the dark, cluttered room where she kept the instruments. "The music will enter the child's soul," she explained.

Anna said, "Dear friend, he lacks nothing in that respect. He hears music day and night and seems drawn to it. He waves his fists and makes little sounds when I sing to him. Like that! See? I think *he* will be the *kapellmeister*, I once wished to be, and conduct the *kapell* orchestra. I put him by the clavier when I play and when Leopold and his friends make music." Anna smiled fondly.

The nuns passed Joachim around, exclaiming at his perfection, praising his beauty. Sister Erentraud held him longest and gazed into his eyes most fondly, her plain face transfigured. The child studied her intently and she was sure he could see into her soul. When she yielded Joachim to his mother's arms at last, she sighed. "Anna," she said hesitantly, "if you can give him your gift, you will be a happy woman."

Anna smiled at Sister Erentraud. Little Joachim wriggled and burbled. "He likes that idea," Anna said, "don't you, little one?"

12

1749

"YOU LITTLE TYRANT YOU!" Anna teased as she changed Joachim's wet and soiled dress. It seemed to her that she, her mother, the nurse and the servant girl had all become slaves to the child. Just two months old, he flailed his arms and legs, chirping and cooing, smiling and drooling. Though she was weary and sick from being with another child already, Anna laughed aloud at Joachim's antics. She was captivated by his weakness, his need of her. She was held to him by such strong bonds as she had otherwise felt only when composing held her in thrall.

Leopold came in, bringing the smell of wet October on his cloak. He bent over Joachim. "Hello, little one. Have you composed an opera yet?"

"Your son may not have *composed* an opera, Leopold," said Anna, "but I do believe he is trying out his voice. Listen to him now, *pianissimo*, but a while ago he bellowed *fortissimo*. Opera may well be his calling!"

Leopold put his arm around Anna. "Herr Eberlin asks after you, my dear." The *Kapellmeister* took an interest in the families of his musicians. "He says that you should take your rest, to save your strength for the babe and more to come." Leopold cocked his head to the side and raised a skeptical eyebrow and hung his woolen cloak on its wooden peg.

Anna laughed ruefully. "Everyone has advice. Herr Eberlin means well, but he has always regarded me as flighty and undependable, though I never once was absent or even late when I sang in the *kapell*, and I mastered even the most difficult parts quickly." She sighed. "Reassure him, my dear, that I am kept far too busy for the distractions that worry him. Oh Leopold," she added softly, "I do long for the time to compose." Her last composition was her hymn to St. Margaret, the modest effort that lay with her other compositions under the linens and lavender.

"I know, my dear," sympathized Leopold. "Surely it is superstition that your womb will wither if your brain is at work." But he had come to wonder: could it be true? Everyone said so, even some of the most enlightened men. Uneasily, Leopold wondered if his wife's insistence on playing the clavier during her first pregnancy now caused Joachim sometimes to make a fuss and spit up the nurse's milk. Leopold was surprised to discover that his son was an ill-regulated and selfish creature, without regard for his father's wish for quiet or sleep. His stern admonitions had little effect on the boy, who bawled more lustily when he heard his father's scolding voice.

Though he would not say so, it had begun to trouble Leopold that his wife cared so much for music. He saw no such inclination in other women. What had seemed to him entirely endearing at first - indeed, the very avenue to her heart - seemed now, perhaps, a little unnatural. In so uncertain a world, where ancient ways and superstitious rites must needs yield to more enlightened thinking, in a world where an ordinary man might rise through his talents and hard work instead of rank, one wanted a virtuous wife who would keep one's home in good trim, give birth to and rear healthy sons. Indeed, his house was well-kept, the child lovingly attended to, but as so much changed in the world, one wanted stability in a woman, not newfangled ideas. Daily Leopold grew more aware that one did not prosper either at court or in society by deviating from accepted views, and while he hated narrow prejudice, ambition urged him to hope that his son would occupy his wife's entire attention. It had begun to rankle that Anna's native gifts were greater than his own.

Eva Rosina came in from the kitchen, where she had bedeviled the servant, finding cobwebs and dust the girl had missed.

Joachim's contentment gave way to a howl. Anna picked him up and he hiccuped and burrowed into her dress.

"Here, I will take him to nurse," said Eva Rosina. "You give your husband something hot to eat, Anna. He is wet and cold." Eva Rosina was always eager to take the child from his mother. Ever since she helped him into the world, taking him from her daughter's bloodied nether regions, Eva Rosina envied Anna, who had a husband and also the son she herself had never given to either of her husbands.

Anna yielded the child to her mother, though she loved the way he snuggled and kneaded into her body.

Leopold was irritated by his son's crying and was glad to see him taken out of the room. He wished his mother-in-law would mind her own business, but he knew better than to quarrel with her. "Mother Pertl," he murmured, bowing slightly.

Anna, also irked that her mother was so quick to order her about, quelled the retort that rose. "Come," she said to Leopold. "We are all in a temper, the day is so gloomy. The stew is ready and there is bread and coffee."

Leopold told Anna the day's news as he supped. "The Archbishop has issued an edict," he said while she nibbled a crust, "that Jews must not buy victuals in the market before certain times. No vegetables before nine, nor cattle before eleven of the clock and no fish at all."

"But why?" Anna asked, astonished.

"It is thought, I suppose, that the Jews come early and buy up all the best of everything. Someone must have complained after a Jew got the best cut of beef."

"It is so wrong!" Anna exclaimed. "There are so few Jews in Salzburg, yet they are so much feared!"

That afternoon, Anna took Joachim, well-wrapped in shawls against the drizzling cold, to Margarethe Arnstein. Since their first meeting, the two women had become fast friends. There was no one to whom Anna could speak as plainly, and Margarethe had taken to Joachim as if he were her own. A thin sun had broken through the clouds to play with the Bohemian crystals Margarethe had hung by linen threads in the deep casements, where they caught the light and flung it in a dazzle of color across the clean white walls.

"Leopold has told me of the edicts," said Anna. "I came to say how sorry I am, my friend. It is very wrong,"

"The taxes we must pay, merely for the privilege of being Jews in Salzburg, have gone up too," said Margarethe tightly. "The Archbishop imitates the impositions of the Empress in Vienna."

Anna reached for Margarethe's thin hand. "Leopold sends his greetings," she told her friend. "He thinks as I do."

"Please thank him. And your mother?" she asked politely, ready to change the subject, "she is well?" Though she trusted Anna, she must always remember that the Mozarts were of the court. There must be no report of resentment from the Arnsteins, so she must guard her tongue.

"Oh, we are all at sixes and sevens!" Anna exclaimed. "Mama orders me around, as if I were simple. Leopold brings others' advice that I should forego all hopes of music. I cannot help but wonder if those he quotes are his own thoughts. I suppose he is fearful of his honor, should it be known that his wife wants to compose. He dislikes Joachim's crying and my mother's high-handed ways. I am often sick when he wants me. I am put off by food and hungry only for music. I know these are small things, compared to the insults you have felt," she conceded, "but I wonder if I am especially wicked to want music so?"

Margarethe reached for Joachim and smiled as he lay contentedly on the rich claret-colored wool of her dress. He followed the rainbow lights that darted and quivered on the wall. "Hardly wicked," Margarethe said. "Why should you not feel the press of your genius? I know you possess it, without any doubt. It is like a hot coal, with little chance of bursting into a brighter flame without fanning, but still it smolders and wants stirring."

Margarethe was silent, playing with Joachim's small hands for several minutes. "Thank you for coming today, Anna," she said at last. "Your fellow feeling cheers me. I was not at first sure that I could trust you, even though you honored me at our first meeting with your secret." She paused, as if she hardly dared go on. "I," she said slowly, "have my own secret. I . . . write . . . poetry. If he knew, my father would be angry." She shook her head, her mass of curly hair caught up in a coil at the nape of her neck. "I cannot imagine what he thinks I should do all day, without husband to please or children to tend, with servants to do what is needful. But he does not inquire. He allows me what books I want and even," she looked significantly at Anna, "newspapers."

Anna was impressed. Newspapers were held to be unfit reading for women.

"Whatever I like," Margarethe went on, "my father procures for me. He is, in so many ways, an indulgent man. Perhaps he understands my isolation here. He even brings me all the English novels I can read, and he is not averse to poetry, so long as I but read it. He would never allow me to write my own, for fear that I would disgrace him and jeopardize his position, which I admit, is always tenuous, for the Archbishop can always find other Jews to arrange for his loans."

"What do you do with your poetry, then?" asked Anna.

Margarethe's thin hand, adorned with a king's ransom of rings, lay lightly on the child. "I have a hiding place," said Margarethe, looking around her, as if to be sure no one other than Anna could hear. "Sometimes, when there is no one at home, not even one servant - who, after all, might be a spy - I take them out and read them." She laughed softly. "I declaim to my heart's content. But," she added, "no one else will ever read or hear them. It is as if I had children, but they are all stillborn." She stroked Joachim's small head, with its whorls of fine, fair hair.

Anna was silent. What if this child of her heart, who lay on her friend's lap, had never taken a breath outside her body? "I cannot imagine it," she said, "the loss you feel. I am selfish to complain, for at least a few of my pieces have had a hearing, though not in my name. May I read what you have written, Margarethe?"

Margarethe was startled. She paused, considering. It was a risk to give anything she had written to Anna. News traveled like fire in Salzburg. Anna could see she had confronted her friend with an awkward decision, but she was disinclined to withdraw her request.

Margarethe rose abruptly. "Here, hold Joachim. I will be back in a moment," she said, leaving the room.

Joachim, who had fallen asleep, fidgeted briefly, then curled into his mother's neck where his soft breath came and went evenly against her skin.

Margarethe returned with a small parcel done up in oilcloth. She took a deep breath. "Here," she said, "keep them from all eyes but yours, Anna."

"I am honored," Anna said softly. "I will keep them safe and out of sight. I will carry them wrapped up with Joachim in his shawl."

"How does Leopold look upon your composing?" queried Margarethe.

"In our courtship, he encouraged me," said Anna. "But now I am his wife and he wishes to be agreeable to his friends. And I suppose he fears the Archbishop, who is, after all, his - our - bread and butter." She eased the babe into the cradle of her arms. "He is entirely caught up in his own composing, performing and teaching. In such odd times as he can find, he works on his manual of violin instruction. And then there is all the scheming and maneuvering at court, which takes his time and attention. How can I explain? He reads everything he can acquire or borrow and he seems to correspond with everyone in the world - writers, musicians, scientists, inventors - and his scientific interests . . . . You cannot imagine, Margarethe, his microscope and flasks and this and that, the clutter of his things - instruments, too, harpsichords and claviers, violins and gambas and lutes. I think there is not room either in our apartment or in his mind to allow for my need to compose. Mama keeps at me that Leopold must be master in his own household." She sighed.

"And, of course, Joachim and day-to-day matters keep me occupied. Everything takes longer. There is so much mess - he is wet or dirty or spits up on me and I am always stained and smelly and do not sleep well. I cannot get anything done without interruption."

Anna glanced at the small, jeweled clock that sat on Margarethe's table. "Oh my," she said. "We have overstayed." She wrapped the sleeping child in his shawls, tucking in the packet of poems. "I do not know how to explain it. I have so much, but still I am not content. I want more, even if it is just two minutes to myself to think of what I might compose. But if I had it, I would want more. Perhaps everyone is right, that music *is* a distraction. It is sure I am divided . . . ."

Over the next weeks in such moments as she could spare, and when there was no one at home except for little Joachim, Anna read Margarethe's poems. She read them slowly, for they were dense, as rich with varied color as the dress Margarethe had worn when first Anna met her, deep iridescent threads weaving together in a dark fabric. A few days later, when the servant girl could watch Joachim, she took back the packet of poems to her friend, held firmly against her bosom under her shawl.

"I do not know how to use language as you do," said Anna, "but it seems to me like music." She reached for Margarethe's ringed hand. "I wish, my dear friend, that you could make these known."

"Your knowing what I have done means much to me," whispered Margarethe."

As the months passed, Joachim grew and changed. He babbled joyously, made his own two hands his playthings, learned to reach for such objects as Anna held within his reach, studied the shifts of light and shadow on the walls.

He had only just begun to sit by himself when everything changed. He began to turn his head aside when Anna tried to spoon pap into his mouth.

It dribbled down his chin and dried on his little shift. He grew thin and listless. He cried and no one could comfort him. His stools ran loose and he arched his small body in pain. Her mother, friends and physician suggested remedies, which availed nothing. When she had tried all else, Anna sang to Joachim with all her brilliance and strength, offering him the beauty of her voice for his health and repose. Frantic and oppressed, Anna spent her nights hanging over her son's cradle to be sure he breathed. His sleep was broken and fretful.

Joachim died in Anna's arms on a cold February day when snowfall muffled all sound. He had lived just under six months, and the new babe in Anna's womb had quickened not long before. She sat near the stove, holding her dead child in her arms while his perfect little body grew cold.

With heavy heart, Anna wrapped the child in a warm shawl. "Fetch Fraulein Arnstein and Frau Gilowsky and send word to my husband at court," Anna told the servant girl, who sat beside her weeping. "My mother will be in later, when her work is finished."

In the hours that followed Anna felt such desolation as she had never known. "Why?" she sobbed. "What has this child done to offend? How have I sinned that he should be punished?"

Margarethe sat up very straight. "Anna," she said firmly. "You did nothing wrong. It is a mystery, some error in Nature, not your fault."

"But I *did* wrong," Anna said. "I have wanted what I cannot have. This is my punishment." Aloud she blamed herself, but secretly she turned against God, who could snatch a tiny babe from his mother's arms.

"They say we should not care so much," mourned Marianna, "that these little ones are given us to tend for a while and that we are taught humility when they die. But how can that be?"

Leopold, too, was beside himself at the loss of his son. When her friends had left, he held Anna tightly in his arms and spoke in broken tones. "I know it is God's will, my dear," he wept, "but it is hard."

Gently Anna put the baptismal dress on little Joachim before she wrapped him in his shroud, thinking of his ecstatic smile, his joy in music. Before long he would be nothing but dust, a ground for worms to turn. "Stitches in air," Anna murmured, holding the little bundle for the last time.

Leopold took the child to be buried in St. Peters churchyard. As soon as he had gone with his pitiful burden, Anna took out her hymn, written to St.

Margaret. She put it in the stove and watched the flames curl and blacken the pages, which collapsed into ash. The death of a child was too high a price to pay for a composition. But she rebelled at the injustice. If she must give up composing to bear and rear children, then it was wrong that she must grow to love a child only to have him snatched away.

13

1749-1751

IN JUNE ANNA GAVE BIRTH TO Maria Anna Cordula. It was a difficult birth after long labor. "Less than a year since her son's birth," muttered Eva Rosina to Theresa. "Not long enough." The child was unusually small with an unhealthy bluish tinge to her face and fingernails. "She will not likely live, Anna," said Eva Rosina as gently as she could.

Anna, too tired and weak to care, was listless, little comforted by the women gathered to help her. She did not intend to give her affection to another child, but her soul reached out to cradle the little one. After just six days, Cordula joined her brother in the black soil of St. Peter's churchyard. Anna went often to visit her children who lay beneath the summer's grass.

In September, just over a year since Joachim's birth, she was once again with child. She grew thin. "You must eat, dear one," Leopold said, but not even the daintiest dishes tempted Anna. Maria Anna Nepomuzena Walpurgis was born eleven months after her short-lived sister. Music made her tetchy. She screwed up her face and whimpered when Anna sang or touched the clavier. When not gripped by colic, she lay inert, incurious. She died in July after only two months of life.

In two years, Anna had borne and lost three children. She felt as if she wore a borrowed life that fit her ill. She sat as much out of doors in the sunshine as she could, exhausted by her effort and stunned by her losses. She knew that her husband, her mother and her friends, both in town and at Nonnberg, stood ready to help her, but they seemed no more than shadows moving at the edge of the blank glare of summer light, which seemed to her bright but not warm. She did not visit Margarethe, nor warm to her overtures. The servant girl kept the house cleaned and meals prepared, though the apartment did not shine with scrubbing and polishing as when Anna paid attention. Some days she walked across the river to the gardens at Mirabelle, where she could sit by herself.

She went into every church she passed, but could not pray. Why were these babes planted in her womb, twined in her heart, and then torn away? Why did God need her children, who had so many others? If it were God's plan to take her infants to his breast, she thought, he was cruel beyond measure. If it were not his will, but some other agency, then he had not the perfect power and knowledge she had been taught.

Leopold feared to lose his wife as well as his children. "Walk out with me, Anna, where the air is cooler," he cajoled. He tried to distract her from her sorrow with tales of the plots and contretemps at court, which amused, exasperated and angered him. "The harm that Firmian did!" he expostulated, as they walked through shadows thrown by buildings on either side, "to espouse enlightened principles and then send all the Calvinists and Lutherans away from Salzburg! To this day we live in a false peace and lack a useful ferment of ideas."

Anna did her best to listen, but these were old complaints about the late Prince Anton Firmian, Leopold's first archbishop.

"And now," Leopold exclaimed, sure that this news must rouse her from her torpor, "Archbishop Shrattenbach has decreed that women must sit apart from men at concerts and comedies. He thinks he will prevent immorality. Anna, did you hear what I said?" asked Leopold.

Anna nodded, hardly hearing. "Mmmm," she murmured. What affairs of state could compare with the tender lives that had been untimely snatched from the earth? The trees began to turn, but she hardly saw the carnival of color.

"Shall we have friends in to make music tomorrow, Anna?" Leopold asked, frantic to arouse some interest.

She nodded, but how could she find delight in what she could not have? The world had decreed, it seemed, that she should have neither music nor children. What then was her purpose upon the earth?

"Come, Anna," Eva Rosina chided her. "You are not alone in your loss. Many women suffer as you have." She was right. Many other women had lost their babes. Anna thought of all that sad traffic of little souls, coming from God and returning to Him, the thousands of small hopeful stitches in buried baptismal gowns and shrouds. She wished Him kinder to women.

At last the physician Silvester Barisani took Leopold aside. "Send her to Gastein," he urged. "Let her take the baths."

Despite the expense, Leopold was desperate to recover his cheerful companion. He paid out the money for a carriage and inquired until he found the wife of a merchant willing, in return for her fare, to travel with Anna to Bad Gastein. He put coins in Anna's purse, kissed his wife and handed her into the carriage, which took her up, up along a narrow and winding road through the pass in the Hohe Tauern mountains, and then down into the narrow valley of the Gastein Ache River, the horses bracing themselves against the steepness of their descent.

For four days Anna bathed in springs reputed to have remarkable curative powers for nervous disorders and other bodily ailments. She felt her body relax in the hot waters that came, almost boiling, from the earth. Though her own lodging was a modest guesthouse, she admired the extravagant inns and hotels where, she heard, the King of Prussia had stayed and, from time to time, the Imperial family from Vienna. She was among perfect strangers: she passed strangers on the paths; ate meals, cooked and served by strangers; sat at table with strangers; and walked with strangers to admire the falls that tumbled into the river. None of the people she saw meant anything to her nor wanted anything from her. She hardly opened her mouth to say more than "yes" or "no," "please" or "thank you."

On her last day, Anna walked to the higher of the two falls. She put her face up to feel the mist from the great plummet of water that had drawn her back, again and again.

"They call it Kesselfall," said a plump woman standing at Anna's elbow.

Anna saw that she was dressed in mourning. "Because the water boils, as it would in a kettle," Anna observed, nodding. "The water just comes and comes and comes. There is no end." The sight and roar of it, the cool mist that conjured up rainbows, were like spring cleaning. God, she thought, had much to attend to beyond her babes. Suddenly she was curious to know the bereaved woman's story. "I am very sorry," said Anna, "to see that you have lost someone dear to you."

"Yes," said the woman. "My husband, after a long illness."

Anna was moved to put her hand on the other's black-clad arm. It was solid, warm. "Have you children?" Anna inquired.

"Yes," said the woman. "Three living. I lost others, but the three have grown up and all have their own families. They are a comfort to me. Her eyes filled with tears."

Anna felt her own tears start up.

"Ah," said the woman. "You have lost children, little ones, from the look of you."

Anna nodded. She told this stranger of little Joachim and his two small sisters, how they had consumed her strength, how their deaths had rendered her indifferent, how she neglected her husband, her mother, her friends, her music. She talked and talked to someone she did not know, a stranger, connected only by loss.

The woman held her hand out as if to grasp the shimmering mist that hung before the falls. "I think," she said, looking deeply into Anna's weeping eyes, "that you will have living children. And you will regain your husband and your friends, even your music again." She must have been, thought Anna later, a fortune-teller - perhaps a gypsy, though she had seemed respectable enough.

When the carriage returned through Salzburg's gate, Anna felt a surge of love. Each red roof and church spire, each tree and cobble looked familiar and dear to her. Her apartment in Getreidegasse, though shabbier than she remembered, and in need of a good turning out, embraced her with familiar associations. Leopold held her against him, their bodies recognizing one another with gladness.

Anna's spirits returned. Strength flooded into her limbs. When, only months after her return from Bad Gastein, the signs came upon her that she was once again with child, she felt strong and eager. Marianna had had a daughter, Katherina, who was well-made and healthy and Anna rejoiced with her friend.

After Joachim's death, Leopold had let lapse the work on his pedagogical treatise on violin playing. Now he returned to it in such time as was not taken up with other duties. He asked for his wife's views as his manuscript grew, and she suggested ways to make the work less formidable, for Leopold's learning sometimes overwhelmed his subject. "Use more common terms," Anna said. "Compare the lines on which composers set their notes to a ladder. The steps of a ladder go up and down, as do the tones represented by the notes. Everyone knows a ladder and will understand."

Leopold once again shared with Anna his passion for music. "Science should be spent to shape good instruments," he insisted. "That is time better spent than time and ink spent explaining why some intervals please while others do not. As I see it, Anna, music is the one work where a man's head and heart are joined perfectly to invent what best honors and delights God. I believe," he said, stretching to clasp his hands behind his head, "that music must be the very voice of God. Man's task is but to hear it."

"And that is why shoddy workmanship in all the realms of music - in the making of instruments, in poor instruction, in the natterings of theorists who do not practice but only preach - so angers me. To blather offends against God. So does," he added, "the neglect of music by princes and public alike. To give music but scant regard offends both Reason and Nature."

Anna, on good terms again with music, nodded. She sang on every occasion, at rest, at work, at gatherings of their friends. She set down ideas for small compositions, ignoring her mother's admonitions. "Once, when I was a girl,' Anna mused, "my mother told me about Mercury. I think he was a trader and thief. In any case, he survived the great flood, walked at the edge of the waters as they drew back and found the shell of a tortoise, the strings of the animal still attached. He picked up the shell and plucked the sinews, which gave forth sound. In this way lyres and harps came into the world. Then it came to him that a stick, pulled across them, could set the strings in motion." She smiled, remembering the days when her mother had told her such tales.

"I remember that story!" exclaimed Leopold. "I read it as a schoolboy in Augsberg. I will put it in my *Violinschule*."

"Be sure to offer your instruction in small and careful steps," Anna admonished, "so that the pupil will not lose heart."

"The rest is a sign of silence," Leopold finally wrote, paring this simple sentence - at Anna's suggestions - out of several more that were cluttered with words. Anna thought this elegant, as were many other sentences when they were finally crafted.

The birth of a daughter, in the middle of the night that ended July and began August, was easy compared with the earlier three. She was baptized Maria Anna Walburga Ignatia, but Anna called her Nannerl from the moment she saw the squalling mite. The child was sturdy and alert, a pretty babe, with fair curls, a healthy appetite and a happy disposition. Once again, Anna was held in thrall. Her faith came rushing back.

"Be careful, Anna," Leopold warned, "lest you be disappointed once more." But he too was taken with his daughter and held her, sang to her and talked to her in a baby tongue.

Anna's friends, pleased with her return to good spirits, were quick to visit the new child.

"She will flourish," said Marianna, whose own daughter wriggled in her arms.

'This child will live to a ripe old age. I feel it in my bones, and if they are right about rain, why not about this child?" predicted Margarethe.

"There is something about her," said Theresa. "This one will live."

The priest at Anna's churching pronounced, "Man born of a woman, living for a short time, is filled with many miseries. Who cometh forth like a flower, and is destroyed, fleeteth as a shadow."

Anna paid little heed to the priest's gloomy preachment. The lovely Kyrie, "Lord have mercy, Christ have mercy," filled Anna's heart with the hope that this girl child, who had come forth like a flower, would be long upon the bud and blossom her full season.

Anna's happiness was marred by the death of her beloved Sister Gisella, who had been ill for some time of a wasting disease and had seen the baby Nannerl only once. "Here is your musician, Anna," croaked the old nun so weakly that Anna had to put her ear to the withered lips to hear. "Look at her fingers! Look at that fine head, filled with genius, like your own, Anna!" When Sister Gisella declared that her final days were come, Anna was summoned to her bedside. "Anna is the nearest to a child she has," said Abbess Eugenia, herself grown very thin and bent. Anna sat beside her old friend. "My daughter Nannerl," she said to Sister Gisella, "will be a musician, dear friend. That I promise you." Anna held the frail hand until it grew still and cold. She had wept with her mentor for joy over her healthy daughter. Now she wept with Gisella's sisters in sorrow.

"Gisella lived a good life on earth," commented the Abbess dryly, "and now the music of the spheres will likely improve."

In some measure, Anna thought, Sister Gisella was as much her mother as the woman through whose loins she had entered the world. The nun had touched Anna with confidence and hope, had told her that her genius was a precious trust and must not be neglected. Over and over through her life, Anna continued to find Sister Gisella at her side, a comfortable ghost who reassured and cheered her.

Old age threaded its way like a minor key through Nannerl's baby days. Eva Rosina's infirmities of body and temper increased. She slept through many a day, sitting gnarled in a shawl, and in conversation or at table she nodded off. Having brought her only living grandchild into the world, she was not interested in much else. She watched the child with hooded, blurring eyes, rousing herself to hold her and tell her stories. When Anna spoke to her mother, she was not always sure the old woman understood. Eva Rosina ate and drank little. She needed the chamber pot incessantly, but often soiled her clothes. When she spoke, it was of her ailments, though sometimes - only when Anna sang or played - she complained that music interfered with her rest.

Nannerl had begun to sit up by herself when Anna was again with child. She felt no apprehension about the impending birth. Nannerl's good health, she thought, had ended the curse that had plagued her childbearing.

14

1752-1756

LEOPOLD AND HIS FRIENDS WERE GATHERED in the Mozart's front room, packing up their instruments when Anna came home with seven-month-old Nannerl wrapped in shawls against the severe February weather. Without waiting to greet the musicians Anna burst out, "Some of the relics of St. Ruprecht are gone-stolen! And the young count of Thurn and Taxis is suspected! Nannerl sit here with Herr Adlgasser while Mama hangs up her cloak." Anton Adlgasser held out his hands for the child. "Your mother brings astonishing news," said Anton to Nannerl.

"But it cannot be true!" exclaimed Leopold, red spots appearing on his cheeks.

"It is all over the market," said Anna, putting her hand on her husband's arm.

Joseph Meissner, who could sing tenor parts as easily as bass, was also distressed. "Are you speaking of that young dandy who goes about with Father Egglstainer? How can this be, when Father Egglstainer makes such a parade of godliness?"

Meissner's father, Nikolaus, one of Leopold's colleagues at court, who had that afternoon played on the horn, chimed in, "That young dandy, who goes about with Father Egglstainer? But surely a man who makes such a parade of godliness . . . ."

"That's just it," said Anna. "There is muttering against Father Egglstainer, too. Some say he has sold indulgences to the simple folk in the countryside, corrupted the young count, raided the town treasury. There is talk of his acquaintance with Pietists."

Leopold, frowning as he unclipped the frog from his bow, loosening the hairs, had grown quite red in the face. "The old count did not raise his son to steal relics from the church! And Father Egglstainer! Just yesterday I heard him proclaim in the marketplace that women, being more amorous than men, have only the purpose of conceiving, suckling and breeding up of children. Therefore, the old fraud said, if we value morality, women and men must stay apart in public. It strains credulity."

"It's only gossip," Anna admitted, sitting down tiredly. As always, when she was with child, she felt unwell. "Who knows what is true?"

Leopold felt great consternation. His first employer, the old count - for whom Leopold had himself engraved his six sonatas on copper - was a man of honor. It was troubling that his wastrel son, falling in with the brazen hypocrite of a priest, might pull down the good name of Thurn and Taxis.

Still, there was much else to occupy Leopold's mind. The best families of Salzburg now enrolled their children under his instruction. He was always occupied with one or another of his projects. The instruments he bought and sold were considered to be of good quality and he could be trusted to charge a fair price. Compositions for the court fairly burst from his pen. His correspondence was large and he was proud that what he called the intelligentsia of Europe answered his letters.

Through the months of Anna's fifth pregnancy, the news of the scandal trickled out, enraging Leopold and all his circle of acquaintance. Father Egglstainer had, it appeared, either put the young count up to no end of deviltry or at least not tried to stop him. The fat priest continued to posture and declaim about public morality, yet it was on every tongue that he would do almost anything for money - misappropriating donations to the church, making off with statues and relics. The young count, it seemed, cheated at cards, did not pay his gambling debts and did whatever the priest put him up to. The old count, ailing and feeble, could not control his son, who drunkenly challenged all comers to duel, and the church did what it could to keep Father Egglstainer's misdeeds quiet. "It would not do," huffed Leopold to Anna, "to admit that churchmen are merely mortal. No! They hear us confess to our sins, but their own are covered by pious claptrap!"

Father Egglstainer, emboldened by having sold away church treasures at a great price - no one could discover to whom or where - tried to shift the blame to the several Jews the Archbishop relied on to secure loans. There was no room in Salzburg, proclaimed Father Egglstainer, for a race that suckled their young like pigs, that looked out their windows at Christian processions when they passed, even though it was forbidden, that dealt in poison, ritual murder, usury and all manner of deviltry.

"Enough!" thundered Leopold, upon hearing of Father Egglestainer's most recent calumny. "I will have something to say about this scoundrel. He has done more harm than any Jew could aspire to."

Anna felt her pains come on a blustery day in early November. As she held Johann Carolus Baptista Amadeus after her ordeal, Anna smiled weakly at the women with whom she had shared so many births. "At last," she said, "another son. Leopold will be pleased."

When he entered her room, so recently the preserve of women, he took the child from her. "Amadeus means beloved by God," he said. "He will be a man of honor, unlike some I could mention."

"Amadeus," murmured Anna. She liked the name, which honored Amadeus Pergmayer, who had stood godfather to all her children, their dear friend. Such a name reminded God to love and care for the child who had arrived upon the earth.

Nannerl, who had only just taken her first unsteady steps, was enchanted with her brother. She rocked his cradle, hung on the nurse's knee when she suckled him, stroked him when Anna held him. She talked her little language to him, amusing Anna and Leopold with sounds she must have heard them make.

Anna was uncomprehending when the child beloved of God died at three months old in the middle of the night. She awakened on a February morning to find him stiff and cold in his cradle, though the stove was burning and he was well-wrapped in warm blankets. She grieved that her poor child had made his journey to death in solitude.

Nannerl was puzzled. Over and over she toddled to his cradle, making small mewing sounds.

How tough the heart is, marveled Anna, grieving for the beautiful little boy with clear gray eyes. Over and over she had felt her own heart break. She had now delivered four children - Joachim, Cordula, Walpurgis and Amadeus - to death. But she could not descend into the stupor of mourning that had afflicted her prior to Nannerl's birth, as the child's needs and wants were perpetual. "I have had enough of birth," Anna declared to Marianna and Margarethe. "My body has served its purpose," she said. Her belly was flaccid, marked by the swelling and shrinking it had undergone. "I must find out how to keep from more getting of children."

"Shh!" cautioned Marianna, herself large with child. "You must be discreet. You know as well as I do that it is not thought good to interfere with Nature, but if you should drink savin boiled in beer, who would know?" Others of Anna's friends had ideas, all passed along in low voices, like stolen goods from thief to thief. Anna tried them all - the savin in beer, saying the Rosary after she and Leopold were together as husband and wife. She boiled teas of parsley and marjoram. She drank stinking ram's urine and carried around with her the tiny finger bone of a stillborn babe that Henriette Weisner gave her. She took the ergot that Eva Rosina secured for her, careful to keep it a secret.

But her own concerns must yield to Leopold's. There was music needed for the installation of the new Archbishop, the Count of Schrattenbach. Further, he had written and had printed, at his own expense, a pamphlet, bitterly lampooning Father Egglstainer's corruptions. Leopold paid several young boys a pfennig apiece to hand it out in the marketplace. Though many of his friends praised the lampoon, Leopold was shortly summoned by the Cathedral syndic and, for disrespect to the Church, ordered to stand at attention in the marketplace at its busiest time, while his pamphlet was torn to pieces before his eyes and scattered about his feet. Then he was to pick up the scraps and make public apology to the good priest, whose reputation had been offended by his sallies.

"I cannot, Anna," he insisted, his face red and his hands clenched. "I cannot apologize to those who sully the good name of the Church and my patron. The old count's probity is beyond reproach."

"Oh, Leopold. This is a dreadful thing. But what if you defy them?" Anna asked. Leopold was so proud a man and his anger had come not from disrespect, but care for the well-being of Salzburg.

"Then, I suppose," said Leopold, spitting out the words, "I will have to search elsewhere for employment. I am sorry, sweetheart, to burden you so when you are still grieving the child."

After much deliberation, Leopold finally conceded, persuaded by his colleagues that he must stay in Salzburg. He knew well that he had not the money to uproot his family and to seek his fortune in some other place.

For the rest of his life, the memory of Leopold's humiliation was like a live ember in his soul. He remembered with painful clarity how his transgression was announced to every gaper assembled to take home a pound of wurst or a cabbage, how he had been ordered by a church functionary to speak his apology louder, how his fingers had felt like lead as he gathered the scraps of the pamphlet that had poured out from good intentions. He would never forget those moments of public obloquy. He would never again trust that good would prevail.

Barely seven months after Amadeus' death, Anna was again with child, despite her attempts to prevent it. Only her duties to her daughter and her aging mother kept her from despair.

Nannerl, at two years old, had grown fast on her feet. Music enthralled her. When Anna sat at the harpsichord, Nannerl asked to sit beside her. "Nan p'ay! Nan p'ay!" she insisted if Anna did not give over the keyboard.

"Nannerl!" Eva Rosina ordered, "stop that noise. Do not encourage her, Anna."

Eva Rosina criticized everything Anna did. She hardly stirred from the house now, and was often ill and bad-tempered.

Marie Crescentia Fransiska de Paula, Anna's sixth child, who was born as every flowering tree in Salzburg burst into spring bloom, succumbed after a little less than two months. A flux drained her poor little body faster than Anna and the nurse could drip herbal teas into her. She never kept down the nurse's milk. She was buried in St. Peter's, where the largest part of the Mozart family lay.

Anna gagged on the taste of the bitter fruit, which, said the priest, Eve had eaten on behalf of all womankind. How could it be just, Anna wondered, that she - thousands and hundreds of thousands of women later - should be required to pay so dearly for the first woman's small disobedience. Anna dreamed, some nights, of throwing herself into the River Salzach, which rushed so quickly through town. But the needs of her living child, her husband and her dying mother kept her anchored to the world.

Anna was disquieted to learn she was once again with child only a year after Franziska's death. She could not, she thought, bear any more pain and loss.

Nannerl, at four and a half years, had learned to pick out simple tunes on the clavier. She had made up little songs of her own. She loved to practice so that she could show her father, who delighted in his precocious daughter.

She needed no coaxing to play for his friends when they gathered to make music. She and Anna sang together as well, and when Anna sat down to compose - which she did now infrequently - the child asked for a piece of paper and a pen as well.

Leopold's thoughts were much in Augsburg, for his mother had come into some money, which she had divided among her other children. When Theresa Hagenauer set off for Augsburg for a visit with her sister, Leopold sent with her a petition to his mother that he should receive his equal share, which he planned to use to pay the expense of publishing his book of instruction for aspiring violinists, the *Violinschule.* There was no response from Augsburg, for his mother's anger at Leopold had become her consort.

Anna again felt most unwell. She could not interest herself in Leopold's schemes. She was tired and vomited morning and night. "It is all I can do to put your dinner on the table, feed Nannerl and cook up the messes Mama wants," she said when Leopold complained about his mother.

"It's very hard when no one takes the least interest in me," said Eva Rosina querulously, having overheard Anna. "Nannerl neglects her grandmother. She has not come at all today."

"Yes she has, Mama," said Anna, as she combed her mother's thin hair. "She came in three times to sit with you already today, remember?"

"You are wrong, Anna," said Eva Rosina. "You make up stories to plague me. I always said . . . ." Her voice dwindled as she dropped off to sleep.

Eva Rosina had barely spoken for several weeks. Her skin hung from her bones and her breath rattled in her throat. She wanted nothing but to sleep, and she grew so thin that the counterpane covering her scarcely revealed her form. One morning, Anna wakened early, dreaming that her mother had called out to her to come. She went to find her laboring to draw breath. Anna held her in her arms as darkness gave way to light, cradling her head and holding her hand. Nannerl came into her grandmother's room, wearing only her shift, to watch with her mother.

"Wrap up in this quilt with me," Anna whispered, glad of the child's warm body against her own.

Eva Rosina gasped for breath and clutched her granddaughter's hand. All at once, her sunken, haggard face, which had not smiled for many months, changed, becoming rosy, smooth and beautiful. She looked as she must have when Wolfgang Nicolaus first saw her. For a moment, Anna knew her again as she had been so long ago in St. Gilgen, on her knees in the garden or standing in the hot kitchen, her sleeves rolled up as she chopped vegetables and sorted eggs. For a fleeting moment, Eva Rosina might have been going out the door to attend some woman in need, or about to sing, her chin tilted up, her light blue eyes happy and her hair floating about her face. But then as Anna and Nannerl watched, her skin took on the look of tallow and caved in at her eyes and cheeks. Her breath came less often and finally not at all. Anna laid her down gently and rested her head on the old woman's chest. Her heart had ceased to beat.

Anna bathed her mother's limbs, now empty of flesh, and wrapped her in the finest linen she had. She buried her, Eva Maria Rosina Puxbaum, the Widow Altman, the Widow Pertl, who had lost her daughters Clara and Gertrud, whose five grandchildren lay beside her in death. Even Leopold, who had found her such an irritation, was surprised by his sorrow.

The birth of Anna's seventh child was the most strenuous and difficult of all. She longed for her mother, who knew what to do. The new midwife, Frau Hertzl, had different ways, which made Anna apprehensive. The darkness of the room seemed to bode ill and the quivering shadows of her friends on the wall oppressed her spirits. The pains tore through her body unrelieved by the posset which had sometimes helped in the past. Anna cried out to St. Margaret for delivery from all and heard no answering comfort.

A tiny, frail boy was born at last, misshapen from the ordeal. He was hurried off to the cathedral by Leopold, who had him baptized Johannus Chrysostomus Wolfgangus Theophilus Mozart, a great name for so very little flesh.

Anna bled greatly after this birth, her womb having been damaged by the clumsy midwife, and lay to mend in gory sheets, which her mother would never have allowed. Later on, Anna counted the injury to her womb a fortunate one; her childbearing ended with this last difficult birth.

Anna kept the new babe next to her in the bed. The insignificant creature to which she had given birth was, she thought, like the last piece of goods on the bolt, a bit askew, his skin minutely creased. One ear was misshapen, a small defect in light of the likelihood that he would soon join his brothers and sisters in the cold earth of St. Peters churchyard. She could not bear to be apart from him when he died. It seemed to her a lonely matter to struggle so to enter the world, and then to leave it without friends.

PART 3

15

1757

ANNA SHRIEKED IN SURPRISE AND PAIN and Leopold hurried to the kitchen.

His wife sat gasping on the floor in a sea of steaming soup. Leopold took in her situation and felt a surge of irritation. How could he accomplish anything when his wife rushed about too quickly and dropped the dinner? "Why can you not be more careful?" he scolded. What he meant to ask was, Are you hurt? How can I help you? She was injured, he could tell that, but he stood at the top of the kitchen steps, frowning, not sure what to do. He drew his brows together. Why could he not be gentler with this woman he loved? All he could think of was the pull of the task that sat on his writing table, as if it were a magnet and he a piece of iron.

Anna still felt the hot, heavy kettle that had tipped when she set it too near the edge of the stove. She had grabbed for it, searing her hand. The hot liquid had splashed up her arm as she pulled back. Now she squatted amidst her drowned and greasy skirts in the middle of the spoiled dinner, rocking her arm against her breast as if it were an infant in need. In the next room, the baby, now a year old and sick with earache and fever, howled piteously, while six-year old Nannerl stood at the top of the kitchen steps, one bare foot curled around the other. She too was feverish. "Mama, get up!" she whimpered, smearing her tears and snot together.

Anna knew she had been working too fast. The servant girl had stayed at home to tend her dying father and Anna had been trying to prepare the dinner, care for two ailing children, clean the house, get out to buy bread before the bakery shut its doors, and iron the shirt Leopold needed for court. She knew Leopold was right. She should have been more careful. But all she could feel beyond the furious pain was anger. Why did he blame instead of help? "Get Theresa," gasped Anna, breathing hard to surmount the insistent burn.

Anna could always count on Theresa Hagenauer, more friend than landlady. She came up the stairs quickly from her husband's shop, sturdy and sensible, bringing extra water to cool the fires in Anna's hand and a tincture made from the fruit of mandragora to dull the pain. "Swallow just a little, Anna," she said. "It can be dangerous." Theresa went for the sobbing Wolfgang, who curled against her, hiccuping. She reassured Nannerl and, one-handed, washed her face. Settling the girl to entertain her brother with the rag poppet Anna had made for him, Theresa helped Anna to change her sodden clothes for a soft old dressing gown.

Having brought Theresa to his wife's aid, Leopold retreated to his work, but he was distracted. He had much to do to finish his *Report on the Present State of Music at the Court of Salzburg*. Herr Wilhelm Marpurg of Berlin had asked for a survey of music in this city with its great heritage of music and architecture. Leopold, flattered by Marpurg's praise of his *Violinschule*, was pleased with the commission. When Anna had interrupted him with her mishap, he had been writing of himself as "1st violinist and leader of the orchestra." It was not, he knew, strictly true. He was still fourth violinist, but he intended to rise to the higher position and was well-regarded as a prolific composer, even if nothing from his pen - aside from the sonatas he had long ago engraved himself - had issued in print. He was deviled by the thought that he should have done more to comfort his wife. But surely it was her task to keep the household in order. He might well have been away at court altogether. He did not like to think how she would have managed in that case. He ran his hand through his hair, pulling it loose from the bit of ribbon that held it back.

Theresa fetched her own servant from below and together, their skirts tucked up, they mopped Anna's kitchen floor. The servant carried the spoiled vegetables into the street for the pigs and poured away the dirty water, bringing more water from the tap and extra ashes for scrubbing. The mandragora made Anna drowsy, but she was still too wrought up to lie down on her bed. Theresa made her sit on the kitchen steps. The children were peacefully occupied in the hallway behind her. "Stop nattering, Anna," Theresa ordered. "You can't do much good with your poor arm. It's light work for two." That evening, while Anna slept, Theresa brought in bread and the excellent stew for which she was justly famous. She stayed, as well, to clean the dishes.

When Leopold came to bed, Anna woke up groggily. Leopold asked, "How is your poor arm, my sweet?" The candle flickered on its stand.

"I am stupid from the mandragora," said Anna, "but still it pains." She shook her head to clear it. "But I wonder at you, Leopold. All I wished for was a kind word, not blame." Her tongue was furred and thick. "I can take myself to task for carelessness. But I help you in everything, so why could you not help with the children? Something. Say you were sorry?"

Leopold raised his quizzical eyebrow. He held out his hands helplessly. "I did not know where to begin," he said, his voice low. "I have so little practice taking care of children, especially when they are not well." He gestured broadly and Anna pulled her wounded arm aside to keep it safe.

"And I was wearing court clothes," Leopold went on. His eyes were troubled. "I am sorry, my dearest. I was not kind." It was hard for him to apologize, harder since his public mortification over the affair of Father Egglestainer and the young Count of Thurn and Taxis. To be thought wrong about anything, it seemed to him, was a danger.

Dimly, as she slid back toward sleep, Anna felt a swelling in her heart. She loved Leopold that he could so swallow his pride. But once again she roused herself. "Could you really not pick up the baby nor take Nannerl on your lap, just for the moment?" she asked groggily.

Leopold moistened his long index finger to douse the light. "I could have, I suppose," he said, "but I would not have known which thing to do first. Everything seemed to need attention all at once." He sounded puzzled. How did she do it, he wondered briefly. Gently he put his hand on her forehead, which was hot.

He has such tender, cool hands, Anna thought, a musician's supple fingers. "I am in awe of you," Leopold went on, "your command of household tasks. You know what comes first, what second, and so on." He had often noticed that Anna could do many things at once - comfort the baby, stir the pot, get something that Nannerl asked for, and carry on a conversation with Theresa, Marianna, Margarethe or some other friend. All at the same time! He seemed able to think of only one thing at a time. It seemed to him that what people said must be true, that women were better adapted to keep the house in order, that Nature had made them especially well-suited for such things. "Above all, my dear, if I hold the baby when he cries, or Nannerl, who will write on the present state of music in Salzburg? . . . ." His voice came to her as from a distance.

Sleep claimed her, though all the night long a ribbon of pain threaded through her restless dreams. She dreamt that she sat at the clavier, strange, dissonances issuing from her injured and throbbing finger ends. Someone - Anna could not tell who - poured pot after pot of soup into the fragile instrument, boiling the finish, ruining the wood, loosening the strings. "You spoiled it!" shrieked Nannerl, as the clavier drooped on its stand and melted like a candle. "Mama! Mama!" cried the baby. Anna ran around, driven to pick up all their possessions and hold the children against the tide of soup, which rose around her. Then she was in St. Gilgen, weeping as invisible hands shut the warped lid of the harpsichord and carried it down the stairs, while Leopold rubbed his hands and said, "Genius, my dear, must not spill soup." She ran about, looking everywhere for lost buttons, brewing remedies for colds and fevers, comforting the children, finding and mending lost stockings, washing soiled linen, cooking up messes to appease finicking appetites, patching torn frocks and the seats of trousers worn thin. She found mice in the larder, no matter that she had just scrubbed it, and green wood smoked in the stove.

When Anna awoke, she was tired, weak and feverish. The tale of her mischance had traveled quickly and friends and neighbor women dropped in and took the children with them so that she could sleep, succumbing to the belladonna prescribed by Silvester Barisani at Leopold's request. The women brought in their best stews and an occasional joint or fowl for the Mozarts to eat.

Anna floated in and out of awareness, sometimes back in St. Gilgen as a small girl, where townsfolk admired her brilliant compositions; sometimes at Nonnberg, where the nuns shared the tasks of provisioning and cleaning, making time to sing their Masses. She wandered into sunlit rooms - hundreds - each with a clavier, clean, well-tuned and inviting. Anna opened her mouth and heard a host of instruments, perfectly pitched, her voice soaring above them.

When she awoke, the bedroom was still. Someone must have taken the children away. She would rise in this precious silence and go to Leopold's desk, write down the sounds she had just heard. Instead, sleep claimed her again.

In the several days it took her to recover, Leopold finished Marpurg's report. "I am happy to say," he told Anna, as she laced up her bodice, favoring her right hand, "that the present condition of music in Salzburg is thriving thanks to the Archbishop's interest and generosity, and thanks as well to the travelers who come here from other lands, bringing their music with them." The children were playing in high spirits, wearing clean clothes, Nannerl's hair neatly braided. "Look, Mama," she crowed. "Woferl can walk like anything now!" The baby took five unsteady steps toward her, grinning, then sat down suddenly, his eyes round with surprise.

Sometimes, when all the work was done, Anna took the children to hear her husband's compositions played at the Cathedral, in one of the other churches, at the university, or in fine weather even out of doors, in the gardens of Mirabell or outside of town at Hellbrun. Nannerl was absorbed and attentive wherever there was music, while Wolfgang was delighted by everything he saw or heard.

Anna, like the wives of the other musicians, sometimes attended musical events in the Archbishop's residence. On these occasions she was always torn, enjoying the music and the splendor, but well aware that such occasions were a reminder to his servants that their employer was rich and powerful beyond their most extravagant dreams.

"I want to go to the Archbishop's house too!" Nannerl said wistfully as Anna dressed, letting her best silk fall over the hoops that made her skirt large and graceful. "Oh, Mama, you look like a queen." Wolfgang played with Anna's uncomfortable court shoes with their high heels, pointed toes and ribbons that tied across the instep.

"I know you would like to come, sweetheart," said Anna, arranging the lace fichu that crossed her bosom. "Someday you will."

"And then I will play for the Archbishop," Nannerl announced confidently. "Tell me all about the palace, Mama."

"Well," said Anna. She knew that Nannerl wanted to hear her tell about the palace just the way she always did. "The floors are inlaid with all kinds of wood in fancy patterns and polished until you can see yourself in them. There are more candles than we use in a year, ten years more like, set in crystal chandeliers that sprinkle light around like summer rain. Papa and all the orchestra will wear handsome red coats with silver braid and there will be such elegance of clothes and wigs as I cannot tell you. And fine food, too! Your friend Frau Gilowsky will be there, and Frau Antretter."

"Here, Woferl. Give Mama her shoes. Ach! They could use these to torture prisoners into confession. Now be good, you two. Mind Marthe and say your prayers," she said, putting on her shawl as the servant girl came in to scoop up Wolfgang.

An evening at the Archbishop's palace always made Anna aware that at home she and Marthe made the candles and that the Mozarts retired early so as not to burn them up too fast. The floor reflected nothing but the effects of daily scrubbing. Their food was plain. On the other hand, at home she need not wear shoes that pinched. Despite all the show of the Archbishop's life, he could not hire music any better than what was heard almost daily in the Mozart's homely quarters. Leopold's friends came in from court, sometimes for cards or a game of target shooting and always there was music to follow other entertainments. The older children tended the little ones in play, though Nannerl most often came to sit with her mother to listen and sometimes sing with her.

Despite all his musical retinue, Anna wondered if the Archbishop had the small daily music she and her children shared. She made up little songs to sing her children - lullabies, songs that told the stories she remembered from her youth, songs her own mother had sung to her. Many a day, as Nannerl helped her mother with the household tasks, learning how to do the things a woman must know, the two of them warbled together like meadowlarks, the small birds Anna remembered from her own earliest days whose song had embroidered the still air of St. Gilgen. Nannerl's voice was as pure and sweet as a stream of clear water. She had long since teased her mother to teach her to play on the clavier. The minute Anna sat down at the keyboard herself, Nannerl wanted to play. While Anna attended to her many household duties, the child often climbed up to the clavier by herself and picked out her own pieces. Leopold, amused by her efforts had to shoo her away, as if she were a flock of poultry, when he wanted to use the instrument.

When the house shone and provisions had been fetched in from the market, when the mending was caught up and dinner simmered on the stove, Nannerl said, "Mama, will you teach me now?"

"Yes," said Anna. Holding the squirming Wolfgang firmly with one arm, she sat with Nannerl at the clavier. "My mama sat with me just so at the harpsichord, Nannerl, when she was young and beautiful and not the least bit cranky."

Nannerl straightened up, flexing her slender shoulders. "I didn't know Grossmutter then, did I?

"No," said Anna. "By the time you were born she had suffered many losses. She turned her mind against music. But when I was a little girl, younger than you are now, she played so beautifully and sang - oh, how she sang! She taught me at first, before Sister Gisella taught me. Sister Gisella, my dear teacher, was sure you would be a musician, Nannerl, even when you were just a babe of a few weeks."

"I will be," said Nannerl. "I will be a musician."

Wolfgang squealed, "Me too, me too."

"Little echo," Anna smiled.

"Did you want to be a musician, Mama?" asked Nannerl.

"Did I? Oh, my yes, I did. I still do."

Nannerl looked puzzled. Mama was Mama. Sometimes Nannerl heard women sing in the Cathedral or in concerts or plays, but Mama sang at home, while she worked, and when people came or the Mozarts went to another house for music. Papa was the musician.

Anna ruffled little Woferl's fine curls. "I was about four years old. Some musicians came to our house in St. Gilgen from Salzburg. I think it was in the spring, and they played compositions by Heinrich Biber. He was once *Kapellmeister* in the Archbishop's court, but long dead by then, of course. And I thought, I will be like Biber. I will write my music down and people will play it even if I am not there."

"Well," said Nannerl, thinking that there had been enough talk about her mother. "I will be a great composer when I grow up, as great as Papa and Herr Eberlin."

Wolfgang chortled happily, reaching for the clavier keys.

Anna shifted him so that she could nuzzle his cheek and kissed him happily. "Nannerl will play just now, Woferl, and I will teach you later, when you are a big boy."

16

1758

USING SOME OF LEOPOLD'S MUSIC PAPER and her strongest needle, Anna stitched together a notebook for her daughter. She copied into it exercises and easy pieces for the child to learn. On a gloomy, rainy day, when Nannerl had helped her tidy the rooms and dust the instruments, which she did with earnest pleasure, Anna said to the seven year-old, "What a help you are, Nannerl! Now, I have something for you. You must shut your eyes and hold out your hands." She reached up, onto the top of the wardrobe, drew down the notebook and placed it in the child's outstretched hands.

Nannerl's eyes flew open. "Oh, Mama!" she exclaimed. She sat down, leafing through the pages, smoothing them with the tips of her fingers, as if the paper were some fragile fabric. "My very own music book! Thank you, Mama!" She hugged it to her plain brown dress and her rosy face shone with pride and joy. Anna thought she had never seen a child so lovely, her blue eyes glowing like the colored glass in a church window, her soft curls framing her face. The Archbishop's candles, though there were hundreds lit at once, could not light the room more brightly.

The image of Gertrud's face when she spoke of Saint Wilgefortis flooded Anna's memory. Nannerl's face was like that. Anna knew at that moment that the divine force of genius coursed through this child. She, Anna Pertl Mozart, must tend that spring, given by God to flow in this small body. She remembered how she and Gertrud, having discovered a freshet in the woods, had pulled back from it the sticks and dead leaves that threatened to smother it so that it burbled freely.

Two year-old Wolfgang played happily with scraps of wood Anna had persuaded a carpenter to give her. While Anna taught Nannerl to play the first of the pieces she had copied into the notebook, he stacked them carefully, then knocked them down, chortling with pleasure.

Nannerl learned fast and played accurately. Her hands were light on the clavier. She sat at her lessons diligently and had soon mastered the exercises and pieces her mother had written down. She treasured her notebook above all things. She always washed her hands before she touched it and asked her mother to put it away each time she finished her practice, so that it would come to no harm. Often, when she had it out, she sat with the notebook on her lap, looking at the music or stroking the pages.

One day, when Leopold sat at his desk to compose, Nannerl pulled a heavy stool next to him, sat up on her knees and busied herself with an old pen and his inkwell, imitating her father, who went away every day to make music for the court. So long as she made no noise, he had no objection to her company. When he paused, from time to time, to consider some phrase or harmony, his long fingers settled gently on the little head from which the curls fell forward as she gnawed on her lip and blotted her paper. Nannerl concentrated intensely for so young a child.

When her father went out, Nannerl brought Anna her smudged and spotted page. "Look, Mama, I composed just like Papa. Come," she said, pulling at her mother's hand, which was covered with the juice of onions, "come and hear it."

"Patience, Nannerl!" said Anna. "I have to wash off the onions or we will both weep." She picked up Wolfgang, who had been watching her and stirring his own imaginary mess in a bowl with a wooden spoon, and set him astride her hip. Nannerl sat at the clavier and played what she had composed, an ungainly little dance, but tuneful and cunning.

Anna was dumbfounded. "Did you do this by yourself, my child?" she marveled. "Without help from Papa?"

"Yes, Mama. I sat very still, just the way Papa does, and I wrote down the notes. But first I heard the way it sounds inside my head."

Tears filled Anna's eyes. Nannerl was so small to harbor so great a gift. Her bones were light as a bird's.

"Mama," complained Wolfgang. "I want to play." He squirmed on his mother's hip and pushed at her.

"I will teach you, Woferl," said Nannerl importantly, "but not for long. I must practice for Papa. Put him up here, Mama. Please," she added, remembering to be polite.

Absently Anna lifted Wolfgang to the narrow bench. Anna pictured herself in St. Gilgen, her mother sitting by her side to teach her at the keyboard as now she - that daughter - stood by her own daughter. Anna had often heard it said that it was unnatural for a woman to compose, that such a practice would wither the womb. She had sometimes worried that, by wanting to compose herself, she had in some way injured the womb in which seven infants had rested before their birth, so that only two had survived. If she encouraged Nannerl, did she endanger the child who would grow to womanhood and bear children of her own?

All afternoon Nannerl practiced her piece. Wolfgang, marched or scampered around in time to his sister's music, then lost interest and played with his poppet, till he curled up with it and, his thumb in his mouth, slept. Nannerl added ornaments and flourishes to her little piece, as she had heard her father's friends do.

When Leopold came in later that day he brought Andreus Schactner and Wenzel Hebelt for some hours of music. These were Nannerl's particular favorites. Andreus was jack of all instruments, the chief trumpeter in the orchestra who also played on any instrument that could be strung. He wrote poems and plays and was not ashamed to work with his hands on any piece of wood, repairing instruments as cunningly as Anna patched and mended clothing. Wenzel, shy to a fault, blushing whenever he was spoken to, played the violin and composed. He was so fair and freckled that he seemed to lack eyebrows and eyelashes and to wear a perpetually startled expression. He was always kind to Nannerl, who chattered enough for both of them.

"There can be no doubt of the excellence nor the quantity of your composition, Leopold," Andreus was saying as the three men climbed the stairs.

"And they are well aware," said Leopold, in heated indignation, "that Lorenz Mizler invited me to join his Society for Musicology in Leipzig, and though nothing came of it, that was none of my doing."

Wenzel, silent but attentive, nodded vigorously.

"Listen to this, Anna," said Leopold. "I am to have the post of second violinist."

"Surely that is good," said Anna, puzzled by his dour countenance.

"*Second,* Anna, not *first*, not *konzertmeister* . . . ." said Leopold, wondering that his wife did not immediately understand the slight visited on him.

"Of which your husband is surely deserving," said Andreus. "He is so well recognized for his composition and as author of . . . ."

"Ah," broke in Leopold, "Here is my sweet daughter, hard at work to learn her music lesson. Climb down, now, sweetheart. Papa and his friends want to play."

"Look, Papa!" objected Nannerl, waving her little composition with excitement. "Look Herr Wenzel. Look Herr Schactner. Look at my piece. I wrote it all by myself. Listen. I will play it for you!"

But Leopold, already short of temper because of his failure to receive the promotion he believed should be his, had no patience. "Get down, child," he ordered. "You heard me."

Nannerl, usually compliant, insisted, "But Papa, listen. I composed a piece myself!"

Anna could see that Leopold, embarrassed by lack of preferment at court, would not be crossed by his daughter in the presence of his friends. "Get down at once!" he said crossly.

Wenzel looked up at the ceiling. Andreas picked up the baby and played with his small fingers.

Leopold was in a fury. "Maria Anna Walburga Ignatia!" he said, his voice cold. "You must not defy your father."

Wolfgang, surprised by his father's tone, began to wail. He had already, in his two years, shown a marked dislike for hard or sudden noises.

Nannerl paled. Her eyes grew large. She knew better than to resist her father when he spoke in that voice. Slowly, crumpling her composition in her hand, she climbed down and went to her mother. But Leopold's wrath, once aroused, was no small thing. "Disobedience in a girl is unnatural," he fumed. "My daughter should know her place and not defy her father!" Seizing the child by the arm, he hustled her, now weeping, to the kitchen. "Stand there and face the wall," he ordered. Anna followed them. She had taken Wolfgang from Andreas. Both children sobbed. "And you, Anna," said Leopold harshly. "You must not to speak to Nannerl. She is a bad girl."

Anna felt Nannerl's pain all the way up and down her spine. She paced, rubbing Wolfgang's back until he cried himself to sleep against her shoulder.

Should she disobey her husband to speak to her child? If Anna spoke, Nannerl would learn defiance from her mother. But if Anna did not speak, she would join Leopold in cruelty. Better defiant than cruel, she thought.

Nannerl's sobs had quieted and Anna heard the men's low voices in the other room and then the beginnings of a trio, but the music was hateful to her and likewise the men who played it. Bouncing a little to soothe the sleeping baby, Anna moved closer to where Nannerl stood, drooping and defeated. She put her hand on her daughter's head and spoke softly, so that Leopold would not hear her. "I am sorry," she murmured. "Papa has not been here all day. He does not know how you worked and practiced. He came in thinking of something else."

Nannerl glanced at her mother, her face white and eyes blank.

"Your father loves you. You know that, but sometimes he is quick-tempered," Anna urged, quietly. But she thought, why do I justify him to her, whom he has wounded? She needs my help. Just now he does not deserve it. "Your piece is so good, Nannerl. Play it for him another time, when he is not so tired and distracted."

Nannerl did not answer, though a shudder like a sob ran through her body.

Shifting the baby, Anna drew Nannerl against her. If she had to choose between her husband and her children, she thought, she would always choose the children.

Nannerl stood in exile through the evening meal, a silent and joyless occasion. Anna banged the dishes on the table and would not speak to her husband. She could tell that Leopold, too, was still angry.

"Now," he said coldly as he wiped his mouth, "you must go to bed, Nannerl."

The child went off to sleep without a morsel of food.

Anna dared not oppose her husband in this mood. She feared to feed the flames of his anger. She knew that when he felt wronged, nothing would quench his passion, which would die down with time. He would taste ashes of remorse in his mouth the next day, she thought.

In the morning, after he had gone to court, she searched the house, but could not find the piece of paper with her daughter's smeared notes written on it. "Where is it?" she inquired of the girl.

Nannerl shook her head, her lips pressed tightly together. She would not speak of her piece again. Nor, Anna noticed, was she ever again at ease with her old friends Andreus and Wenzel.

"I love my husband with all my heart," Anna confided to Maragarethe, "but sometimes I feel it harden against him. Sometimes we are as much at one as the waters of the Salzach and neither of us can run along nor dash against a rock without the other. But sometimes we are like currents speeding in opposite directions. You know how it looks when a storm whips up the waters and throws them at cross-purposes? Sometimes I hardly know him. He seems a stranger."

Margarethe nodded. "I have no experience of a husband," she said thoughtfully, "but my father does not often show affection, though he demands that I serve him. He provides for me, but his rule is harsh. Sometimes I think he is an utter stranger to me."

Anna took a cup of the good strong coffee that Margarethe's servant handed to her. "What a treat. Two ladies, no children, peace and quiet!" The children played with the wooden toys that Margarethe kept in a small old chest under the watchful eye of a servant in another room. I swear, Margarethe, you live like an empress. Look at these cups! The light comes through the rims!"

"A Jewish empress!" laughed Margarethe. "Not likely!"

"So," Anna went on, "I stand up for the children, doing as Leopold forbids. But often they too drive me to distraction. It is confusing. I would cheerfully lay down my life for them without a moment's hesitation. Just a glimpse of the back of Nannerl's neck or Wolfgang's misshapen ear takes my breath away. But sometimes I cannot abide their constant need of me. Sometimes I want to wake up widowed and childless. Of course I do not really mean it," she said crossing herself.

Only Margarethe was privy to the perplexities that riddled Anna's life like the woodworms that bored into unprotected instruments. Once spoken aloud, Anna's troublesome thoughts seemed less unnatural and wicked. She felt more connection to Margarethe - a spinster, a Jew - than to the busy Catholic matrons who were the constant warp and woof of her life.

Margarethe entrusted to Anna as much as she received. She told Anna that she had loved once. Her suitor had mistaken her brusque humor for rejection and had traveled the world without asking a second time for her hand. Thus she served to this day as her father's companion and hostess.

"Leopold is a good man, a good husband, and who could have better children? But sometimes, Margarethe, a wicked spirit takes hold of me and I am so angry at them, so full of spite, so tired of their wants. I try with all my heart to understand Leopold. He has much to do, I know that. But when the evil spell is on me, I am hard-pressed to ease his burdens."

Margarethe listened to her friend intently, making the small encouraging noises that signified, Yes, yes, I understand.

"I hear it said that everyone marvels at your husband," Margarethe commented. "They say he has a discerning mind, that his *Violinschule* is a great and useful work, that no one composes so many symphonies, serenades, dances and church music in so short a time."

"Yes," said Anna. "He is admirable. He works without stint. How can I begrudge him?"

"Tell me," said Margarethe, "who it is keeps his house clean. Who puts dinner on his table every day? Who mends his linen and tends his children?"

Anna raised her eyebrows. "Just guess!" she said, laughing dryly.

"And tell me as well," Margarethe said, "if he had all those things to do for himself, when would he compose and play and teach and so on?"

"He could not," Anna said.

"Then," said Margarethe, "it takes at least two to do what Leopold does. His accomplishments are not his alone, but yours as well. You help him compose every piece. You love your husband and your children, never doubt it," she said. "But they need and take so much *from* you."

Margarethe's words were like a cool lotion on abraded hands.

"They give much to me as well," Anna admitted, "affection, amusement. Leopold brings home the money that puts bread on the table. He never raises his hand against me. But you have hit the nail," she mused. "I want Leopold to know that his compositions are, in some measure, mine. Somehow, my need to compose has given way to his. I long for what everyone says Nature did not intend."

"Well," said Margarethe. "Where did that longing come from if not from Nature?"

Leopold and his friends spoke often of Nature, which ordered the world. For them, Anna thought, Nature meant God. Sometimes, in her opinion, they mistook the arrangements men had made for their convenience for Nature's ordering. When she thought of Nature, it was the things no man could regulate, the squirrels that flew through trees and plants that flowered from seed. It was her charge to see that her children's natures were allowed to fly and flower. But she had also to teach them about the world that men had ordered.

"Well," sighed Anna, as she rose to gather her children from their play, "whenever I hear anyone speak of Nature, I know it means I will cook and clean."

17

1759-1761

IN THE MOZART FAMILY, music was the common language. Anna sang as she went about her daily tasks. She sang with her children and often sat with Nannerl at the clavier, holding little Wolfgang on her lap. She sang with Leopold and with the many friends who came to their house to make music. Leopold often played his violin, and Nannerl had been known to lift her father's instrument carefully from its case and put it under her chin in imitation of her father. Even Wolfgang made up little tunes while he played at other games and piped up with perfect confidence when his mother and sister sang. He adored Nannerl and wanted to be like her in everything, not least in making music. He was eager to learn from his mother and father as well. All three were glad to teach a child of such cheerful aptitude.

For Leopold, music was inextricable from his ambition to rise to greater worldly prominence. He was well-regarded as an able and prolific composer, a dependable performer, a pedagogue whose reputation extended throughout the German-speaking world, but always he yearned to advance to higher position.

Music was the native tongue of Anna's soul, but the claims of music were countered by those of the children - dearer to her than her own life - and Leopold, by the incessant tasks to be done. She had little time either to compose or to study the new music that flooded into Salzburg. Her musical gifts - genius, Leopold had often said in earlier days - collected verdigris and dust, no matter how brightly she sang about the house.

Leopold had taught Nannerl at the clavier for nearly a year when she asked her mother to reach down her notebook from the top of the cupboard. Shyly Nannerl showed her father her most treasured possession.

Leopold nodded. "This is excellent, Nannerl. I see that Mama has already written down some exercises. Excellent, excellent! See here." He took up his pen and dipped it into the inkwell. "I will write here, in French - that is the language of the world. *Pour le Clavecin. Ce livre appartient à Mademoiselle Marie Anne Mozart 1759.*"

"What does it mean, Papa?" Nannerl asked.

"It means, 'For the clavier, this book belongs to Mademoiselle' - you know what that means - 'Marie Anne Mozart, 1759.' " He held the page at arm's length, admiring what he had written. "Here," he said. "We will cut this off and stick it to the front of your notebook, where all can see, and I will write more compositions in it for you to learn."

That evening Leopold sat with his wife as she finished the day's mending. "What a quick study Nannerl is, Anna."

Anna pulled her shoulders back to ease the ache of bending over her sewing and trimmed the wick of the tallow candle that had begun to smoke. "Nannerl does learn quickly," she said, "and has such a fine touch. What do you think, my dear, am I right about her genius?"

"Mmmm," said Leopold, "genius. Who can tell? Nothing is as simple as I used to think. People say the female cannot . . . ."

"But you do not hold with all *that*?" said Anna.

"Well," said Leopold slowly, "I do not, precisely, but no one can gainsay the Archbishop . . . . We must think about what is good for the girl, my dear, and you know yourself that a woman has such distractions . . . ." Since his humiliation by the Cathedral chapter in the matter of his lampoon, Leopold had grown more cautious.

"I am surprised at you," said Anna crossly, putting out the candle and rising. She was shaken. "I will bank the fire in the kitchen. See to the stove in here, if you please." But what Leopold said was true. There were indeed distractions, she thought as she unlaced her bodice and took off her skirt.

Anna thought of the painting she had seen at the pilgrimage church of Maria Plain, just outside of Salzburg, where she and her husband had gone to pray for a sick friend. In the painting the Holy Infant reached for his mother with delight just as she drew a cover up over him, his legs pulled up, ready to kick the cover off. The child wanted to play; his mother wanted him to sleep. Perhaps the Jungfrau Maria longed for his nap so that she could do whatever it was her soul cried out for. As she lay in the dark, Anna thought of the Jungfrau, giving birth in pain and mess, not knowing any better than she, Anna, how to raise a baby. That child, got by God, must have strayed into mischief, just like Nannerl and Woferl. He must have rubbed his dinner in his hair, must have been sent to stand in the corner to learn right from wrong.

Rocked in the cradle of near-sleep, with Leopold's heavier breathing beside her, she was startled awake by a sudden longing to return to St. Gilgen, where she had been so sure that she could do as she liked with music. What was it like, St. Gilgen? She had only the most fragmentary memories, the poppies that cupped sunlight in the burnished grass, the sound of the meadowlark, the lapping of waves. Leopold would not, she thought, take her there: it was an insignificant town, lacking architectural glories, great learning or citizens of note.

Nevertheless, in the morning Anna asked Leopold whether they might make the short journey to her birthplace.

"But why, Anna?" he asked. "There is nothing to see there."

"I know," said Anna, "but still, I should like to go."

"Well," Leopold temporized, "maybe. Someday." He was preoccupied. Would Eberlin consent to double the winds for the *serenata* he had written? There would be extra expense, but what a fine effect they would make. He could not think about sentimental matters just now.

Anna had little time to brood about returning to her birthplace. She had only just sat down to work on the church sonata she had started three weeks before when Nannerl came screaming into the room.

"A mouse!" she shrieked, "in my shoe!"

Wolfgang came grinning behind her, holding the stiff, mildewed creature by the tail.

"Woferl," Anna said sternly, but began to laugh. She tried to scold the little boy, but his face so shone with delight that she had not the heart. "Come here, my sweet," she said to the weeping Nannerl. "Woferl, you were naughty to torment your sister. Go throw that disgusting - ugh! Take it out of my face, you little scamp. Shh, Nannerl. You are well enough." She laughed again. "I am sorry, my dear, but your brother's face! The imp!"

When she picked up her church sonata later in the day, she had forgotten her intention and she saw no virtue in the few measures she had achieved. And then Elizabeth Antretter asked for her help in the repair of the fine Brussels lace that adorned the sleeve of her green watered silk. The garment had hung so that mildew affected the flounce, which had rotted in several places. Now Elizabeth's husband, Ernst, the Provincial Chancellor, had been summoned with his wife, to meet dignitaries from Vienna and Graz, and Elizabeth needed Anna's skill. "Bring the children," she said to Anna in the chilly marketplace. "They will enjoy a day in the country. And we may not stay there long, as Ernst is looking for lodgings in town."

The lace was difficult to repair. While Anna took it in hand Nannerl took her brother, both dressed warmly against the November chill, to wander the extensive orchards. They happened upon the beekeeper's hives on the far side of a small apricot orchard, where in summer the bees feasted. Woferl picked up little stones and threw them without much result. Nannerl, to show him how to throw, aimed some larger rocks at the hives and broke them. The children were frightened when the bees swarmed out and even more so when the bees dropped down dead in the cold air. The beekeeper came on a run, shouting curses. "Run, Woferl!" shouted Nannerl, and grabbing his hand, they raced away from the old beekeeper.

Back at the Antretter's house, Elizabeth admired the flounce that was as good as new, thanks to Anna's deft fingers. "I know Leopold would object if I paid you for your work. But perhaps Nannerl and Wolfgang could use these suits of clothes my niece and nephew have outgrown. See, they are perfectly good, still."

Anna would not have accepted payment from Elizabeth, for the Antretters were friends. Ernst had often spoken up on Leopold's account with the Archbishop and other men of influence, but Anna was happy to have the offered clothing for her children, as were Nannerl and Wolfgang when they inspected their new finery.

That night, as Anna tucked the children into their thick feather bed, Nannerl looked away from her. "Mama," she said, "some bad children at Antretters' broke some beehives with rocks."

Anna was preoccupied, only half listening. "Mmmm," she said.

"The bees came out and fell down on the ground. Dead," piped up Wolfgang.

"Oh," said Anna absently. "Poor things. I suppose it was too cold for them. Bees like summer weather best."

In the morning, Nannerl felt poorly and stayed abed till late. Wolfgang hung onto his mother's skirt, to her intense annoyance, whining and sniveling, always underfoot. Finally, near to noon, Nannerl came dragging out to the living room, where Anna had finally sat down to comfort her ill-tempered son. The girl's face was pale.

"Mama," she said. "We did it, Woferl and I. I threw big rocks at the hives. Woferl threw little ones."

"Is this true, Wolfgang?" Anna asked, sternly.

The child buried his face against his mother's dress. "Yes, Mama. Me too." His voice came out muffled by her worn blue wool. "The bees were going to bite us, but they fell down."

What should she do, wondered Anna. Should she whip them both soundly or lock them in the cupboard? She remembered the desolation of such punishment. "I want you both to stand here. Look at me," she said. "Understand what you have done. Those hives are the Antretters', in the care of their beekeeper. He takes much trouble to weave those hives and fill them up with clay. He raises rosemary and feeds the bees with it so they will not starve in the winter. All this so that you two can have something sweet on your bread. And now you have broken all his hard work to pieces. The gardener will be angry with the beekeeper, who did no wrong. Frau Antretter is always good to you and gave you clothes to wear, but now she will have no honey."

Brought face-to-face with their misdeeds, the children's eyes grew big.

"And think of the bees," Anna continued, her mind going every which way as she searched for the right words. "They are small creatures, but they have families, just like ours, mother and father bees and bee babes." Was that true? I know nothing about bees, she thought. But she went on. "Now some are dead and will never swarm in the summer, nor drink the nectar from flowers."

Both children began to weep.

"I'm sorry, Mama," whispered Nannerl.

"Me too," choked the boy.

In spite of her anger at them, Anna felt a surge of affection for the two little wrongdoers. "I know you are," she said, drawing them both to her bosom. "You're not bad children, but you did wrong and now we must go back to Frau Antretter so that you may tell her and the beekeeper you are sorry."

She bundled the children up straightway and took them a long walk through the wintry streets and fields. Nannerl, haltingly and in small voice, explained their misdeed to Elizabeth Antretter. Wolfgang piped up, "Me too," from time to time.

"Thank you for telling me," said Elizabeth. "Go down now and talk to old Otto. Ask him how you can help repair the damage."

Old Otto was angry. "I seen what happened," he grumped. "I could'n'a stopped you for my old lame leg," he said. But his heart melted when the children confessed to him. "You must come in the warm weather an' I'll show you how to make the hives and you can help me do't."

When it came spring, the children learned from the old man how to make beehives with their own hands, while he told them stories about the busy insects. They became fast friends, always running to greet him when they called on the Antretters.

"Well, in that case, all ended well," confided Anna to Henriette Weisner, whom she often met at the water pump of a morning. "But there are so many times I don't know what is best to do." She had many skills: she could play on the keyboard, though she hardly had time; her voice was flexible and resonant; she could make lace, mend, make candles, soap, noodles and sauerkraut. But no one had ever taught her how to be a mother. Her recollections of her own mother were too few, too enchanted by memory, to provide the guidance she needed. The nuns provided no model either, for there were many of them, one for this task, one for that.

Henriette nodded. She often shared stories of her own children's escapades. "You can take comfort," she told Anna, that they tell you what they have done. Mine are not so forthright."

It seemed no time had passed at all until Nannerl changed into a beautiful, thoughtful, slender young girl, clever and industrious. Woferl grew from a spindly wisp into a lively, good-natured little boy who made every task into play. Though he was a sickly child, Anna began to think he might live to grow up after all. Both children showed aptitude and appetite for the music that pervaded the Mozart household.

That year, when Nannerl was just ten and Wolfgang nearly five, Salzburg had the hardest winter in memory. The snow fell day after day, night after night. Every morning Anna awoke to a white sky from which whirled whiter flakes. The shops were empty, for traders and farmers could not drive their wagons through the deep drifts. The servant girl could not make her way to Getreidegasse, so Anna had more work than usual. She had to bring up fuel herself and slog through the snow to take the chamber pots to the river while the children slept or Nannerl looked after Wolfgang. Anna had stored dried fruit and had hung up summer sausages and hams against just such a season. She went out for bread, but every time she did, her shoes filled up and her hems grew sodden with snow.

Wolfgang was wild with excitement. Several times a day he teased to go frolic in the snow. But when Anna sent him with Nannerl to flounder in it, he fussed to come back inside, where their wet clothes steamed by the kitchen stove and smelled like sheep. While their shoes dried, they padded about in stockings. Wolfgang liked to slide on the floor and wore holes in his stockings faster than Anna could mend them.

Before long, both children were restless and cranky, though Nannerl did her best to help her mother. She played games with Wolfgang, invented tunes with him at the clavier, told him stories. She showed him how to figure on a slate, but her brother ran around and wrote sums on all the walls and furniture. Anna lost her temper. "Wolfgang Gottlieb," she said loudly, her hands on her hips, "you are a very limb of Satan. Stop it right now. Come here and sit on my lap."

The little boy, impressed by his mother's fury and instantly contrite, felt feverish, she thought. "You must wash all that writing off," she told the top of the child's head. "Right now. You do not want your father to come in and see his house all marked on and chalky. Maybe, if you ask her nicely, Nannerl will help you."

But Nannerl, tired of being indoors, was out of sorts as well. "Oh, Mama," she objected. "I clean up after Woferl all the time. Do I have to help him? I want to play by myself on the clavier just now."

Anna's anger had flared when she saw her son's mischief, but that was now replaced by doubt. Should Nannerl always have to fetch and carry and clean for her brother? The little boy ought to be made to amend his own rascality, but it was too big a job for such a mite. If she did it herself, Woferl would learn no lesson. "You go practice," she said to Nannerl. "Wolfgangerl and I will scrub off the numbers."

And so the two of them cleaned the walls and furniture, Anna working fast and Wolfgang dribbling dirty water up his shirtsleeves.

"Look, Mama!" Wolfgang crowed, as his cloth left its glistening trail where the numbers had been and a river of water on the floor where his rag dripped. "I can scrub like you!"

"May I have my notebook?" Nannerl asked, returning from the front room. "I have not looked at it for a long time."

Anna wiped her hands on her apron and reached the notebook down for Nannerl, while Wolfgang played in the puddles he had made. He is only a lively child, thought Anna, not a bad one. But he tries my patience all the same.

"Mama! Mama, look!" cried Nannerl, running back into the room.

Her wet hands held back, Anna saw a note in Leopold's hand written in the margin of a Wagenseil scherzo. "Hold it still, Nannie. 'This piece was learnt by Wolfgangerl on 24 January, 3 days before his 5th birthday, between 9 and 9:30 in the evening.'" Nannerl pointed out other notations, written in her father's hand. Throughout the notebook, in the margins of several minuets, an allegro, a march, and a second scherzo, by Wagenseil, Leopold's hand had recorded his son's achievements.

"In my notebook," Nannerl whispered. She stroked the cover with its precious label in French. She read its meaning out in a choking voice. "This book belongs to Fraulein Marie Anne Mozart, 1759.' He wrote down that it belongs to me, but he did not write what I learned, Mama. He wrote about my *brother* in *my* book."

Anna took the child into her arms. "Oh Nannerl," she said. "I'm so sorry. But sweetheart, it is the way of things. You are his daughter, but Wolfgang is his son." To be sure, the little boy had made great strides, but how could he not, surrounded on every hand with teachers? Other boys, only a little older, would be apprenticed to masters to learn their trade. Why should her husband make a portent of their son?

Nannerl was in a rare temper. "And here," she said, "My brother did not write these dances!" she exclaimed. "Papa wrote them and then put Wolferl's name on them!" Swiftly she ripped the offending pages out of the notebook, flung the book on the floor while she ran to put them in the stove.

Wolfgang did not understand why his sister wept, but he was nevertheless sorry. He picked up the notebook, dampened by the water on the floor, smoothed its pages and handed it quietly to his mother.

Nannerl wept until her head ached. She was silent and withdrawn all day and held herself apart from her brother. She was angry at him, but confused because he had done her no wrong.

When the children were tucked up for the night and the fires banked, Anna reproached Leopold. "She could not understand why you would write of Wolfgang's accomplishments and not of her own," she said. "She has learned as fast and as young as he, after all. Nor could she understand why you would put her brother's name to your own work."

Leopold, who had taken Anna in his arms under the cold covers, pulled away from her. "She's a selfish girl," he said. "She wants everything for herself."

"She shares almost everything with Woferl," objected Anna. "But that notebook is her prized possession, something particularly hers, and you used it to record his triumphs. You did not write down what she learned, so it seems to her you think more of him than you do of her."

Leopold too was weary. He had worn cold, wet trousers all day at court, where tempers were also bad and nothing went right. And now his wife saw fit to scold him. Nannerl was a fine little musician, no doubt about it. But what good would it do her? The boy, on the other hand, might have a great future, if not in this court then in others. If his father was balked by petty men, why should his son not be trained up to take the world by storm? It was a new idea, but one that increasingly occupied his thoughts.

Leopold continued to write simple compositions of his own in Nannerl's notebook and to record Wolfgang as the composer. Nannerl never again protested. She had lost her interest in her notebook. It was no longer hers as it had been.

18

1761-1762

YOU WILL NEVER GUESS what Leopold has in mind," said Anna to Margarethe. Without waiting for an answer, she went on, "He has made up his mind to take the children to Munich to play for the court."

Margarethe frowned. "How has that come about? Here, let me take your cloak. Anna," she exclaimed, "this is much too thin for such weather!"

Anna waved her hand. She had taken a light cloak in her hurry to tell her friend the news.

"Do you remember when Leopold's friend Georg Robinig died? And Leopold traveled to Munich to pay his respects? He did not tell me then, but he had another purpose in mind. He returned sure that Munich is ready to hear his children. He assures me that they will not be shown as trained monkeys but as true musicians. He says he will be a mother hen, see to their meals, make sure they are not up until all hours. They will want for no comforts, he says."

"You will not go along?" queried Margarethe.

"It seems not." Anna was, in truth, a little hurt not to be included in her husband's plans. "I have not pressed Leopold," she said slowly. "I have thought that, maybe," she took a deep breath, "maybe, left to my own devices, I will try my hand at composition once again, find out if I can do anything when I have no distraction."

"Then by all means, Anna, wish them Godspeed," said Margarethe heartily. "Why not be a spinster for awhile? What can it hurt? Wolfgang is nearly six and plenty of children of that age work for masters more severe than Leopold. Nannerl is a sensible child. It will not hurt her to earn plaudits outside of Salzburg."

I think," mused Anna, "that Leopold counts most on Woferl. He is burning to show off his little boy, present him as a prodigy of Nature. I have to admit, proud mother that I am, he is a fetching sight."

"He is," said Margarethe firmly. "Those plump little cheeks and large eyes, and his curls. And he is still so small. He beguiles everyone who sees him."

"Ever since Leopold enrolled the boy to dance in Herr Eberlin's opera for the Archbishop's name day, my husband has had it in mind that it is time the boy earned him some money," said Anna. "He does have a pretty way about him, when he is not driving Nannerl or me mad with his pranks. And I grant you, he has learned fast and plays nimbly upon anything with keys. There is nothing he likes more than to climb up on a stool beside his father when he conducts at court and wave his arms in imitation. All the orchestra treat him as a sort of pet. Leopold has devised some tricks for him, silly things that impress people who know no better, like playing when the keys are covered with a cloth."

"He has none of Nannerl's accuracy or feeling, not yet," said Margarethe, nodding her agreement, "but he is surprisingly accomplished for a child so young."

"Is it too much of a burden," Anna asked, "to expect Nannerl to take care of him away from home? He is such a tease and often plagues her. Am I right to let them go at such tender ages?"

"I suspect," Margarethe offered, "that Leopold will do as he pleases, Anna. I doubt you can stop him if his mind is made up. And what, after all, can be the harm, even if Nannerl is hard pressed? She is a sturdy child and she will surely win applause - and money - for Leopold. She is such a beauty, Anna."

Anna nodded. "Thank you, my friend," she said gratefully. "You are right. I cannot oppose Leopold. You have set my mind at rest."

She had much to do to ready her family for this venture. Leopold was well supplied with fine dress for court. She made a suit for Wolfgang out of the material from one of Leopold's that had grown shabby at elbows and knees, and another from new goods. She made two dresses for Nannerl, cutting them down from one of Margarethe's and another of Theresa

Hagenauer's. She raided her own dresses for lace to adorn Nannerl's finery and made some new edging for Wolfgang's linen. Leopold had new shoes made for each child and Lorenz Hagenauer, who also made him a generous loan for the journey's expense, gave them fancy shoe buckles from France. Anna even stitched some undergarments of linen, wanting her husband and children to wear everything fashionable. She assembled a packet of remedies, the black and margrave powders, some sweet marjoram for the cold, dill to aid digestion, some mandragora for Nannerl's headaches, oil of almond for coughs and colds. She also packed Nannerl's tattered dolly, though she was too old to play with it. She thought it might keep her daughter company when she slept in a strange bed. She put in Wolfgang's chewed and ragged blanket. He would want it to rub against his cheek as he dropped away to sleep.

On the night before their departure, when the iced Epiphany Cake was set on the table, Wolfgang shrieked with delight to find the pfennig baked into his slice. "I will take my pfennig to Munich," he said grandly. "I will tell them I am King of Twelfth Night."

Anna hugged her little boy and was nearly overcome with misgivings. Wolfgang still seemed very small and frail as she thought of him setting out on a journey without her, but she would not burden them with her fear. "Well," she said. "Do not forget. Kings may eat from golden plates, but what they eat comes to muck too. They are just like you and me."

"*They* do not think so," observed Nannerl.

"I would still like to be a king," said Wolfgang.

During the night a light rain fell and then froze, turning Salzburg to a city of crystal. The morning air was sharp as a knife. Warmly wrapped against the cold, Nannerl and Wolfgang carried down to the street the last of the smaller things that would travel with them to the Bavarian capital. The Getreidegasse, usually a-bustle soon after dawn with the sound and motion of beginning commerce, was silent. Perhaps the merchants, the journeymen, apprentices and even servants had lingered a little in their warm beds. It seemed that the Mozarts alone in all the world were up and about.

The coach, which carried the mail to Munich, seemed to Anna roadworn and shabby. She hoped it would not be too drafty. The unmatched horses, snorting steam from their nostrils like dragons, moved restlessly, shifting their hooves on the frozen street. Wolfgang flew to the coachman, with whom he was instantly the best of friends. "Will you drive very fast, please?" Wolfgang urged the driver. "Look, Mama," he said, grabbing his mother's hand and pulling her close to the horses, "the horses are smoking! They want to go fast!"

Nannerl was excited and apprehensive. Two red patches showed on her face. A lovely young lady at eleven, she was dressed warmly in her newly made green wool, a red flannel petticoat, a cloak with a deep hood and her prized gift from Margarethe, a fur muff to keep her hands warm. Her hair was caught up behind in a simple but stylish way that Anna thought the child could manage herself.

Anna had showed Leopold how to do the children's hair. But he was all thumbs and fretted about it. He was vain about his own appearance - he was, Anna thought, a fine figure of a man - and it mattered to him that he and his children should look their best, display good manners and mix easily with nobility. Leopold always wished to be thought higher born than he was.

Wolfgang, but a few days short of his sixth birthday, was dressed like a small gentleman. He swaggered importantly in his gray britches, fawn vest and warm undervest, his blue coat with wide cuffs trimmed in braid, and the thick stockings his mother had knitted for his feet, which were always cold. Anna had cut his cloak down from one of Leopold's. Wolfgang was wild to be off, galloping behind the snorting horses.

Leopold was scarcely less excited than his children. His dear, familiar face was intent and felt feverish to Anna's touch. But Anna knew him well. Once they were away, he would regain his calm. Anna had carefully packed away in the trunk extravagant lace for his throat and cuffs and for the children's finery as well. No one in the Bavarian court of Maximilian Josef in Munich could complain that the Mozarts lacked elegance!

Leopold had arranged this venture with his friend Count Ferdinand von Seeau of the Archbishop's court, who had a relative, one Joseph von Seeau, in the court of the Bavarian Elector. Joseph von Seeau, who superintended theatrical events for the court, was reputed to be a glutton and a gambler, often in his cups. He had secured for the Mozarts an introduction to the Elector, a music lover who was willing to present Nannerl and Wolfgang as novelties to his guests at court. It was, after all, deep winter and entertainments were not so easy to come by. Furthermore, the Elector had a cousin who maintained an extravagant establishment. Leopold had every confidence that the Elector, his cousin and all who aped nobility would hear his children.

Leopold calculated that the Munich journey would show him whether the children might be presentable at other courts in Europe. Would he make enough from this endeavor to justify the expense? With Hagenauer's loan and one from the Archbishop as well, Leopold must make the venture profitable or be a debtor. Leopold worried perpetually about money.

"We are sure of a warm reception, Anna," Leopold had reassured her the night before, when she expressed her doubts about the whole undertaking. She worried that her children might be seen as vagrant entertainers, mountebanks or gypsies, traveling from place to place and holding out their cups for money. Anna knew uneasily that Leopold sometimes strained the truth or modified details to fit what he believed. It worried her, for untruthfulness seemed to her the worst of mortal sins. Her husband and children could not pass for what they were not, nor should they jeopardize their souls for small gains. No matter how gorgeously her family went, no one would ever mistake them for highborn: Leopold and at least Wolfgang would always have to earn their bread: no matter how gifted. It was Anna's fondest dream that Nannerl would be able to do likewise.

Leopold had taken her hand. "You remember Andreas Bernasconi, Anna. I played in the orchestra when his opera came to Salzburg. Now he conducts the court orchestra in Munich. He will introduce us to the best people, as will von Sccau, and once we are heard at court, all else will follow." He had squeezed her hand and stood to stride up and down the room, punctuating his speech with his long fingers. "Just as important, Anna. Wolfgang will learn the musical styles - and the manners - of other courts."

He has already left Munich and gone on to other cities in his mind, Anna thought.

"To be sure," he continued, "Munich has not the splendors of Mannheim, with its unparalleled orchestra; but it is just the place to begin. Some day," he had added, a far-off look in his eyes, "if all goes well, I will take the boy to the Italian cities and France, and who knows maybe even as far as London. But it will do him good to see that Germans, too, appreciate music."

"You must not forget your daughter, Leopold." Anna reminded him. "She will likewise learn from this journey."

"Of course, my dear," Leopold amended, "of course, of course. Nannerl will appeal for her beauty and her proficiency as well. She too will gain much as we go our way."

When Leopold had explained his travel plan to the children, Nannerl had inquired, "What about Mama? Will she not come with us? Who will take care of her?"

Anna had hastened to reassure Nannerl. "Here in Salzburg," she said, "I am among so many friends. I will miss you and count the days till you return, but I will be safe and well." Anna worried that she had taught Nannerl to think always of others first. How could she come to anything as a musician unless she grew more selfish?

Wolfgang's immediate thought upon learning of the journey was that he would ride fast in a coach and go where he had never been before. "There will be many rich people who will clap their hands when I play, Mama," he said happily. Everything was, for him, an adventure. As far as Anna could tell, he was - except for loud noises - quite fearless.

Anna held her children tightly and kissed them a thousand times. They were going so far. She might not see them ever again, for who could tell what evils they might encounter on their journey? Leopold engulfed Anna in his arms, holding her so close that she could feel his heart beat against hers, though both were thickly wrapped in the warmest wool. He whispered loving endearments in his wife's ear.

"Take good care," she urged him, "and never forget my love. Watch over my little ones. There is dill for Woferl's digestion and mandragora for Nannerl's headaches. I have packed everything. See that they get to bed early . . . ."

'Yes, yes, my dearest," answered Leopold, putting his index finger gently on her lips, "we have everything we need."

To all that Anna had carefully packed, Leopold had added many sheets of music and several copies of the *Violinschule*. The little square clavichord was carefully wrapped in a heavy horse blanket, tied about with thick cord. Leopold's violin was stowed in its leather case, the bow wrapped separately and riding atop everything else. At the last minute he had added Nannerl's little fiddle, also well-wrapped.

Finally, Leopold boosted the children up and gave Anna a last kiss before he swung himself into the carriage. Once they were all settled and warmly wrapped up in blankets, Anna handed up the large basket packed with bread and cheese, sausage and sour milk, some preserves and a flask of beer. She had tucked in some of the little sweets from Hagenauer's shop as a special treat.

"God be with you," Anna cried out as the coach creaked into motion, wood and leather groaning, the fastenings of harness jingling. The heavy wheels made racket enough to wake the dead and the breath of horses and coachman streamed back over the carriage like banners. Anna watched while the coach clattered away up the street under the shopkeepers' signs.

The street had wakened in the time it took the trio of Mozarts to be off. Shopkeepers and their boys began their work reluctantly, as if longing for their warm beds. Maidservants carried steaming chamber pots to the river. Anna pulled her shawl tighter about her head and shoulders and walked quickly down the street to the baker's, where she bought a loaf hot from the oven. She held it inside her shawl, where it warmed her like a fragrant stove, and walked home, enjoying the glitter of each church spire and tree. It was as if all Salzburg was fashioned from the famous Bohemian crystal.

She was alone for the first time in her life.

19

1762

THE FAMILIAR ROOMS WERE SILENT, DISHEVELED. The floor creaked underfoot. Thin January sunshine, which out of doors had made the ice-covered trees glitter, picked out the dust indoors.

Anna felt panic rise, a flock of starlings with their black wings clapping. She brewed up some of the precious supply of coffee and cut off a thick slice of bread to eat with the butter she had salted away for the winter. The bread's yeasty fragrance slowed the beat of her heart. She stirred up the fire in the kitchen stove and sat to warm her stockinged feet in its mouth. She could hear her heart ticking like the great clock on the Town Hall at midnight. Inside the Town Hall was the hateful statue of the sow suckling Jewish children. Margarethe, she thought - wounded almost daily by the world that hated her kind so casually - frequently had her house to herself, for her father traveled a good deal. She was often lonely, but in loneliness came the chance to work on her poetry, searching out just the right word, the right rhythm, the right resonance. Such a brave woman, Margarethe, to write words that begged to be spoken, to have them fall on silence and yet to persevere.

Anna ate and drank slowly, crumbs falling in her lap. She had never in all her life sat like this - alone - savoring the taste and fragrance of her food entirely at her leisure.

The silence stunned her. How noisy we Mozarts are! During the day the children asked questions, shouted or gabbled in play, wept, whined, argued and laughed. The harpsichord and violin sounded, and other instruments as well, for musicians came and went all day. Someone or another was always singing, shouting, humming, laughing or crying. The pot's bottom scraped across the clay stovetop, pewter clattered onto its shelf or the table. There was the scouring sound of ashes on the kettle, the sibilance of the broom, the tapping and hurrying of feet, the bubble and pop of the stew on the stove. Even at night, when Anna had to use the chamber pot, she could hear the creak of the cooling stoves, the children's breathing or turning, Leopold's snore. Now the rooms were as quiet as a church, quieter, for even in church at odd hours you could hear a priest's footfall or someone cleaning or a bird stirring about in the belfry.

Time lay before Anna like unbroken snow, which might last for weeks, even months, or might melt away sooner. A truly devoted housewife, Anna thought, would turn out the trunks and wardrobe, finish the mending, which had once again grown to a pile, or set up a new piece of lace. Instead, Anna fed the fires in all the stoves to warm the entire house, an extravagance, since she was the only one at home. She would have to economize, but surely on this first day of solitude, she was entitled to burn a little extra wood. Meanwhile, the sunshine had gathered strength and now streamed through the small kitchen window. She had her crumbs swept up and the bedding shaken out in a trice, but she forbore to start other household tasks. When the servant girl appeared, Anna sent her away without loss of pay, until Leopold and the children should return. She imagined the coach carrying her family, growing ever smaller in the distance and finally disappearing.

Hesitantly, as if she trespassed, she sat herself at Leopold's writing desk. The walls of the room seemed to fall backwards and a wide space to open up around her. She had the impression that she sat amid fields starred with flowers. The sky stood open, as if it were the lid of a great harpsichord. A vibration in the air commanded, "Now, compose! This is your opportunity! Seize it!" She heard it distinctly, as a decree from Heaven. "Compose! Try your hand!" It was God's voice she had heard. Common sense said no, God did not speak in such a way, straight out, to so ordinary a person. But she heard it clearly. "Compose!"

This was what she had hoped for, to have time and space to set her mind on composition, as she had not for so long. Not that she had given it up altogether, but during the years of childbearing she had rarely had energy or time, nor since the children's' birth. Such scraps as she had done had been mere variations on the themes of others. Now she had time, for no one needed her for anything: she would see what she could do.

At first, to break the unaccustomed silence, she played on Leopold's best harpsichord, singing the arias, playing the music that lay in stacks on her husband's shelves. Her fingers loosened and limbered, and joy flooded through her. Then she let invention rule her heart, improvising but writing nothing down on paper. Memories of her early days bubbled up. She felt the icy Wolfgangsee grip her ankles, and her toes, magnified by the water, curved to grasp the slippery stones. She saw her father laughing from high upon his horse, felt the cool of the airy little church of St. Gilgen and heard the deep hush of the woods. She smelled the moist earth and saw her mother, down on her knees in the garden, with her head turned to speak, her hair streaming around her face. She stood before Sister Gisella at Nonnberg, remembering how it felt when the color and sound of the world had rushed back into her body with her voice. She saw Gertrud standing in the orchard, a basket full of sun-warmed plums on her hip.

Then Anna saw the terrible look of surprise and anguish on her dead father's face, Gertrud's body blackened with bleeding pox, her mother's skeletal hand, Sister's Gisella's fluttering chest as her spirit escaped, her own infants placed one after another in the dark soil.

Harmonies of pain and loss ran through melodies of delight. She was whole again.

When finally she stopped, her neck and shoulders ached. The sun had moved from the back windows to those that faced Getreidegasse. She was tired, happy, ravenous. She had not thought to prepare her dinner and took some of the small supply of money Leopold had left to the tavern across the square to buy a cutlet of fowl to eat with her bread.

Having supped, Anna still had some hours of daylight and used them to stretch her limbs, striding eagerly over the covered bridge and up the long road that led travelers toward Linz. She walked all the way to Witches' Tower at the edge of the town wall. The familiar landscape lay all around her, but transformed and strange. Standing alone, at the top of the Linzergasse, she felt again the vibration that came like a voice: "Compose!" She knew that, whatever people said, it was not wrong of her to attend that voice and obey it.

As she walked carefully down the slippery Linzergasse and back across the bridge, Anna passed familiar faces and greeted them, but held inside the gleeful secret that she was alone, that she had her own work to do which no one need know about. Despite uncertain footing, she was free, strong and able and would sit to her own composition tomorrow.

She did not wish to be alone as evening fell into the empty rooms. Luxuriating in her choices - to stay at home, to worship at the nearby Collegiate Church or any other church, to visit with friends - she climbed to Nonnberg to hear the nuns' vespers. Wrapped about by the lovely voices, she paid silent tribute to Sister Gisella, the bride of God, who had composed and known of other women who composed. Anna felt she might stand, someday, arm in arm, with these women through time and scattered over the earth. To her mentor's departed spirit she prayed, "Be with me, dearest teacher. Guide me."

"You will know what to do, Anna," Sister Gisella seemed to answer.

In the chapel stood the carved figure of the Jungfrau Maria, her child on her hip and her familiar expression of quizzical calm. She was a woman, a virgin and a mother, both despised and honored. She had carried God's son in her body, brought him into the world. She had bathed him, taught him, chased after him and grieved his death. No one knew what the Jungfrau might have wanted for herself. The carved figure had done nothing but stand so through the centuries, fixed there in wood, holding her babe on her hip. But the real mother of God, the woman of whom the statue was but a picture, what needs had bitten at her? Through the transom came the clear voices of the nuns singing the psalms and the magnificat. The Jungfrau had no voice to tell her story. The nuns, also virgins, had no children. Could she, a married woman with children, sing her praises to God in her own voice? Did she have to choose to be either a mother and wife or a musician, but never both? I do not have to choose just now, she thought. I am alone for awhile and may use the time I have as I wish. When the vespers ended, Anna stayed a while, while other worshippers left, so that she could make her way back to the apartment on Getreidegasse, cherishing her loneliness.

At dawn, when church bells rang, she was already up. She had washed and breakfasted and had before her a quire of Leopold's ruled paper, neatly set out beside his pen and inkwell even before the room was properly warm. She had meant to begin with something easy, perhaps a simple dance, to remind herself how it was done, but an idea had come to her from her night's sleep. She would write a symphony out of the memories of her early years, of childhood and the countryside. It would have a slow dark movement, to honor the loss of so much she had loved. That sadness would be framed by the brightness of the countryside and the beauty of what she had not lost.

Anna had dreamed her hand would race across the paper. In her dream, the notes dropped onto the ruled staves almost of their own accord, in just the right places, with perfect neatness, so that she would not waste Leopold's paper, always of the best quality, for he hated cheap material. She had imagined she would hear in her head exactly the sounds she would write down, that her knowledge of composition had survived and broadened with all she had listened to, and that she could compose something of real elegance and taste. Now she found she had forgotten some of what she had learned from Sister Gisella. It came back to her, but she was rusty.

Further, she was plagued by her dear friends. All morning, one beloved neighbor after another knocked at her door to offer companionship and hospitality. Anna was touched and exasperated. How could she find out whether there was even a pinch of genius left in her nature when she had such sociable friends? She did not want them to know what she attempted. Word must not get around Salzburg that Leopold Mozart's wife presumed. Each day she rose, well before sunrise, and worked by candlelight. During the day, when she was likely to be interrupted, she could play on the clavier and sing to her heart's content, for everyone knew she liked to do both.

Anna was surprised by the difficulties she encountered in writing her chamber symphony. She could hear it so clearly. She wanted string and wind bands both, as well as the horns that Leopold so fancied. She struggled with the harmony and modulations, the rules of composition like a game that drew her more deeply toward what she had imagined.

"It is not easy," she confessed to Margarethe as the afternoon shadows fell, chilling the melting snow.

Margarethe had been ill. She lay on a chaise in an old wrapper, very pale and tired. But her eyes were quick and bright as always . "Are you so surprised, my dear?" she asked. "How long has it been since you really put your mind to composition?"

"Oh," Anna shrugged, "a long time. But Leopold makes it seem so easy. He sits down and straightway his page is covered with notes. He is not plagued with doubt."

Margarethe's face reflected Anna's distress. "You are unaccustomed, Anna, nothing more. Leopold composes every day. People pay him money to do it. They admire his work and give him ideas." She coughed and lay back to catch her breath.

Anna was contrite. Here she was, asking Margarethe for comfort when she was ill. "What can I do for you?" Anna inquired anxiously. "Shall I ask the servant for something? Shall I get you another wrap?"

Margarethe waved a narrow hand to dismiss her ill health. "Think of it, Anna. You have not had instruction since you were a young girl. The world tells you you cannot compose, that you are selfish even to want to. How can it be easy?"

"Oh Margarethe," sighed Anna. "As always, you comfort and strengthen me, even when you are not in the best of health." She took her friend's hand in her own, feeling its slender bones through the skin.

"And you me, Anna," said Margarethe. "We strengthen each other."

On each of the precious days Anna had for herself - some pure and blue with glittering sunlight, some drifted deep in snow - she ordered her time as she liked. She brought water from the tap and swept down the steps and kept the rooms tidy and clean, save for one thing: she did not sweep away a spider who spun her web above Leopold's desk. As Anna set her notes down on the paper, she often glanced up to see the insect hard at work, spinning a finer lace from her very body than Anna could make with her fingers.

Anna kept the hours for composition as a sacred office, wherein she drew from her innards what she understood - and more than she understood - about the world. Each day was like a lying-in: turned inside out, she delivered what had grown inside her. Each day by mid-afternoon, she was tired, stiff, sore, in need of recovery.

20

1762

"OWWWW," WOLFGANG WAILED. "You're pulling, Nannerl! Papa, make her stop!"

Nannerl was trying to get Wolfgang's hair right, the way Mama did it. But it was such fine hair, curly and snarled, and he had slept on it so that it wanted to stand up where Nannerl wanted it to lie down. She could not manage to comb it deftly, tie on the ribbon and keep Woferl happy and chattering the way Mama could. Her own hair was not much better. Mama had showed her how, but it was harder than it looked to get it just right.

Leopold was penning a dedication to the Elector for the minuet he had helped his son to write. His neck cloth was awry and his coat unbrushed. "Nannerl," he scolded. "Be gentle with Woferl."

"But Papa," wailed Nannerl with frustration. "I can't do it right. Look, this part sticks out no matter how I comb it."

"Well," said Leopold, "do the best you can. I thought your Mama had shown you how."

"Papa," complained Wolfgang, himself mightily out of sorts, "I have to look good. The Elector will not like it if I look shabby."

"You are right," said Leopold. "Let me try, Nannerl." It is not so difficult at home, he thought. Why does it seem impossible to keep body together with soul in Munich? Here I am, trying to launch a genius into the world, and find myself having to fiddle with hair and buttons and holes in stockings. He brushed the boy's hair back but he could not hold it in a tail while he tied the ribbon, nor could he get the awkward bend in the child's hair to lie down flat. When he tried to think about how he tied back his own hair, his hands refused and he could not do it.

"And look at mine," cried Nannerl, despairing. "I look like that old woman who lives under the bridge and asks Mama for alms. I tried to mend this little tear here on the side of my dress, and look! It is not at all as nice as Mama's mending. It puckers out so."

"Well," Leopold said, "There is nothing for it. We must find a wigmaker. It will be an expense, but what can we do? You cannot manage and I cannot either. Your mend is fine, Nannerl. No one will notice. Maybe, if you don't like it, Frau Bruger will help you with it." Frau Bruger, the widow who had let them rooms in her house, was both too voluble and nosy for Leopold's taste, but he had to admit she had helped when he was at his wit's end.

With the wigmaker's and Frau Bruger's help, Leopold and his two children were very trim when they were presented to the Elector later in the day. Nannerl and Wolfgang wore powdered wigs, which had cost far more than Leopold could have imagined and made their heads hot and itchy. Their clothes were neatly mended and brushed, the lace fresh and elegant. Nannerl had been hard-pressed trying to get everything in order, and Wolfgang had played the clown until she was beside herself and had to crawl into bed with a headache.

The Elector, Josef Maximilian, received the Mozarts in his splendid apartments with the greatest cordiality. Never had Nannerl and Wolfgang seen so extravagant a gathering as attended the Elector.

Earlier Herr Bernasconi had told Leopold what line would best advance his case. "The Elector composes in the old style, but is inordinately proud of what he does, Herr Mozart," the Italian had coached his German friend. "He is only a fair composer, and he overvalues his skill with the viols."

"I understand, Majesty, that you are yourself a composer of note," said Leopold as he straightened from his bow, "and skilled in the playing of the viola da gamba."

"Indeed, Herr Mozart," returned the Elector, his face coloring with pleasure. "And I am told you have brought us a genius who will surpass us all. And your girl too. Let us hear them without further ado."

First Nannerl, poised and confident as far as anyone could tell but alternating hot and cold inside, played three difficult sonatas with the greatest precision and feeling. The last was her own composition. "How well you play, young lady," exclaimed the Elector. "And it has not ruined your beauty. Come here and take my hand and tell me about that last piece. I have never heard it."

Nannerl went to him shyly, let him hold her small hand in his chilly fingers. "I composed it myself," she said quietly.

"Did you now? That is surprising," said the Elector. "You must take care, my dear, that you do not spoil that fine complexion with such efforts and never get a husband."

Seeing that their prince was pleased, the assembled company exclaimed at Nannerl's performance. "But surely," said one lady, whose coiffure was a tower of powdered hair, feathers and ribbons, "your father composed that last piece."

"No," said Nannerl. "I did, though my mother helped me on one of the hard parts."

"Well," said the lady, glancing archly around her to knowing smiles from the other ladies, "to be sure."

They think I am lying, Nannerl thought. They think I did not compose the piece, but I did. Mama has taught me better than to lie.

The ladies petted Nannerl and fed her dainties from the sumptuous table. "Such a beauty!" they exclaimed. "Such fine lace!" "Such a complexion!"

Leopold had saved his son for last, thinking he would arouse even greater admiration. "You have heard my daughter, Sire, who is only eight years of age," he said, "but now you shall hear my son, who is but four years old. And yet, he is already a composer and will play on the keyboard without seeing the keys."

Nannerl was astounded. Could her father have forgotten that she had reached eleven years and that Wolfgang had, only a few days before, reached his sixth birthday?

Wolfgang strode importantly to the front of the room and made an extravagant bow to much applause and some laughter, but he had to be helped up onto the bench before he could reach the harpsichord keys. "Now, young master," said Leopold, "I will put this scarf over the keys to hide them."

Wolfgang, who had practiced this trick, played the little march easily and everyone who was gathered to hear him oohed and ahhed.

"And now my son will play his own composition," said Leopold, and Wolfgang played a tune of which his father had set down the notes as the child hung on his arm. It was not really, thought Nannerl, Wolfgang's own. She was uneasy that her father would so easily say that it was. What would Mama think? Mama always said that lying was the surest way to hell.

She sidled up to Leopold during the applause, when the same ladies who had fluttered around her like gorgeous butterflies carried Wolfgang off to flatter him and stuff him with sweets. "Papa," Nannerl whispered, "you forgot that I am eleven and Wolfgang is almost six. Maybe you should tell them." Leopold tilted his eyebrow up and looked down at his daughter. "Never mind, Nannerl. I mistook, but no one will mind. You acquitted yourself very well, my girl, a little fast, maybe, in the last allegro, but on the whole, very well done indeed. And we are sure to receive handsome presents," he whispered.

The ladies of the court found Wolfgang very amusing. He was puffed with importance and before long grew queasy from all the rich food he ate. He pulled on his sister's arm. "Nannerl," he complained. "My stomach hurts. I think I have to be sick."

Nannerl was struck dumb. Her father was listening to a thin, voluble woman, whose face had been ruined by the pox. "Papa," she said, tugging at his sleeve.

"Not now, Nannerl," he said. "You can see I'm engaged just now."

Nannerl was perplexed. Where could she take her brother? Who was it good manners to ask? She wasn't sure how one found a privy or a basin in such a great palace. Looking about her frantically, she wished for her mother, who would know what to do. "Come," she said to Wolfgang, taking his hand and pulling him toward the door they had come in. She could not remember all the rooms they had come through, but she raced with him back the way they had come. "Here," she said at last, finding a great potted plant. "Be sick in this."

Wolfgang gagged and sickened into the pot, bringing up the delights with which he had gorged himself. Nannerl used her lace-trimmed handkerchief to wipe her brother's face. "We have to go back now," she said, "or Papa will wonder."

"But Nannerl," whimpered Wolfgang, "I feel bad. I want to go to sleep."

"Soon," said Nannerl. "We have to find Papa."

It was a long evening and the children were exhausted long before they had returned to their rooms. Nannerl, longing for her mother, sang to the homesick Wolfgang until her voice wavered and dwindled and she fell off into her own deep sleep. Leopold sat in the rickety chair, his long legs stretched out. He had been rewarded handsomely for his children's performance and he was content with this venture, but he longed for someone to talk with, to examine each phrase the children had played, to discuss this nobleman and that wife, this courtier and that, to revisit the fine rooms in which the Mozarts had been entertained. He missed his wife, and not only for her mending and her skills with the children's hair.

The small wigs sat cockeyed on their stands in the room lit by only one candle, which was not so smooth and well-shaped, Nannerl had noted, as her mother's candles. Leopold thought of the Elector's expense of wax candles, of the great silver platters, of the gold leaf that covered the decoration on the walls, of the red brocade on chairs, and the fine porcelain. He sighed and noted approvingly that Nannerl had hung her clothes and her brother's up on the pegs so they would not wrinkle. "What a good little maid she is," he said to himself. "Anna has done well with her. And really, she plays astonishingly well, though the boy will gain on her."

By the next day, Wolfgang had recovered his high spirits. Still wearing his night shift, his fair hair disordered, he entertained his father and sister by acting the fat old Count Seeau. The child staggered around the room, pushing out his little belly, smacking his lips. He seized the bundle of twigs that leaned against the wall next to the stove for cleaning up ashes and bits of wood. "See here my good Mozart," he shouted, brandishing the broom, "I am fighting against all the Turks."

So precise was his imitation that neither Nannerl nor Leopold could help laughing.

Wolfgang mimed the gulping and gobbling count at table. The boy sank his little chin down, as if it rested in a wreath of jowls, jumped up and strode around the room, huffing, gobbling and muttering. "And now, my good man, I will give you lots of money!"

"Woferl," protested Leopold, "you are unkind." But he laughed until tears ran from his eyes. The child had caught the immense, greedy, boastful old man to perfection.

"I did not like his dogs," said Nannerl. "They smelled bad and they slobbered."

"And they licked me right in the face," said Wolfgang, imitating their slurping tongues.

Leopold, wiping tears from his eyes, said. "My year's pay changes hands in an hour in the Count's card room. Why, a whole army could eat from his plate alone and never go hungry."

Nannerl said, "He *is* a whole army, to hear him tell it."

"Well said, Nannerl," said Leopold, still chuckling. "And now, my dears, we must get ourselves up for a ride. Bernasconi will send his carriage so that we may drive out and dine with the Count Sonnleithner. And then we will attend with him at Bernasconi's Italian opera. That will be a treat, and then no work at all for us until two days from now. Nannerl, you must get your new piece for four hands finished so that you and your brother can learn it by then."

"I hate putting on this wig," said Nannerl, sighing as she tucked her hair up underneath. "I miss Mama. When can we go home, Papa?"

21

1762

TWO AND A HALF WEEKS PASSED. Rumors flew that the Austrian Empress would make peace with the Prussian king after seven long years of war. Some said that paper might be used to pay for goods instead of gold or silver. Adelheide Althaus had taken it into her cranky head that Leopold Mozart had left his wife behind for good and did what she could to whip up gossip. But what kept Anna's entire attention was her symphony. She worked on it with all her might, and then, exhausted but restless, walked vigorously.

When at last Anna's symphony seemed to her finished, she thought of Leopold's colleague, the singer Joseph Meissner. In his most recent letter from Munich, Leopold had asked her to tell both Hagenauer and Meissner of his children's triumph at the Elector's palace. Hagenauer would spread the news in town, and Meissner would see to it that the Salzburg court buzzed with Herr Mozart's success. Anna thought Meissner the kindest of men who owed Leopold something for having stood witness at both of Meissner's marriages. His sister Sabina's splendid voice had resulted in her appointment at the court, though she was still very young. Anna knew well that singing was different from composing. The Archbishop might command silence for women in church, but even he agreed that sopranos and mezzo sopranos were necessary. Anna thought that Meissner would surely understand that women might be driven by musical impulses. And most important, Leopold called Meissner a man who knew how - and when - to be discreet.

Quickly, so that no doubt could dissuade her, she carried her bundle of manuscript tightly under her cloak to Herr Meissner. "My dear Frau Mozart, you are most welcome. Tell me," he inquired, showing her into his front room, "what news have you of the travelers?"

"Thank you," she said, yielding her cloak to his servant. Sitting, her hands shaking, she smoothed the manuscript pages on her lap. "Leopold wishes you to know that he is received very courteously. The children have played several times for the Elector and have appeared also in the best houses in Munich, and my husband judges his journey a success. Oh, they have played as well for the Count von Seeau. Nannerl even wrote a piece for four hands, which she and Wolfgang played at court. My husband says Wolfgang takes to the gypsy life wonderfully and tries his hand at composition, though of course his father does most of it."

Herr Meissner was slender, always nattily dressed and of grave demeanor. He nodded, touching the tip of his nose with his middle finger. "Good news, indeed! I will see to it that word of this success gets to the right ears. Your children are greatly gifted, Frau Mozart. And your girl's composition, hmmm, I will not make too much of that."

Anna did not fully attend to Herr Meissner, for her own composition seemed to burn through her dress. "Herr Meissner," she said, her tongue suddenly large and heavy, "I too have presumed to try some composition of my own. It is just a . . . I cannot tell . . . . I wondered . . . . Would you be willing to look . . . ?" She stood and thrust the manuscript at him. Suddenly her work seemed to her very paltry scratchings on papers with bent and ragged edges. "Perhaps you would be kind enough to tell me if it has any merit at all?" There was a pounding in her head and ringing in her ears. Her own voice came to her as if from a great distance. "It is nothing, just an attempt. I have not composed anything, nothing serious, for many years."

Meissner's heavy-lidded eyes opened wide. "My dear Frau Mozart!" he exclaimed, "I am astonished. How can you trouble your head about such things when you have so much to occupy your time? But of course," he said, again rubbing his nose, "you are without your family just now and time, no doubt, lies somewhat heavily . . . ."

Anna, dazed, could not tell whether Meissner was merely surprised or disapproving.

"But," he said, leafing through the pages, "of course I will look at what you have done."

Having sought his opinion of her work, which had filled her with such joy and strength but which at the moment seemed so puny, Anna wanted to seize the pages out of his hands and throw them into the stove which made the room seem much too hot. She could not, of course. He would think she was mad. There was nothing for it but to inquire after the health of his family and go away, torn between pride and shame.

Anna felt like a drunkard as she stumbled home, head throbbing. Though it was not yet midday, she fell into a deep slumber. She dreamed she was in the marketplace, but no one saw her, so caught up in their gossip were the people she hardly recognized. "How dare she?" said one, who wore the baker's apron but a different face. "Compose?" asked the tanner's wife in her stained dress, "for shame!" There was the face of one of her dearest friends set upon the heavy carter's body. "Impossible!" she shrilled, in tones Anna had never heard her use. "The Archbishop will have her up on charges," said another woman, whom she spoke to every day when she fetched water, but her face melted and became a vulture's; "they will pull her bones from their sockets to get at the truth." "She will come to a witch's end," sang a bloody haunch of meat in the butcher's stall in a soaring soprano. "Her husband and children are dead, all dead now," said the fishmonger, "did you know?" He took up a monstrous fish and put it in Anna's arms, where it weighed her down so that she sank to the cobbles to support the strong-smelling creature. Her fingers ran up and down its scales, discordant, untuned notes. "My children! My husband!" she cried out, asking for help, but she could not budge from the spot and no one would look at her. The Cathedral bells tolled and she was conducting an opera, whose chorus sang out, "Dead, all dead," and then she was dragged at the back of a cart up the Linzergasse to the Witches' Tower, where she was held in muffling darkness.

The Cathedral bells were ringing as, slowly, she awoke. She knew she had dreamed. What she had seen and heard were fancy's invention. But however unreal, it lay heavily upon her. Her children were far away. Wolfgang might have fallen under the wheel of a carriage and Nannerl might have taken a fever. Their lodgings might have caught fire. Smallpox might be abroad in Munich. Who knew when Leopold would return or a letter with news would reach her?

She had slept away the morning. She would clear her head by going to the market for bread and milk, but as she tidied herself and walked out, she was oppressed by her dream and its unreal but convincing images. She hurried through the gloomy winter streets, her cloak gathered tightly about her, and whom should she encounter but Herr Meissner, who hailed her in the most amiable manner.

"Frau Mozart, I am glad to find you. I was on my way to call upon you, but here we have met in the street. I wished to speak to you about your chamber symphony."

Anna glanced around her, dreading that someone might hear him.

"I like it," he said, surprise in his voice. "I found it somewhat awkward in places. In the cantabile, here, in the sixth measure, where the expected fifth is missing - here, you see?"

"Yes," Anna said, "I do." She saw at once what changes were needed.

"But," Meissner went on, "I thought it deeply felt and full of taste. Some new ideas. Interesting, quite interesting." He rubbed his nose.

Anna looked at him in wonder. Her dream had seemed so real. She had been sure he would find fault with what she had done, condemn her for doing it.

"I especially like the part - here it is, where you used the octave in this surprising way. It takes you a little aback, but you have prepared so well." Meissner studied the score, nodding his head in time to unseen musicians, humming a little and smiling.

"The trouble is," Meissner continued thoughtfully, "as you must know, the Archbishop is distinctly opposed to women being heard in any public way. I know, I know," he fluttered his fingers as she opened her mouth to speak, "women sing in the *kapell*. He doesn't like it, but it is really necessary. Castratti are fine, of course, but have not the same flexibility and warmth of voice . . . ." He worried his poor nose again. "I have heard our Prince say it often enough," he said slowly, "that when women put themselves forward, children run about beggars." He smiled ruefully. "I fear if he knew that Leopold had a composer for a wife, he might make it more difficult for your husband to advance. And if Leopold expects leave to take his children about from one court to another, as he has told me he wishes to, he will need the good will of our Prince Archbishop." He pondered again. "I think he is wrong about this, Frau Mozart, indeed very wrong, but there it is."

Anna was covered with joyous confusion. How could she thank him enough? She let her cloak fall away to grasp his hand, which she shook up and down like a pump handle. "Thank you . . . . I. . . Dear Herr Meissner, thank you with all my heart." When she realized she still held his hand, she let it go quickly. She had to stand there in the snow to chatter about this and that. But all the while her spirit had taken wing and wheeled above like a hawk riding the heights.

The gloom had lifted from the day and she went about her business, smiling at everyone, mentally revising and improving her little symphony, Pertl Symphony she would call it, for her maiden name. Perhaps no one would ever play nor ears ever hear what she had made, but she knew every note, which resounded in her head, performed there by the best musicians who could be assembled. She determined to hurry home and clean, sure that before long her husband and children would return to her. She turned the apartment upside down, swept and scrubbed, took everything out of cupboards and chests and washed in corners, crushing lavender buds to release their fragrance. She tidied Leopold's room, dusting his books, neatening his stacks of music and papers, trimming the wicks of candles and lamps.

She studied the spider who had made its web above the table at which Anna had composed. The small gray creature was repairing a hole made in the web by one of the insects it had trapped in its graceful but deadly construction. "Frau Spider," Anna apostrophized, "you have been hard at work as I have. You have your calling, as I have. What you spin out of your body is both useful and beautiful." She moved her head to the side, so that she could see the light glint from the fine silken threads the spider had thrown out. Its carefully connected web was anchored by lines that ran from Leopold's shelf to a book whose spine stuck further out than the others, to the candle stand to the edge of the table to the inkstand and the wall. Anna's breath caused the web to vibrate slightly, and the spider stopped its silent spinning, holding perfectly still. "Your art and your necessities are one," Anna mused. "You live in the midst of your work and your dinner comes to you." She laughed. "Anyone would think I had run mad, to speak out loud to a spider."

"I do not know," she said, still amused to find herself conversing with an insect, "how you get children or if you have a husband and whether you care that your web is constructed just so." She sat and leaned her head on her hand. "I do not think I will be able to go on with my work," she said softly. "Meissner says it would hinder Leopold and bring censure on us all. But you know, Frau Spider, Meissner said what I did had merit. I felt it, truly, and I know that given the time and opportunity, I could compose good music, maybe even great music." She sighed. "I cannot stand in my husband's way, and in my children genius appears to be at work. Perhaps I must make it my task to give whatever genius I have to them." She stood up and shook herself. "I must sweep away your web or give up any claim to housewifery, good Frau Spider. My apologies. It is the way of the world in which we must both live." Carefully, making sure that the spider could scurry away unhurt, she swiped away the spiderweb.

The apartment was clean and she laid new fires in all the stoves, shook up the bedding and reordered the larder. Everything shone from her exertions and now, while new snow fell, she could make the changes she had in mind for her symphony and go to the tavern to bring back a pitcher of beer. Then she went to church to give thanks before retiring, glad that her house was in order.

The next day, Leopold and the children returned with a puppy, the gift of Count Seeau, and tales of their adventures in Munich. Leopold was full of schemes for further travel. "Vienna, next," he said to Anna. "The children will conquer Vienna as the Turks never have. And you must come, my dear. We missed you sadly."

Never, not once, did Leopold or the children ask Anna about her time alone. What, after all, could possibly happen to Mama, at home, in Salzburg?

They had not been home for so much as an hour, strewing the clean house with crumpled clothes, instruments, pages of manuscript and assorted gewgaws, when Anna herself doubted that she had lived by herself for the space of three weeks, or composed anything at all. She knew very well that she was delighted by the safe return of her loved ones, and yet she felt a strange sense of sadness and loss. She chided herself for unnatural feelings and weakness and laid her symphony tenderly away in the trunk.

PART 4

22

1762

EIGHT MONTHS LATER Leopold took his entire family to Vienna for a little over four months. Upon their return, Leopold was summoned to the Archbishop, who wished to hear whether his money had been well spent. Leopold dressed in his most splendid wine-colored coat, shirt, lace and freshly pressed hair ribbon. He carried with him his newly polished Viennese shoes to keep them clean. Though Leopold had bowed to an Empress and her consort in Vienna, his bow to his own Prince, the Archbishop Schrattenbach, was deep and deferential.

"I should be pleased, Mozart, to hear how you and your son fared in the Austrian capital," said Schrattenbach, putting his right hand over his left to still the bothersome tremor that afflicted him. Though in many ways an easygoing monarch, he disliked any sign that he too was subject to mortal decay.

Leopold was eager to report. "My son played for Her Majesty, the Empress, and all her family at the palace at Schönnbrun, as I am sure you have heard, and we were received most graciously. On our way to Vienna, we were in Passau for five days before the Bishop heard the boy play." Leopold could not, of course, say that he had lingered, despite the Bishop's flagging interest, knowing that the prelate had designs on the Archbishop Schrattenbach's throne.

"I believe you also took your girl, Mozart? And your good wife?" inquired the Archbishop, biting his lip.

"Yes, Excellency. Marie Anna - Nannerl, we call her - played in a masterly fashion and won plaudits in Vienna."

"Ah, Mozart, no good will come of it. It is not natural for the female sex, not natural." Schrattenbach shook his head. "But go on."

"It was our good fortune, Excellency, that the Count Palfy in Linz and the Counts Herberstein and von Schlick, whom we encountered on the boat from Linz, all took a great fancy to both of my . . . to my boy, and prevailed on the Archduke Joseph to persuade his mother, the Empress, to invite us to court. From there, there was no end of invitations. The Count Colalto, the Count von Zinzendorf and his lady, the Prince Colloredo-Metz and Wallsee, the Countess Kinsky and the Princess Trauton . . . ." Leopold loved the taste of these noble names on his lips.

"Yes, yes, Mozart, all those who glitter in Vienna, I know them well." The Archbishop waved his good hand. "But you were gone much longer than the time I granted."

"I must apologize, Excellency," pleaded Leopold, who had wanted to enumerate more of those whose notice had amplified his own stature by making much of his children. "First, my boy contracted the scarlet fever and had to be kept in bed for some time, and afterward, when he was well, he was obliged to play for those whom we had been forced to put off. And then, just as we were about to return to Salzburg, we heard the news that the Hagenauer children were infected with smallpox, and I was afraid to bring my children back into town and since we were wanted in Pressburg, it seemed wise to delay."

The Archbishop frowned. "Well, Mozart. There are those who say we are too generous, paying you while you gallivant to other courts, where undoubtedly you received handsome presents, and those who think we should not lend you money from our treasury for your expenses."

"In my opinion, it is money well spent, Excellency," said Leopold, bowing, "as everywhere I was able to remind those who marveled at my children that but for Salzburg and your Excellency's generosity . . . ."

"Yes, yes," said the Archbishop. He was used to flattery.

Meanwhile, Nannerl was deep in conversation with her bosom friend, Katherl Gillowsky, whom she had known almost since birth as their mothers were such friends. During her sojourn in Vienna, Nannerl had missed Katherl sorely. "You would be amazed," said Nannerl. "I met the Archduchess Johanna, who told me to call her Johanna, even though she is - was - an archduchess. She was so kind to me. She told me I should compose in her household when she married, for she could choose who would compose for her and perform in her court even if she could not choose whom she would marry." Nannerl stretched, glad to be at home and wearing old, soft everyday clothes again. She lowered her voice, just as the Archduchess had. "She said she might have to marry someone who was fat and ugly and had spots on his face if her mama told her to. She said it was very tedious to be an archduchess and to live in a palace with hundreds of rooms and servants everywhere. And she sent us beautiful suits of clothes. An ivory-colored taffeta for me, with all kinds of ruching and frills." Nannerl crossed the room and took the dress from the wardrobe. "Look, Katherl. Isn't this the most beautiful . . . ? And here is what she sent for Woferl." She stroked the lilac watered silk, touching the gold braid with her fingertip and tears filled her eyes. "Oh, Katherl, it is so sad. She died while we were away in Pressburg and the river was so high we could not get back. We finally had to cross on a smaller river that had frozen solid. Poor Johanna," she said, as tears ran down her cheeks. She had not, until this moment, wept, though she had felt like it from the moment she had heard of the Archduchess's death. Part of her sorrow was for the Archduchess; part for herself and the hopes the Archduchess had raised.

Katherl, as short and merry as Nannerl was slender and elegant, took the dress and the small suit from her friend so that no tears should stain the precious fabrics, and put them back in the wardrobe. Having rescued the dresses, she put her arm around the weeping Nannerl. "Did you meet the Archduchess right away, when you first got to Vienna?" she asked.

Nannerl dried her tears. She did not have long. Mama had gone for bread, but on her return she would need Nannerl to help unpack the trunks and sort all the crumpled clothes and music, gloves, ribbons and trinkets. Papa had already taken out the rich presents, the rings, snuffboxes and sword, and seen to their storage. "It was about a week after we got there," Nannerl said. "We played for the Court several times and Johanna invited the composer Marianna Martinetz so I could meet her. Marianna is Spanish, the daughter of the Master of Ceremonies for the Nuncio from Rome, and her compositions have been played in the best houses, even at court. The Archduchess said she had heard Marianna's masses performed at church and that they were excellent. Marianna is older than we are, maybe twenty, and very beautiful in that haughty Spanish way. She can speak any number of languages and the famous poet, Metastasio . . . ."

"I have heard of him," said Katherl, looking pleased.

"Well, he hung over her, bringing her sweetmeats, carrying her cushion, jumping to take her empty glass from her hand as if she were sickly. We could not talk at all for the constant interruptions! And then Johanna *commanded* Marianna's parents and Metastasio to leave us alone so we could walk in the orangery by ourselves. It smelled delicious," Nannerl said. "There were gardeners everywhere, snipping and watering and bowing to the Archduchess, but she ordered them all to go away, and when an archduchess tells people what to do, they do it! Johanna told Marianna that I am a composer and asked her how I should do when I am older."

"What did she say?" asked Katherl, winding one of her copper curls about her finger.

"Marianna said it was very hard," Nannerl said. "She said her father has to plot and flatter all the time. Of course he knows everyone. And also the Dowager Princess Esterhazy lives on the first floor of Marianna's building and the Princess has taken Marianna up." Nannerl sighed. "Even so, Marianna says everything is uphill. She hears it whispered that what she composes must be the work of others that she palms off as her own. Mariana said one lady told her that her womb would rot from too much thinking! "

"Marianna's parents won't let her do anything else but compose and perform," said Nannerl. "She says no one will let her lift a finger for herself. Imagine, Katherl! She said she envies me, *me*! Because I can compose *and* do all kinds of other things like cook and clean and knit and walk about whenever I want to!"

Woferl was just then talking to his dearest of many friends, Cajetan Hagenauer, sixteen years old and very large and wise. "The Archduchess was a kind girl, but she died. She took my hand - she was still alive then - and took me about to meet all the people in the court and showed me the animals as well. I liked the menagerie best of anything. There were all kinds of animals in cages, and you could watch them walk about and eat and sleep. There were some big bears and a tiger from India, and Indian crows, with green and blue and red feathers. And they had dwarves in the court, too!"

Cajetan smiled at his little friend. He loved the way young Wolfgang hung on him and admired him. "And you played well, and your sister?" he asked sternly, to remind the child who was the elder.

"Oh, yes," said Wolfgang, carelessly. "Nannerl plays much better than I do. I just do tricks and everyone claps and claps. I liked going to Vienna on the boat much better than all the palaces where we played. I got to stand in front and watch until it got too cold and stormy, and then Mama made me go inside. But the palaces were good, too. There was gold everywhere and people wore finer clothes than here."

"Don't let the Archbishop hear you say that!" laughed Cajetan. "He likes to think that Salzburg is the richest and finest city in the world."

"Well, it is," said Wolfgang stoutly, "because you are here, and all my friends, and I can wear old clothes and play out-of-doors."

"I was surprised that the Empress is not much older than I am. She looks older, though, a little stout and her skin has a powdery look. I had not thought I would ever talk with an empress!" Anna told her friends gathered briefly outside the bakery.

"What was she wearing?" Marianna asked. She had left Katherl with Nannerl so that the girls could chatter awhile as their mothers now did.

"I was surprised about that too," laughed Anna. "Her dress was rich, very heavy, a sort of dull blue color, velvet and brocade, but it did not suit her. It did not seem to fit just right, and she wore her own hair, which has gray streaks, caught back by a fillet with a small, rather fusty jewel on her forehead. She was not at all splendid. There were portraits on the wall in which she looked much better than she did in the flesh."

"You expected a fairy princess," observed Theresa dryly.

"Yes," said Anna, "but oh, my, the dresses all the other women wore! I was a wren among peacocks. There were miles of silk and jewels enough to pay the wages of everyone in Salzburg. And hair piled so high, each hairdo must have taken a week to construct. I cannot imagine how the ladies sleep."

"Was she pleasant to you, the Empress?" queried Theresa, who dressed richly enough, but always in sober colors.

"Mmm," said Anna, musing, "she asked about our journey and about the children's health, but she was always looking over my shoulder, as if to see if someone important stood just behind. She was very kind about the children, letting them play for her family and praising them, and then sending them off to see the menagerie with a bevy of archdukes and archduchesses."

"I did not really take it amiss that she could not attend to me. Think what she does! She can order men to go off and fight in a war." Anna shook her head with wonder. "It also occurred to me that an empress can never know whether she has true friends or not. Everyone must bow and scrape, even though they may dislike her or oppose what she does. I could not bear my own trials," said Anna softly, "without friends I can trust. Who can the Empress trust without reservation, when there are always such schemes afoot, each man - each woman too, the wives and mistresses - seeking advancement and privilege?" She paused. There was such a tumble of impressions in her head from the four months away from Salzburg.

"She has done great things, like abolish torture - can you imagine if the Archbishop tried that! - and then she must turn around and teach her children right from wrong and how to live well in the eyes of God. There seemed to be tutors and governesses for the children, but surely the Empress herself must teach them as well. And all of them, boys and girls alike, princes and consorts to princes, must learn how to manage such a great household. She commands whole cities of servants who clean and launder, cook and wash up, make the beds and stoke the fires and carry out the slops. Just think of the chamber pots to be emptied for a hundred and fifty guests!"

"Did you like Vienna, I mean the city?" asked Marianna.

"You cannot imagine how glad we were to get there," Anna said. "We had come through a terrific storm and were cold and wet, tired and hungry, and there was your man, Hans, who took us in a dry carriage to the White Ox. What luck that he was there, Marianna, and how kind of you to ask him to meet us. After we had changed to dry things, he took us to a tavern for a good hot meal. He seemed to me an angel." Anna reached for Marianna's hand. "And you, Theresa, you and Lorenz were such help. I fear my husband has asked too much of you, borrowing money from Lorenz, then expecting him to go to Lauffen to make the case that Leopold should be appointed Deputy *Kapellmeister* when Eberlin died, and then asking you to arrange for masses to be said when Woferl was ill and . . . ."

"Don't give it a thought," soothed Theresa, though in point of fact she had commented to Lorenz, during her friends' absence, that Leopold presumed rather much on their friendship.

"But yes," said Anna, remembering Marianna's question. "I did like Vienna. It seemed very gay, though also large and noisy. I had not known so many kinds of people had existed in all the world. Leopold says there are almost a thousand houses! How could you know everyone in such a place? There are market stalls for selling more goods than I thought the world could hold. There is one whole alley where men and women of fashion select their silks and velvets, brocades and muslins, buckles and gloves, lace and ribbon, buttons - everything. And there are pits for baiting bears and cocks and dogs, and puppet shows and plays on street corners, and drunken men reeling about and women of the night - oh, I saw one accost a man quite flagrantly by day. And when people were hanged or punished, or when there were processions, there were so many more people than we are used to here. Oh, and there were Hungarian oxen that came herded in, accompanied by such a procession - clowns and jugglers, a street band. One of the oxen broke loose and there was a great chase and revelry, and when it was caught, it was slaughtered on the spot, poor beast."

"We hoped you would return somewhat sooner," said Marianna fondly.

"Yes, Leopold intended to. He no doubt told the Archbishop that it was illness that kept us so long," she confided, "but I think it was that he fell in love with Vienna and all the nobility, and the way they made much of him and the children." She forbore to tell her friends that it had troubled her when Leopold had represented himself as *Kapellmeister* of Salzburg and when he let the Viennese believe that his children were younger than, in fact, they were, so as to increase the astonishment of those who heard them.

"And Nannerl?" inquired Theresa. "How did she do?"

"Oh, very well. She amazed all who heard her and was beside herself to meet the great Christoph Wagenseil, whose compositions both children have played. He was loud in his approval and kissed Nannerl's hand and then took Wolfgang on his knee and was altogether kind. Nannerl was also able to meet a young composer by the name of Marianna Martinetz. But Nannerl had a dreadful shock when the Archduchess Johanna, who had taken up my daughter very kindly, took sick and died. Poor Nannerl was most grieved by the loss." Anna thought of the beautiful child and her mother, the powerful Empress, who had had to bury her child. Her grief would be as sharp as any mother's. Rank was no protection against death.

"And Wolfgang?" asked Marianna. "How did he fare?"

"Oh," said Anna, smiling, "the little scamp did very well indeed. He is getting to be quite an accomplished musician, you know, but what he liked best were things quite removed from the music: the boat we traveled on, the carriages when they went fast, the animals in the Empress's menagerie, the spectacles on the street." She glanced at the sun, which seemed to make its appearance on this winter's day especially to welcome the Mozarts back. "I must be getting along," she said. "There is so much to do after such a time away."

"It is good to have you back," said Theresa warmly.

"Yes, it is," concurred Marianna.

"Do you know," said Anna, lowering her voice, "Leopold has it in mind to have the children's portraits painted in the finery the Empress sent to them. Think of it!" Only the nobility and the richest of burghers had portraits made.

It was to Margarethe alone that Anna confided Leopold's plans, already afoot, for a much longer journey, "as far as Paris and maybe even London," said Anna, shivering.

"And you will go?" asked Margarethe.

"Yes, I must. I think it is not good for the children to be made so much of. They are adorable miniatures to the fashionable, who care nothing for their health. I must teach them to tell the truth, when they are surrounded by falsehood, make sure they eat sensibly and say their prayers and so on." She could not tell even Margarethe that, away from home, Leopold was less careful of the truth, less careful, even, of the children's bodily and moral well-being than in Salzburg. Swamped in adulation and swayed by nobility, Leopold sometimes lost his bearings, Anna thought. She must go along to protect her children from, among other things, their father's enthusiasm. "I have to admit," she said, "that I do wish to see such far-off places, though I do not like to be away from home."

Margarethe put her arm around Anna's shoulders. "I have missed you," she confessed.

"And I you, you cannot think how much," said Anna.

23

1763

THOUGH KAPELLMEISTER EBERLIN had died in the summer between the Mozarts' journeys to Munich and Vienna, no one had yet been appointed to replace him. Leopold took that to mean that the Archbishop did not intend to appoint Giuseppi Lolli, the Vice Kapellmeister, to Eberlin's post. The Archbishop's generosity in providing funds for the Mozarts' travels also suggested to Leopold that he might be preferred over the fat Italian.

"Everyone in Vienna," he said to Anna, "took me for Salzburg's *Kapellmeister*."

"Because you let them think so," said Anna a little tartly. She had not approved of her husband's failure to correct the misimpression.

He hardly heard her. "You should see Lolli," said Leopold in disgust. "The Italians laid their plans during Eberlin's illness, while I was still away in Munich." To him, the Italians, who scorned honest Germans even in German lands, seemed capable of anything. "There was Lolli, coming from Mass alongside His Grace today, making calves' eyes, tripping over his own shoe buckles, '*Si signore, non signore, qualunque cosa dica*,'" simpered Leopold in imitation of his rival.

"Well," said Anna, "had Lolli been away from Salzburg, you would not have sat quietly in the corner counting stitches." She would be happy with the increase of salary the *kapellmeister's* position would bring, but it still seemed unreasonable that her husband should expect to be both absent and preferred.

There was a pounding on the door. "Ah," said Leopold with satisfaction, "It is Loronzoni. Be sure the children are ready, Anna." He went down the stairs to let in the painter, who was to make portraits of the children in the dresses the Empress had sent them, and of himself, in his finest brown plush.

Pietro Loronzoni was a pompous little man who never ceased to brag that he had painted both the high altar at Zell am See and the side alters at Strobl and Mariaberg. He had pitted yellow skin and bad teeth, and his neck cloth was stained as if he had wiped his lips on it at table. Leopold would have preferred someone less dissipated, but it was expensive to have portraits made. Leopold was determined that his friends and associates would always be reminded what a figure he and his children had cut in the Viennese court, even after the children had outgrown their imperial dress.

"Oh," Anna exclaimed when she saw the children dressed in their finery. "I might take you for royalty! Here, Wolfgang, let me tie your ribbon and your lace is crooked. Nannerl, you must wear my earbobs."

"No, Mama, you wear them," said Nannerl. "Hurry and change your dress."

"Come," said Leopold. "We must not waste the artist's time."

"Surely you cannot want me to paint this child," protested Pietro Loronzoni, as he examined Wolfgang. "Too thin and pale." Behind his hand he added, "God will no doubt spare you the expense of bigger shoes for him!"

"My son has been ill," Anna said coldly.

They had all been ill since their return from Vienna, first Wolfgang, then Nannerl, then Leopold. Anna had felt the same malaise spreading through her body like an army on the march as she nursed her husband and children, but she had not herself had the time to take to her bed.

"Surely you can fatten him up in your picture," Leopold urged the artist. "See, he has put on the suit the Empress herself sent to him in Vienna." He lowered his voice, as if confiding a great secret. "The Privy Paymaster brought it right up to our door after my children played for Her Majesty and the Emperor. The Empress held my boy in her lap and let him kiss her cheek as if he were an archduke. Just make him a little fatter and put some roses in his cheeks, fill out the waistcoat and so on." His long fingers sketched an art he knew nothing of as Wolfgang strutted about, his small ceremonial sword clinking and his shoe buckles rattling.

"And the girl," said Loronzoni, studying Nannerl, "I brought along the dress ready-painted." He unrolled a canvas with a rose-colored dress that wore a blank space where the head should be. "This has one hand, as you requested. A hand of such beauty and difficulty. I am used to being paid well for such a hand."

Nannerl frowned at the canvas. "Ready-painted?" she asked blankly.

"It is so costly," soothed her father. "Signor Loronzoni will charge me far less if he does not have to paint the dress."

"And white is very difficult," wheedled Loronzoni.

Anna would not dispute with her husband in the presence of this egregious man, but she was angry. Leopold raised no objection to the cost of painting Wolfgang in his imperial suit.

Nannerl stroked the glowing ivory silk that reminded her of the Princess Johanna. She too knew better than to argue with her father, especially in the presence of a stranger. "What about Mama?" she asked. "What should she wear?"

"Oh," said Leopold vaguely.

Anna interrupted him. "This is not a good hand," she said, studying the ready-painted figure to which the artist intended to add her daughter's head. "The flower grows right out of the finger, and my daughter would never wear the dress you have painted, with such a board of a stomacher, for no one could perform trussed up like that. And look at that shoulder." She pointed to the left side. "It vanishes altogether. And the thumb is hidden!"

Leopold broke in, "Remember too that you said you would do just a finger and a half for the boy, like this." He posed with his hand on his side, three of his fingers folded under and out of sight.

"But I must add the keyboards," said Loronzoni, "and all that braid on the boy's suit and the brocade of the waistcoat. And he will not sit still, I doubt."

"I told you what I could pay, Signor Loronzoni," said Leopold brusquely. "If you do not wish the commission . . . ."

"No, no," said Loronzoni quickly, "but a man must feed himself. I expect many important commissions . . . ."

Anna could hardly make out what the ill-favored Italian said, for his German sounded Italian and he spoke very fast. Loronzoni was not much of an artist, in her view.

It was worse than she had expected. For some reason, Loronzoni had the boy put his hand in his vest the wrong way across the placket, as no one would ever do, and the lower half of his other arm grew out of the background draperies with anatomical impossibility. Leopold had arranged to sit for the artist himself, but to save money he hid one of his hands in drapery and showed only the fingertips of the other. Anna grew so irritated with the untidy, bombastic artist who imperiously demanded food and drink, that she hardly minded that Leopold had decided not to pay for her portrait. She wanted the artist out of the house with all her heart.

When Margarethe, out for walk, came to visit, she examined the portraits that hung on the wall. She wished to be polite, but she thought them very bad. "Leopold's is better than the children's," she said, once Anna had invited her to be candid. "Was Nannerl much disappointed not to be shown in the Archduchess's dress?"

"At first she was," said Anna, "but the artist - so-called so offended her that she came to think she did not want his eyes on that particular dress. She was more put out that her father had decided not to have my portrait done. I told her I did not mind, that I was glad to have that creature out of the house. I would not have liked him leering at me."

"Why did Leopold not have him do you?" Margarethe inquired gently, knowing that it might be a sore point.

Anna was silent a long time. She had pondered the same question. "He has changed in some way," she admitted, trusting her friend's discretion. "He is wholly taken up with his advancement at court - and beyond - and he sees forces arrayed against him - Lolli, all the Italians. Even his mother, for heaven's sake, because she still holds it against him that he left Augsburg all those years ago! And now that young Michael Haydn has arrived at court to be *Konzertmeister* . . . . Leopold finds him gifted but brash - not in the least respectful and too fond of drink. I think," she said carefully, "that my husband had hoped for more notice from the Archbishop." She sighed.

"I am no longer - maybe I was never - the center of Leopold's universe," mused Anna. "It is all Wolfgang, now. Nannerl plays better than her brother and half the compositions that Leopold says are Wolfgang's are really hers. She taught him most of what he knows about the violin, though now, of course, Leopold has taken over his instruction. In Leopold's mind, it is all about his son and only his son. My husband used to think differently of women, but it seems now to serve him better to hold the common view."

Margarethe studied Leopold's portrait. She thought it was an accurate impression of the proud, learned, richly dressed and somewhat supercilious man into whose hands her friend had given her life.

Anna said softly, "At first he knew me as a musician and admired my work, but I think he has forgotten that. It is inconvenient, a hindrance to him. I think these," she gestured at the paintings, "show the family musicians." She snorted. "And you can see that Nannerl is but *part* musician. See where that little length of rose-colored ribbon attaches her head onto the body - any woman's body?" She stood up and touched the canvas with its slick covering of paint. "It is not good, Margarethe, for the children to be puffed up with pretensions," said Anna. "Paying someone to paint a few fingers and lavish clothes does not change the fact that they must work for a living."

The Mozart children had been commanded to perform at court for the celebration of the Archbishop's birthday in late February. They were resplendent in the clothes the Empress had sent them and Leopold made sure that everyone knew from whence the finery had come. The festivities were lavish. No one could fail to attend without giving offense, and therefore everyone of any importance was there. Immediately after the Mass, said in the Prince's honor, Archbishop Schrattenbach stood in the Cathedral to make an announcement. He was more gorgeously arrayed than was usual even for ceremonial events. His small, rather delicate and girlish features were, Anna thought, nearly overwhelmed by the scarlet velvet and gleaming white fur of his voluminous robes. Around her the company stirred and rustled. "We have been too long without a *Kapellmeister*, and so we have named our good Signor Lolli to that post. Herr Mozart, too, has been advanced to the post of *Vice Kapellmeister*." Anna watched as the flushed Italian, ornately curled and trussed up in taffeta, affected modesty. Leopold, his face set, bowed punctiliously. He would never let on how deeply the second prize he had won rankled. Not even the exclamations and applause awarded to his children, who had indeed progressed in mastery and musicianship, soothed his burning sense that he had been conspicuously wronged.

"So," said Leopold, once the children had drunk warmed milk and settled in their beds. "Lolli has his post, we Germans being too barbaric, our souls too simple. We clearly have not mastered the fine art of flattery. Oh Anna," he said wearily, "Lolli cannot hold a candle to Eberlin, whose goodness he ridicules. All the Italians insult Eberlin's memory by rolling their eyes when they speak of him, though never when the Archbishop is by, of course."

Anna felt a flood of sympathy for Leopold, who had honored and revered old Eberlin, the fatherly old man who had known enough to hire the youngster. "I know," she said softly.

"To think, Anna, how I was treated in Vienna, where everyone knew the *Violinschule* and honored my children and I was taken for *Kapellmeister* of Salzburg." He pondered, pulling his lower lip between his thumb and forefinger. "Perhaps I ought to try my fortunes elsewhere . . . ." He stared off into space. 'Here I will never have my due."

Anna thought of her composition, interred under linen in the bottom of the trunk. She thought of Margarethe's poems, hidden from all who might understand and cherish them. She had some idea how it was never to have one's due, but she said nothing: it would be no solace to her husband to know of her stillborn hopes or those of her friend.

Leopold put on his nightshirt and his warm dressing gown and paced restlessly, while the candlewick grew long and smoked and the tallow puddled. "Anna," he said at last. "It seems to me that God may have entrusted me with a greater task than my own success. He has sent Wolfgang into my care. The boy is not an ordinary child at all, but a miracle. He learns so fast, with such a will, and is so adept . . . ."

Anna had put on her own nightshift. She was aware that her husband was talking more to himself than to her. He paced and paced, stopping from time to time to pass his hand over his face. He pulled the ribbon out of his hair and flung it carelessly aside. Anna picked it up, unobtrusively, when his back was to her.

"I swear to you, Anna . . . ."

She put up her hand to stop him. "Leopold, dear one," she urged, "you are tired and disappointed and must sleep. Tomorrow . . . ."

It had been a difficult day and the candle was nearly gone, flickering and smoking, throwing her husband's long shadow dancing upon the wall, where it rose and fell with the flame.

"No, Anna," said Leopold harshly. "You must understand. I am balked here. I have enemies. I have given my all to the court but can trust no one." He stopped and wheeled to face her. Anna, you will be my witness." He laid one hand on his breast and held the other up, as if taking an oath before a magistrate. His voice was hoarse. "I hereby solemnly vow, before God, with my wife to witness, that I will give my life to making known what has come to pass in this humble dwelling in Salzburg," he paused, "and that my life's work will be the education and nurture of my son's gift, which God has given to the world."

Anna reeled in astonishment. How often had she heard Leopold rail against vows? He was a man who held that reason was the greatest of all faculties and that contracts between reasonable men were the foundation of all society. He wrote long letters to the enlightened thinkers of the civilized world and received long answers, too. Anna had heard him argue at length, in many companies of his most respected and enlightened friends, that a vow before God could be no kind of contract at all, for it could bind only one party, man, but never God. Yet here he was, Leopold Mozart, taking a vow to God!

"I thought," said Anna, "that you did not hold with vows." She could see, even by the wavering light, that her husband was covered in sweat. Was he ill?

Leopold sat down heavily. "In the ordinary course of things," he admitted, "you are quite right, quite right indeed. A vow is a kind of bargain in the dark, as God's ways are inscrutable. But in this case to take a vow may not be amiss. God has, in this instance, declared himself quite clearly, by setting this child down here, in my humble household, to delight and astonish the world. He has genius, my dear, of a sort never before seen."

"Well," Anna observed with some asperity, "I suppose that whenever a man takes a solemn vow, it is *always* a special case. What about Wolfgang? Does he have a say in the matter? You have always said a child must be free to choose what he will do. And what about Nannerl?"

"Anna," Leopold said, restraining his exasperation, "you fail to understand. Wolfgang is not *like* other children. He is not of the same clay as his sister. She is a good musician, no doubt, gifted to the bone, but she is a girl, Anna. What can possibly come of her gifts? She must marry and bear children. *You* of all people should understand, Anna," he pleaded. "But the boy is altogether different. There is nothing he may not conquer with the right backing. Any good father would give his son what he needs to do his work, and Wolfgangerl is still a baby, too young to choose aright. He is hardly out of skirts! Of course he loves music and the attention it brings him, but ask him and he would just as leave stable the Archbishop's horses! I cannot allow him to squander his gift as if he were no more than a blacksmith's son!"

Leopold knelt before his wife and clasped his hands against his breast. "Anna," he said, "so many light minds these days scoff at miracles. But this child. . . ." He shook his head, unable to find the words. "I must," he pleaded, "be his herald to the world, which is full - as Salzburg is - of greedy, ambitious and dishonest men."

The smell of smoking tallow filled Anna's nostrils. The cheap candle's flame sputtered and sparked in its melted puddle. Leopold's shadow came spinning in to meet him as the room grew dark. She took her husband's hand and led him to bed, where they clung together until sleep claimed him.

But Anna did not sleep. Leopold was, as she knew full well, a man given to enthusiasms. This was not the first time he had abandoned reason under the pressure of strong feeling. He had left his schooling for music; married her, a woman without any fortune; and would now make of her son a cause. Well, she determined, she would take no vow but she would nevertheless protect both her children from their father's passions.

24

1763

IT SEEMS VERY ODD to take out these warm cloaks in June," said Anna, carrying an armload of their heaviest clothes from the hallway.

Margarethe, who was helping to pack up the children's things, chuckled. "Well," she observed, "they'll be going right back into trunks again."

"Leopold says we will be away this time for months, maybe even years," said Anna. "He thinks we may extend our journey as far as London. Oh, Margarethe, I cannot imagine going so far!" Though Salzburg was a commercial crossroads to which merchants traveled from the orient and darker places still, Salzburgers rarely went so far afield. As far as Anna knew, no woman in Salzburg had ever traveled such a distance.

"Are you frightened?" Margarethe inquired.

"Yes," Anna admitted, "because I have never gone among strangers in lands where few will speak my own tongue. And there are dangers. Brigands, illness, accidents - and we will meet, at long last, Leopold's mother, whom I have learned to fear." She smoothed her good wool cloak with its fur lining. "I could have used this warm a cloak in Vienna last winter, though my husband was as good as his word and ordered this one made immediately upon our return."

Anna and Margarethe sat in the bedroom, while in the front room the children played a game, laughing and talking companionably. Nannerl would strike a chord on the harpsichord and Wolfgang would name the notes, improvising upon them. Nannerl would set a melody and Wolfgang would fit a bass to it, so that their four hands played as if connected to one body. "I marvel at Nannerl's proficiency," said Anna. "Her musicianship grows by leaps and bounds." Nannerl, now twelve, had never known an interruption in her music as Anna had during her early years at Nonnberg.

"And Wolfgang is so quick," said Margarethe.

"Yes," said Anna. "What he hears once is his altogether, and he invents upon it. I have no doubt of his success. His native talents and Leopold's determination assure that he will flourish. But when Nannerl plays," she confessed, "especially her own compositions, I am led to hope that my daughter may, after all, achieve what I have not. And then I worry that my hopes for her are mine, not hers."

The women worked in companionable silence. "How will you travel?" Margarethe asked sadly, for she would miss her confidant.

Anna caught the mournful tone and spoke its twin. "Leopold has decided," said Anna, threading a needle to mend a small rent in a pair of Wolfgang's breeches, "to purchase his own carriage. He has even hired a servant to travel with us this time. It will surely help, for travel is difficult, but these are great expenses," she worried. Neither woman, each dreading the separation to come, could say aloud what she most dreaded - to lose the other for a time, perhaps altogether.

Leopold was sure that their takings would meet and exceed his outlays, for travelers from the Viennese court had carried news of his children to many other cities. He had taken particular pains that a letter of his own devising had already reached an Augsburg newspaper with an account of his children's triumph - and his own virtuosity. His mother, he thought with satisfaction, would surely see that Leopold and his children had been warmly welcomed by the Empress in Vienna.

Anna's apprehension about meeting her mother-in-law grew during the ten days the Mozarts spent in Munich, only a day's journey from Leopold's birthplace. The children astonished the Elector of Bavaria and several dukes and princes, but Anna's mind was on Leopold's mother, whom she would finally meet. She knew that the Widow Mozart was a fiercely observant and upright Catholic, the more ardent because of the many Lutherans who were at home in Augsburg. Leopold called his mother "a woman to strike terror into God." Anna could sympathize with her mother-in-law, who had reasonably wanted her eldest son's attendance following her husband's death.

But that offense had occurred when Leopold was young and hot of blood. Surely by now, more than two decades later, the old lady would have forgiven her son.

"Mama," asked Wolfgang, as they drew ever closer to Augsburg, "is Grossmutter fat or thin?" The seven year-old child, still small for his age, asked one question, it seemed to Anna, for each revolution of the carriage wheels as they beat against the rutted summer highway.

"What do you think?" asked Anna. "Look at Papa."

Wolfgang squinted at his father. "Thin," he pronounced, then leaned his head against his mother. "When will we get there, Mama?"

Anna, stroking her son's fair hair, thought that this winsome child, small and pale, would win the heart of a stone, much less a grandmother. As for Nannerl, she was a comely girl of twelve, slender and graceful with a pretty manner.

Nannerl was composing in her head an aria devised as a quartet for a new opera she had in mind as the coach jounced and swayed along the rutted road. Her body ached, but she was distracted from discomfort by hearing how the menacing low tones of the villain's bass underlay and connected the unsuspecting soprano, the busybody mezzo and the yearning tenor. None of the characters knew what the others knew, thought or hoped, but together, ah, together! She heard Wolfgang's incessant questions as the quibble of mayflies, which were still abroad in late June.

Everything irritated Leopold, his son's excited chatter and whine, his daughter's absorbed silence, his wife's quiet reassurances. The closer they drew to Augsburg, the less freely he could draw breath. A weight pressed on his chest. He was torn between fierce desire and cold repulsion. At one moment, he imagined that his mother would welcome him and draw him to her bosom; at the next, he felt her push him from her with her hard hand. Anna would no doubt wonder - and ask - why her husband would take his family to lodge at the Three Moors Hotel on the Maximilianstrasse, when his mother, brothers and sisters lived in town. It never occurred to Leopold that were he to explain more to Anna, she might inquire less.

The night before Leopold had dreamed that old Frau Mozart, eager to make amends for the injustices she had done to her eldest son, came to greet them and found them in the most expensive quarters Augsburg could provide. She saw that her son had made his way in the world and gladly gave up the grudges she had treasured. Leopold had wakened that morning with immeasurable lightness of heart, but now with every inch that he moved closer to his childhood home, he felt more burdened and bound.

Anna was astonished by the unaccustomed elegance of their lodging and felt both surprise and disappointment that they had not gone directly to her mother-in-law. She supposed that Leopold meant them all to wash and brush the dust from their traveling clothes. Anna had discovered she must walk on egg shells where Leopold's mother was concerned, for he was both evasive and short whenever she inquired. To Anna it was inconceivable that she, in like circumstances, would not rush to lay eyes on her son and his family. She hoped that when Nannerl and Wolfgang were grown, they would not hesitate to come directly to her when they arrived in Salzburg from their travels.

Wolfgang capered about the room, sniffing like a dog into every corner. "Papa," he pleaded, "may I have my fiddle. I want to play something."

Leopold unwrapped the small instrument for his son. This was what his hard-hearted mother would miss, this genius who had sprung from her son's own loins, who would rather play and compose than run about the streets like a costermonger's son.

"Should we not go to your mother?" asked Anna gently.

"She can come to me," growled Leopold. It sounded to Anna like a curse. "I will not go to be turned away at the door."

Anna protested. "She would never turn her eldest son away!"

But Leopold was adamant.

"But think, Leopold," Anna urged. "She has grandchildren she has not met, and Nannerl is her namesake. Can you not now make your peace?"

"Anna, you know nothing of this," said Leopold coldly. He ached to do as she asked, but he could not. "Kindly do not trouble yourself about it."

But Anna *did* trouble herself. All during the days when Leopold sought out the people of influence who could arrange for concerts - all Lutherans, of course, for the Catholics did not extend themselves to hear the traveling prodigies - Anna wondered how she might go about to reunite her husband with his mother. In their chambers, Leopold raged at the old lady, for it was surely her doing that the Catholics kept away when the children performed. "My mother kept even my brothers away!" he exclaimed. He paced back and forth in silence. "Well" he said finally, wiping his hand over his face, "I will go to Herr Stein this morning. He has asked me to bring the children to inspect his newest claviers, for which he has invented an improved escapement device. And I may purchase a traveling clavier. Are you ready, Anna?"

"I think," said Anna, who had an idea, "I will not come with you, my dear. I have something of a headache and should rest." She knew that they would not return in a hurry. Both children would have to play on every instrument in Herr Stein's workshop and the enthusiastic inventor would show them his every innovation. But the moment she was alone, she walked out and away from the hotel and, asking directions of a respectable man, made her way to the house in which Leopold's mother lived. It was wrong to deceive her husband, but surely it was a greater wrong for two grown people, tied by blood, to occupy the same city and never lay eyes on one another.

When Anna was shown into the room in which Frau Mozart stood, she recognized her at once as her mother-in-law. Thin, erect and hawk-like, she had Leopold's skeptical pitch to her eyebrow. Frau Mozart examined Anna as if from a great height. "Yes?" she said coldly.

"I came to meet you," said Anna, flushing, "as we have not had occasion . . . ."

"Nor will," said Frau Mozart, running her eyes up and down Anna's figure, memorizing, thought Anna, the stitches in her bodice, which suddenly seemed to Anna very crooked and uneven.

Anna took a deep breath. "Leopold is your son," she said quietly.

Frau Mozart hesitated and sat down, but did not invite Anna to sit.

Anna, only dimly aware of the room, noticed that it was dominated by a large, dark, bloody painting of Christ suffering on the cross.

The old woman raised her Mozart eyebrow and said, "Did my son send you?"

"Oh!" exclaimed Anna, "You are so like him. I had no idea. He is out with the children your grandchildren, Maria Anna, whom we call Nannerl, and little Wolfgang - he is seven, no longer so young. Nannerl is twelve. Both are gifted musicians, taught by your son, who has brought them to Augsburg to perform. And then we will go on to more of the German cities and the Lowlands and then perhaps to Paris, maybe even to London." I am prattling like a child, she thought, noting that her mother-in-law held herself stiffly upright and appeared unmoved by what Anna said. "I know there is something not right between you and your son and thought perhaps . . . ."

Though uninvited, she sat down, feeling that her legs would buckle.

"What do you know of my affairs?" inquired Frau Mozart, pursing her lips.

"Very little," Anna admitted. "I know that Leopold was unhappy - hurt - that he did not inherit equally with your other children." She quailed at her own boldness, but she did not think her mother-in-law would suffer her to stay long. She must say what she had come to say. "I told him he did not need your money, but he does need a mother . . . ."

"Did he tell you," snapped the imperious old woman, "of the way he turned his back on his father's intention that he should be a priest, running away to Salzburg, consorting with heretics who would undermine the Church? Did he tell you how he left behind his widowed mother, when he was most needed? Did he tell you that he asked his mother's help in claiming citizenship in Augsburg, leading her to think he intended to return to his home city? Did he tell you that he spoke to his mother through his publisher rather than directly?"

Anna noted that Frau Mozart spoke of herself as if she were someone other.

"Why," continued the old woman, "should any of his *mother's* wealth go to a son who has embarrassed and deserted his family in the eyes of all Augsburg, though as a child he was given every advantage?" She paused, nearly breathless from her listing of grievances.

"I knew some of this," said Anna slowly, "and I am sorry. Children are so often hard for their parents to understand. Already my children have desires I know nothing of. But Leopold is older now, and wiser, for he has children of his own. He was a rash youth when he left, and I am sure he acted, as he often does, out of enthusiasm. I think it pains him to be divided from you. Surely by now, you and he could make your peace."

"Then he must confess his wrong and beg my pardon - and the priest's as well - for sins committed against the commandment to honor mother and father," said Frau Mozart. "I will not come to him. He must come to me. I have never wronged him in the least."

The image darted through Anna's mind of Leopold forced to apologize in public for his pamphlet, which had lain scattered like snow at his feet. He would never so humble himself again, she knew. He would not have done so long ago without the threat of ruination.

"Will you not come, perhaps, to hear my children play then? Tomorrow at the Three Kings Hotel or two days after that? They would so like to meet their grandmother. And Leopold will see that you reach out to him and his hardness of heart will dissolve."

"No," said Frau Mozart firmly, standing up and smoothing her long bodice into her skirt. She was plainly dressed with absolute neatness in fine but somber fabric. She clutched the heavy silver cross she wore around her neck.

Anna knew she should stand up, that the interview was ended. But stubbornly she sat where she was. "My mother died shortly before my son was born. She had grown old and infirm and it was her time. But once she was gone, I thought of things I had never told her, how much she had given me even in the hardest times, when we were so poor we had only bread to eat . . . ."

"If my son had to marry without my consent, and to marry a woman without means, he must not cry of poverty," said Frau Mozart.

"No," cried Anna. "That is not what I meant. Leopold frets about money, but we have plenty. I meant that you and your son should meet and put an end to your grievance while you can, so there will be no regret."

She saw just the least flicker of yearning in the older woman's eyes and her body inclined a little toward Anna. But it passed and Frau Mozart stood even straighter than seemed possible, so tightly held that Anna thought she might shatter if touched.

"Do not trouble yourself," said old Frau Mozart. "You are a stranger to me, and so is my son." She showed Anna to the door without another word.

At night, when the children were tucked up in their beds, a messenger came with a note for Leopold. It was in his mother's handwriting. It bore no greeting.

> *Do not send your wife to plead your case. You must know that I require an apology from you. Otherwise, you will find few Catholics among your admirers. You must make do with Lutherans.*
>
> *Anna Maria Mozart, born Sulzer*

Leopold stared at Anna, his face white and drawn.

"What is this?" he inquired in a low voice. "You went to my mother?"

Anna felt her heart drop to her shoes. "I did," she confessed. "I wanted you to reconcile, and I wanted her to know our children. I asked her to come to hear the children play tomorrow. But she will not unless you come to her first. She is still angry because you left for Salzburg and did not become a priest."

"How dared you, Anna!" Leopold's voice was loud and harsh. He felt utter incomprehension that his wife would interfere in his affairs.

"Leopold," she whispered. "The children."

He dropped his voice. "Anna," he said. Even though he spoke quietly, his voice was fierce and angry. "If you go behind my back and try to thwart me, what am I to do? When the world opposes me, at the very least, my wife might not."

"I did not go to oppose you," Anna said, "but to try to mend what has divided you. Perhaps I should not have gone. Perhaps I should have asked you, but you would not have allowed me, and I hoped a word would unite you. But she is like you. She nurses her grievance as if it were a child, and it grows bigger and stronger every day. And you too. You nourish twin angers and they keep you apart. She is an old woman, Leopold. Her face is lined and sorrowful. What if she dies and you have not made your peace with her?"

"Then she will die," said Leopold, "with her sins to keep her company in Hell."

"Leopold!" exclaimed Anna, aghast, as her husband took himself to bed, where he lay rigid through the night, unforgiving and furious.

Anna lay troubled in the dark, blaming herself for visiting the old woman. Poor Leopold, she thought, to have suffered such severe and unrelenting judgment. No wonder he had run from Augsburg the moment his father had relaxed his grip. Leopold had sworn his candlelight vow to advance Wolfgang's fortunes with the same sharp fanatical glint in his eye that Anna had seen in his mother's. Sick with foreboding, she slept.

25

1763-1764

THE MOZARTS TRAVELED ALL FALL through German cities – Ulm and Stuttgart, Ludwigsburg, Schwetzingen, Heidelburg, Mannheim, Frankfurt, Mainz and Coblenz. As soon as he arrived in a new city, Leopold sought out the great and influential men and presented his letters of introduction. He took his wife and children with him to walk out in public of an evening, that they might be seen and talked about. He put notices in newspapers and worked feverishly to create an appetite for the prodigies he had brought to town. Everywhere, the children were heard and admired.

Nannerl's virtuosity brought applause in every company. Anna often found herself near tears as she listened to the music her daughter's slight body and slender fingers could conjure from what was, after all, no more than a wooden box with strings and ivory jacks. "You can do what few women can," Anna told her, "I am sure of it. Remember what the Archduchess told you, that you could be a musician in her court."

Nannerl nodded. "But she died, Mama," she said softly.

"There will be others like her," said Anna.

Wolfgang played on all the great German organs, on every smaller keyboard instrument and on his small violin, astounding those who heard him with his dexterity and command. He could sight read and improvise with startling facility. Anna frequently heard her son echo his father and Nannerl, but every now and again she heard a turn of phrase that made her catch her breath. Perhaps, she thought, his gift is as great as Nannerl's. But when he was not performing, Wolfgang grew restive and homesick. He tormented Nannerl, hiding her stockings and her comb, writing silliness in the margins on the pages of her compositions and then, when scolded, fell to sobbing that he missed his friends in Salzburg. He was, Anna reminded herself, only a small boy.

Anna had much to do just to keep everyone's clothes in trim. The children perspired when they played, and their clothes, both under and outer clothes, had to be laundered without washtubs or places to spread or hang the wet things. Leopold was hard on neck cloths and hair ribbons were twisted into strings. Sebastian Winter, the servant Leopold had brought, made all the arrangements outside the Mozarts' lodgings, but he would not lower himself to do woman's work.

The late summer's heat, which shimmered in Frankfurt and Coblenz, gave way to cold rain. Wolfgang caught a chill, and Leopold was overcome with terror. Suppose this child, in whom all his hopes now resided, were to sicken and die? Leopold's care for Wolfgang grew so assiduous that Anna feared he would stifle the child. When Wolfgang was well enough to travel, the Mozarts moved on to Aachen, where the Princess Amalia, sister to the King of Prussia, tried her best to persuade the itinerants to go to Berlin rather than Paris, promising Leopold that he should be *kapellmeister* and his daughter court composer. "It is nonsense, Anna," Leopold said. "The Princess is without funds here in Aachen. Her brother, the King, has no regard for her, because she will not do his bidding as she should. He keeps her on a short string. Her promises are worth nothing."

"But Leopold," countered Anna, "how many such offers to be court composer will Nannerl have? Should we not, at least, consider it?"

Leopold frowned. Anna, it seemed to him, opposed him in everything. Sometimes when he looked at her, he saw his mother and had to shake his head to clear away that impression.

In Brussels, where granules of snow swirled in the cold wind, Anna put her foot down. "Leopold, we must stay for awhile. The children are exhausted. They are out late every night and eat at odd hours. I need time to have all the clothes cleaned, and there is mending I cannot do in the middle of the night by cheap candles."

Prince Karl, the Governor of the Austrian Netherlands, had commanded the Mozart children to entertain him, but as was his wont he was too deeply engrossed in debaucheries to remember his casual demand. Though Leopold had agreed to stay a while at Anna's request he worried about the costs and blamed Anna for them. "Every day I must pay out money for our room and our meals," he complained. "You will not be content until there is not a thaler nor a pfennig left in my pocket."

Anna was firm. "Here the children go to bed early and sleep late. They go out of doors, even in the bitter weather. Their faces have color in them again. They need the rest, my dear. And it takes time to get the heavier woolens and the cloaks out. I have found someone to wash and iron our clothes properly, but all the shoes are full of holes and the heels run over. Please to take them to the cobbler, Leopold, and have yours repaired, too. Sebastian cannot, for he is seeing to repairs to the carriage."

Leopold demurred. "The boy has so recently been ill, Anna, to go about in stocking feet." He knew he should do as Anna asked but disliked leaving his son. "What will you do, Woferl, while Papa is out with the shoes?"

"Oh," said Wolfgang mischievously, "tweak my sister's braid and put spiders in her soup."

Leopold frowned.

"Leave him," ordered Anna. "He is with me, and I will not turn him out-of-doors to run about unshod."

"We will practice on the clavier, Papa," Nannerl told him. "We do not need shoes to do that." But once Leopold had gone with a sack of shoes, Nannerl stretched luxuriously, like a cat in sunshine, and sat down on the floor. Wolfgang curled beside her. "When can we go home?" he asked.

"Hush, Woferl," said Nannerl. "Papa will be very unhappy if he hears you complain."

"Well, Papa is not here, so I can complain all I like."

"It *is* nice," mused Nannerl, "just the three of us, and no concert tonight, and we can just sit and talk about anything at all."

Anna put down her mending. "If you had three wishes, Woferl, what would they be?"

"Go home, go home and go home!" he shrilled, not waiting an instant.

"And you, Nannerl?"

Nannerl put her head to the side and pondered so long that Wolfgang began to tickle her. "Stop it, Woferl. I am thinking. I do not object to traveling. Maybe I would wish to go to Berlin, if Princess Amalia could really get a post for me. Maybe," she said shyly, "my opera would be played. But I would like to go home, too. Do you have wishes Mama?" she asked hesitantly.

"Mmm," said Anna. "I suppose I would go home. But you know, I wish we could all go - sometime - to St. Gilgen, where I was born. It is only a little place, but quiet and pretty and I should like to see it again. And I wish . . . ." Her voice trailed off. She could not say it, not to her children, but she wished for the old easy familiarity with Leopold. He had been distant and distracted ever since Augsburg, as if the unpleasantness about his mother still weighed on him. "Well," she said, picking up her mending, "if wishes were horses, then beggars would ride. You told Papa you would practice and I must finish this shirt. When you have finally played for the Prince, Papa says we must go on to Paris."

The children groaned in unison. "Princess Amalia said that in Paris, the ladies wear their hair as tall as buildings," observed Nannerl.

In Paris, Leopold's letters of introduction were of no use whatever. "The court," Leopold fumed, "is everything. No one will do anything until the court does."

Anna disliked Paris from the moment she arrived. It was, for one thing, too big. The Parisians pointed proudly to the domes, spires, palaces, and the plentiful goods in the market. But the air was evil smelling and black with smoke. The water tasted odd. Anna pitied but feared the throngs of ragged beggars, many of them crippled or mutilated, their hollow faces grimed and devoid of any expression. Some, she was told, were soldiers from the late war, wearing rags and unable to feed the starving wives and babies who had followed them to the field and back. Multitudes of noisy people selling their wares, whining for alms, shouting orders and disputation, crowded into the dark and fearsome alleys. Had she been on her own, Anna would have left for home after the first day, but she knew her children needed reassurance and she imagined that Leopold himself, though he would never let on, felt as frightened and repelled as she did, so she held her tongue and did not complain. Nevertheless, she hated Paris.

The Mozarts were taken in by the Count van Eyck, the Bavarian diplomat, and his kindly wife, the plump, good-tempered daughter of Count Georg Anton Arco, Chief Chamberlain to the court in Salzburg. The Countess paid no attention to Anna's lack of rank, asking her about needlework, the raising of children and cookery. She advised them on the proper clothing, for - despite all Anna's efforts in Brussels - new suits and dresses were necessary for Paris. The Countess played merrily with Nannerl and Wolfgang, lending them books and her large clavier with two manuals and letting them romp all through her apartments while Leopold was out and about looking for influential friends.

"It cannot be good for my children to perform day and night, to practice every hour, to be always on display," Anna confided to the Countess. "I sometimes think Woferl has not the leisure to grow tall, and surely he needs some time to be apart from his father." She confided her concern that Wolfgang seemed at once too young and too old for his age. "He is so gifted, I know that and everyone says so, but he is also a little boy . . . ."

The Countess put her hand on Anna's arm sympathetically.

"Perhaps I worry too much," said Anna, "I worry that the boy will succeed and that Nannerl will not. I suppose I am foolish."

Quietly the Countess saw to it that Leopold was introduced to the Baron von Grimm and his mistress, the powerful Madame d'Épinay. These luminaries knew everyone and arranged for both children to play for the King and Queen, who were always bored with their sumptuous life and craved novelties. The King and Queen kept the Mozarts at Versailles for two weeks. The Queen insisted that Wolfgang sit beside her at dinner and fed him morsels from her plate with her fingers. Though Nannerl's playing was praised, she did not receive the same lavish attention her brother did. Leopold spoke briefly with the royal couple, but Anna was ignored, which gave her ample opportunity to study her surroundings. What she saw spoke to her not of beauty, but of surfeit and tedium. She smiled when required to, but the splendid retinue made her think of rotting vegetables, rubbed with wax to tempt foolish buyers.

No sooner had the Mozarts returned from Versailles to the van Eyck apartments than everyone in Paris was mad for the prodigies. One lady would drawl languidly to another - both of them laced into embroidered, jeweled and flounced dresses, toweringly coifed, powdered and rouged - that she was having the Mozart boy and his pretty sister to entertain. The second lady, struck with envy, would straightaway send for the young Mozarts to come to her. Thus the children were kept busy in one palace after another, wearing their new finery, performing and being fawned on till all hours.

The Baron von Grimm, a witty and energetic man with large teeth and immeasurable influence, gave the children rich presents. Others saw what he did and did likewise until Leopold's newly purchased trunk was full of watches, knives, writing cases, toothpick holders, snuffboxes, lace collars and shawls, ribbons and caps, elaborately worked swords and rings. Leopold kept a careful inventory of each gift, its giver and its likely value and was careful to send word of this little treasury when he wrote to Salzburg. He took in presents of money as well, handfuls of ducats and louis d'or. He copied the Baron's dress and Anna noticed that his walk took on a little of the Baron's uneven gait. He even began speaking in something like the Baron's drawling way.

"I am worried," Anna told Leopold, "that the children's heads will be turned. They are not real to these people, who want only to be amused. But when they are bored with our children, Nannerl and Wolfgang are nothing to them. And morals here are very low. You cannot see the women for the simpers painted onto their lips, and nearly every man of influence flaunts his mistress quite openly. Some of the mistresses seem more powerful than the King's ministers!"

"Well," said Leopold, "mistresses are not limited to France." Secretly he agreed with his wife, but somehow he could not, of late, bring himself to let her know of his concurrence on anything.

He was right, thought Anna, thinking of the Mirabell in Salzburg, a palace built by an earlier archbishop for his Jewish mistress, who gave him fifteen children. Still, in Salzburg as a rule, one was not so open about adultery, which might cause an ordinary woman to be publicly whipped, dragged through the streets wearing the heavy iron scold's bridle with its dirty gag, even driven from town. The French men seemed to marry prudently, then take mistresses for pleasure.

Leopold undertook to have four sonatas engraved in Wolfgang's name, for the Parisians especially favored the work of German composers in print. The sonatas that Leopold had engraved were not, in fact, Wolfgang's alone, for Nannerl had done a good part of the composition. Both children were especially fond of a striking adagio, which was entirely Nannerl's.

After one performance, Anna was standing with the Comtesse de Tessé. The Comtesse spoke kindly to Anna in her halting German. "Meine gut Madame," she said. "Vous haf giffen consideratión . . . uh, uh . . . zu inoculatión pour die smallpox, n'est ce pas? Pour les enfants . . . uh . . . die kinder. Inoculatión ist gut."

Anna was touched by the effort the Comtesse made to speak in German, particularly as her own French was even more halting.

"Ah, zere ist die Comtesse van Eyck." In rapid French the Comtesse de Tessé summoned the Countess van Eyck. "Come, Maria, and tell Madame Mozart, if you will, that she must have her children inoculated against the smallpox. Everyone is doing it."

"It might be a good idea," said the Countess to Anna, "since your children are exposed in so many places as you travel. My husband and I have been inoculated."

That evening Anna told Leopold what the two generous countesses had advised. "Both of them have received the inoculation and have come to no harm," she said.

"No, no," said Leopold. "I cannot do that. Wolfgang has been entrusted to me by God and we must rely on God's grace for his protection."

Anna felt weary; her husband spoke only of their son and not their daughter. "But if it would keep them safe?" She stressed "them" slightly. "You have always been interested in the newest inventions, and if men of reason think it right. . . ," she pressed.

"No, no, do not think of it," said Leopold.

Anna was silent, looking at the floor. "Leopold," she said at last. "How often have you told me we must cast aside superstitions in favor of reason and science? But ever since you took your vow . . . ."

Leopold's look was grim.

" . . . .you have seemed in the grip of something . . . ."

"It is not science," said Leopold hotly, "theses inoculations. They are nothing but fashion. These are Parisians who have rejected all religion. Their priests go about the street looking no different from any man. You must understand. God has laid a special . . . . But you do not understand." Leopold put his head in his hands. Why would Anna bedevil him with ideas beyond her comprehension. "You will not. Pray do not trouble me about this further."

Leopold was right: Anna could not understand his objection, though when the Countess van Eyck explained to her that it took a long time for inoculation - a month of isolation - Anna thought, perhaps that was it. Such an ordeal would be hard on her children, who were already tired from their incessant work. It troubled her to think that Leopold might have other motives: to isolate the children for a month would mean they could not perform and thus would not bring Leopold any money. There was something else, too, some pricking of fanaticism in Leopold these days, but she no sooner thought so than he was her sensible husband again, making arrangements, keeping track of his takings, seeking out the most influential people to know, the most accomplished musicians for the children to meet.

The dreadful news came at breakfast that the Countess, who had kept to her bed for several days with a severe cold, had coughed up blood during the night and lost consciousness. For five days, Anna and Nannerl did what they could to help the Countess, who had no family in Paris, but then, as if a candle's wick had broken, suddenly the Countess was dead. The Mozarts were plunged into mourning for their kindly mentor along with the rest of the household. The Count, dry-eyed and pale, thanked them for their help and told the Mozarts they must stay where they were so long as they sojourned in Paris. "My dear wife would have wished it," he said, his voice cracking.

Anna felt such sadness for the dear Countess, who had died far from home, from family and friends. Both children were desolated and even Leopold stopped for awhile to weep. "It is not right," cried Wolfgang, who had climbed onto his mother's lap, though he was too big to hold comfortably. Anna thought he was feverish. Nannerl took to her bed with a headache, trying to stifle the sobs that made her head hurt worse. It occurred to her that two of the women who had furthered her musical hopes, or promised to, had now died, the Archduchess Johanna and now the Countess Van Eyck. The thought flickered at the edge of her mind that those who sponsored her might be doomed for their efforts.

From grief and fatigue, the children both fell ill. Leopold gave them Vienna laxative water and called the German doctor who cared for the Swiss Guards. So far as Leopold was concerned, Paris itself had undermined his children's health. "The French are not to be trusted," he said. "Their music is execrable and they are a wicked, secular people. The Parliament would have arrested the French archbishop if the King had not ordered him into exile, and all because he backed the Jesuits." He shook his head and wrote to the Hagenauers in Salzburg, asking them to have special masses said for the children's sake at the Maria Plain and Loretto Churches. Anna, fearful that the children might suddenly cough up blood as the Countess van Eyck had, sat with them night and day, until she was too tired to wake, and then she slept beside them. She dreamed of women dancing a minuet in red-lacquered high-heeled shoes, holding their extravagant skirts out of the decay and filth of the streets.

"I want to go home," Wolfgang muttered in his sleep.

Anna woke and put her arm around his feverish body. So far as Anna was concerned, Paris was a place of death and disorder. Nothing good could come from so corrupt a city. "So do I," she whispered.

26

1764-1765

THE MOZARTS CROSSED FROM FRANCE to England by boat on whose shifting decks one could keep neither one's balance nor breakfast. Leopold, dismayed by the cost of the crossing, was the sickest of all and walked off the boat pale and dizzy, to be accosted by hordes of rough fellows, all shoving and shouting in their rapid English tongue. Anna, holding her children's hands tightly, moved closer to Leopold, who tired and nauseous though he might be, at least knew a little English.

"May Nannerl and I go down to the water?" begged Wolfgang, whose cheeks were red in the brisk seaside wind. Anna looked to Leopold for advice. So far from home, in so strange a place, she had no idea what was safe.

"You go with the children, Anna. Just over there. Porta will find our trunks." Leopold, too, was frightened by all the clamor. He was uncertain what to do, but he could not let his wife know this, for she had wanted to return to Salzburg from Paris, and it would not do to show her his weakness and fear.

Leopold had actually been relieved when his servant from Salzburg had left the Mozarts for a better post in Paris. Leopold had asked his Parisian friends' advice and hired the Italian servant, Porta, who was fluent in several languages and had crossed the Channel many times before. Now Leopold turned gratefully to the swarthy little man, Porta, whom Anna had disliked from the moment she set eyes on him, thinking him both arrogant and ingratiating. "Our luggage," Leopold said. "And then conveyance to a decent place where my wife and children can rest." Leopold had left his own carriage in Paris to be reclaimed upon the return journey.

Anna let the children run to the water's edge, where, as in Calais, they marveled at the mountains of water that advanced on them, crashing, collapsing and sliding back, leaving behind lacy scallops of foam, long banners and strings of watery vegetables. From the white cliffs, birds came screaming overhead, alighting to eye Anna and her children and to squabble with other birds over invisible scraps. The strong, unfamiliar odor of the sea was bracing to Anna.

"Look at that!" marveled Nannerl. "The water never stops coming in and running away again, forever and ever!"

Wolfgang squatted down on his haunches and pressed his hand on the wet sand, studying a dead fish that had washed in, iridescent white belly up. The wind tore the ribbon from his hair and he was left with curls blowing around his face, as if he were a small girl.

Porta hustled the Mozarts away from Dover to London. After the first night, Leopold, recovered from the crossing, found the Mozart's lodging in St. Martin's Lane, and Porta found a tailor to make them English clothes. Word that the Mozart prodigies had arrived spread quickly and they were sent for almost at once by King George III and Queen Charlotte, who received them without ceremony in their own living quarters.

The King seemed to Anna a kind, bluff man. Queen Charlotte spoke to them in her native German. "Ach, it is good to speak my own tongue. You bring relief from this English, which has no order. Come child," she said, drawing Nannerl to her with one hand. "You too, my boy. Tell me about your travels. Sit here. I will have the servant bring beer, ja? And I have ordered dinner. What do you think of liver dumplings?"

"Oh," exclaimed Wolfgang, "I like liver dumplings above everything!"

A queen, Anna thought, sitting down with the Mozarts to liver dumplings! What would her friends in Salzburg think? Leopold was engrossed with the King in a discussion of the ungrateful American colonies, where there was little understanding that the colonists must pay taxes for the recent war or that they must stay on the eastern side of the mountains to avoid inciting the savages. If Leopold was impressed with the King's acumen, the King was taken with Leopold's grasp of the matter.

The King and Queen were musical enthusiasts. The Queen played tolerably well at the clavier and admired the children's virtuosity without reservation. "You must hear the late Handel's music. Glorious, glorious," said the Queen, "and attend the Concerts of Ancient Music and meet our good Johann Christian Bach, the Concertmaster, and we must present your dear children in a concert at court."

Leopold was gratified by their warm reception. The King and Queen, their carriage passing the Mozarts as they walked in St. James Park a few days later, stopped, leaned out and greeted them warmly. Hardly had the Mozarts' new English clothes arrived than they were invited to appear at court. The children played splendidly to great applause, which served as some small compensation for the meagre present the Queen made to Leopold. Of greater importance was that she had told Bach to see to it that everyone of any importance in London attended the performance.

Johann Bach immediately took up the Mozarts, introduced them to all the musicians in town and showed Leopold how to arrange for public concerts. Bach, who quickly became Johann to Nannerl and Wolfgang, taught them what he had learned in Italy. He introduced them to their first *fortepiano*, which, he said laughing, "these English want to re-christen *pianoforte*. They change everything to suit themselves!" With Leopold's blessing, the young Concertmaster gave the children composition lessons and showed them many other courtesies as well. While Leopold was out and about and Johann had leisure, he took Anna and the children to see the wonders of London. He told Anna what shops she should visit and how to ask for what she wanted in English. He looked at Nannerl's opera and pronounced it "grand," which fired eight year-old Wolfgang's desire to compose an opera as well, for Johann had become his hero. Nannerl, now thirteen, promised her brother that when they returned to Salzburg and had a little leisure, they would compose an opera together and perform it in their front room for all their friends.

Leopold congratulated himself on coming to England, though he swore he would not go on to Holland, as some urged. He took in more money than he had ever dreamed he would earn from his children's first concert, which he advertised in extravagant and not-quite-truthful handbills. Anna could not reconcile herself to Leopold's understating her children's ages: at thirteen and eight, they were astonishing enough without being represented as twelve and seven.

The Mozart children were in great demand, composing, practicing and performing until all hours. Though neither complained of the quantity of work their father required of them, Wolfgang often broke down in tears, begging to return home to Salzburg to his dear friends and to the opera he and his sister would compose there.

The Mozart family had arrived in London late in April. At the end of July, Leopold caught a chill, which worsened. Finally, he took to his bed with a fever, inflammation of the throat and pain in his chest. When he did not improve after several days, Anna sent a message to Johann Bach, who immediately sent his doctor. Leopold required severe measures. His innards were purged with a clyster till he groaned. The ill humors were bled from his trembling body. Finally, when he still did not mend, the doctor ordered Anna to take the whole family into the country so that Leopold could breathe the purer air and rest.

Anna was terrified. Here she was in this strange place, where she knew how to say "Hello," "good-bye," "please," "thank you" and little else. What if Leopold should die? How would she get herself and her children back to Salzburg, where she would know what to do? There were so many things to think of. Which first? Which second? Her husband's breathing was labored. Anna, Anna, she chided herself, taking a deep breath. This will not do. One thing at a time. It does no good to think what might happen. I must find a place for us all to live. She felt some regret at the thought of leaving the now-familiar apartment in St. Martin's Lane, in a neighborhood where so many foreign artisans lodged. She called Porta, whose arrogant disobedience increased now that Leopold did not govern him. "You must fetch Herr Bach. Here is a note. Go directly, Porta. Do not dally." She spoke sternly, for Porta slouched disrespectfully and never looked her in the eye. She knew he often took his time, watching London spectacles, the cockfights and bearbaiting. Once she had come upon him jeering at some poor miscreant who writhed in humiliation and pain in the pillory.

Bach came immediately. He asked to see Leopold.

Anna shook her head, fighting the desire to burst into tears. "He is asleep, Johann, and I need your help. We must find other quarters. In the country. The doctor says so, but I do not know . . . ."

Bach mused. "Chelsea is said to have clean air, so near to the river. I know a Dr. Randal in Chelsea who has rooms to let. My driver can take you, but he must put me down at court, where I am wanted in an hour. Give me paper and pen and I will give you a letter of introduction to the doctor."

The children came in just then. Nannerl had gone out to buy dinner at the eating house some ten minutes walk away, and Wolfgang had seized the chance to go along. He loved to peer at all the strange sights and to chatter with anyone at all.

"Yes," said Anna with decision. "Nannerl, I will go to see about a house in the country. You and Woferl have dinner and offer Papa a little of the fowl, cut up. Where is Porta? Gone, as usual. Nannerl, you can call on Monsieur Couzin downstairs if Papa needs anything." She knelt by her little son, whose eyes were enormous. "Now Wolfgang, Papa must have quiet, so you are not to sing or talk loudly. And please, Woferl, help Nannerl."

It took all day to make arrangements. The distance was great, the roads crowded and bad, and it took some time to find Dr. Randal, but by dark, Anna was back. She had found lodging in Chelsea with the good doctor. The top floor was small and shabby, but clean with a high-ceilinged room that gave onto a grassy orchard. Dr. Randal had given her a good price, though Anna had to root through Leopold's things to find out what monies they had to live on. She was relieved to find that they were not short of means.

All through the night, once the children were tucked up and Leopold asleep, Anna padded around in her stocking feet, sorting their possessions and packing the trunks. They had acquired far more than they had brought with them, and it required her ingenuity to fit it all in. When day broke she sent Porta for a cart to carry their trunks and a sedan chair for Leopold, who had to be half carried down the stairs. Anna rode with him and put the children into the carriage Johann had kindly sent. She hoped it was right to send them off alone, but what else could she do?

By midmorning she and Porta and Doctor Randal had carried Leopold up the stairs, and Anna had settled him in a freshly made bed, where he slept, exhausted by the journey. The children had arrived safely, and the baggage was piled in the entryway. Nannerl and Wolfgang examined the new quarters closely. Porta vanished.

Days became weeks. Light hurt Leopold's eyes, the slightest noise grated painfully on his ears, and food sat uneasily. He grew thin and was so weak that Anna had to hold him when he got out of bed to use the chamber pot. He spoke little, falling into a sleep at every opportunity. Anna was hopeful that he would live, but worried that he would not regain his strength of either body or mind.

The children could not play the clavier nor sing. "Run outdoors," Anna told them. "You have worked hard ever since we left Salzburg. Now it is time to play." It seemed a safe neighborhood and the children roamed about, making friends, becoming, Anna thought, quite English. She sat often with Leopold, mending, to reassure him when he woke that all was well. She had given up sending out for their meals, which were too expensive and not to her liking. The shopping was laborious because she did not know the names for cuts of meat or vegetables and the money confused her. She had only the few cooking utensils she had finally shyly bought. Anna's dislike for Porta grew daily. He was disrespectful. She suspected he charged her more for goods than he paid, pocketing the difference. He was both furtive and pompous, and he was never to be found when she needed him.

"Mama," said Wolfgang, "help us think of an opera story, and we can start on the music right away." The three of them spent many hours, whispering ideas and scribbling down music, which they could not sing or play, but only imagine. Anna marveled at Nannerl and Wolfgang who thought almost as one, coming up with the same ideas at nearly the same moment. When they were not working on their opera, the children worked on first one symphony, then another.

"We want horns," Wolfgang murmured. "All the music here has good parts for horns."

"Right here," said Nannerl, excited. "First the oboe and then the bassoon and then the horn takes it up, like this." She started to sing the tune, but her mother hushed her, glancing at the next room, where Leopold lay in his unaccustomed silence.

"Anna," Leopold called weakly. When she went into his room he fretted about his son's progress. "Woferl will fall behind."

"Oh, sweetheart," Anna exclaimed. "I think you must be getting better. It has been so long since you worried. Woferl is working this minute, composing a symphony. He and Nannerl. And they have run about out-of-doors and Wolfgang has grown so tall, you will scarcely know him. Shall I bring them in to see you?"

"Yes, let me see them," muttered Leopold, "I must write to Hagenauer to have masses said."

Anna took his hand for a moment, then called the children. They were shy to see their usually masterful father so thin and wearing a wrinkled nightshirt, his hand raised very feebly in greeting. Wolfgang hung back, burst into tears and hid his face in his mother's skirt. Nannerl's face was set and pale. They think their father is dying, Anna realized. "Your father is better today," she said. "He took broth, but he is still weak and we must not tire him. Kiss Papa and let him sleep now. He will soon be up and about."

"We composed some symphonies, Papa," Wolfgang said, his voice small. "We put horns in."

"Shh," cautioned Nannerl, seeing her father's eyelids droop.

"Good boy," said Leopold and dozed off. The children tiptoed out and then ran shouting in the small orchard next to the house, romping and tumbling until they were hot and dirty and needed to wash in the tub that Anna filled from the stove. Anna felt strong and capable, though she had grown thin. She made all the decisions, worked and played easily with the children, and saw them look up to her in a new way.

Slowly Leopold's health improved. He was surprised to find that the household was well-ordered, the children happy. It disturbed him a little that Anna had managed so well without him. He insisted that they remove again to London and exerted himself once more to promote a set of public concerts.

"It is not going so well this time, Anna," Leopold sighed, coming in, tired from his efforts, his strength not what it had been.

In the next room, the children played on the clavier. "No, this way," insisted Nannerl, demonstrating. "Oh, I see," said Wolfgang. "But what if you put this chromatic . . . here, like this?" "Magnifique!" shouted Wolfgang, and the two fell to giggling.

Leopold frowned. "We did not get much of a present from the Queen from the last performance, though they . . . ." He thrust his head in the direction of the children . . . . "played for four straight hours. Still, she gave us fifty guineas for Wolfgang's sonatas. But Parliament will open late, so none of the nobility have returned to town, and then, Bach says, they will be taken up with Italian opera and will want only oratorios during Lent. Everything costs so much, and we used up such a lot of money when I was ill. I must really take in more. I will try to sell the Paris sonatas here, and Haganauer will put a notice in the papers in Salzburg and send them to Augsburg and Nuremberg . . . ."

Anna reached for his hand. He worried too much.

"But here is the real news, Anna. The King has sent me an inquiry. Would I consider acting as his secretary in the matter of . . . ."

"We would stay here?" Anna inquired, feeling suddenly chilled. "Permanently?"

Leopold sighed. "I do not know, Anna. They say the King is often not in his right mind these days and the colonies are in revolt. There are riots and tumults and refusal to pay taxes . . . ."

Porta rushed in shouting. "Everyone is in the streets! Weavers with banners and placards who want the government to ban silk. They say the French silk weavers take their jobs." He was panting with excitement.

"Porta," Anna said mildly. "Herr Mozart was speaking and you interrupted him."

The servant paid her no attention, turning to Leopold. "No one knows their place in this city. They should all be taken up by the constables and sent to jail. What do they know of French silk?"

"Porta!" said Anna firmly. "You will apologize for rudeness to me and to Herr Mozart."

"I do not," said Porta grandly, shrugging elaborately, "apologize to a woman." He looked at Leopold for approval.

Leopold was deeply distressed. He still felt too weak for altercation and did not want to lose Porta, who might be dishonest but knew London.

"Then," said Anna slowly, but distinctly, "you must find other employment, Porta. "I cannot pay wages to someone who is insolent."

"Anna!" exclaimed Leopold.

"No, Leopold," said Anna. "All the while you were ill, Porta was rude and dishonest. He kept back money and was never to be found when he was needed. I will not pay good money for this man's holiday in London. Get your things and leave," she put her hands on her hips, "at once."

Nannerl and Wolfgang, having heard raised voices, came to stand in the door, but Leopold did not see them. "Anna, you forget yourself," he said. "I hired Porta. It is not your place to dismiss him."

"It is," Anna rejoined. "It is my place when he is rude to me. I should have discharged him sooner. Go, Porta. Herr Mozart will not help you."

"Now go on, Leopold, tell me about the King's offer."

27

1765

WHEN PORTA FLOUNCED OUT, Anna felt as if she, her husband and her children were formed of the thinnest crystal. The merest touch might shatter them, the shards and slivers wounding the hands that must sweep them up. Anna took a deep breath and said, "You must trust me, my dear. He really is a bad man."

"He is," piped Wolfgang. "He told me I was a lapdog. I am not, Mama, am I?" He crossed the room to hold her hand.

Nannerl also moved to stand by Anna. "Papa, Mama is right. He was horrid, always looking down my dress." She shivered and reached for Anna's other hand.

Leopold felt dizzy and weak. He was balked by his wife and now his children.

Anna too was lightheaded, not from illness but from the strength she felt. "Now do tell us," she said, sensibly, "what is it the King wants?"

"Oh," Leopold said, shaking his head to clear it of all that stood in the way of his memory. It seemed so long ago that the royal emissary had sent for Leopold. He had worried for several nights, turning the idea this way and that. Now there was the sound of people chanting and shouting outside the window, the weavers Porta had mentioned, no doubt, coming along Thrift Street. If he were to accept the King's offer, he would have to think about such things rather than occupy himself with finding ways to present his boy. But if he said "no," what doors might be closed to the child? "The King sent one of his minions," he said dryly, "to inquire whether I might consider the post of undersecretary to advise the secretary about the colonies. It seems that we, the King and I, see eye to eye . . . ."

"But Papa!" wailed Nannerl, "I have such hopes for The Hague. Mama, tell him. Jan - the Count van Waldereen - has been so kind. He is quite sure that the Princess will want me to . . . ." Nannerl could not say aloud what she most hoped.

The young Dutch envoy had urged Leopold, in the strongest terms, to travel to the capital of his country, where he promised rich rewards in the household of the Princess of Nassau-Weilburg, sister to the Prince of Orange.

"Jan says the Princess plays the clavier very well and will want Wolfgang too, and that she is truly generous with the musicians in her court and will pay for everything," Nannerl pleaded. Privately the Count had told Nannerl that she might receive a commission for an opera. But they must not dawdle, he warned, as the Princess was soon to give birth to a child. Nannerl dreamed about the Count, his handsome face and slender figure, the particular fineness of his linen, the delicate gestures his long fingers made when he spoke. She could tell he was taken with her as well. At night, she dreamed about him. "Mama," she pleaded. She had told her mother of her hopes, how one opera might lead to another, how it seemed a rare possibility.

"Well, I want to go home!" shouted Wolfgang, stamping his foot. "Home to Salzburg!"

"Shhh," hissed Nannerl.

"Well, maybe we could go to the colonies," Wolfgang temporized. "They say that over there, boys ride horses without saddles, just like the savages. Could we go there, Papa?"

"I think it would be a good thing to go to The Hague, Leopold," Anna said quietly.

Leopold was used to telling his wife and children what they would do. But since his illness, they had ideas of their own. This tempest of opinion disconcerted him. "We have been in London now an entire year," he said. "We must return to Paris to reclaim the carriage. I have sent our furs to Paris as well, and the weather here will soon turn cold. I had thought we would go on to Milan and Venice, maybe even as far south as Naples. You have both learned much of the Italian style from Herr Bach, but far better to see and hear for yourselves!" What he really wanted was to show the overweening Italians, with their contempt for anything German, what these

German prodigies of Nature could do. He did not want the position the English King offered. Nevertheless he was flattered, and he feared that to refuse the King might have consequences.

"But Lorenz writes that you must not stay away much longer, Leopold," cautioned Anna. "The Archbishop will not pay your wages forever while you remain away. Surely it would make sense to travel through The Hague and from there, towards Salzburg."

Nannerl put her hands on her hips, just as her mother had stood when she told Porta to leave. "Papa," she insisted, "we *must* go to The Hague."

Nannerl surprised Anna with the strength of her determination. She had always been such a biddable child. But this strong-willed young woman standing before her and speaking so strongly to her father was no child. Her beauty was striking: creamy skin and searching blue-gray eyes, red lips that needed no rouge, a rich endowment of gleaming ringlets, which she braided and pinned up behind. She had already a woman's shape. She would have, Anna knew, few such opportunities as the Count van Waldereen had held out to her. "It *is* something to consider, Leopold." Anna knew that it served her purposes to speak quietly. She imagined that Leopold was still angry at her over Porta.

Nannerl could not bear to think that she might not go to The Hague. Already ideas for the opera she would compose were flooding into her mind. She hardened her heart against her father. Secretly she decided that she would not go to Italy nor stay in London, no matter how he might rage against her and punish her. She did not know how she would fare on her own but somehow she must go to The Hague to have the chance of an opera.

Leopold passed his hand over his face. He needed a barber. The angry noise of the weavers had passed and Porta had stomped down the stairs, stopping to demand his pay and passage back to Paris. In this room with his wife and children, Leopold felt alone, weighted by cares and unsure what to do. Something had broken, some gyroscope or compass that had, till now, kept him on course. Suddenly it came back to him that he had taken a vow before God. His wife had opposed him then, too. But a vow was a serious thing. Perhaps Nannerl was right and Wolfgang would be well-received in The Hague. "I will refuse the King," he announced, "but it will not hurt those in Salzburg who are so eager to hurry me home to know that I have been asked to stay here in London." He stood up, full of decision. "We must organize some concerts, for we have used up guineas at a great rate. And then. . . ." Nannerl held her breath. "Then we will go to The Hague, as you wish, my dear."

"Oh Papa!" Nannerl cried, throwing her arms around him. "Thank you. This is wonderful, Mama. You will like it, Woferl, I promise you will."

"Well," sighed Wolfgang, "as soon as you have made your opera and married your Count, then we can go home."

"Hush!" said Nannerl, cuffing her brother lightly.

"Thank you, my dear," said Anna, putting her cheek against Leopold's. She felt that he pulled back a little from her touch.

It was six months before they sailed in clear fall weather from Dover to Calais. Nannerl's hopeful countenance withstood news of the Emperor's death widowing the Empress who had treated the Mozarts so kindly in Vienna. It withstood her brother's and her father's colds, which made them tired and cross, though Wolfgang played on every organ he came upon, including the great cathedral organ in Antwerp. Having left their own carriage behind in Paris once again, the Mozarts traveled first in hired coaches, then on a barge, then in another hired coach, moving slowly through the towns and villages where the streets were cleaner than Anna's table in Salzburg.

The Count van Waldeeren had been correct: the Mozarts were eagerly awaited and warmly welcomed in The Hague. But Nannerl woke on the day after their arrival too ill to dress for court. She could not stand the touch of stays around her waist and an inflamed throat kept her from speaking. She could hardly swallow. Coughing tore at her and left her feeling bruised and weak. She lay weeping, unable either to sleep or to rise from her bed, while her father and brother were received by the Prince of Orange and his sister, the Princess. The Count van Waldeeren sent his fondest wishes to Nannerl.

"He says you must come the very minute you are well," Wolfgang reported to Nannerl. "He kisses your hand." The child seized Nannerl's hand and showered it with wet kisses. "And look, the Princess sent a custard and some flowers to cheer you, Nannie," he said. "Please get well. I don't like playing when you are not there."

But Nannerl only felt worse. She was restless and ached in every joint, and her stomach hurt. All she wanted was sleep, but no matter which way she turned, she found no comfort. Alarmed, Anna asked the landlady to send for her doctor, who diagnosed the dreaded typhoid fever. He recommended bleeding and shrugged, unable to do anything further.

Anna and Leopold took turns watching over their daughter who lay burning with fever, often unconscious, while Wolfgang amused himself in the next room, scribbling out his ideas for music, practicing on the small traveling instrument, conducting invisible orchestras from the keyboard and singing in his fine, clear soprano. When he tired of music, he played games with words and numbers, teased the landlady's lazy cat, who woke only to stretch out his claws. Wolfgang was lonely. His mother and father were wholly absorbed by Nannerl.

Wolfgang stole into the room where his mother watched over his sister, walking on tiptoe so that the heels of his shoes would make no sound. Nannerl had told him he must creep about like a mouse when his father had lain so ill in England. He imagined himself as a small, sleek and furry creature, with tiny reddish toes, ears cocked like the petals of a flower, his long tail flowing after him. He must not rouse the cat, who slumbered by the stove and would like to make a merry meal of him.

Wolfgang tiptoed into the bedroom and leaned his head against his mother. "Mama," he whispered. "I was working on one of the symphonies that Nannerl and I wrote in London. She will like what I did." Pulling on a strand of his hair, he asked, "Is she going to get well?"

Anna took her son in her lap. He was getting too big to be held like a baby, but poor little soul, he needed her just now as he had in infancy. "Oh my dear boy," she whispered back, stricken at having neglected this child on behalf of the other. "Who can be sure of anything? If we lose her, Woferl, we must try to remember that God has taken her without any sin on her head."

"If God takes Nannerl," Wolfgang declared with a scowl, "He is not good!"

Anna understood. She knew she should reprove him for such views, but what use was it to say what the heart refused?

Wolfgang clung to his mother for a moment, then slipped from her lap. "I will play what I have composed for her, an Andante in G minor. Help me bring in the clavier, and I will use my music to make her well," the boy said.

Why had Anna not thought of it? If anything would urge Nannerl to turn away from death, it would be her brother's playing, which was now not only technically marvelous but moving as well. Anna helped Wolfgang carry the clavier to Nannerl's bedside.

"Nannerl," said Wolfgang, putting his mouth close to her ear, "listen." He played and then spoke to her again. "I changed this to be the way you thought it should be. And listen to what I did with the A-sharp! I got that idea from Herr Graaf, the *Kapellmeister*. Isn't that good?" The children had composed this symphony together in London. Leopold had copied it out, putting Wolfgang's name as composer. Wolfgang and Nannerl had talked about changes, and now Wolfgang had made them.

Nannerl's eyelids fluttered open. "Tres fatigue," she said. "Todmüde. Tired to death. Very, very tired." Throughout her illness, she had spoken in a mixture of tongues, as if she were not sure what country she was in.

Wolfgang kept playing, singing the parts for oboes and horns, conducting as if the room were filled with a whole orchestra. His sister fell into a deep sleep.

By the time Leopold woke to take his turn at watching, it was evening. He came into the sick room, examined his daughter and said, "I think we must rouse her and speak to her of what may come."

"Oh my dear, no!" cried Anna. Leopold's words were terrible. How could Anna, who had laid so many infants in the ground, talk to this child of death? She shut her eyes to gather her thoughts and knew that Leopold was right. They must hold out to Nannerl what comfort they knew.

Leopold woke his daughter and knelt by the bed, his arm under her thin shoulders to raise her a little. Anna knelt on the other side, holding the child's hand. They could hear Wolfgang in the next room, singing the tunes he was setting to paper, talking to himself and imaginary others from time to time. Anna's heart ached for him, feeling the loss he would suffer in addition to her own and her husband's. When sister and brother sat together to compose or to play at the keyboard, they were as one person with four hands. If Nannerl died, so would a piece of Wolfgang.

"Nannerl?" Leopold whispered. "We must speak of what may come if it is God's will that you leave us."

Nannerl fixed him with her eyes, though the lids were heavy. "Oui," she whispered. "Ja. Sterbensakramente."

"Yes," said Leopold. "I will go for the priest to give you the final sacrament in a minute. We will not let you die without it, my dear. But if you pass from the earth, Nannerl, it will be a happy death. Such is the death of all children." His voice quivered. "You have not sinned, my daughter. There is nothing - nothing - to keep you here if it is God's will. The world is all vanity. Everything - fame, riches - nothing but vanity. The only thing real, at the end, is God, who directs our every step." Leopold meant what he said to Nannerl, even though he pursued both fame and riches avidly. He saw no contradiction, however given he was to Reason. A deathbed changed everything.

Nannerl stirred. "Ich habe die Schuld. My fault," she whispered. "Je desire everything." It was clear to Anna that speaking was a great effort for the poor child. "An opera. I wanted an opera. Not right. Wollen die Oper. Die Eitelkeit. Vanity."

"Nannerl," said Anna, "I have prayed for you every hour. You are the child of my heart. Even God cannot love you more." She held back tears, forcing her voice to be calm. "I have no doubt if He takes you, He will press you into service to write music for Heaven to sing. You will have an opera."

Nannerl's lips twisted slightly. "Nein," she murmured. "No opera." It cost her dear to speak. Exhausted, she fell asleep. Her father eased her head down on the pillow, but Anna would not let her hand go. Leopold went for the priest while Anna put her head down on Nannerl's narrow bed and slept along with her child.

The priest's ministrations quieted Nannerl, who slept deeply through the night as Anna watched, waking just as the sky began to lighten and as the cocks began their morning fanfare. "Mama," Nannerl said, her voice shaky and low. "Maybe I will not die after all." She was silent a long while.

Anna drew back the curtain to let in the morning. Nannerl had not spoken so clearly nor in such steady German for weeks now. "Nannerl," she exclaimed, smoothing the coverlet that had been tossed while her daughter slept, "I think you will soon be strong again, and you will play for the Princess, and who knows, maybe she will . . . ."

"No, Mama," said Nannerl, in a voice so low Anna was not sure she really heard it. "I cannot." Within minutes the girl was deeply asleep again. She slept quietly, her skin cool to the touch, her breathing deep and easy.

Nannerl recovered at last, though she was weak for a long time. She went often to church and thought about all the pious women whose stories she had heard. They had renounced what was dearest to them in their devotion to God. It seemed to her she had a great lesson to learn and must search to discern what it was.

She did not sit at the clavier nor at her composition, for Wolfgang had fallen ill with the typhoid and she was sure it was her fault.

28

1765-1766

WOLFGANG LAY ILL FOR NEARLY A MONTH, never approaching death's door as nearly as Nannerl had, but nevertheless causing his sister and parents great consternation. Leopold, beside himself, tried to assign the fault. God would not dangle such a prodigy of nature just within reach of mankind and then snatch him away. He blamed Nannerl and Anna and the Dutch doctors. He crossed himself and knelt by Wolfgang's bed while the little boy-the very purpose of his life-slept. "I must go out to pray for the boy," he said to Anna, his voice rough with worry, his shirt fastened up askew and his hair tied carelessly.

"I will go with you," said Nannerl, who blamed herself for her brother's illness far more severely than her father ever could. Had she not been beguiled by the handsome Count van Waldeeren's promise of an opera, they might not have come to The Hague, where she had brought contagion into their quarters. She had felt earlier that she bore responsibility for the deaths of the Archduchess Johanna and the Countess van Eyck, both of whom had supported the delusion of Nannerl's genius. Everyone said that Nature had decreed that no woman could have genius. It had come upon her during her own illness that had she not entertained so unnatural and selfish a notion, her friends might still be alive and Wolfgang would be well and merry. The deaths of others might be charged to her account.

"Before you go," said Anna, "please ask the landlady for more bed linens. Wolfgang has soaked his again. Poor woman, she will be glad when we do not wear out her sheets any longer."

Anna said her own prayers for her son as she bathed the poor child's burning skin with cool water. She thought he would recover; he was not - thank God - as ill as Nannerl had been, but he was restless with the fever and had grown stick thin.

Anna was heartily tired of nursing ailing children. She went about her tasks as always, sponged her feverish son, tried to tempt him with the rich Dutch cheeses and milk, dressed Nannerl's hair every day and worried because her daughter preferred to cross the square to the church than to sit at the clavier. After Wolfgang's fever broke, Anna entertained him with stories about her early life. She told him the tales she had heard in her own childhood about dragons and warriors and animals, her limbs aching with inactivity. She longed to walk out by herself in the brisk December air, looking at the Dutch, their houses and shops.

Throughout Wolfgang's illness, anxious inquiries and lavish presents came to the door, for he had become a favorite at court and in the houses of the great Dutch merchants. But while others worried, Wolfgang was oddly happy. He lay deep in a featherbed and under a feather tick, too weak to practice, compose or show off. He wandered dreamily in and out of the imaginary kingdom he had named Ruck. Nannerl had helped him make it up, but he could bring it into his mind without her. In Ruck, he was no one and could do as he liked. He knew just where the stables and the fields were, and could ride the spirited horses over every hill and dale. He rode a great, black stallion, whose mane flew back like silk into his face as it galloped, flying over the turbulent river that circled the kingdom to keep marauders out. When he was finished riding, he groomed and stabled his horse himself, feeding it apples redder than rubies. He romped with all the kingdom's children, climbing trees, swimming naked and playing at rowdy games in the streets. No one ever told them to go indoors or punished them for tearing their clothes. In Ruck he was dirty, sunburned and carefree.

Leopold marked Wolfgang's recovery by attempting to resume their nightly ritual. For years, father and son had ended the day with a lullaby sung in the child's light treble, his father's lower voice in harmony. Leopold would query, "Does my son love his father?"

"Next only to God," Wolfgang would answer.

Then Leopold would smother the boy with kisses and carry him off to bed, undressing him tenderly and tucking him up for the night.

But on this night, when Wolfgang was tired from his first day out of bed, he shook his head. "No more," he said. "I want to go to bed by myself."

"Wolfgang Gottlieb Mozart!" exclaimed Leopold, wounded.

Nannerl, just coming into the room, saw how pale her brother looked and crossed the room to put her arm around him.

"Nannerl," said Leopold irritably, "I am surprised that you should encourage your brother to rebel against his father!"

Nannerl looked up, surprised.

Anna, a step behind Nannerl, caught her breath.

Leopold expected the usual childish homage, the confirmation of his son's fealty at the end of every day. Wolfgang was too tired from the day's exertions at the clavier to utter another sound on his father's behalf. Nannerl had merely seen her brother's need and offered him comfort.

"Leopold, my dear," Anna said softly. "See the circles under Woferl's eyes. He must go directly to bed."

"I will take off my own clothes, Papa," whispered Wolfgang. "I am not a baby anymore."

Leopold could not but retreat. He had received a powerful blow to his very being, which resonated as if in an empty chamber or a deep valley. He lay by Anna's side tormented by fears that he would lose his son, whose genius Leopold had vowed to give his life to nurture and promote. Finally, unable to endure his own lurid premonitions, he reached for his wife, who slept soundly, caressing her with an ardor he had not shown since his own illness and recovery in England.

Anna surfaced from the velvet depth of her sleep reluctantly at first, but as she awoke, she returned his passion. It had been some time since they knew one another as husband and wife.

When at last, replete, Anna and Leopold lay looking into the darkness, rich with the satisfactions of their bodies, Leopold said quietly, "Woferl does not love me, Anna."

Anna reached for his hand. "Of course he does, Leopold. But he is not a babe any more. He will grow up, whether it suits us -" she had begun to say "you" "- or not."

"You do not understand, Anna," said Leopold, his voice still soft so as not to wake the children, but nonetheless charged with intensity. "I took a vow. I have a sacred obligation to protect and to further the boy's genius."

"Oh Leopold," sighed Anna, "there are so many things . . . . Woferl is not a puppet. He will grow up and change and have a mind of his own."

"But his genius . . . ." objected Leopold.

Anna turned on her side, where her husband's profile was barely blacker than the room's winter darkness. She shifted the comforter up over her shoulder. "Genius," she mused. "You used to say I had genius. Nothing has come of it. And Nannerl? Why have you taken no vow to further that bright spark in her?"

Leopold sat straight up, dislodging the covers. "It is not the same," he said sharply.

"Shhh," Anna warned, but Nannerl had wakened at her father's brusque exclamation.

"You know yourself it is not the same, Anna," whispered Leopold. "What can Nannerl do, unless I bend my every effort on her behalf? And even then . . . . What would become of Wolfgang if I did that?" His mind, which had been at peace minutes before, was in turmoil again.

Anna was silent for a long time. Then she said softly, "Once a person marries, there is the other person's good repute to keep." Her husband had to strain to hear her. She had never told him about her chamber symphony, swept away from her life like the spider web she had destroyed as she readied the house for her husband's and children's return from Munich so long ago. "And then come the children. But Nannerl . . . . There are women who make a life of music, dearest. We have seen such women, and Nannerl's soul needs . . . ." She did not know Nannerl's soul, but she knew her own.

Leopold, when he was fair, had to admit that his daughter's native gifts were as great as his son's, but he also knew the world. Nannerl's career could never reach the pinnacles that he envisioned for her brother. Wolfgang was the promise that his father's life would come to something splendid. The child must not be allowed to squander the gift that God had placed in the frail and all-too-mortal frame.

Nannerl's feet were cold. She put them against her brother. Sleeping, she had been filled with the joyous and tender notes of a serenade. For a while she had lain, half awake, ravished by the sound. And then, coming more fully awake, she had heard most of what her parents said. She lay in stony silence and prayed for an end to this upsurge of music that tempted her. In the depth of her soul it seemed to her that the deaths of the Archduchess

Johanna and the Countess van Eyck were debts that she, Nannerl, was bound to pay. She had ignored these warnings but had been reminded by her own near death, and then her brother's illness, how serious her weakness was. Music made her selfish. She must give up her own ambitions and join her father in upholding her brother's talents, which she must never think to rival. Nannerl's feet took warmth from Wolfgang, and she drifted to sleep again.

By spring the Mozarts were back in Paris, and by summer they had left for home, traveling from French to Swiss to German courts, the children performing everywhere and reaping generous gifts of money, rings, watches and other costly trinkets. Nannerl performed, for her father insisted, but she refused to compose. To Leopold it was proof that his daughter's genius was, indeed, inferior; to Anna, worrisome evidence of lingering ailment; to Wolfgang, the loss of his best playfellow.

As they reached Augsburg, Anna resolved to say nothing of Leopold's family. It was his own business whether he would search out his mother and his brothers. But as luck would have it, Leopold encountered his brother in the marketplace.

"Is it you, Leopold?" asked Aloys Mozart, a shorter, rounder version of his older brother. His good-natured face, framed with chestnut curls, lit up. "Have you come home to Augsburg then?"

Leopold felt caught, like a fox in a hunter's trap. His heart leaped at the moment he recognized his brother, and yet he tugged and strained against that clamp of affection that bit into him like teeth. "No, no," he said, "we have stopped for a short while to rest the horses." He thanked God that Anna and the children had stayed behind in their lodgings. They would have been only too willing to visit with any of the Augsburg Mozarts. Leopold spoke with his brother almost against his will. "You may have heard that my son is a great musical genius," he said stiffly, but then with increasing enthusiasm. "We have traveled far and wide and have been entertained in every court, by kings and electors. Why, the French king and queen kissed my children often and gave me great sums of money. The English king and queen as well. And the greatest men of every land. Just yesterday they played here for the Elector. You can scarcely imagine how well I have done in taking this child to every German town, to Swiss towns and those of the Lowlands. So I am now, in spite of my mother's intentions, a wealthy man."

It often suited Leopold to exaggerate his poverty; now it suited him to boast of his takings.

Aloys put a hand on Leopold's arm. "Leopold," he said, "our mother is very ill. I think she may not live much longer. Surely, in her extremity, you might visit her. It would gladden her old heart."

The thought darted through Leopold's mind, Oh, how good it would be to receive my mother's blessing before she dies! But it shimmered only an instant, with the iridescence of a dragonfly, before it was gone. "I cannot," he said, tightening again. "She has never begged my forgiveness for preferring my younger brothers. She has wronged me."

"But brother," said Aloys, "*she* thinks you wronged *her*. You and she are like twins. And now she has been stricken with apoplexy and cannot speak, walk or even feed herself. My wife and I look after her, but it is you, always you, she wants. Come, brother. You will be the better for making your peace with her in this life."

Against his better judgment, Leopold went with Aloys, who lived nearby, and greeted his sister-in-law and such children as were in the house at midday. When he entered his mother's room, she struggled to sit up and her piercing dark eyes fixed on his face. She looked to Leopold like a withered husk, wrapped in shawls and blankets.

His heart beat hard against the cage of his breast. "Mother?" he said in low tones.

Her claw-like hand came up and covered her eyes. Her other hand, from out the covers, pointed feebly in her eldest son's direction.

Leopold started back as if she had pronounced his death sentence. "I must go," he said to Aloys, who had gone to his mother's side. "She does not wish to see me."

"Who knows?" said Aloys. "Who knows what she means?"

His pretty, plump wife explained, "She often puts her hand thus. She may wish you to come closer."

"No," said Leopold. "She does not want me here. I must go." He was drowning in the old woman's presence and felt he must leave to breathe again. "Farewell, brother." He gave his sister-in-law a hurried bow and turning, fled down their stairs like one deranged. He ran until he came back to his family's lodgings. "Come," he panted to Anna. "We must leave immediately."

"But Leopold . . . . Why? It is late in the day. We cannot travel by night. We would break a wheel or be overtaken by brigands. You know that. What is it?" she asked, catching at his hand. The children, hearing alarm in their mother's voice, left their play and joined her.

Nannerl took her father's other hand. "Papa, are you ill?" she asked.

"Papa?" queried Wolfgang, "Papa?"

"I saw my mother," Leopold said, his voice but a whisper.

"Oh, Leopold. I am glad," exclaimed Anna.

"She is ill, near death. She covered her eyes and told me I should leave," muttered Leopold.

"Your mama would not do that, Papa," exclaimed Wolfgang in disbelief.

Anna's heart sank. "Are you sure, Leopold? I remember how cold my mother seemed to me in her old age. Perhaps . . . ."

"I know what I saw, Anna," said Leopold. He felt more like himself now. The image of the dried-up old woman - as brittle as a fallen leaf, her face drawn into a lopsided scowl, one hand covering her eyes, the other pointing towards the door behind him - was as clear as if it had been branded in his mind. He straightened up. "But you are right. We cannot travel by night. Nevertheless, we must be gone by sunup. The Archbishop has ordered me to return and now we must make haste."

PART 5

29

1766

IGNORING THE LATE NOVEMBER COLD with its whipping flurries of snow, Wolfgang and Nannerl craned out the carriage windows, watching the passing countryside give way to the houses of Mülln. The Mozarts would not stop to see Cousin Pertl, who lived in Mülln; they were too eager to be at home.

"The Cloister of St. Augustine!" Nannerl exclaimed, quivering like a violin string, just plucked.

"Our Lady's Gate!" screamed Wolfgang, who could not sit still for a minute. He darted from his mother's side to his father's and back again.

Then they were through the gate and rolling along the cobbles, passing the Ursaline Convent, the Charity Hospital, clattering at last down Getreidegasse, with its shops and signs and bustle of merchants and late-day shoppers. Empty carts going out of town passed them, making a great rattle on the cobbled street.

It seemed to Anna both achingly familiar and utterly strange. Each city they had visited had its own character, she thought, just as did each person she knew. This was her home, and yet she returned, after three years, a stranger in a city that seemed smaller than she had remembered, older-looking. The life of the city, the lives of her friends and neighbors, had gone on without her. Salzburg had been her fixed point during the long years of traveling. Common sense should have warned her that there would be changes, yet she realized she had expected that everything would be just as she left it. Here was a new sign - a locksmith, from the giant iron key that hung over the shop door - and the saddler's sign hung askew from a bent hook. What other small, and even great, changes had occurred?

Finally they stopped in front of the Hagenauer's shop, and the horses snorted, shifting their weight so that the carriage creaked. Lorenz and Theresa appeared, their two youngest children clamoring at the carriage

"Oh my goodness!" cried Theresa, wrapping Anna in her strong arms.

A swirl of cold air from the snowy mountains carried the smell of the yeast from St. Peter's baking and brewing. Tears came to Anna's eyes. "I had forgotten that smell!"

"I thought about Cajetan more than anyone," said Wolfgang, a catch in his voice.

Anna cradled her son's head against her. "He is wrought up and tired," she said softly to Theresa.

"Listen, Woferl," said Theresa. "Cajetan heard you were coming and sends his greetings. He is eager for you to visit him." Wolfgang's dearest friend had joined the monastery in the Mozarts' absence. Wolfgang had lamented it then, but now the reality that his older friend had left everything for a life of godliness struck a fresh blow.

"Did you see kings and queens and talk to them?" Cajetan's younger brother asked Nannerl.

"We did," said Nannerl, "but I would rather see you than all the kings and queens in the world. Where is your sister?"

"She is gone to visit our cousins," said the boy. "Come," he urged. "Tell us all your adventures."

"Hold up, my boy," said Lorenz. "Let the travelers catch their breath and let us help carry their baggage up. Here you!" he called the servant in the shop, "Get a man from the market to help carry." Lorenz directed the unloading of the carriage, while Leopold arranged to have the horses stabled and the carriage stowed.

"I had forgotten the feel of these stairs," said Anna as she and Theresa carried an armload each of small baggage up to the Mozart apartment. The worn stones fit under her feet as no other stairs on their journey had. "Oh Theresa, look what you have done!" For the fires were lit, the apartment shining clean. The beds had been aired and the larder stocked. "I had expected cold, dust, mouse droppings and nothing at all for supper," Anna laughed. "But how could you know when we would arrive?"

"Lorenz had a letter from Augsburg," said Theresa. "Leopold sounded in a great hurry to leave. My husband calculated that you would arrive tomorrow, but I had a feeling in my bones."

"Anna, you must tell me everything. You have been to the ends of the Earth and back. And how the children have grown up! Did they truly accomplish everything Leopold wrote about?"

"Where to begin?" Anna said. "Yes, the children were splendid. We were away such a time and they learned so much! Everywhere, Leopold found teachers, especially for Woferl. But I do worry about Nannerl. She is not herself since her illness in The Hague. And Leopold is in a state since he saw his mother in Augsburg. She was dying, I think. I met her, did I tell you? Oh, Theresa, I am in a muddle. I have missed you so much!"

That night Leopold was up, too agitated to lie still, long after his wife and children were finally asleep. Carefully moving the clothes and shoes and other daily detritus aside, he pulled all his treasure out of the trunks, all the tributes to his son's artistry, and calculated how to display it all. He was not sure what was best to do: if he paraded his takings, no one would understand that there had been great expense on the journey. He did not want to be thought a rich man. On the other hand, who would understand the esteem in which his son - his daughter, too, come to that - were held unless he could show the presents they had received? He counted nine pocket watches, a dozen gold snuffboxes - one of which the French king had filled with forty louis d'or, though Leopold thought he could safely call it fifty - a good three dozen gold rings set with precious stones, and all sorts of handsome oddments - lace collars and cuffs, shawls, ear-bobs and necklaces, fruit knives, writing tackle and bottle holders, brooches, two small swords, one with a jeweled handle, and nearly two dozen toothpick boxes. He had also bought goods cheaply in European markets, sure that he could sell them in Salzburg at a tidy profit.

He sorted through the newspapers with their admiring stories, many of which he had written himself, all of which he knew by heart. "All the Overtures will be from the Composition of these astonishing Composers," said one; another, "Herr Mozart, director of the music of H. H. the Prince Archbishop of Salzburg, has been in this capital for several months with two children who cut the most delightful figure. His daughter, aged eleven, plays the harpsichord in a distinguished manner; no one could have a more precise and brilliant execution. His son, who this month reached his eighth year, is a veritable prodigy. He has all the talent and all the science of a *maitre de chapelle*." Leopold turned the paper so that this encomium was on the outside and smoothed it. "Prodigies of Nature," his children were called, and he himself, "Father of the celebrated young Musical Family, who have so justly raised the Admiration of the greatest Musicians of Europe . . . ." His friends would see the glory he had sown and the rewards he had reaped and would understand how his absence shed splendor on Salzburg. He thought of his colleagues at court and wondered if they would comprehend this comet that had come streaking across the night sky to hover over Salzburg. Just look what the world thought of his endeavors!

In the morning, Anna found that her house had become a museum, trophies covering every surface. She had much to do, the sorting, laundering, mending and storage of the light clothes. The shoes must go to the cobbler's and the children's wigs to the hairdresser. Nannerl would need new monthly rags, and the medicines were depleted and in disarray. She would need to hire a servant and would ask Theresa's advice.

"I will ask some of our friends in this afternoon," Leopold told Anna, "maybe Schactner and Hebelt, Meissner, Haffner . . . Gilowsky and Barisani, perhaps, as well."

Anna knew he wanted to show off his treasure so that word would spread quickly. "Could it not wait for tomorrow?" she pleaded. "It will take me some time to put all this away." Her arms took in the opened trunks in the middle of the room, their contents spilling out every which way. "And I must find a servant . . . ."

"No servant!" said Leopold vehemently. While he wanted his friends to know of his children's success, he was not eager for strangers to know that there was treasure in his house. Nor did he want to be deprived of the story he would tell at court of the expenses of his journey. Nevertheless he agreed reluctantly that Anna could clean up before he invited his particular friends.

There was much to do, but Anna knew that she would - must - go to market to see her friends first, to assure herself that she was truly at home. While she was still in her dressing gown, her hair in its long nighttime braid hanging down her back, Father Beda Hübner arrived to take Wolfgang to see his friend Cajetan at St. Peter's Monastery. Hardly had she dressed when Marianna arrived with Katherl, Nannerl's best friend. The two girls could hardly wait to be off.

"I wonder," Anna mused, delighted to see Marianna looking so well, "what Nannerl will tell Katherl. There has been a change in her, Marianna. Nannerl will not compose, though she performs. She will not talk to me about it. She was terribly ill, you know, in The Hague. We called the priest in for final rites. Oh, Marianna. I could not bear it. To lose her would be bad enough, but to leave her there, in a foreign graveyard, apart from my other babes . . . . You know, we were there, in the Lowlands, because the Dutch ambassador to England assured her that she was wanted - not her brother, so much - and that she might even get a contract for an opera. And then, before she had a chance to appear, she was taken ill - so ill. We despaired. And Woferl, of course, had the attentions of the House of Orange to himself."

"We heard that Wolfgang contracted the typhoid as well," said Marianna.

"He did," confirmed Anna. "Typhoid is not a laughing matter, but he was never in mortal danger, thank God." She crossed herself quickly. "But tell me about your dear ones. Wolfgang pined for Franz - for all his friends. Indeed, he often wept for them. Now he is off at St. Peter's to be sure that dear Cajetan has not forgotten him."

The marketplace was thronged with friends. "In Paris do they really dress as grandly as the fashion dolls show us?" one wanted to know. The waxen dolls of which she spoke were dressed in the latest styles, meant to promote consumption of French luxury goods - gold and silver lace, silks and brocades, velvets.

"A doll can give no idea!" Anna exclaimed. "Yards - no, miles more like - of silk and lace and embroidery and gold and silver. The skirts are enormous! They are a fortune of silk and velvet. And the jewels! It takes all morning for ladies to dress. The décolleté is so extreme, you hold your breath, fearing a breast will pop out at any minute. I was told the priests inveigh against extravagance, as they do here, but to no more effect. Extravagance is the point! And the hair! Servants have to climb up on ladders to do the hair. The ladies can hardly move for their vast piles of hair.

"What about London?" inquired Eleanora Haffner. She looked, thought Anna, shockingly thin. An educated woman, who read everything she could lay her hands on, Anna thought she might be Chancellor were it not for her sex. "We hear that the colonies in America refuse the taxes levied on them."

"There was much talk of it," said Anna. "There was talk of everything, more than you can imagine. People in England say anything without fear. I saw a woman preaching out-of-doors and nothing was done to her. There is even a sect they call Quakers, among whom are women considered the equals of men!"

"Anna," marveled Babette Möll, who had put her market baskets down to embrace her neighbor, "you have gone so far and seen so much. Have you come back a very wise woman to shame us all?"

Anna laughed. "I do not know that wisdom is to be found in the places we were." She pondered, aware that her friends listened to her with new respect. "I had to manage everything when Leopold was ill in London." She laughed. "I even fired his miserable Italian servant. Leopold was scandalized. He could not believe my temerity. I do not know that I am wise, but perhaps I have grown bold."

Though Anna's friends were reluctant to let her go, the November cold sent them on their way. Anna stopped briefly in St. Peter's churchyard to visit the graves of her five children. Grass had grown up around the small stones, but she would let it grow until spring. How long ago it seemed, since her body and spirit had been seized by that time of childbearing and loss. She had been not long out of the convent and not wise to the ways of the world, still so sure of her genius. She had only just married the handsome, worldly and fastidious Leopold when she was held hostage by one infant after another, loving and then losing all but two. Those two were now dearer to her than her own life or any promise it had once held. Why, she thought, I have changed. I have seen privation and loss, as well as splendor and power, in the greatest cities and courts. I know more than I did. And I am now the *mother* of genius.

"It is hard to believe!" Margarethe exclaimed. "You have dined with the English king and queen in their own quarters . . . ."

"And watched French royalty stuff itself - and my son," Anna said dryly. "It is true, I have been far from home and seen much. But you have traveled, Margarethe. You know what it is like. Under all the satin and velvet and gold and silver lace, what are the gorgeous creatures of France and England but *women*? Half of them, it seemed to me, were bored nearly to distraction with their fine lives. And had I tried to rival them, I would have heard lectures about the arrogance, thoughtlessness and immorality of an artisan's wife aping her betters. In any case, it does not take me the morning to dress, which is just as well, as I have better things to do."

Margarethe nodded.

Anna went on. “The children have become quite remarkable. But Nannerl puzzles me. She has the idea she must not compose, but will not tell me why.”

Margarethe frowned. “Not compose?”

“Wolfgang, on the other hand, will take the world by storm,” Anna said. “He has no doubts, and nothing is impossible to him. Everywhere we went men tested him, putting before him the most difficult works, which he could play at first glance. He and Nannerl composed so much together. He does not understand, anymore than I do, why his sister will not sit down with him to compose any more.” Anna turned the palms of her hands up.

Margarethe shook her head.

“Leopold has changed too,” Anna continued. “I think it has to do with his mother. You will surely think, Margarethe, that I will never stop talking.”

“Go on, go on,” said Margarethe impatiently. “I want to hear.”

“I wrote to you about my visit to Leopold’s mother in Augsburg. Oh, Margarethe. What a time I had getting letters off to you. Leopold disliked spending money to send them and I finally kept back a little that he gave me for meals so that I could send you a letter now and then. I took sheets of his paper when he was out. I have become a sneak, my friend,” Anna admitted. It had always seemed to her that to lie or cheat were the worst of sins because if you could not trust people if you were not worthy of trust then nothing made sense. Such betrayals in word or deed seemed to Anna to merit an afterlife in Hell. She had not precisely lied to Leopold in these instances, but she had deceived him.

“In any event,” she resumed, “Leopold went to see his mother on our return to Augsburg and came away convinced that she had ordered him to leave.” Anna crossed to the window and stood looking out. “I worry now, because he will not leave Wolfgang alone. He wants entire control of the boy, the more as Wolfgang sometimes pushes him away and insists on some separation between them. I fear for them, Margarethe. I fear Leopold will do to my son what his mother did to him and that he will lose what has become the chief object of his life.” Anna sighed. “It does no good for me to remonstrate. Leopold is quite clear,” she paused, reluctant to admit what she now knew well, “that like others of my sex, I have inferior understanding.”

“Oh Anna,” Margarethe exclaimed. “Surely not.”

"It is not so much a new thing," said Anna, "as more apparent. It is the belief that everyone holds and Leopold wants everyone's good opinion."

"You, too, have changed," said Margarethe, studying her friend. "You have traveled the world and observed much. There is about you a sureness that I did not see before."

Anna nodded. "Yes, there is truth in that. But I have talked quite enough. Now tell me about yourself, your poetry, everything. I have been away for three years, but they have been three years for you as well."

30

1766-1767

THE NEWS CAME IN A LETTER from Aloys Mozart in Augsburg. Leopold's mother had died. All of her children but Leopold had gathered at her bedside. She had confessed her sins, though she could hardly speak, been forgiven and received the final rites. Leopold was stunned. He had believed, despite everything he knew, that she would come to him, beg forgiveness and hold him once more in her arms.

He held out the letter to Anna, who read it and put her arms about him. She wished he had made his peace with the old lady.

Leopold let Anna hold him, shuddering, for a long while. "She was not kind to me," said Leopold softly, "but I had not thought she would die so soon. She is gone." He gathered himself. "We will not speak of her again."

After his mother's death, Leopold grew more reluctant than ever to let his son out of his sight. Where he had tasked the child before, he now set before him twice the work to master. The child must learn Italian, work at sums, read books about ancient history and science, compose keyboard concertos based upon sonatas written by the men they had met on their travels - Schobert, Eckard, Raupach and Johann Bach. He secured for his son a commission to write part of a sacred *singspiel,* set to a text by the merchant Ignaz Weiser, from whom Anna had bought many a length of woolen and silken cloth. Leopold drew up on paper a scheme for the disposition of Wolfgang's every waking hour.

For the most part Wolfgang did what his father charged him to do, most often cheerfully, for he was a good-natured boy. Sometimes, however, he longed to run about and play with his friends and sulked when his father forbade it. When Leopold was displeased he grew cold and distant, and Wolfgang was quick to come back to him, to regain his father's favor.

Wolfgang's part of the *singspiel* took him more than two hundred pages to set down. He often asked Nannerl for help. "I cannot, Woferl," she would say. "Elise Hoffmann is waiting for her lesson." Or some other pupil. Or she must go to church, repair a dress, wash her cascade of hair. He could not understand her reluctance and sometimes stamped his foot in frustration.

"The music must be just so," he confided to his mother, "because it is the first and foremost commandment. 'You must love the Lord thy God . . . .' I want to *show* that in the music, the part about 'all thy heart and all thy soul and all thy mind and all thy strength.' " He measured the untidy pile of paper with his fingers. "Herr Adlgasser and Herr Haydn have not written down so many pages, because they do not make so many mistakes. Look at this! Look at all the mistakes! But Papa will write my part over so the pages will be clean." The child had smudges of ink on his face and forefinger and spots on his shirt.

Anna examined his pages, noting the passages he had written and then crossed out. Already, she thought, he can tell when he has done well, when he has not. "Let me have that shirt, Woferl, before the ink is set. Change first and then run out for awhile and get some color in your cheeks before your Papa comes in. Go on now."

Wolfgang blew a kiss at his mother as he danced past her, in his haste, letting his clean shirt hang out. He was always eager to be out where there were people and bustle, the more the better.

Nannerl too had gone out. She was required to give a lesson to the son of the Prince Colloredo, the imperial envoy to Spain. Prince Colloredo had come to Salzburg to stay with his brother, the Bishop of Gurk, who had recommended Nannerl as the most accomplished teacher for the Prince's son, a sullen and surly child whom the Bishop fondly prayed could be civilized.

"The Prince pays hardly anything," Nannerl had grumbled at the morning meal, "and his wretched son would far rather be shooting or riding to the hounds or just lying on a couch giving orders to the servants. He has no interest in music and dislikes to do as I tell him."

"But the Prince will dine with the Archbishop, Nannerl," Leopold had said, "as you know since your brother will play for them at dinner. I hear it will be an exceedingly grand affair. So smile and bear it, my dear."

Nannerl sighed and drank her coffee pensively. What a waste, she thought. No doubt her father was right, but thank God for her one excellent student, young Rudi Kurtzmann. She tried not to envy her brother's commission to compose part of Herr Weiser's oratorio. Envy was a sin. She had determined not to compose again, but composition was an itch she could hardly forebear to scratch.

"I had to change so little of Wolfgang's work, Anna," marveled Leopold later. He showed her the neat stack of manuscript pages in his hand. "See here, I made some few changes here, and here, where the phrasing was not just right, and I put in some dynamic markings. And of course it needed to be set down without blots and crossings out. But what Woferl has done is remarkably good."

"Mmmm," agreed Anna, noting the names of the singers on the first page. "I hear that Fraulein Fesemayr has set her cap for Anton," she commented, putting her iron, which had cooled, back on the stove. "Woferl says her voice is good - all the voices, come to that, but hers especially." She dug her fists into the small of her back and arched herself backward to relieve the ache that ironing always brought on.

The oratorio was a great success. Wolfgang was the talk of Salzburg. "I know better, of course," said Theresa, walking companionably with Anna to St. Peter's bakery, "but some suspect that Wolfgang did not compose his part of the oratorio at all. It is just for something to talk about of course, but at the pump this morning I heard mutterings that Leopold composed whatever the child laid claim to."

Anna laughed and rolled her eyes. "Leopold proved his son to the world," she said, "but not to his neighbors, who suspect that foreigners can easily be gulled."

"What is said," Theresa rejoined, her hands on her hips, her voice raised to mimic those she alluded to, "is that 'Herr Mozart wishes to travel abroad at the same time he draws his pay at court.' 'When he travels, he palms his own works off on the boy and garners riches past belief.' 'He wants to journey to Russia and Sweden and maybe even the American colonies, where gold lies in piles on the streets.' 'Nonsense,' says I, but I am thought to be in on these nefarious designs, friends as we are."

Anna grew serious. "Leopold will be livid if he hears such talk," she said, "and how could he not hear?"

Sure enough, Leopold had heard the rumors before the morning was half spent. It is the Italians, he thought, always the Italians, who will go to any lengths to hinder me and my son." He cursed that he had not traveled to Italy as he had intended, rather than to the Low Countries. Had he triumphed in Italy, the Italians would have had no thunder. Leopold demanded to see the Archbishop, fearful that his principal would be influenced by such foolishness. "It appears, Excellency," he said, "that some in your court disbelieve in miracles, though they claim to be good Catholics. And so my boy's gifts are thought a fraud and taken lightly."

"Well, Mozart," said the Archbishop, who had put a large sum of money into his *Vice Kapellmeister's* travels with his children, "I cannot stop people talking. "

Leopold, as it happened, had an idea. "Excellency, my son was often tested wherever we went, as far as England and France, to everyone's satisfaction. I propose that you devise a test. Prove, once and for all, to everyone, that - though I have taught my son what I know - his genius stands on its own. Give him a task, Excellency, a cantata - perhaps, a passion cantata for the coming Easter week. Hold him apart from me, where there can be no doubt whose work it is. And be sure the word gets out."

"To satisfy the doubters I would have to lock the boy up, keep every mortal away from him. Otherwise, it would be said you had found a way to help him," smiled the Archbishop.

"Then lock him up, Excellency. Give it out that he will not see a living soul for a week, if need be, that he has nothing to hand but paper, ink and a text."

"How old is your son, Mozart?" queried the Archbishop.

"Just gone eleven, Excellency," answered Leopold.

"Somewhat hard on one so young." mused the Archbishop.

"He will not mind," Leopold said.

But Wolfgang did mind. "Papa!" he objected, when Leopold, much pleased with himself, told the child of his unusual commission, which would still all lying tongues. "Papa! I do not want to be locked up. I would rather be whipped in the streets! At least there would be company!"

"Leopold!" exclaimed Anna, equally aghast.

"It is not punishment, my son," Leopold explained, startled by the boy's opposition and angered by Anna's, "rather, an opportunity to put paid to foolish rumors. You will have a fine apartment in the Archbishop's residence, with a bed just for you and meals sent in from the Archbishop's very own kitchen. The Archbishop is fond of you and I think he will provide the daintiest food."

Wolfgang was not comforted. "I do not *want* to be locked up!" he repeated. "I will not do it." He stamped his foot.

Leopold's face darkened. "You will do as you are told," he declared. "I am your father and will hear no more foolishness. We must quell false reports spread abroad by small men. Tomorrow you will go to the Residence. I will hear no more about it."

"Mama!" pleaded Wolfgang, on the verge of tears.

Anna leaned down to whisper in his ear. "Let me speak to your father alone. Here, take some money. I left shoes with the cobbler yesterday. You can run across the bridge and get them. And some sweets as well for Nannerl and yourself."

Wolfgang put on his warm cloak and ran off. His mother would stop his father. Wolfgang had seen her dismiss Porta in England, despite his father.

Hardly had he run down the stairs than Anna turned to her husband, her face very flushed. "Leopold," she said firmly. "You must not do this. This is wrong."

Leopold thought he had never seen his wife before. His plan, accepted by the Archbishop as if it were the Prince's own idea, would make clear, once and for all, that Wolfgang was possessed of talents uncomprehended by those of common clay. His wife aligned herself with those coarser beings, unable to understand the brilliant gift that God had entrusted to him. How could she have once seemed to him so fine, so pure, so perfectly fitted to understand him and to answer his needs? "Must not, Anna?" he said coldly.

Anna pressed her thumb and forefinger into her eyes and tried to still an anger that frightened her. Outside, the fat flakes of a wet April snow fell thickly, settling in small drifts on the window ledge. "Leopold," she said quietly, "think of your son. He is an affectionate and sociable boy, no longer a child, but hardly a man. He tries hard to please you in everything. Whatever your intention, to him this scheme is punishment. He will suffer greatly, and," she added, "he will blame you."

Leopold could not relent. The die was cast and now everything depended on his son's proving himself to Salzburg. Leopold thought he must, no matter what it took, still the lying tongues of the Italians and anyone else who doubted. Still, the thought that his son might blame him was like a knife in his belly. It was like a woman to stab a man as he but did his duty. "You do not know the world, Anna," he said.

"I know more than you think," she said, "and I fear for you as well as your son. Your mother - no, let me finish," for Leopold had started and held up his hand to stop her. "Your mother made her plans for you, and you have never forgiven her. You left her. I would not have you lose your son in the same way."

"I have forbidden mention of that woman in this household," said Leopold, coldly, "and I will thank you to remember it. You do not - you *cannot* - possibly understand."

Neither Anna nor Leopold knew that Nannerl, who had earlier taken to her bed with a headache, had awakened to their raised voices and had crept softly to the adjoining doorway. She listened, not knowing what had happened but uneasy that her parents would dispute so angrily.

"I understand more than you give me credit for, Leopold," Anna said. "There is gossip. There will always be gossip. What does it matter? There is no harm in Wolfgang's being taken for what he is, a mightily gifted child whose father helps him. Of course you help him. How else would he learn?"

Leopold felt that his head was caught in a vise. One part of him heard wisdom in what Anna said, but the larger part rose up to quell it. "Anna," he said heavily, "I have always treated you well. I have never yet beaten you nor the children. Yet you have defied me, over and over. You went to my mother in Augsburg without my leave. You dismissed my servant, even though I objected. You oppose me, your husband."

Anna hesitated. "Once," she said softly, "you thought well of me. You put your name to my compositions." She held up her hand to forestall his objections. "I know it was for my benefit and I was - am - grateful. But what I mean is that you found no disgrace to owning my work. Now you find me deficient in understanding, even understanding of my children, for whose sake - and yours - I have given up music. Am I to have no realm . . . ?"

Leopold interrupted her. "Perhaps you did not give up music in time," he said hotly. "There are five graves in St. Peter's to prove it."

Anna gasped.

Nannerl pulled back from the doorway. Could it be true, that her mother had lost so many infants because she desired to compose? Her father was right: Wolfgang must perforce be the brightest star - the only star - in the Mozart firmament. Her mother could not possibly understand true genius.

It seemed to Anna that she had lost something much weightier than an argument. She felt sick, diminished, bereaved. In a small and useless gesture of defiance, she refused to pack up Wolfgang's clothes for his sojourn at the Archbishop's residence. Instead Nannerl performed this task, feeling scorn for her mother, while Wolfgang watched his sister mutinously, muttering all the time. Everyone, he thought, had turned against him, his mother because she had not interceded successfully, his sister because she did what her father asked. His father's betrayal he could not even contemplate.

Anna and Leopold moved around each other warily, with excessive care and politeness. Leopold thought Anna had deserted him when he most needed her. Anna tried to keep in mind that her husband had recently lost his mother and that he had returned from his successful journey to find less adulation that he had grown to expect, but all she felt was anger and emptiness. "I will think of you every moment," she whispered to her furious son. "I will see if I can arrange for Cajetan - I always forget he is Father Dominicus now - to look in on you and hear your confession."

Father Dominicus was glad to go to Wolfgang in his captivity, staying longer than it took for the child to confess. Cajetan's voice was the only one Wolfgang heard for the entire week. His friend brought news and a small flute, a gift from Anna. "She says to remember the bird woman of her old story," said Father Dominicus, "She says you will know how just such a pipe carried the prince through fire and flood."

Wolfgang played the little flute when the walls seemed to press in upon him. They were fine high walls and there was a stove decorated with gilded scrolls. The floor was an intricate parquet which he studied at length, trying to decide which pieces were put down first, which afterwards. He tried running about the large apartment, but there was nowhere to go and his legs grew heavy with the effort. He imagined his mother as she cooked and cleaned and talked with her friends, enumerating each dish and all of its ingredients. He thought of poor Nannerl and how she must trudge out to give lessons to dullards. She was always good to him. How he missed them, Mama and Nannerl!

His father loomed large like a great thunderstorm that boiled over the mountains, flattening the grasses and turning the air green and the leaves to their silver sides. His dreams were troubled by the terrifying winds that drove sticks and leaves across the squares and made the horses lay their ears back against their heads. Papa's will was lightening and thunder. Perhaps it was true that he must love the Lord his God with all his heart and soul and strength, but he had better obey Papa at all costs.

As for Leopold, no sooner had he worked his will than he was riven with anxiety. What if Anna were right, that this test was too hard on the boy? What if he could not compose in such circumstances and his father looked the fool to everyone at court? What if he should hate his father for subjecting him to a week in isolation? What if he fell ill and died? What if one of the Italians, to defeat a rival, found a way to send in poisoned food to the boy? He could say nothing of his fears and doubts to anyone. He was locked up in his own prison of anxiety. Lucky Anna, he thought. She had the best of it with her gaggle of chattering friends in the market and at the pump. Lucky Nannerl, whose particular grace was to accept the world as it was.

It was an anxious week. Anna went to Father Dominicus every day to have news of her son, to send him messages and small tokens of good cheer. Nannerl was quiet and withdrawn. Though Anna longed to comfort Nannerl, she did not want to tell her of Father Dominicus' visits, lest Nannerl drop even a word to her father. Once again she deceived her husband, for he would surely see her little scheme to comfort her son as undermining the perfection of his plan. To sin, Anna decided, was the price she must pay to ease the terror of her child. But there would be an account against her at Judgment Day.

Wolfgang easily completed the passion cantata, which was performed on Good Friday in the Cathedral. The circumstances of its composition were widely bruited, and soon those who had doubted that young Wolfgang was a composer in his own right proclaimed to the world that they had known all along how greatly this child, a true Salzburger, was gifted.

Leopold was gratified by the outcome of his scheme. His son had a new commission, a Latin comedy for the University in May, to be followed by an exhibition of his playing at the harpsichord. Then they would go to Vienna and after that to Italy. They must go quickly, while Wolfgang was still young enough that everything he did excited admiration.

31

1767-1768

THE CARRIAGE JOLTED EASTWARD along the baked road, trailing dust. Its shadow went before them in the late September sun, which spangled the red roofed villages, the quiet fields and tall pine forests. Both Nannerl and Wolfgang had fallen asleep, the girl leaning against Anna on one side, the boy curled up on the other with his head on her lap.

"In Vienna, Wolfgang will be recognized for what he is," Leopold murmured.

Anna studied her husband's thin intelligent face, lit as if by a fire that burned without consuming. "What he is, Leopold," said Anna without any hope that her words would be heard, "is a boy not yet twelve."

Startled from his reverie, Leopold said quietly, "Do not oppose me, Anna. I will have my way with my son."

Anna did not answer. Uneasiness had lived with them like an unwelcome guest since Leopold's test had kept Wolfgang locked up for a week. Anna knew the breach must be mended. Her anger had given way to perplexity: how could she protect her children, one of whom needed more of her father's attention, the other less? Certainly not by continuing hostility toward her husband. "Her Majesty must continue to mourn the loss of her husband," she ventured. "She has such a task as Empress. I know that her son rules with her, but still. . . ." She kept trying to introduce conversation in matters of no moment to either of them.

"Mmm," said Leopold, not really listening. His head was full of his son's prospects. He was taking his family to Vienna for the marriage of the Archduchess Maria Caroline to the King Ferdinand of Naples. Music would be wanted for the festivities; ballets, serenades, symphonies, divertimentos and dance music would be required, and an opera for every day. Surely he could get some part of this work for Wolfgang. Leopold's great plan was to contrive that the new Emperor Joseph II, now co-regent with his mother, would commission Wolfgang to compose an opera. That would set Vienna on its ear and lead to untold opportunity!

Now that Leopold knew the wider world, Salzburg was too small a stage for his son's talents - and his own, for that matter. In Vienna, that great center of music, he would drop a word here, an allusion there, about the English king's offer and how he had turned it down, bringing his talents back to his own German people. Surely he would find some desirable post for himself. He had left a set of six of his son's symphonies with the copyist in Salzburg: these had been commissioned by the Prince von Fürstenberg in Donaueschingen when the Mozarts had passed through on their triumphal return from England and Paris. The copyist, Estlinger, was under instructions to give the finished symphonies to Frau Hagenauer to forward to the Prince, along with a flattering letter. The Prince von Fürstenberg was well worth courting, for his connections in Vienna were extensive. With such backing, if he - Leopold Mozart - stepped carefully, he might find excellent preferment for Wolfgang, even though his son was no longer the amusing miniature of five years earlier. Nannerl would woo the highborn, playing in the best houses. She might beguile some nobleman who would regard her beauty more than her birth. At seventeen, she would be an adornment to any nobleman's household.

Anna was unready for this journey, which came less than a year after their return from the last one. She was not, she had decided, an apt traveler. She did better at home, where she was firmly rooted, drawing her nourishment from familiar people and places. She was often lonely in strange towns, and found untoward events - illnesses, accidents, the peculiar exigencies of daily life - more difficult far from home. There was no doubt that Nannerl and Wolfgang had learned vast amounts from their travels, but she thought it hard for them to leave friends and the stability of home. It seemed to her that on tour her children worked too hard and were likelier to contract foreign contagions.

In Vienna, Leopold found lodgings on the top floor of the goldsmith Schmalecker's house. Nannerl and Wolfgang, warmly remembered from their earlier visit, were immediately in demand to perform at every gathering, and there were operas and plays to attend daily. Wolfgang received a commission to write incidental music for a small part of the royal nuptials. It seemed Leopold had been right, that he and his children might have a great future in this city. Anna relished the splendid array of musical events, and thought that, should Leopold decide to stay, she could make the friends that were essential to her happiness.

Then, in mid-October, all Vienna was rocked by the news that the Archduchess, having asked that her bridal finery be hung where she could see it near her bed, had died of smallpox. Vienna mourned the little Archduchess as well as the loss of festivities, which, in the preparation, were more elaborate than any in memory, with the King of Naples trying to outdo the Imperial Court in the magnificence of arrangements.

Wolfgang was agitated by the death of someone just his sister's age. "Was she the one with curls and dimples?"

"No," said Nannerl, also shaken. She remembered how she had grieved the earlier death of the Princess Johanna. "Maria Caroline was sallow and had straight hair pulled back in a ribbon. She wanted to stay behind and read a book - remember? - when we went with the Archduchess Marie Antoinette to see the menagerie. *She* was the pretty one, all frills and flounces."

"How could a princess die so young?" Wolfgang asked. It isn't right." He plunged into a piece of work, a duet for two sopranos which he, with his clear, high voice, and Nannerl could sing together.

Nannerl understood what her brother felt. If royalty could die young, why not ordinary people like the two of them?

All Vienna shared the young Mozarts' fears. The smallpox was abroad, like an invasion of Turks, cutting down rich and poor, young and old. No one was safe. One of the goldsmith's children died and two more fell ill.

Leopold felt himself in a house whose timbers were weakened by woodworms and flying ants. His hopes were collapsing around him and his only thought was to get Wolfgang away from contagion. "Dr. Laugier has offered sanctuary in the country. Woferl and I will go to him," said Leopold to Anna. "The servant will stay with you. Send him out for whatever you need and stay indoors. Keep Nannerl away from the Schmalecker children."

"You and Woferl will leave this pestilent house?" Anna asked coldly, "in which your daughter, not to mention your wife, will remain?"

Leopold heard Anna as little more than a buzzing insect objecting to a windowpane. "Please to put together some clothes for us to take," he said.

Anna planted herself in her husband's way. "What of Nannerl?" Anna repeated. "Her health is of no concern to you?"

"Oh, Anna," said Leopold impatiently. How could he explain to his wife? She was unreasonable so often of late. Everything rested on his son. "Nannerl may have had the pox already," Leopold said, as if to a half-wit. "You remember the spots she had when she was an infant. I must look out for the boy. He has never been strong."

Anna was cold with fury. "As you looked out for him when the Archbishop locked him up? You were willing to risk his very sanity. Listen to you, Leopold. In France, when inoculation was spoken of, you would have none of it. 'We must trust to the will of God,' you said. Now that there is smallpox in the house, where is your trust in God? Only on behalf of Nannerl? But you will take Woferl away to better air? I cannot stomach it, Leopold!"

Leopold had taken a vow, and it was clear to him that he was bound by ordinances beyond those that governed most people. Anna balked him and frustrated his designs, as if she were in league with those wretched Italians in Salzburg, envious and second-rate musicians who saw in Wolfgang a threat to their preeminence. Was she, like them, jealous of the genius that resided in her own son? She had seemed perfection to Leopold twenty years before, but he had mistaken her. She was no more than common clay.

"Anna, I cannot ask Dr. Laugier to take in a whole family of refugees," he said with exaggerated patience. "I know best about these things. I will send for you and the girl when I can."

What was Anna to do? She might quarrel with her husband, but she had no means to defy him. She had no money of her own to leave the Schmalecker house, no friends independent of his in Vienna. She remembered, as clearly as if it were yesterday, the terror that had swept the convent when the smallpox had raged through Salzburg, the brutal illness that had seized Gertrud and tormented her as a cat tortures a mouse, and then killed her. Every day Anna awoke alone in her bed and crept to Nannerl's side to see that she was still cool and breathed easily.

Nannerl understood clearly that her father had chosen her brother's life over her own. She wandered about the rooms abstracted, without purpose.

She sat at the clavier, but did not play. She tried to sort her thoughts, but they were a jumble. Her mother loved her, she knew, but what good was love without the power which was her father's? She knew that she must look to win her father's approbation.

"Nannerl," said Anna, "why do you not compose something? Something grand, maybe an oratorio? Something for your brother once we are reunited?"

"That is just what I must not do, Mama," said Nannerl with heat. "When I compose, I am hungry to compose more."

"And why should you not?" asked Anna.

"Oh Mama," sighed Nannerl. Why could she not understand? She was silent a long while. She did not want to confide in her mother, but she was her only companion, shut up as they were. "You remember when I was so ill in The Hague?" she asked.

Anna nodded. "We nearly lost you," she said.

"It was my fault," said Nannerl hesitantly, "I mean, that we went there at all. I was proud and ambitious."

Anna was aghast. "You think your illness was punishment? For what?"

Nannerl nodded. "For wanting an opera, music, composing."

"It was no such thing!" Anna protested. "You had an invitation from the Princess herself, who paid all the costs. Papa did not blame you."

"He told me it was all vanity," said Nannerl, speaking so low that Anna had to strain to hear.

"But that was to make it easier to let go, if," Anna crossed herself, "it was necessary. Why should you not follow the leading of your genius, Nannerl?"

"Oh, Mama," said Nannerl, impatient. "A woman cannot have genius. Everyone says so. In London, I was sure I *had to* go to The Hague, but I was tempted, misled by false passion and ambition. I should not have insisted on having my way." She paused, then said slowly, "I made a vow, before God not to compose." Her voice trembled. "But it is hard. I bend to my desires." Like you, Mama, she thought, I am weak. "I have to pray for submission all the time."

Another vow, Anna thought. And *I* am considered unreasonable! She put her arms around the slender girl. "Oh, Nannerl," she said. "I have wanted you to compose, to be a musician as I could not. Perhaps it is wrong to want for another what one cannot have. And you are right. Your father holds and many others too that only men have genius and can make their way in the world. But think, Nannerl, think! You and I have seen, and with our own eyes, women musicians who are able to earn their bread. We know they can do it. Papa means well and he holds you dear, but," she sighed, "who can stand in his way when he is carried along by notions?"

Nannerl shrugged free of her mother's arms. Not you, Mama, she thought bitterly. You cannot give me what I want, what I need. She struggled to keep from weeping.

Anna went to the window. The streets were nearly empty. A storm must be brewing, she thought, for the air had grown dark and turbulent at midday. She saw a lone woman, her hair flying about in the wind, clutching a shabby cloak about her. The bent figure staggered to the corner and turned into the broader Karntnerstrasse, where Anna lost sight of her. "Your father has always said that a vow cannot be binding," said Anna slowly, "for one cannot enter into a contract as a equal party with God. Yet he himself has taken a vow . . . . Yes," she said, seeing Nannerl's brows lift in surprise. "I was witness, though not a willing one."

Anna continued. "When I was younger," she said, "your father admired my work and often put his name to it."

Nannerl had overheard her parents quarreling about some such thing in Salzburg, though at the time it had made no sense to her. "Tell me," she insisted.

"When I went to Nonnberg," said Anna, "I lost everything - father, mother, even my voice. I stopped speaking, singing, playing at the harpsichord." Conjuring her memories, she told Nannerl how Gertrud and Sister Gisella, had brought her back to life. "The nuns gave me confidence," she said. "I thought I could do as I liked in the world. And your father, oh, what a handsome, dashing suitor, Nannerl. He who seemed to want my music as much as I did. But then . . . ."

At that very moment Leopold himself burst through the door, breaking off Anna's story. Anna and Nannerl had not seen him for many days. "Pack up your things," he ordered. "Now! There is no time to waste! We will travel to Brünn, where the brother of our Archbishop resides. Come, now, quickly!" Leopold was peremptory, for he was ashamed of himself. He knew it had been a shabby thing to leave his wife and daughter behind.

With only an hour or so to gather together their possessions, Anna and Nannerl joined Wolfgang and Leopold, who took his family to the cleaner country air of Brünn. But upon their arrival, hearing word that the smallpox had spread to this Moravian capital, they fled further east to Olmütz, where, in the damp and smoky inn, Wolfgang showed signs of fever. "This cannot be!" Leopold exclaimed as his son raved and tossed about in a rapidly advancing delirium.

After a long night, through which Anna watched the boy so that Leopold could sleep, Leopold rose early and went out to church, where he spoke to the Count Podstatsky, Dean of the Cathedral. The Count, who had five years earlier been impressed by the Mozart children in Vienna, was appalled to see Leopold nearly out of his mind with fear for his son. "My good Herr Mozart," said the Count, a small neat man, whose bald head shone, without a wig, "you must bring your family to my house at once. I will send my man, Boris," he said. "And once you are well settled, you must join me for some of the fine brandy from my cellar. No, no," he said to forestall Leopold's rather limp protestations. "I am not afraid of the disease in the least. My household had it some years ago."

True to his word, the Count Podstatsky had his servants prepare the rooms in the west wing of his grand house, where Leopold carried his sleeping son, warmly wrapped in Anna's fur cloak. Anna was more grateful than she could say to the Count. The Mozarts' every need was met, freeing Anna to sit by her son's bed. When Wolfgang complained that he could hardly see anything, the Count's physician cautioned Leopold and Anna that he must not use his eyes, but must lie in a darkened room till they should amend. The pox sores came out all over Wolfgang's body, until finally his fever broke and the scabs fell off, leaving red spots on his face.

"Mama," Wolfgang said one day when he had recovered most of his strength, "does Papa not love Nannerl?" Leopold had ridden out with the Count and Nannerl had gone to church.

"Of course he does, Woferl!" answered Anna.

"But he left her behind - and you," said Wolfgang.

"I cannot explain it," Anna answered, ashamed of her husband as he appeared thus flawed in her son's eyes. "You are his only son," she explained, "and he sets great store by you. He also thought perhaps Nannerl had had the pox as a baby."

After a while, Wolfgang dropped off to sleep and Anna covered him up, thinking how his fair skin was marred by the scars of the pox.

Leopold commented that evening on the seriousness he saw in his son. "There has begun," he said to Anna, looking up from the letter he wrote to the Hagenauers, "a new period in his life. He has been spared by God for the work that lies before him."

32

1768

THE HAPSBURG EMPRESS MARIA THERESA kept abreast of the affairs of her empire by means of the complicated system of rumor and gossip. She knew of the Mozart family's arrival in Vienna and she knew that the pox, which had taken her daughter and so many of her subjects, had driven the family away from the city. But now they had returned. There was no harm, the Empress thought, in having them in to play a little, to raise the spirits of her grieving family. There could be no festivities nor large parties so soon after such losses as her realm had sustained. On a cold Tuesday in the middle of January, the Mozarts were received in Empress's private quarters.

"I understand," said the Empress to Anna, "that your children have both suffered from the pox." The two women sat aside from the young Emperor, who was extolling the virtues of his new-fangled clavier to Leopold, Nannerl and Wolfgang.

"Yes, your Majesty," said Anna. "My daughter was not so sick as the boy. As you can see, my son's face still bears the scars."

"But your daughter's complexion is fresh as a flower still, and a good thing. She will need her beauty to marry well," observed the Empress.

Anna was not sure whether she should mention the deaths that had sent the palace into mourning, but it seemed cruel not to acknowledge this woman's sorrows. "I was saddened, your Majesty, to know of your losses," she said shyly. "It must be doubly difficult with everyone looking on." There could be no pause in the affairs of empire while a great prince mourned. And an Empress owed her duty to her realm first, then to her family.

The Empress, who looked much older than she had five years ago, touched Anna's cheek with her jeweled fingers and reached for her hand. "You are very kind," she murmured. "You find us much reduced, Frau Mozart. The whole of Vienna mourns for those newly buried." She smoothed the fine black silk of her dress. "You will find that we have given up amusements, which suits my son very well as he is set on economies. We have not the concerts in court we once did."

Across the room, the Emperor Joseph II, a man of decided opinions, held forth on the undesirability of women playing any instrument but the keyboard. "It is entirely unsuitable for a female to play on the flute or the horn, since she must purse her lips suggestively and must be seen to give visceral support for the tone." He shuddered. "Nor must she embrace the cello or viols with her legs, nor strain her neck for the violin, which will make an unsightly scar under her jaw. No, no," he said, peering far too closely, thought Nannerl, at the front of her dress, "the clavier shows off a woman's arms to great advantage. See here, how the lace falls from your sleeve as you place your hands on the keys." His long, pale fingers stroked Nannerl's arm.

Nannerl, gritting her teeth, did not think it seemly to pull her arm away from an Emperor and was glad when he turned his attention to Wolfgang. "A great boy you have grown to be, Herr Mozart. No doubt you will now compose whole operas and conduct them by yourself!" The tall, pale young emperor laughed heartily at the idea.

"Yes please, your Majesty," said Wolfgang.

"And how do you think the musicians would like to play and sing for a mere child?" The Emperor laughed again.

"Your Majesty," said Leopold firmly, "my son is ready to serve you with the finest comic opera you can imagine, an Italian opera buffa."

"Fine, fine," said the Emperor carelessly. "You must speak with Signor Affligio about it. Tell him I said so." But he paid more attention to Nannerl's *décolletage* than to the idea of an opera composed by a twelve year-old. While Nannerl flinched away from the Emperor's attentions. Leopold was puffed up with the thought that the Emperor had just promised Wolfgang his opera. It even occurred to him that the Emperor might be attracted to Nannerl.

"Good Heavens, Leopold!" Anna exclaimed when her husband observed to her that the Emperor had shown a decided interest in their daughter.

"Royalty may flirt with a woman of Nannerl's station, but never marry. That he must do for policy, not passing fancy! Leopold, think!" What, she wondered, had happened to her husband, who prized reason and boasted that he knew the world?

Leopold did not answer. His wife was too earthbound and ordinary to see the prospects that extended like magnificent formal gardens before him. An opera for his son, followed by court appointment, the Emperor's interest in the beautiful Nannerl! Now he must talk to Signor Affligio, the Italian who held the franchise for all Viennese spectacles, who arranged for all entertainments from ballet and opera to the more profitable animal baiting. Rumor had it that his titles were of dubious provenance, that he was an unscrupulous gambler and seducer, and that he had been the friend of his legendary countryman, the rake who called himself Casanova. Still, Leopold would carry with him the Emperor's promise, which Affligio could hardly overlook.

Nannerl had found the Emperor's attentions distressing, another affliction to remind her that she was, by Nature, limited by her sex. She could not oppose Nature. How often had her father told her so? She had been sternly taught by the typhoid fever in The Hague, and the smallpox she had suffered in Olmütz was but a reminder. If an emperor were to lay siege to her, what recourse had she? Her father was her best protection, but would he come to her aid? Her mother certainly had no power to oppose an emperor. Nannerl spent as much time as she could in church, praying that God would still her turmoil.

Leopold approached Giuseppi Affligio. It was a royal command, he said, that his son, who had triumphed in Paris and London, was to write an opera. The Empress and her son the Emperor would attend and bring with them all of Vienna. Affligio, preoccupied with the cost of supporting a troupe of French dancers, agreed reluctantly to take on the dubious project. If the Emperor had indeed endorsed it, the boy might compose the music for Goldoni's libretto, *La Finta Simplice*.

Wolfgang did not like the story, which concerned a foolish romantic plot involving old men, their beautiful sister, a scheming maiden and her brother. It was to be a long opera with over twenty arias and a symphony to alert the audience that the opera was about to begin. "Nannerl," he wailed. "I need you to help me."

"Oh no, Woferl, I cannot," said Nannerl, holding her hands up in front of her, as if fending off an importunate swain's advances. "Do not ask."

"Of course you must help him, Nannerl," Leopold insisted. "You must not be selfish."

Nannerl paused. If she were ordered, how could she refuse? It was not the same thing as composing for her own sake. If there were several voices in the Mozart family, why should her brother not have both of them - all of them, come to that. That her mother had given up composition was an example of selfless devotion. If it were true that Wolfgang was a miracle sent by God, then the entire family must make sacrifices. Thus reassured, Nannerl sat down at the score with her brother. "To begin with, all these men are silly asses," she said. "Give the really good songs to Rosina. Look here, where she sings '*Ho sentito a dir da tutte le più belle*,' you can set these phrases as A and B and then repeat them, but with a different modulation."

Wolfgang saw at once what she meant. "Here," he said, "just where these three notes come in, this little fanfare, repeated later, but turned around .... And here, where Cassandro says he is not drunk, the strings can wobble .... Like Signor Affligio, in his cups!" They giggled. Neither of them liked the pompous dandy, who was always turning one calf or the other out to show his legs and the high-heeled shoes he wore with their massive bows and buckles.

Wolfgang thought Nannerl wonderful. She understood what he was thinking before he did. It was she who suggested that he use the symphony he had composed last January and change the ending, increasing the intensity and then changing from duple to triple meter so as to move directly into the first vocal ensemble. It was great fun to work together on the opera, which otherwise stretched before him endlessly. Nannerl felt she was violating no strictures, for helping her brother, who had already outstripped her in virtuosity, was something she did for the sake of others and not herself.

While Wolfgang and Nannerl were finishing the opera, delighting in pairing Rosina's voice with the oboe or with the trumpet in splendid and unusual arias, Leopold had a letter from the Chief Steward to the Archbishop in Salzburg. The correspondence informed him that he might stay away as long as he liked, but that he would no longer be paid to do so. "Here I am, Anna, spending *my* money in order to save the honor of *our* Prince among these Viennese, and he cuts me off!" Leopold paced furiously. So this is how a good servant is prized! I am sent to show to the world what God has bestowed on Salzburg! Why should I return to the very place where the ignorant have refused the evidence before their eyes? I owe it to God Almighty to endure these plots and persecutions as villains rise up against us. If I were to leave now, with my enemies in the field, what reputation would remain behind for my son?"

It was not unreasonable, Anna thought, for the Archbishop to want his servant back at work. "Perhaps," she ventured, "the Prince Archbishop has heard the rumors that you desire to stay in Vienna for good. Maybe we *should* go back home."

But Leopold would not hear of giving up, though he was increasingly frustrated by the delays that plagued his son's opera. At first, when the singers read through their parts at the Baron Van Swieten's palace, with Wolfgang at the clavier, they had applauded the boy's work. But then several wanted their arias rewritten. The performance was scheduled for Easter, but then Coltellini, who had refurbished Goldoni's libretto, insisted he must make further changes, until Easter and then Pentecost had passed. Then Affligio assured Leopold that the opera would be performed for the Emperor upon his return from Hungary.

During this time rumors swarmed thicker than the black flies that came with warmer weather: no twelve year-old boy could write an entire opera; it must be the father's composition. Leopold knew what to do about such empty mutterings, and he arranged for Wolfgang to compose an aria in public. The text would be chosen at random by one of the doubters. But even Wolfgang's masterful setting and orchestration of the text, done on the spot, did not result in the promised performance of the opera. Nor was there any sign of the hundred ducats that had been promised.

"They are jealous, Anna," fumed Leopold. "The famous Gluck, who cannot bear that a child composes better than he, is behind the whole conspiracy. Affligio says the singers do not like the opera. He says it is 'unsingable.' And this after what the singers have told us, that each aria fits its voice like a glove! Affligio reports that the orchestra does not wish to be conducted by a mere boy, but the musicians say they have no objection to the music or the boy!"

Anna laid aside her mending: they had stayed in Vienna so long that Wolfgang's sleeves needed to be lengthened. It seemed wrong to stay, she thought, where there was so much opposition. Leopold feared he might have no employment to return to in Salzburg, and Anna feared he was wearing out all his Viennese friends with his complaints of persecution and conspiracy. What could they do, when there were four mouths to feed and the possibility of no employment?

"I'm sorry, Leopold. You had such hopes for Vienna," she murmured.

Leopold looked at her with gratitude. Perhaps she understood after all what it was to be opposed by villains one could not quite identify and then to be harried by his employer in Salzburg as well.

Wolfgang came into the room, a smear of ink across his face. "Papa?" he queried, seeing his father's dark expression. "What is it?" He and Nannerl had taken to working on another opera, a little *singspiel* that Anna thought better suited to the child's talents than a grand *opera buffa*.

"Hush," said Anna quickly. "Papa is tired, Woferl."

"No, Anna. Why should the boy not know what villains are against us? This Affligio, he promises this and he promises that, but he has no intention to produce your opera, my son."

Wolfgang's eyes filled with tears. He was thoroughly tired of the opera, and now Papa was angry on his account. He pushed his soft, fair hair back from his face. He wanted to go home to Salzburg.

"It is all for spite and envy of this innocent boy," Leopold said, putting his hand on Wolfgang's shoulder, "this *German* boy, a prophet without honor in his own land. In the meantime, my money runs from my pockets like a river. Soon we will live under the bridge and feed on slops fit only for pigs, and wear nothing but rags."

Wolfgang's eyes widened. Was their situation really so desperate?

"Hush," Anna said. "You frighten the boy." She knew that money came into Leopold's pockets, for her children gave concerts nearly every day, whatever the fate of Wolfgang's opera. "You wanted everyone to envy Wolfgang's talents, my dear," she said. "Now you have succeeded and they envy him too much for your taste. You said yourself that the musicians are all on Woferl's side."

Leopold frowned. He wanted more than the good opinion of the musicians. "I shall appeal directly to the Emperor. He will not put up with the shame and calumny that this *Italian* wishes to heap on us."

"It is not a good idea, Leopold," Anna pleaded. "The Emperor has so many preoccupations. He - and I think his mother, too - will not look kindly on having to adjudicate your troubles with Affligio."

"You know nothing, Anna," retorted Leopold, who went straightway to his desk to compose his petition to the Emperor, who was, as Anna had feared, annoyed. There were greater affairs on his mind than this insistent musician from Salzburg, who never tired of advancing his son.

But the Emperor did order Affligio to pay Leopold the hundred ducats. "This is good," said Leopold to Anna, laying out the coins on the table, "but even better," he continued, "the Emperor has commanded that Wolfgang compose all the music for the consecration of the new orphanage chapel."

Disappointed by Anna's lack of enthusiasm, Leopold looked into the next room, where Wolfgang worked on a score and Nannerl practiced at the clavier. "Come," said Leopold to his son, "you must hear what the Emperor has given you to do! His Highness has said you will compose all the music - the mass, the offertory, and a trumpet concerto as well - for the new church at the orphanage. The orphans' choir is to sing, and you are to conduct it yourself. Altogether, Wolfgang, it is a great honor. I understand that the entire royal family will be in attendance. You will be redeemed in every eye, my child."

Nannerl listened reluctantly, not wanting to hear of her brother's preferment. Try as she might, it was difficult to stifle her envy of his opportunities.

It was not until December that the Orphanage Mass was performed. There Wolfgang stood, such a slight figure at the harpsichord, where the great orchestra he commanded could barely see his little arms in their red sleeves. The Emperor had allowed him a free hand, and Wolfgang had doubled the violas, his favorite stringed instrument. He had also added clarino trumpets, trombones and timpani. He had four of the best soloists in Vienna, a choir of thirty men and fifteen young orphan boys with the light voices of girls. Anna closed her eyes to hear the splendid music her child had written. There was much, she could tell, that he had learned from others- his father, Nannerl, Michael Haydn in Salzburg, Johann Bach in London. But he had done some things she had never heard in the works of other composers. This music, written by her own flesh and blood, taught her to hear in a new way. The boy had done everything to please his father, but now he was beginning to speak in his own voice.

When Wolfgang turned to bow to the assembled throng, his face was white from effort and glistened with a fine sweat. Nannerl leaned up against her mother, "It is very good, Mama, is it not?" she whispered.

Anna nodded, tears streaming.

To Leopold, the acclamation was a balm to the abrasions he had suffered. He hurried to the door of the chapel, basking in the adulation of those who had, not so long ago, been sure his son was a fraud and impostor.

"Ohh!" Nannerl exclaimed, remaining in the pew with her mother, "those trumpets! And the exclamations that start the Kyrie and come again at the Agnus Dei, but this time mournful because Christ has gone from the earth . . . ."

"Yes," mused Anna, "it is almost as though one were *there*. That beautiful soprano voice, coming out of nowhere, announcing 'He is risen!' Your brother remembered that it was the women who stayed with our Lord in his suffering and then took care of his broken body and sat by him to grieve."

Nannerl nodded. If she entered a convent like Nonnberg, she thought, perhaps she could serve God by composing such Masses herself. The tug of war, her father's preference for Wolfgang and her mother's insistence that Nannerl too should compose, would not touch her there.

Wolfgang, having taken the congratulations of the multitude, was at last free to greet his mother and sister. "Mama! Nannerl!" cried the boy. "Did you like it? The Emperor said it was first rate!"

"First rate, indeed!" exclaimed Anna, and "Wonderful!" cried Nannerl, almost as one, as they fell together, laughing and hugging.

"Now," said Leopold rejoining his family, "we can go back to Salzburg with our heads held up. I will order the horses tomorrow."

"Make sure you get fast ones, Papa!" said Wolfgang. "The faster, the better!"

33

1769

LEOPOLD HAD SET HIS SON TWO TASKS: Wolfgang must finish recasting his serenade into a symphony appropriate to take on their trip to Italy, and he must master a passage from Virgil. Wolfgang had developed an affection for Francesca Henschen and wanted nothing more than to write nonsense verses to her; far better than to parse the dull Latin passages his father set him! Still, he was an obedient youth and had quickly done as instructed. In need of diversion, he went into the front room, leaving the papers, ink and books neatly stacked as Papa required. Mama was sorting through the summer clothes brought back from their sixteen-month sojourn in Vienna, and Nannerl was mending a seam in the waistcoat Mama had embroidered for her son on the journey. "I think I will go out now," said Wolfgang, gently tugging the tendrils out of the tightly coiled braid of his sister's fair hair.

"To see the fair Francesca?" Nannerl teased him back.

"And why not?" answered Wolfgang, grinning. "I must go before Papa retur . . . ."

It was too late. Leopold came up the stairs and through the door. His face darkened as he took in the scene. He did everything for his son's benefit: this very morning he had endured Lolli's pretensions and young Michael Haydn's excuses. Such dullards as he must countenance! Were it not for the care he took of his son's reputation, Leopold might have advanced his own interests. At least his wife and daughter occupied themselves with useful pursuits, but his wastrel son had nothing better to do than pull his sister's hair! "Wolfgangus Theophilus," he said sternly, "I am surprised to find you lolling about with nothing better to do than torment your sister. I thought I had given you some occupation."

Wolfgang colored. His father always believed the worst of him. "I have finished the trio already," he said sulkily. He would not tell Papa of his pleasure in the G major movement for strings alone, the violas divided into separate voices as violins usually were. It was like coming home after a great occasion at court. In the minuet you could hear the people strutting about, trussed up in their finest clothes, uttering the expected platitudes. Arriving at the trio was a relief, as if tight clothing were loosened and dear friends could speak intimately of their tenderest sentiments. Wolfgang's mind was still full of the lush viola tone. "And yes, Papa, I finished the Latin, too," he added.

"So quickly?" inquired Leopold skeptically. "I will look over what you have done to correct the mistakes you likely made in your haste. But first, Anna, listen to what I have written." He shrugged off his cloak, which sheltered a small sheaf of papers. He held them up and read, " 'Your Serene Highness, Most Worthy High-born Prince,' etcetera . . . . "

"Etcetera, etcetera," parodied Wolfgang, bowing low, pointing his foot and flourishing his forward hand in ornate circles of deference.

Nannerl held her breath, sure that her father would be angered by Woferl's dramatics.

Anna felt weary. She did not know how to come between her husband and her son. Wolfgang was unkind, but she knew that he chafed at Leopold's constant demands. Still, she reminded herself, it was not unusual for boys of Wolfgang's age to work for hard taskmasters.

Leopold was not amused by his son's antics. "Woferl!" he admonished. "You must listen, too. You will not always be above composing such petitions. They are as needful as symphonies." He continued to read. " 'Your Serene Highness was recently most graciously pleased to permit . . . ', no, no - Woferl, run and dip this pen in ink. I want to change this. Ah, yes . . . 'ben-e-vo-lent-ly to permit me to remain some months longer in Vienna with my family, but your Highness gave orders that my salary should be withheld until my return. Since, however, this stay in Vienna was made against my will . . . .' "

"It was not, Leopold!" Anna interrupted. "You chose to stay."

Nannerl tightened her lips, wishing her mother would not contradict her father. Wolfgang rolled his eyes.

Leopold scowled. He went on, raising his voice a little, " *'against my will* and turned out to my disadvantage, I now therefore most humbly address to Your Serene Highness the request that I should not only be paid for the past month, but that you will also be most graciously pleased to give your gracious command that the arrears should also be handed to me. The greater this beneficence may now be, the more shall I endeavor to render myself worthy of it,' etcetera, etcetera."

"Etcetera, etcetera," echoed Wolfgang with another extravagant bow.

"This letter will come at an advantageous time, just before His Grace's birthday celebration," explained Leopold, drawing his brows together and pursing his lips at Wolfgang. What do you think?"

"Excellent, Papa," said Nannerl, hoping to forestall any more wrangling. She hated it when Mama and Papa argued.

Wolfgang looked expectantly from his father to his mother. Unlike Nannerl, he did not mind when his parents were at odds, which seemed more frequent than he remembered. He liked to see his mother oppose his masterful and confident father. Perhaps one day he would have the strength to do so himself.

Anna put down the summer coat she had been turning inside out when Leopold came in. "You asked my opinion, but you will not like it if I give it," she warned.

Leopold made an impatient gesture with his long-fingered hand.

"Very well, then," she said. "You stayed in Vienna of your own free will and for your own purposes. And you do not need the payment you request, my dear, as your children have brought you plenty of money. And there is this too, that you will soon ask the Archbishop for leave to travel again. It may not be wise to ask for so much. My advice is to leave well enough alone. There, now, I told you that you would not like to hear my thoughts."

Leopold found it galling enough to have to truckle to his employer without being taken to task by his wife, who should provide nothing but encouragement and praise to ease the difficulties of his life. He had invited her advice, but what he had wanted was her approval.

Leopold sent his "most submissive and obedient supplication" to the Archbishop, but did not immediately tell his employer that he would soon ask leave to travel to Italy. He determined to stay in Salzburg long enough to remind the Prince how valuable his son's services were. Then Wolfgang would travel with Leopold to Italy. He would not take Anna with him this time. She was too much inclined to interfere with what he thought best for his son.

Had anyone asked, Leopold would have said he was happily married, but increasingly he resented and feared Anna. Her offenses were numerous: seeking out his mother in Augsburg, dismissing the Italian servant in London, opposing the test that had proved Wolfgang's genius to all of Salzburg. And in Vienna, when Wolfgang had needed to marshal every resource, she had sometimes interfered and demanded that he take rest or go out-of-doors to do nothing more than waste his time. Leopold did not like to think about Anna's anger when he had taken Wolfgang out of the Schmalecker household to avoid the smallpox: it flickered at the edge of his awareness that he had been at fault in that instance and it seemed very wrong in his wife that she had made him see it.

He prayed that Nannerl would not grow up to be an interfering woman. The child had taken it into her head that she would ask for admission to the Nonnberg convent, but young Joseph von Mölk, older by three years than Nannerl, had paid court ever since their return from Vienna. She would be a fool to refuse von Mölk, though Leopold thought she seemed disinclined to encourage him. Either way, Leopold would be expected to come up with a dowry.

"Your daughter," Anna said, "has earned you a great deal of money with her performance and composition. You might consider that she can pay her *own* way."

Leopold looked at Anna as if she had spoken in a foreign tongue - one which he himself did not speak. Where did his wife get her crack-brained ideas, he wondered?

Anna was surprised when several weeks later the Archbishop ordered his Exchequer to pay Leopold for two of the several months he had overstayed his leave. Of far more moment than Leopold's back pay, though, the Archbishop had ordered that Wolfgang's Vienna opera, *La finta simplice*, be given its premiere performance for his name day celebration in May. All the best singers of his court would take part and surely would do the opera justice.

Wolfgang was equally pleased about another new project. Cajetan Hagenauer, now Father Dominicus, had requested that his dear friend Wolfgang compose the music for his first celebration of the Mass. Cajetan hoped that working on this composition would ease the pangs the boy felt at losing his playfellow to the monastery.

Leopold began to plan the journey he and his son would make to Italy. He wanted more than anything to dazzle the overweening Italians with Wolfgang's mastery of every musical form. Let them speak slightingly of German genius after they had heard his son! In the time he was not needed at court, he penned a new preface for the second edition of his *Violinschule.*

Father Dominicus' first Mass, with Wolfgang's splendid music, was a great success. Lorenz Hagenauer invited Salzburg's most eminent citizens to a lavish celebration in honor of his son. The festivities lasted all afternoon, ending finally with a concert given by Wolfgang and Nannerl.

Though Nannerl had said so to no one, she thought of this as her farewell performance. She wore her most elegant dress, a blue-green watered taffeta with Brussels lace at the neck and sleeves and a rich velvet underskirt. Mama had dressed her hair to true Parisian height and fastened it around with a blue-green satin ribbon. Nannerl played pieces of her own earlier composition to perfection, allowing her passion for the music to carry her to depths and heights she had avoided since it became apparent that her own ambitions had deadly consequences. She intended to approach the Nonnberg sisters as soon as her father and brother had left for Italy. But this afternoon, feeling that there was no harm in indulging herself since she meant to renounce what she loved, she surrendered herself entirely to the music.

Joseph von Mölk had asked Nannerl if he might walk her home following the festivities. She did not wish his company but could think of no excuse. She walked along in a euphoria of the music she had made, the applause it had brought.

"It truly amazes me," he said in his fusty way, "that you should play so well, Nannerl."

"And why is that?" she asked absently. She did not much like Joseph, but her father reminded her often that she could do worse than to set her sights on a von Mölk.

Joseph had a round face with small eyes and wore a head of his own fine brown hair, of which he was unduly vain. "Because, it is well known that a woman cannot, by her very nature, truly distinguish herself in music," he said pedantically.

First cold, then heat rose in a flood through her entire being. She thought she might burst out of her stays, the silk and velvet that bound her. She imagined an explosion of scalding blood and tissue. Joseph had just heard her play splendid music of her own composition and nevertheless said what she had done was impossible! She could not risk a word.

Joseph went on, having no idea what turmoil his words had set into motion. "From time immemorial," he said complacently, "there have been instruments about, and pens and manuscript paper, yet show me the work of any woman that has achieved greatness. Show me any woman who holds a high post in any sovereign's court." He touched her arm. "Nannerl, I should tell you, I intend directly to ask your father for your hand."

Nannerl felt his touch as an insult. She thought she must surely drown in the tide of emotion that swept through her. She clasped her hands together to keep from hitting out at this dullard who considered himself her suitor. "You must not," she gasped.

"No?" He raised his negligible eyebrows.

"No," she said. "I must not marry."

"But Nannerl," he said. "We have known one another from childhood, and you are eminently suitable to make me a good wife."

"No," she said, shaking her head. She realized that she must not be rude to Joseph von Mölk, whose family were friends with her family. "I can say no more just now. You have," she choked on the words she must say for courtesy's sake, "done me an honor and I am sorry, but no. I mean to enter Nonnberg soon." She fled up the stairs to her house, where she flung herself on the bed and beat on the bedcovers until she was spent.

The following day Margarethe came to Anna's house for a visit. Her father was away, so Margarethe was free to come and go. The sounding insects in the trees and the unusually warm October air streamed through open windows, filling both women with contentment. "Tell me about Wolfgang's Mass," said Margarethe. She must learn about such occasions more through report than attendance, as Jews were not often welcome.

"I liked it," Anna reported, "though not so well as his Mass for the orphanage in Vienna." What a pity that her friend could not hear for herself, connoisseur of music that she was.

Nannerl joined them. Her eyes were still swollen and she was abstracted and restless. "I must go," she said at last. "Fritzi Zitterbarth wants his lesson, and I have lingered overlong because I like so much to see you, Margarethe." She kissed her friend and her mother.

The two women watched Nannerl, usually so lithe on her feet, leave the room slowly, as if weighted down.

"She is the ghost of herself!" Margarethe exclaimed.

Anna nodded, worried. "Tell me what *you* see," she said.

"Her beauty, for one thing. It has always been so rich, so abundant - the way her lips curve, her enormous eyes with their dark lashes, all that luxuriance of hair, her fine complexion. But she has skinned back all her hair into a braid so tight it pulls her eyes sideways. She has been weeping, I think. And she is so thin. Everything about her seems rigid, bound, somehow, as if she wished to confine herself in the smallest possible space." She put her slender ringed hand on Anna's arm. "I was startled. I do not mean to alarm you, but she looks most unhappy."

Anna studied her hands. "She played brilliantly at the Hagenauer's party, Margarethe, and yet I think she cried herself to sleep afterwards. She will not tell me why."

"You have no idea?" asked Margarethe.

"For a long time, she has insisted that she should not perform nor compose, though Leopold has insisted that she must. She took her illness in the Hague as a warning from God that she was doing what is unnatural in a woman. In Vienna, Leopold made her help Woferl with his opera, and she obeyed him, but under protest. It seemed to me she wanted to and thought she should not." Anna let out her breath, puffing her cheeks. "She tells me little, as if I were the enemy. There is none of the easy conversation we once had, though she is polite, correct. She confides - so far as I can tell - in no one. She seems more drawn to Leopold than to me, though she is distant with him as well. He calls her sulky, and she *is* withdrawn."

Anna had told Margarethe how Leopold had chosen his son over his daughter in Vienna when the pox had raged through the capital. "Leopold has always preferred Wolfgang," she said softly now, "neglecting to credit Nannerl for her work, attributing hers to the boy as well as his own."

"And all the world seconds him," sighed Margarethe.

Both women were silent a long while. Finally Anna said, her voice low, "I fear Leopold, Margarethe. He would pull Wolfgang's strings as if he were a puppet. Here is a boy of thirteen years, eager to make his way and Leopold . . . . He wants to take Wolfgang to Italy - alone, just the two of them."

"Nannerl will not go?" inquired Margarethe. "Nor you?"

"No," said Anna. "Nannerl says she will go to the nuns at Nonnberg. Oh, but Margarethe, I see the yearning in her eyes when Leopold speaks of the Italian cities. Leopold says I must stay behind as well, and I know he wants me far off, unable to interfere with his schemes."

"All my life my father has had absolute control, Anna" said Margarethe, rubbing her hands together. Her voice was low, matching her friend's. Only finely tuned ears could hear their discourse. "If my father knew how I defy him, writing poetry meant to be read, who knows what he might do?" She shivered. "I tend to his needs. He gives me the money I need to order his household. He is not a kind man, Anna," she said hesitantly. "A rich man, yes. He sees that I have food to eat, a roof to shelter under, clothes to wear and books to read, since I am so much indoors, but my passions, my soul . . . . These are frivolities, he thinks, of which I have no need. But I defy him. I come to you, at least when he is away, and I write my poor poems. Wolfgang, too, will defy his father one day, if he is leashed too tightly."

Anna felt tears rim her eyes. "Oh Margarethe," she said, "what would I do without you?"

Margarethe squeezed Anna's hand in answer. "Now, what will you do about Nannerl?"

"You know that I have wanted her to have what I did not," said Anna, "to compose, to have music. I have hoped the way would open for her. But," she said slowly, "she must choose her own path. I cannot do it for her."

PART 6

34

1769

LEOPOLD AND WOLFGANG left Salzburg in December, taking with them the Archbishop's blessing and 120 ducats from his treasury.

Nannerl longed for equanimity. She had felt numb and tired since Joseph von Mölk's proposal, and she slept fitfully the night before her father's and brother's departure. She had drifted in and out of restless dreams, in which domed Italian cities beckoned and were transformed into gardens, perpetually golden with sunshine, the rich foliage burdened with blooms and fruits. Minstrels wandered the orchard paths, reaching out for the brilliant plenty, the fruit bursting into partitas and chaconnes, sonatas and operas at their touch. Nannerl knew that she must not eat of that fruit. She must endure the punishment visited upon Eve.

And then Nannerl was awake, staring into the dark and railing at God. Why did not other women seem dissatisfied with their lot? Even her mother, once a musician, appeared to wear her exile lightly. Nannerl could only conclude that her mother could not have lusted for music as fiercely as she herself did.

Finally, as the interminable night yielded to the thinner darkness that precedes morning, Nannerl shook her brother. "Get up," she whispered. "There is something I must say to you before you leave for Italy. We can fetch the bread and talk as we go."

His sister's manner overcame Wolfgang's desire to pull the covers back over his head. "It is freezing!" he whispered as he put his thin legs over the bedside. He pulled on his breeches, stockings and shirt and had his cloak wrapped around him in a trice.

Nannerl and Wolfgang found Anna in the kitchen still in her nightshift with her hair hanging in a long braid. She had been up for an hour, preparing a basket of food for her husband and son to take. By candlelight she packed the last of the newly made, mended and cleaned clothes, and on top of that all the remedies she could imagine the travelers could possibly need. She was surprised to see her children up and dressed before dawn. Nannerl looked drawn. Anna could only guess what torments had troubled her daughter's sleep. Her children had never before been separated, except for that brief and terrible time in Vienna when Leopold had taken Wolfgang and run from the smallpox. This separation, Anna thought, would be longer and harder on them both.

Nannerl and Wolfgang hurried toward Brotgasse, the street of bakers, drawn by the perfume of proofing and baking yeast. They were deeply muffled in their heavy cloaks and early morning stupor, and Nannerl could not remember the careful words she had thought of during the night. Trying to stifle the resentment she felt, she burst out, "Woferl, you will have everything in Italy. Everything will come to you."

"Nannie," pleaded Wolfgang, "can you not come too? Surely Papa . . . . "

"No," she said sternly. "I must not. Papa does not wish it. I must go to Nonnberg."

"You are not meant to be a nun," argued Wolfgang. He could not imagine his beautiful, gifted sister bundled up in a black robe and kept behind walls. It was bad enough that his playfellow, Cajetan, had become Father Dominicus, but to lose Nannerl . . . . It would be like losing a part of himself. "What about von Mölk? Can you not marry him?"

Nannerl winced. "No, Woferl, I cannot marry him. The real problem is music: it is a disease in me. Composition especially."

Wolfgang had to strain to hear his sister. He was startled by her half-whispered words. "No!" he exclaimed. "That is not so, Nannerl! Music cannot be a disease."

"It is," said Nannerl, making clear that there was nothing more to say in that regard. "But listen, Woferl. You will learn so much, meet so many of the greatest musicians. Everything will come easily to you. It always does. You will get *scritturas* for operas. Papa will see to it." She held up her hand to stop him. "Not like that foolishness in Vienna, where everything was like one great, complicated plot. But real, signed *scritturas*, with good librettos and the best singers. Wolfgang," she said, turning to face him and grasping his thin shoulders in her strong hands, "I want you to promise me . . . . "

"I will," he said, shaken by the solemnity of his sister's face, her tone of voice and the way her fingers dug down through layers of wool into his bones. "I will, but what have I just promised?"

"That you will always," she said with deliberation, "*always* do your best. For me. As if I were beside you." Nannerl had a notion that if her own voice could somehow find its way into Wolfgang's music, she would not lose everything while locked up in the convent.

Wolfgang studied his sister's dear face. She looked to him pale and unhappy, but perhaps it was the gray morning light. She was so much older and wiser than he. He had always depended on her guidance, her ideas. He shivered and confessed, "It frightens me, to think of Papa and me, just the two of us, without you or Mama."

Nannerl did not want to hear anything against her father. "Papa knows the world," she said - a world that said to her, "music is beyond your reach," and to her brother, "music is your destiny." If Papa did not know best, how was she to understand anything? "Papa knows how to find the right people to advance your fortunes as no one else can," Nannerl said. "He cares about nothing else, Woferl." She was careful to keep a note of bitterness out of her voice.

"It is not so easy," grumbled Wolfgang.

"No," Nannerl agreed, "it's not."

As they neared their home they slowed their steps, knowing that they might never again walk out together like this, sharing their hearts. An accident, a broken wheel on the carriage, robbers armed with pistols, plagues - what dangers lay between them? "All right, Nannerl, I promise," said Wolfgang, solemnly, stopping to face his sister. "In fact, I promise to give the best arias to the women. I will think of you every time I compose anything, operas especially. I will think of all that I have learned from you."

Nannerl put her arms around her brother, holding him for a long time, though the bread was crushed between them. As they went into the kitchen, Anna looked from the misshapen bread to her children's faces and knew that they had said a difficult good-bye.

Once Leopold and Wolfgang were gone, the house echoed dismally. For twenty-two years, Leopold's wants and needs had ordered Anna's life, and for the last thirteen years she had watched her little son grow from an unlikely scrap of squalling red flesh to an accomplished, good-natured boy. Now they had gone for who-knew-how-long and she was left with her prickly daughter, now a woman of eighteen years. I have lived almost fifty years on this earth, she thought, and what I have to show for it are these children, these remarkable creatures, whose flesh and bone were formed within me. Now they are separate from me.

Nannerl prowled restlessly from one room to the next. Disconsolate, she could not sit still but was unsure what to do. She felt the pull and itch of the harpsichord, where she might play the morning away, but she resisted until, berating herself for her weak resolve, she sat down at the instrument and tried to open the lid. "Mama," she called, in irritation. "Have you the key to the harpsichord?"

Anna woke from her daze. "No," she answered, coming to the instrument. She tried to lift the lid. "Locked?" she mused. Together they looked everywhere for the small key. "Leopold, in his haste, must have locked it," said Anna. "Surely he would not deliberately . . . ." Suddenly she heard her heart beating like a great timpanum. She felt the urge to claw and screech and stamp her feet as if she were a child in a transport of temper.

"Yes, Mama, he did," said Nannerl. Papa must have known that she would succumb to the call of the instrument and decided to lock it up, taking the key to Italy. "Dear Papa," she said, though she felt hot anger coursing through her veins. He had known her better than she knew herself, known her weakness. "I must go to Nonnberg now," she said. "Today. Will you come? Please?"

"Are you sure, Nannerl?" Anna asked, putting her hands on either side of her daughter's face and looking deeply into her eyes.

Nannerl nodded and pulled away. "Now, Mama. I must go now." She could not bear to be another minute in the apartment with the locked harpsichord, a signal to her that she must finally act with resolution, having temporized too long.

So it was that Anna walked up the long Nonnberg steps with her daughter, who had dressed as plainly as might be for the occasion. Nannerl had braided her thick hair in a plait pinned up around her head. She had left off eardrops.

But even so, the slatey blue of her plain worsted bodice lit up her eyes and showed off her small waist and long arms to advantage. She was, thought Anna, enough to cause any young man shortness of breath. Joseph von Mölk was only the latest, though Nannerl seemed averse to him.

"Sister Gisella - may she rest in peace," said Anna, crossing herself, "was able to make any music she liked. Perhaps you may do the same, my dear."

Nannerl stopped, dappled in the shadow cast by trees that overhung the wall and the steep stairway. "Mama," she said firmly, "that is just what you must not wish for me. It is to get away from music that I must come here." Secretly, Nannerl harbored her mother's hope, that she might be required to use her gifts in divine service, obedient both to God and the community. If she renounced her ambitions, she reckoned, they might nevertheless be rekindled so long as they did not serve worldly vanity nor come from her own desires. She would be obedient, but there was always the chance . . . . She could not fully admit such scheming to consciousness, lest she undercut her longing for uncluttered vocation.

Anna was glad to pause. "My old bones protest these stairs," she laughed. "I used to skim up and down them, as if they were level ground." She grew serious. "Does it seem to you wrong - I mean somehow sinful - to pursue music?" she asked, not sure where she ought to probe.

Nannerl looked at her mother pityingly. She understood nothing. "Oh, Mama," she sighed. "Can you not see it? How people have died?"

"Died?" Anna asked, puzzled. "What do you mean?"

Nannerl would say no more on the subject. In her interview with the Abbess Emma, Nannerl said merely that she felt a strong call to the Benedictines at Nonnberg.

Abbess Emma was incredulous that a young woman, so beautiful, renowned for her musical performance and worldly in her tastes, should want to join the Nonnberg ladies. Of course, women of all kinds entered into abbeys, but the Nonnberg nuns had followed the Mozart children with close attention and pride. They had secretly hoped for Nannerl's success, even more than Wolfgang's, because the child so much resembled her mother. The Abbess, who had taught Anna needlework and lace-making when she was the plump and merry Sister Emma, still had a lilt to her voice, but she was an old woman now, with seventy-five years on her head and a palsy in her hands. The nuns had been saddened that Anna could not keep up her music nor grown famous for it, as Sister Gisella had hoped. But even Sister Gisella had known - and confessed as much in the chapter - that Anna would not find it easy to pursue a life of music, the world being what it was.

The Abbess raised her hand, which in addition to tremors, was crippled with the stiffness and pain of old age. "St. Benedict has commanded," she said, "that newcomers not be granted an easy entry. The spirit must be tested, to see if the calling is from God or from a lesser source. You may knock at our door, my child, but your knock may not be answered for days or even weeks. If you persist, you will be allowed to enter and stay as a guest for a few days. Then you will live in the novitiate with the other novices. St. Benedict says, 'The concern must be whether the novice truly seeks God and whether she shows eagerness for the Work of God, for obedience and for trials.' "

Nannerl, unable to hear the warning in the old nun's voice, was eager to begin knocking. She was sure that once she was admitted as a novice, the way would open before her, a broad path, plainly marked, without tangled growth or diverging trails, and that the other nuns would applaud her purpose, her dedication, the depth of her renunciation of the world. She knocked by day and stayed upon her knees into the dark of night, praying in the chapel, whose old stones were always cold and damp. She often did not creep into her bed until the wee hours.

And so Anna found herself much alone. One evening, when she sat by herself, working a nearly-finished piece of lace, a strange figure - a young man, by the look of it - came half panting, half weeping up the stairs without knocking. "Anna!" gasped the unknown person, stumbling across the hall toward her. Anna recognized Margarethe's familiar voice, though so odd was the apparition's appearance that Anna doubted her ears.

Margarethe - for indeed it was Margarethe - was wearing a man's clothing, though so hastily and slovenly put on as might befit a tavern drunkard, and her hair was cut short, standing up about her head in uneven clumps of ringlets. Her face was marked, red and swollen, one eye nearly closed.

"Margarethe?" asked Anna, going to put her arms about her friend, who collapsed against her. "Margarethe? What has happened to you? But never mind. Come in and sit down. I have the fire going. Put my shawl around you. You're shivering. I let the servant go for the evening, Nannerl being away. Let me run across to the tavern and get you something strong to drink."

"No, no. Stay, Anna," said Margarethe, still breathing hard. "I knew I could come to you." She sat still, hugging Anna's shawl around her, her eyes closed.

Anna pulled her chair up close and took her friend's hand. "Tell me," she said, fearing that Margarethe had been attacked, perhaps by a robber who saw the rings on her fingers. But no, her rings were still in place. Could it have been someone inflamed to see a Jew in the streets?

"My father found my poems," Margarethe said, gently touching the puffy skin around her eye. "Or rather, not my father, but my servant, Rachael. The hateful girl must have seen me locking them away, or maybe my father asked her to spy. I don't know why she was watching me, but she looked in the locked cabinet in my bedchamber. I kept the key with my ribbons." A wracking sob coursed through her body. Margarethe tugged the shawl more tightly around her shoulders, then sighed deeply and loosened it a little.

"Whatever the case," she continued, "Rachael gave my papers - all of my poetry, written over these many years in Salzburg, and some from even before - to my father, who came storming into my room last night, shook them under my nose and called me 'strumpet.' 'Wicked, ungrateful strumpet,' he raged at me, and threw them one by one into the stove. I tried to stop him, but he grabbed me by the hair - I had plaited it for the night - and he took hold of it and forced me down onto my knees. I had been sitting there embroidering and there were scissors at hand, and he cut off my hair, all the time railing at me, how I had betrayed his trust, how careful he had to be, how if the Archbishop heard what I had been up to, he would be finished at court."

Margarethe touched her unruly hair, which sprang in every direction. "Strumpet," she said wonderingly. "He called me strumpet." She smiled ruefully, though her lower lip was cut and probably, thought Anna, painful. "Imagine, in this day and age! He could not think of anything worse, I suppose. But how could he think my poems would get out and damage him? They were hidden, after all, under lock and key, not published where someone could read them! And then, Anna, with my hair all over me and all over the floor, he went to my wardrobe and with my own scissors, ripped up my dresses, cursing me the whole while, saying that I was an ungodly woman who had brought disgrace on every woman of my race. He left for a few minutes and then he returned with some of his clothes, which he threw at me. 'You want to be a man?' he shouted." She shuddered. "He screamed at me, 'Then dress as a man and make your way in the world.' He beat me about the face and forced me out into the street. I came to you, lurking along the walls, hoping no one would discover me in the shadows. I could not think what else to do."

"You did right," said Anna. Her mind was racing as she fetched cold water and bathed Margarethe's cuts and bruises, gently smoothing on a healing liquor of arnica flowers boiled in water. "Something my mother taught me," she said. Tenderly she combed her friend's cropped hair. "It's so thick," she comforted. "I think with a little trimming, it will look very handsome and be cool and easy to manage. I will trim it, or Nannerl, when she returns."

"Nannerl!" said Margarethe, startled. "I hadn't thought of her. No, Anna. No one else must know." And then, as if struck, "But everyone *will* know. What shall I do, Anna? Where can I go? I have no means." She looked wildly around her. "I will have to go back to my father, beg his forgiveness and submit to his rule. I must give up poetry, for every servant from now on will be a spy."

"Wait," said Anna. "For tonight there is the bed in Leopold's study where his students sometimes stay. Nannerl is out early every morning to knock at Nonnberg, so we can decide what to do when she has gone."

Anna helped Margarethe to undress and gave her a shift to sleep in. "You may have a dress of mine," she said, and kissed her friend as if she were one of the children.

In the morning, when Nannerl had taken her bread and coffee and gone to Nonnberg, Anna found Margarethe awake. "Listen," said Anna, as she sat down in the kitchen to keep Margarethe company at breakfast. "You must go back to your father. I can see no way around it, since you cannot set up housekeeping alone or go to other relations. He will have repented, for he needs you. But your father goes out almost every day, sometimes out of Salzburg altogether, and so you can keep on with your poetry. Hide what you write on your person, till you bring it here. I will keep it for you, in the trunk where I have stored all of my compositions, under the best linen. No one will ever think to look for it here."

Margarethe's head throbbed, the bruises on her face purple, the skin tight and shiny. "I cannot think what else to do," she said. "But how will I even get back to my father's house?"

"Wait till you are sure your father has left. Then you can wear my black dress," said Anna, "and a veil, as if in mourning."

Margarethe nodded gratefully. "If you will trim my hair, I will take your dress for a week while I have some new clothes made." Left unspoken by both women was the possibility that Margarethe's father might refuse to pay for new clothing or even the more essential meals and lodging.

That is how close to beggary I am as well, thought Anna.

35

1770

MARGARETHE'S FATHER DID TAKE HER BACK into the house and paid for new clothing, though he let her know she would live, henceforth, under the strictest surveillance. Anna worried about her friend, but even more about her daughter's state.

Nannerl went daily to Nonnberg, waiting and receiving no answer, and her conviction grew muddy. She went every evening for the vespers service, letting the disembodied nuns' voices revive her spirits as they floated through the transom into the cold stone chapel. She prayed for patience, persistence and clarity, but the distinct voice that had called her to the religious life grew faint. At last, one day, she stayed abed, not going to Nonnberg to knock, not dressing, ignoring the clavier lessons she was bound to give, covering her head and sleeping. She stayed in her bed the next day and the next, neither eating nor speaking.

Anna tried everything she could think of to arouse Nannerl to attention. "Look," she said, "Papa sent the harpsichord key back, with apologies. He did not mean to take it with him." She played on the harpsichord, hoping that Nannerl would be impatient with her mother's lesser proficiency and come to take her place. Anna read Leopold's and Wolfgang's letters aloud, but found no answering spark of interest; Nannerl merely covered her head with the quilt.

After five days, Anna sent for Silvester Barisani, the Archbishop's physician and good friend to the Mozarts. "I see nothing wrong with the girl," Silvester said to Anna, frowning. "She will not get up? Nor take any nourishment?"

"A sip of water, now and then," said Anna. "She neglects her pupils, shows no interest in the letters that come from Italy. Leopold and Wolfgang are in Milan now," she said, answering the quickened interest she saw in the physician's face. The Barisani family came originally from Padua and retained their ties with that city. "Wolfgang chastises her," she said, eager to draw Silvester's attention back to her daughter's plight, "for not answering his letters."

"I believe," said the doctor, "that Nannerl suffers from melancholy. I will send a surgeon to bleed her of these ill humors and send a tonic as well to fortify her blood. But you, my dear Anna, must find something to take her attention. I have seen a number of young ladies lose all interest in life. It is not easy to revive them," he said, half to himself, mystified by the obscurity of the female frame. It was precisely such megrims and vapors that rendered women unfit for the world's work.

Then one day there came a knocking at the door. Anna answered it, then flew up the stairs and into Nannerl's room. "Get up at once, Nannerl," she ordered. "Theresa says that Adelheide Althaus is desperately ill. We are needed to help."

Nannerl did get up, washed and dressed herself and did her hair, though without her usual care. Anna did not mind. Her daughter was upright, took both coffee and bread with a thick slather of butter, and was willing to walk out with her to tend the old lady's needs.

"Old Adelheide must have a hundred years, maybe more," said Anna. "As long as I have lived in Salzburg, she has been a prickly soul, grumbling and predicting ill events." She hurried with Nannerl through the snowy streets to the old lady's apartment above the iron monger's. "It seemed to me she was old when your father and I were only just married, always scolding, always ready to wound with her sharp tongue." The Widow Althaus had been a constant in Anna's life, complaining, criticizing, trading in scandal, petty report and grotesquerie, uttering two nays for every yea. For some years now she had hobbled around on sticks, her wizened face sunk into pits, her toothless mouth caved in.

Nannerl, having lain in bed for some weeks, was not so swift as her mother. "Slow down!" she panted, and Anna slowed her steps. "Poor old thing," Nannerl said, when she had caught her breath. "I came upon some children taunting her one day, calling her a witch. I chased them away and told them they should be ashamed, and then Frau Althaus scolded me for intemperance."

Anna was delighted to see the beginnings of a smile on Nannerl's face. She had not spoken so much since she had left off knocking at Nonnberg.

A tall figure, well-wrapped in a fur-trimmed cloak, fell in step beside Nannerl. It was Armand d'Ippold, who bade them good morning. Armand was a tall, good looking military man, with snapping black eyes, a thick black mustache and black curling hair, which had begun to show gray. It was said he had gypsy blood in him, but that had never bothered the Mozarts, who had always found him lively company.

Anna was pleased that Nannerl fell into conversation with Armand.

After a few moments of quiet conversation, Anna heard Armand exclaim, "But of course you can play!"

"I have given it up," said Nannerl, but the toss of her head was flirtatious.

"What nonsense!" he said. "You play better than anyone. We *must* have you for the ball. We cannot dance, otherwise."

"But what if *I* want to dance?" Nannerl asked coyly.

"Then," said Armand, "you will have to do with a lesser musician at the harpsichord."

When they reached Adleheide's house, Anna gladly left her daughter outside with Armand, absorbed in conversation. She felt a great weight lift to see Nannerl's spirits so improved. She had never thought of Armand d'Ippold as a suitor - he was twenty years Nannerl's senior - but just now, she would welcome anyone who roused the sleeping beauty from her slumbers. As Anna climbed up three steep flights of steep stairs, she wondered how old, crippled Adleheide had managed.

There was no answer to Anna's knocking, but the door was not latched. The room was cold, hoarfrost rimming the windows on the inside. Anna crossed herself as she saw the small mound that was Adleheide Althaus laboring to breathe under a pile of ragged and greasy old quilts. "Cold," croaked the old lady, "cold."

There was no fire in the stove. The wood box held only enough sticks to start a fire, and the larder only a few scrapings of hard cheese and a stale crust. Anna could hear the scuttlings of mice in the walls and found plenty of droppings to show her that the creatures had no doubt fed better than Adelheide.

Nannerl arrived at the doorway, her face rosy. She had a happy, clear look that Anna had not seen for she could not remember how long.

"We need wood," Anna told Nannerl, "and some of the broth I made yesterday - also some clean quilts, one of my nightshifts, herbs and clean rags for poultices."

"Armand is waiting. He said he would help," said Nannerl. "He and I will go back and get what is needed."

With the little wood that was left, Anna started a fire and set a brick in the mouth of the stove. When it was warm, finding no flannel, she sacrificed her pinafore and put the wrapped brick against the old lady's feet. She fetched water and set a kettle to begin warming, then washed the shriveled limbs tenderly, astonished that so little flesh could cover a body. She lay poultices of healing herbs against the open sores on the bony hips and heels and held spoonfuls of warm broth to the nearly lipless mouth, which sucked as greedily as a babe's. Together, she and Nannerl stripped off the filthy sheets and replaced them with Anna's lavender-scented linens, trying to disturb the old woman as little as they could. They covered her with clean feather quilts and began a watch by her side that lasted for nearly a week.

Anna was stricken to think that, in her concern for her best friend and her daughter, she had neglected to inquire after the old lady. Now she and Nannerl took turns sitting with her, returning home to sleep, collect clean nightshifts and steep more herbs to bathe the dying woman's sores. Other Salzburg women stopped in to help, though the Mozart women, having no men to look after, took most of the burden of the death watch.

In spite of their ministrations, Adleheide's breathing grew more labored, the rattle in her chest louder. When at last she died, with an astonished look on her face, Anna felt a larger loss than she would have expected. "Who would have thought that I would feel so sad? Never, ever had she a kind thing to say to anyone. She loved bad news and doom more than meat and drink. Yet already I miss her pickled tongue."

There were many hands to help in the preparation of the old body for its Christian burial. The women worked together, washing the dried out limbs, setting coins on the scaly eyelids, combing through her tangle of thin hair, dressing her in a clean shift and finally sewing the shroud. Many, like Anna, who had rolled their eyes and sighed at her approach, mourned the loss of the cantankerous old soul.

"She would sour milk by looking at it," commented Marianna. "She said to me one time, 'You are very spry,' and told me all the reasons I should be cranky. I was always twice as jolly when she was about, just to spite her." She laughed.

"I've heard it said she was a great beauty in her time," mused Lise Bruner, "though 'tis hard to see now."

"I've heard she was married to a rich and handsome count," said Babette Möll.

"Hmmm," said Anna. "I heard her husband was a merchant, dealing in - what? - I have forgotten. Whalebone? Ivory? Adleheide once said I owed my buttons to her husband."

"And buried ten children before they were old enough to marry," said Marianna.

"She has hardly anything," said Theresa, inventorying her meagre room. "Only threads to wear, odd pots and plates . . . ." The women were sorting through Adleheide's few possessions, as none knew of any kin.

"She boasted once," said Henriette, "that her mother was a witch and her father a wolf. She told me she was left, a changeling, on the doorstep of the Cathedral, to be brought up by the cooper's wife."

"She told *me*," said Theresa, "that her father was an Hungarian prince, her mother a slave girl brought from Africa. She said that her husband was in the Archbishop's employ."

"She told *me*," Marianna said, "she was never born at all, but hatched from the egg of a bird who laid it in a craggy place in Moravia." Marianna was cleaning out the old, black wardrobe. "Wait," she exclaimed. "What is this? Here in the back. It is too heavy . . . . Here, Nannerl, help me move this pile of stuff . . . ." She pulled out a cooking pot, black with age and use. The lid was rusted on. Anna brought the poker to pry it open and Marianna lifted off the lid, peered in and caught her breath. She put her hand in hesitantly to stir the contents.

"What is it?" asked Anna. "Here, let me look."

Marianna looked stunned. "It's money!" she exclaimed, "gulden, shillings, thalers, some half crowns and louis d'ors and here's some kind of coin I do not recognize." She sat down on the floor and poured the contents of the pot out into her lap. Her apron sagged between her legs with the weight of the treasure.

The women goggled, dumbfounded. "It was true, then," breathed Anna. "She had a fortune, but hidden away while she lived a pauper almost, in old rags and without proper food and no heir to claim her pot of gold."

"What should we do with it?" Nannerl asked, dazzled. She sometimes tried to imagine the money she and her brother had earned, all in one place at one time, in a great pile like that in Frau Gilowsky's lap. There must be a fair amount - wherever her father kept it - for they were always handsomely rewarded for their performances. If she had all that money, at least what she had earned, perhaps she could ignore what everyone said and do as she liked.

"We must give the money to the priest. He will know what to do," said Babette.

Marianna sighed. "I know it is not ours to keep, but what would we do with it if it were?"

"I would buy silk and satin, yards and yards of it, to make up some clothes," said Lise, who always imagined that her plainness would give way to beauty if only she had the right dresses.

"I would buy new furniture. Mine is so old and scuffed," said Babette, who was, in Anna's opinion, somewhat house proud.

"I would travel," said Theresa. "Lorenz too. Go everywhere. To London. To Russia. To China. The American colonies. Everywhere."

Anna was silent. She was thinking of Adelheide Althaus, whose face had resembled a dried apple, her lively and malevolent eyes taking in everything, who spoke out of spite, living on crusts and parings and salting away her fortune, day after day, year after year, all the while rich enough to eat well and take her ease.

"What about you, Nannerl?" asked Marianna. "What would you do if all that, or a share of it, were yours?"

Anna looked up, interested to hear what her daughter would say.

"I?" Nannerl said. She thought for a long while. Finally she said firmly, "I would - if it were mine to do with just as I liked - I would give it to my father to advance my brother's fortunes."

"That is very generous of you, I am sure," said Theresa dryly. She had had high hopes for Nannerl's success in the musical world and was disappointed by the girl's withdrawal from composition and performance. "What about you, Anna?"

Anna wondered. She was surprised at Nannerl's intention to promote only her brother's success. "With such a lot of money? Hmmm. I suppose I would do something silly, hire a carriage and go back to St. Gilgen where I was born, just to see what it is really like. I cannot remember very well, and Leopold thinks it foolish to go to a town that has nothing to commend it." She felt uneasy. She would do better to have larger wants. Surely there were greater things to be done with so much money. She would like a bigger house, to be sure, but she would not say so for fear of wounding Theresa, whose house the Mozarts had lived in for twenty-two years. "I know," she said triumphantly. "I would buy a pair of spectacles!"

"Well," said Theresa dismissively, "you hardly need a fortune to buy spectacles, Anna. Lorenz paid only a few farthings for his."

Marianna held out her hands, which she had run through the money. "What a waste," she said softly. "Here she had enough to live as she liked, and she hid what she had, hoarded it, and lived in such a straitened way. Why would she do it?"

It was a question everyone is Salzburg asked everyone else. "Why would she do a thing like that?" Nannerl asked Margarethe, who had eked out a brief visit from a walk to the goldsmith's on her father's behalf. Anna had not yet returned from the bakery, affording Nannerl a rare opportunity to speak privately to her mother's friend.

Margarethe pondered. "I believe your rabbi told a story about a man who entrusted his servants with talents in various amounts. Two of them used the money to make more money, while one buried his share in the ground, where it earned no interest nor bore any fruit."

"My rabbi?" quizzed Nannerl.

"Your Christ," said Margarethe gently. "He was a Jewish man and a teacher, a rabbi."

Nannerl was startled to think in this way.

Nannerl was curious. "Do you read in the Gospels?" she asked

"I read whatever I can," Margarethe said briefly.

Margarethe watched Nannerl closely. She knew of the girl's melancholy, which had so perturbed Anna. "The old lady, Frau Althaus, buried her talent in the ground, where it could not grow nor enrich her life nor the lives of others," she said, noticing that Nannerl clenched her hands in her lap. Margarethe laid her thin and spotted hand on Nannerl's young and supple one. "My dear Nannerl," she said, "I hope you will not bury your talent. I know it is hard . . . ."

"How can you know?" Nannerl shot back fiercely.

True to her word, Anna had not told Nannerl about Margarethe's poetry, nor of Solomon Arnstein's prohibition of his daughter's writing. Anna alone kept these secrets for her friend, as she kept the occasional scrap of poetry Margarethe handed her, lifting out the best linens that weighed down her compositions.

"I am sorry," said Nannerl miserably, ashamed of her hot words.

"You are forgiven, my dear," said Margarethe. "I cannot, of course, know your thinking. I suppose we all have secrets, parts of our lives that are hidden from others, but there is something wrong about putting one's riches in dark closets and letting the lid rust onto the pot." She thought to herself, what a hypocrite I am, to lecture about keeping secrets, hoarding riches! "Perhaps Frau Althaus was afraid," she said.

"Of thieves?" queried Nannerl.

"Perhaps, or friends who might ask her for money. Or perhaps she feared some other thing we might never guess in a million years," said Margarethe. She knew what it was to fear discovery. "Women must so often labor under prohibitions. They often shrink from loving what may fail or be lost. Poor old lady. Who knows why she buried her riches as she did. Our passions are so often secret and, thus, misunderstood." Gazing into the distance she mused. "I saw a lily once. It was in a rich man's orangerie. He said it came from the orient. It was extravagantly marked as if wine-colored velvet had been streaked and overlaid with the richest gold. It was as though God had been an artisan and expended all His effort and material on that one lily. But it lasted only a day before the bloom withered and fell off. And yet, for that day . . . ."

It was a striking image, reminding Nannerl of the passage in scripture about the lily, which even King Solomon, in all his splendor, could not rival. She would like to stay longer, to probe Margarethe's mind further, but the fashionable little clock at her waist chimed the hour, startling her. "Armand said we would go sleigh riding this evening," she said shyly, "and I must put on warm clothes.

Armand, thought Nannerl, was by far the most attractive man she had found in all her travels and he had been there all along, in plain sight.

36

1770

IN HER DREAM, ANNA ENTERED A SMALL CHURCH, where light echoed from candles to crystals to walls. The great parish record book stood open before her, reaching from the floor to the top of the altar. It was written in characters that Anna had never seen before. She searched through the heavy pages, looking in vain for her name, until she realized that Gertrud stood beside her. But when Anna looked her full in the face, it was Sister Gisella's homely countenance she saw instead. Slowly, this face, framed in a white linen wimple, melted and rearranged itself to become Leopold. "It is very cold in Italy. You would not like it. We are perfectly free, my son and I."

Anna drifted slowly, in and out of sleep, hearing Leopold's voice say aloud some of the thousands of words she and Nannerl had read in his letters from Italy. Be sure to save every one of my letters, Leopold admonished her. He wrote them with more than one purpose in mind: he wanted to record his son's triumphs, so that he could write his story down when he had the leisure, and he wanted to impress the important men of Salzburg.

Though her dream troubled her, Anna was not eager to wake up. She had been up half the night with poor Basil von Annam, Wolfgang's friend and son of the Privy Councilor. Basil had been injured the day before, when a drunken Hungarian count spurred his horse, bucking and leaping through the marketplace, toppling carts, carriages and stalls. A cart had fallen on young Basil and injured him badly. Anna, who had both tended to the boy's wounds and comforted his mother, had gone to bed at last with the sounds in her ears of tearing and splintering wood, clashing iron and shrieking people.

Gratefully, she felt herself caught in the undertow of sleep. Nannerl's voice pulled her back towards waking. "Mama?"

"Mmmm," said Anna vaguely. Groggily she sat up and looked around the room. Her dream still claimed her: The familiar furniture looked strange and foreign. Perhaps they were traveling and she had forgotten where they had put up for the night, and yet she knew this was the quilt she had made herself. She pressed her fingers into her eyes and looked again as the room grew familiar. "Nannerl?" she mumbled sleepily. Her daughter sat beside her, still wearing her nightdress. "Where are we? What time is it, Nannerl?" Anna asked, yawning.

"We are here at home," laughed Nannerl. She too yawned and then laughed when her yawn prompted another from her mother. "We will have a duo for yawns. I thought sure the bells had wakened you. They rang eight o'clock only minutes ago. Look Mama, I cannot set this placket in right." She held a tricky piece of bodice in her hands, her fingers pressing back a seam that would not lie flat, the needle stitched into her nightdress.

Anna took the dress and peered at it. She held it close and then at arm's length. "Oh Nannerl," she sighed, "I cannot see anything at all these days. Let me get up and bathe my eyes and perhaps I can tell what to do." It troubled her that her vision was so imperfect. I must get spectacles, she thought, though Leopold will not like my doing so without asking him. He will think me a bluestocking, like those literary ladies in London. Well, too bad. He is away in Italy - *free* with my son. I am here and I will spend a few pfennigs on spectacles.

"Nannerl," she said as the two women sat to their breakfast, "I have it in mind to hire a carriage to visit my birthplace in St. Gilgen. I would be glad for your company." She had made the decision as she dressed. Why should she not go? She thought it unlikely that Leopold would ever take her, as there was nothing notable about the town of her birth. No one important lived there, nor were there particular sights to be seen.

"Would Papa mind our spending money for a carriage?" Nannerl asked cautiously.

"Well, perhaps he would," said Anna, "but he has left us to our own devices, and why should we not amuse ourselves somewhat?" Leopold's salary still came in regularly and he wrote of Wolfgang's endless successes, each of which, she knew, meant money in Leopold's pocket. The boy had impressed the great Padre Martini, who knew everything about music, and Cardinal Pallavicini had called Wolfgang "a famous boy." After one hearing of Gergorio Allegri's *Miserere* - a piece considered so beautiful that no copies were allowed - Wolfgang had written the whole thing down with all its parts out of his head, astonishing everyone. No, Anna need not worry about Leopold's finances.

So it was that Anna bargained with a coachman to drive her and Nannerl over the rough, dry road to St. Gilgen. While he took himself to the tavern to spend the day, Anna led her daughter from the verge of the road, down the winding lanes of St. Gilgen, past the neat houses and well-tended fields. The surrounding forests were richly in leaf, the meadows spangled with summer's flowers and humming insects. Small flashes of remembrance sparked in Anna's mind. "Here is where my sister found a nest of mice," she said to Nannerl, "with the mother dead beside them. I can almost see those wee, squirming, blind bodies and how we marveled at them! Here is the yard where we watched a horse foal." These were not great events to her daughter, Anna knew, for Nannerl had traveled in German lands, to France and England at an early age, but mice and a horse had been great events to a village girl. They came up to the small church, a creamy golden color, its windows and doors edged with white, its clock and bell tower topped with a spire just as Anna remembered, the church yard in flower. "We will come back later," said Anna. "First I want to show you the house my father built, where I was born." Down the lane they walked the short distance to the substantial District Court House, generous in proportion, sturdy, speaking to the world (so Anna thought) of the dignity of the office it housed. "Your grandfather was a well-respected man in this district," she said wistfully, "and he left his mark on Salzburg as well, for he sang in the Archbishop's *kapell.* I used to think," she added, "that the Wolfgangsee was named for him."

They stood at the edge of the lake, which reflected the thick forests and mountains as far as they could see. Anna felt a rush of sensations in her blood, the slippery pebbled cold of the lake on the soles of her gripping feet, the braids of ripples that followed the ducks as they swam toward her to snap up the bread she held out, the tiny emerald frogs that moved lightly when she held them throbbing in her hands, the thick crust of ice that grew out from the shore in winter.

A stout woman came out of the District Court House, a basket over her arm. She looked curiously at Anna and Nannerl. Strangers were not common in St. Gilgen and were regarded with suspicion. Anna, turning, caught her eye and went to meet the woman. "Good day," Anna said. "I have brought my daughter to see where I began my life. My father, Wolfgang Pertl, built this house."

The woman's face, which was red and stern, broke into a smile. "Oh my stars," she said, "little Anna Pertl! I can hardly believe my eyes! Your dear papa is remembered with such honor. And the wrong they did him when he died, carting all his things away, for shame! We had news of Gertrud's death, long ago. And your dear mama's, of course. We hear everything here. Oh, I can hardly trust my senses. Wolf Pertl's girl! And this fine young lady?"

"This is Marie Anna, whom we call Nannerl," said Anna, "and you must forgive me. I do not recognize . . . ."

"Of course, of course, where are my manners? I am Isobel Braun. My father, may he rest in peace, was Hans Dortman. You and Gertrud came to watch one of Papa's horses foal, and my brothers and I watched with you. Now I keep the house clean for Herr Neidermann, who has your father's position, but he is not the man your father was, oh no! Nothing like. Here I am, running on at the mouth, and you would like to show your Nannerl the house you lived in, no?"

Anna caught her breath. "Could we go in? We would not disturb Herr Neidermann?"

"Oh, heavens no! He is away this fortnight and will never be the wiser. I doubt you will remember, you being such a young one when you left. You must have been, what? five? six?"

"I was four," Anna smiled, "and played every day with your brothers Jacob and Willi." These names conjured faces and distinct, sturdy bodies, though she had not thought of them these forty-six years.

Frau Braun led them in and up to the living quarters, done up quite differently now. And yet as Anna looked around her, the years and furniture melted, and she saw in her mind's eye just how everything had looked when her mother, father, Gertrud and she had lived there. "Here," she said to Nannerl, "was our eating table, and in here the trundle beds where my sister and I slept. And here," she stood in the living room, besieged by memories that bubbled up from nowhere, "sat our harpsichord. It was such a beauty, a

Silbermann, as I remember. I can see it, plain as day in my mind, the name wreathed around with painted flowers. I remember it had a gilded paper cutout under the strings. How I loved that harpsichord! Your grandmother and grandfather loved it too." She ran her hand lightly along the windowsill, looking out at the lake on her left, the lane and church on the right. "My mother once told me that on the day I was born, an apricot branch set by the stove burst into flower. Do you do that still, Frau Braun?" she asked, turning back into the room, "cut an apricot branch in the dead of winter?"

"Bless your heart, of course we do. I remember hearing it from my mother, too, how Eva Rosina Pertl brought a babe into the world as the apricot branch flowered, and how that meant the child would reap good fortune."

The word spread around St. Gilgen quickly, once Anna and Nannerl had thanked Isobel Braun for her kindness: Wolf Pertl's younger girl was back in town, and she had traveled the world far and wide. While the young people stared at these two women, who could awaken no memories, the older townsfolk stopped their work to greet Anna, to remind her that her mother had delivered this child or that, to exclaim over some kindness or act of justice Wolf Pertl had done them. When Anna and Nannerl stopped in the tavern for their dinner, the host would not let them pay. "Wolf Nicolaus helped my father when his property was forfeit and held off the Archbishop's men," he said. "What is a little sup compared to that kindness?" "The music your mother and father brought to St. Gilgen!" exclaimed the old inn-keeper. "My father had to pay your mother in honey for my birth," recollected a farmer's wife. And so it went.

Finally, as shadows lengthened around them, Anna and Nannerl returned to the church. It was, as in her dream, cool, orderly and light. They found the parish records and paged back a full fifty years. "Here," said Nannerl, "1720, right at the end of the year, December 25. 'Anna Maria Walburga, legitimate daughter of the industrious Wolfgangus Nicolaus Pertl, Deputy Prefect of this place, and of Eva Rosina Altman, his wife.' "

Anna felt tears prick at her eyes. There was something about seeing it written down in browning ink on the yellowing page! She felt the excitement she had as a child when her father had shown her the words, some in Latin, some in German. "Anna Maria Walburga, legitimate daughter!" "Oh my," she said, sighing deeply. "Here I am, still written down."

Nannerl looked at her mother curiously. Imagine, that seeing this little entry in a record book could move her so! Why would it matter so much?

Nannerl felt that she was seeing her mother for the first time, a woman like herself, subject to strong emotions. "Shall we go now?" she asked, tenderly.

"Yes," said Anna, but her eyes lingered on her name in the record book. She knew she would never see it again.

As they jolted back toward Salzburg, Nannerl asked her mother shyly, "Why did it matter so much that you saw your name in the parish book?"

Anna pondered. "Well," she said, "I suppose it is knowing that there is something lasting about me, some mark I have made on the world, however small. When I am gone, should anyone care to look, there it will be, the notice that I existed. I will leave nothing else, no work, no monument, no other sign of my passage."

"Oh, Mama," Nannerl demurred.

"You will remember me for a while, Nannerl, and Wolfgang and your Papa as well, but my memory of my mother has faded. Someday Leopold will die, you and your brother as well. You have all left something, your portraits on the wall, your compositions and those of your brother and father. The few pieces of lace I have made will rot in time. It is all stitches in air. But my name is written in that book forever." She fell silent. "There are my compositions," she said, more to herself than her daughter, "but I have not put my name upon them, except for my chamber symphony."

Nannerl was startled. "Chamber symphony?" she asked.

"Mmm," said Anna. "When I was younger, I meant to be a composer. You know I sang in the *kapell* before I married your father," she said, "and when you went with your father to Munich - remember? I think you were eleven - I spent the time I had alone composing, to see if I still knew how. It had been a long time and I was very rusty, but I did compose some pieces and linked them together as a chamber symphony."

"And none of us knew," Nannerl marveled.

"You were full of your Munich adventures," said Anna dryly.

When they were back in their Salzburg apartment, Nannerl was insistent: her mother must show her the composition of which she had spoken. Anna, taking care that Nannerl should not know its hiding place, lifted the linens out of the trunk, and gave the pages to her.

Nannerl studied the pile of her mother's work. "These are good, Mama. I especially like the symphony. No one has ever heard it?"

"I showed it to Joseph Meissner," Anna remembered, "and he liked what I had composed. But he told me the Archbishop would not be pleased to know that your father's wife had done what everyone knows a woman cannot do."

"This has sat silent too long, Mama," said Nannerl. "We must have a grand party and perform it. We need not say who the composer is," she said, noting her mother's look of alarm. "We can say the composer is 'Anonymous.' I will gather the musicians. Armand will help me. We can borrow the Hagenauer's and Frau Möll's maids since our poor Marthe is still so ill, and we can invite everyone. Armand will help too."

Their servant, Marthe, was very ill indeed. Anna spent much time nursing her, but her condition worsened. Leopold wrote vexing news of an accident in which he had injured one foot and then was crippled up with rheumatism in the other. Anna was distracted by worry, but nevertheless, Nannerl was determined: they would invite all their friends and entertain them with her mother's chamber symphony. Anna, both fearful and pleased that she would, at last, hear her small efforts of nearly a decade ago, was surprised and touched by the decision her daughter showed. It was good to see Nannerl so full of purpose again.

She settled her new spectacles on her nose and watched Nannerl bustle about with enthusiasm, inviting musicians, rehearsing them, overseeing the refreshments they would serve to their friends - for truly, everyone was invited. To accommodate such a host of friends, there would be performances on three successive nights.

Anna no longer thought of composing. It had been too long and there was too much that she had not learned. Her children had moved into the space that, for a time, she had reserved for music, or at any rate, her hopes for music. It is not music, not my name in a parish record book, she thought, but my children, Nannerl and Wolfgang, who are my true works of art. They too will someday perish - nothing lasts forever. But I made them with my body and nurtured them with my full soul, and they are wonderful. They stand as the proof that my existence means something.

She noticed, with pleasure, how clearly she could see everything, thanks to the spectacles. There were separate and distinct leaves on the trees, beginning to brown at the edges with the end of summer's heat. She could see the fine grain of a loaf when she cut it. She wrote to Leopold and Wolfgang with greater ease. She had no trouble helping Nannerl set her placket.

37

1770

LEOPOLD AND WOLFGANG, having secured a contract for an opera to be performed in Milan at Christmas, wrote of their travels to Florence, Naples, Rome and Bologna, where they slept in fine linen sheets, were waited on by servants, and gloried in fresh figs, melons and peaches.

But in Salzburg, for three days in a row, Anna, Nannerl and their borrowed servants spread a feast on borrowed tables covered with Anna's finest linens, on which real wax candles burned steadily, illuminating the room. And on each occasion, the best musicians in Salzburg performed Anna's chamber symphony. In spite of her frenzy of preparation, Nannerl had found time to make her mother a festive gown of garnet-colored silk, trimmed with the rich black Belgian lace that had been given to Nannerl on their long journey. She did her mother's hair, brushing it up over forms and pads, braiding, curling, pomading and piling it high on her head. "I fear to move!" Anna laughed. She in turn did Nannerl's hair and admired the effect of her daughter's blue-green dress, which flattered her dewy skin and picked out the sapphire lights in her eyes.

"It is right to make this a great occasion, Mama," Nannerl said calmly, when Anna worried about expense. "This may be the only time your chamber symphony is performed. It is good and should be heard." Nannerl conducted from the harpsichord and Anna, watching her daughter's composure, felt something in her unfold like the damp crumpled tissue of a butterfly's wings, expanding and stretching in the air outside of its case. Was it her own music or the efforts of her daughter, the soaring of her own soul or seeing Nannerl happy at music once again that touched her most deeply? Anna did not know which it was. Somehow her own musical ambitions had flowed together with her feeling for her children. Her genius, such as it was, seemed a gift freely given to them.

The applause was enthusiastic and prolonged. "Whose work is it?" everyone asked. "Who is the composer?" Of the guests, only Margarethe, who came with her father, and Joseph Meissner knew the truth, and both were pledged to secrecy. Meissner pressed Anna's hand with greater firmness than was usual as he took his leave. "Your mysterious composer has a great gift," he said solemnly. "'Tis pity we cannot know him here in Salzburg and persuade him to give us more symphonies."

"You are very kind," Anna murmured, coloring with pleasure.

Solomon Arnstein gave his daughter permission to stay after the others had gone. She and Anna sat ignoring the disorder to be cleaned up and leaned back in their chairs in shared satisfaction. Armand d'Ippold, dashing in his uniform and helpful in every way, had taken Nannerl for a walk by the river. Nannerl was glad of the cool air, for she was flushed with the success of her conducting and warm with congratulations for the suite of dances she herself had composed and played for the guests.

"Was it as you hoped?" Margarethe asked.

Anna sighed deeply. "It was," she said. "It was very odd, really, to hear the notes I had written down. It was as if someone else had penned them and they surprised me. I thought them," she cocked her head, "not bad. What did you think?"

"Oh," said Margarethe, stretching in the late September warmth, "I liked them immensely. Especially the second *andante*. And I felt such pride. I wanted to jump up and announce to the world that the composer was among us, sitting right there, and had cooked and cleaned as well as composed." She laughed. "Will you tell Leopold and Wolfgang about all this?" She gestured broadly at the tables spread with the remains of hams, the carcasses of fowls, bowls of bread crumbs, the left-behind peach, apple and empty stem of the grape.

"Yes," said Anna, considering. "Why should they not know that we too have enjoyment. And I will tell them," she said deliberately, "about my chamber symphony and I will call it my Pertl Chamber Symphony. Leopold, of course, knows I have composed - though he does not know I made this work - and it will not hurt Wolfgang to know that his mother has something on her mind beside mending his breeches." She folded her hands behind her head, pressing the pins that kept her elaborate hairdo together against her scalp. "I have had a rare time of it with Nannerl," she smiled. "This was her idea. And this," she smoothed the glowing silk of her dress, "is her handiwork. She has come out of herself, bloomed again, as she did before we went to The Hague. It is Armand, I suppose. And perhaps she has come to terms with more modest ambitions. It is not so easy to know how to nourish genius, is it, my friend, since it comes attached to human beings who have to live in the world? Nannerl's, like your own, must be cut back, in her case, so that her brother's can flourish. Nannerl has had to decide how she will be a musician and a woman both in Salzburg."

Nannerl came in, as if her mother had spoken her cue. She was rosy from her exertions. She had confided to Armand, as she had to no other person in the world, how those women who had endorsed her aspirations had died untimely - the Archduchess Johanna, the Baroness van Eyck - how she had very nearly died herself just when an opera seemed within her grasp. Armand had held her hand, looked with his dark eyes into her blue ones and told her, with the utmost sincerity, that no science in the world could hold her responsible for these events, that God would not have blessed her with genius - he used that word, "genius,"- unless he had wanted it used.

"You did a superb job of it," said Margarethe, smiling at Nannerl. "You did your mother's work proud and I rejoiced for both of you. Shall we clean up these things?"

"No," said Anna firmly. "Tonight you are our guest, Margarethe. Nannerl and I will clean up and gossip about our guests as we do." She smiled. There had been weeks and weeks of hard work, but a time of such pleasure and fulfillment. Nannerl was happy again. Anna had seen her name in the parish record book in St. Gilgen. She had heard her composition played.

Word came from Milan. The Accademia Filarmonica of Bologna had received Wolfgang into membership, a great honor. Wolfgang wrote, rather unhappily, Anna thought, that his fingers ached from composing the many recitatives for his opera *Mitridate, rè di Ponto*. "Mama," he implored in writing, "I beg you to pray for me, that my opera may go well and that we may be happy together again." Leopold wrote of the plots and schemes that seemed to go with the production of any opera, where there were many competing interests. But Count Firmian had secured the commission and composition and rehearsal went ahead. Finally Anna and Nannerl heard about the performances, twenty in all, with Wolfgang conducting in his new suit, which Leopold described as scarlet, lined with sky-blue satin and trimmed in gold braid. The little *maestrino*, said Leopold, was greeted with shouts of approval by the adoring Milanese each time he appeared. "So we see," wrote Leopold, "what the Almighty Power of God can make of us human beings, if we do not bury the talents which he has most graciously bestowed upon us."

Nannerl read and re-read each letter, memorizing each detail. She gloried in her brother's success, imagining what it would be to see one's opera unfolding with real singers, a real orchestra, conducting from the harpsichord, then taking the bows, the adulation. The Almighty God had indeed blessed her brother with extraordinary talents, and she rejoiced for him. Her own success, conducting her mother's little pieces and writing jolly dances, now seemed puny by comparison. It was perhaps true, as Armand had assured her, that her friends did not die on account of her own aspirations. Nevertheless, Almighty God had not seen fit to make her a *maestra*, nor was any Accademia Filarmonica likely to welcome her to membership. Well, she must be content with her lot and rejoice in her brother's attainments.

Nannerl's busy life - teaching, going about with her friends to parties and balls - left Anna alone for a good part of the time. Poor Marthe had died and though Ilsa, the new servant, was young and willing, she was a raw country girl who needed training. Leopold and Wolfgang would be coming home before long, now that the opera was completed. Anna looked forward to their return eagerly, but she also wondered what it would be like to have a man and a boy back in the center of the comfortable household of women. What will they see in us, she wondered, after two years filled with such high living, honors and applause? She was alone in the apartment and had a sudden impulse to see what she looked like. Though the late February air was cold, the stove had burned all day and the room was warm enough for her to strip off her clothes. She pushed a stool under the cloudy and spotted mirror that hung in its gilded frame on the wall. By turning the mirror this way and that on its hanger, she could see herself, though not all at one time. She remembered what she had been as a young girl, narrow of waist, with small firm breasts, slim arms and thighs. She had lost her narrow waist. Her stomach sagged down, the skin wrinkled like linen. The skin under her chin was loose and her arms and legs, even her face had thickened. I was comely once, she thought. I am no fright even now, though all the years and work have surely left their mark.

She turned this way and that, wondering if Leopold, once he had seen all the glittering company in Italy, would find her too plain to want. He was entirely faithful to her, she thought, even though sometimes he flirted a little with the rich and powerful ladies he met in the salons with his son, but it was power, not animal passions, that attracted him. Anna knew that he would never risk scandal nor have the time - nor for that matter the strength - for the kinds of dangerous games that had seemed so common in France. No matter how she strained to see herself in the mirror, to get just a glimpse of herself from top to bottom all at once, she could not.

She stood close to the mirror, looking at her face as she ran the wooden comb through her hair, noting as she did that gray hairs were more numerous now than the light brown she was used to seeing. She turned her face this way and that, holding her hair against her head in different ways, trying to see how she, Anna Pertl Mozart, looked. Her eyes, magnified by the spectacles, were still clear, a deep gray-blue. Her lashes and brows were brown, and her nose long and straight - her son's nose exactly - and her lips still full. Her eyes were ringed with darker skin now in her old age, no longer as fine as the petals of flowers, and the lines that ran from her mouth to slight jowls were deeper. Swiftly she braided her hair and pinned it in place.

As she pulled on her stockings, Anna thought of the accounting she would have to make when, in the fullness of time, she departed this Earth. She fell into a reverie. If her worth were truly in her children, then they would be judged and that judgment would go to her account. The five children that lay slumbering forever in St. Peter's churchyard no longer wounded her as they once had. There was no sin on their poor heads. Nannerl had not the worldly success Anna had hoped and prayed for, but she was pleased that her daughter had found Armand, who was willing to recognize the talent that was the pivot of her life. Wolfgang was well launched. Success usually fed on success, and he would likely do well. Leopold would not rest, she thought, until Wolfgang had achieved - what? Anna was not sure at what point Leopold would let go of the boy so that he could find his own way, as every man finally must.

They are leaving me, Anna thought. Nannerl will marry, perhaps Armand, and her husband will be at the center of her life. Wolfgang will find steady work in some court or other, marry, and I will rarely see him unless it is in Salzburg he finds his way. She felt uneasy, thinking of Wolfgang employed by the Salzburg court. Would the son displace the father? Would Leopold's need to hold on to and promote his son cripple the boy?

She shook herself. These were fruitless thoughts. Ilsa would be back soon, as would Nannerl, wanting her dinner. She finished dressing, cleaned her spectacles and basted the joint over the fire.

Nannerl came in with letters. "They are in Venice," she reported, "and will be in Salzburg by Easter. And listen to this, Mama. Papa says, 'we are only sorry that we cannot remain here longer. It is indeed a pity, for we have got to know the whole nobility very well; and everywhere, at parties, at table, and, in fact, on all occasions, we are so overwhelmed with honors that our hosts not only send their secretaries to fetch us and convey us home in their gondolas, but often the noble himself accompanies us on our return . . . .' Oh, Mama. My brother will be spoiled and think us very dull." She sighed, for when she read the letters that came from Italy, her contentment often left her. She could not help but envy the honors and opportunities her brother received.

Anna grimaced. "They will have to pass over the mountains in this dreadful weather," she said, for it had been an unusually harsh winter and travelers' reports from Innsbruck were of high winds and heavy snowfall.

It was time to clean house from top to bottom in preparation for the Blessing of the New Fire, when everyone in Salzburg went out into the dark streets to receive the fire that rekindled their hearths, relighted their lamps and lit the Paschal candle in every church.

"I love the Blessing," Anna said to Nannerl, "after this season of cold and gray, when everyone is testy and it takes too long to dress." Struck anew from flint onto a tinder, the new fire burned brightly, reminding everyone that spring would return, in spite of the snow that turned into slush and ice.

Anna and Nannerl carried their candle home, shielding it from the snowflakes that fell sputtering into the flame, exchanging greetings with their friends and neighbors, who carried their own new fires shining in the snow. They climbed back up the stone stairs to their apartment and relit the stoves, the candles and the lamp, their shadows dancing a *pas de deux* on the wall. They both felt the peace of the household, sparkling from their exertions and the flame of the new fire. They went back out onto the street and walked to St. Peter's church to see that the Paschal candle also burned with new and brighter flame.

Anna reached for Nannerl's hand as they returned home. "Your father and brother will be here soon," she said. "They will find you happier than when they left."

"Yes," Nannerl acknowledged, "and yet - oh, Mama, it is hard not to envy my brother. Was it hard for you . . . ?"

But Anna did not answer, for a carriage was stopped in front of their house, and there were Leopold and Wolfgang, hauling down their boxes and trunks in the snow.

"We had not expected you so early!" Nannerl exclaimed.

"We could hardly wait to get here," exclaimed Wolfgang. He spoke in an unfamiliar man's voice.

"You have been out," said Leopold.

Anna thought she detected a note of reproach in his voice. "Lighting the Paschal candle," she said, "It is the festival of the New Fire."

"Yes, yes," he said impatiently. "Well, here you are at last. Let us go up. No, Wolfgang. You must not carry such heavy things. Nannerl, take hold of this trunk and help me carry it up."

38

1771

WE PRESSED THE HORSES VERY HARD," complained Leopold, "so that we might be here sooner. The weather was filthy over the pass. I feared for our very lives." This morning, he was in turmoil, unaccountably disappointed by everything he had hurried toward. He and Wolfgang had been welcomed warmly, plied with Anna's good stew and given basins of hot water to clean the dirt of the road from their aching limbs before they slept. Nevertheless, Leopold felt vaguely wronged, misunderstood.

When Leopold looked askance at the stew Anna had warmed and set before him in a wooden bowl the night before, Anna had said, "We have no roasted partridges nor figs nor melons, my dear." In truth, she was annoyed that her husband, who had written from Bologna of the fine fruits of the countryside, seemed to expect Italy's summer fare when it was winter in Salzburg.

The apartment was too small and crowded. Anna looked older, more worn than Leopold had remembered. Nannerl had somehow escaped him; she looked to her mother now rather than to him. Leopold's grievance extended even to his son, whose joy at embracing his mother and sister was unalloyed. Leopold felt himself outside of his own family.

The night before he had dreamed of being stranded in drifts of snow, buffeted by the gusty winds that drove needles of sleet through him as he slipped towards the sheer edge of the narrow, winding and half-hidden road. Wolfgang, hovering by, laughed at the danger, while Leopold ground his teeth and cursed. In the distance he saw Italy's golden sunshine beckoning. In a shaft of sunlight sat a bowl of rosy apples in the crockery bowl on the table, and Anna, untouched by years, looked up, surprised, smiling at him. But when he waked and saw the white light of winter, in which the canary warbled with full throat, everything still looked as reduced, worn and shabby as it had by candlelight the night before.

"I had forgotten how cramped we are here," said Leopold, looking about him with dissatisfaction. "In Milan," he said, "we had a very large room with a balcony and windows and a fireplace. And a separate sleeping room." In memory, the apartment he had shared with his son in Milan was much brighter and more comfortable than it had seemed at the time.

From the travelers' open trunks and boxes spilled a tangle of clothes, shoes and treasure Anna had never seen. There were more manuscript pages than she had imagined existed in the world. Everything was in need of sorting, mending and laundering. Anna stretched and sighed. The house that she and Nannerl had occupied so companionably for two years, which had been clean and ordered only yesterday, was cluttered with gear and filled up with male voices.

Nannerl had risen early to go to church. Now she sat herself down on the floor, her skirts spread about her, and begun sorting through manuscript pages, reading the notations eagerly, hearing the instruments and voices in her mind as she set the pages in order. How her brother had grown musically! These were very, very good indeed.

Wolfgang had sprung from his bed, glad to be at home. He found his proudest possession, his own razor, and carefully shaved the minuscule blond hairs from his upper lip. He put on a dressing gown, his old clothes being far too short and tight, and skipped into the front room where he tickled Nannerl. She looked up in wonder at her brother. "I wish I had composed these," she said.

Wolfgang smiled at her. He valued Nannerl's praise more than all the counts and princes in Italy. He went to the canary cage and spoke to the canary, "Has Nannerl not taught you to sing any better songs than that, little bird? We will teach him together, will we not, Nannerl?"

Leopold frowned at his frivolous son. "You will have better things to do than teach a bird to sing, Woferl," he admonished.

Anna hardly recognized her son's new tenor voice. She doubted that he could still sing soprano parts as he had. "You brought back a splendid wardrobe, Woferl." She held up the red silk suit coat lined with blue satin in one hand and an embroidered waistcoat in the other.

"Oh, yes. When I am decked out, you never saw so fine a fellow," Wolfgang teased. He put on the red and blue coat over his old dressing gown, preening and mincing around the room. He snatched a wig from out of a box and put it cockeyed on his head. "Behold," he announced, "Signor Cavaliere. But look Mama, that cravat is ripped, and all my stockings have holes in them. Knit some new ones, Mama, or I will be a fright. Nannie, I will put on some clothes and then, please you, dearest milkmaid, princess, peerless beauty, to walk out with me." He flung the wig back to its box, but it fell on the floor. "I might get lost," he said, pretending an infant's lisp.

Anna peered at him over her spectacles. "You might consider helping me sort some of these things," she said mildly.

Nannerl straightened the stacks of manuscript and stood up, shaking out her limbs, which were cramped from sitting. She could never, in a thousand years, compose such pieces and in such quantity. She doubted that she had ever had a pfennig's worth of the genius that had been lodged in her brother.

Leopold said impatiently, "He has better things to do than clean and sort, Anna. He will be wanted at court." He did not know how to impress upon his wife that his son had conquered Italy, that he had been toasted and fawned over by royalty and nobility wherever he had gone.

Anna pressed her lips together, refusing to take her husband's bait. She did not know how best to persuade him that their son, however gifted, still walked upon the earth, a mortal boy, and should be instructed as such.

When brother and sister had left, Anna glanced at Leopold, who looked very down in the mouth. He had felt an unreasoning surge of rage and jealousy that his son would go out without his father. "Let me give you some coffee," said Anna and went to the kitchen to grind the beans and brew the rich drink just as he liked it, with a froth of boiled milk. They sat together at the scarred old table as they had sat so many times. Anna, though sensing her husband's distance from her, was determined not to quarrel with him. "You must be very tired from your journey." She knew how hard travel was. She knew, too, that he had been so cosseted in the Italian cities that home must seem very plain.

She put her hand on his. "Has your injury entirely healed?" she inquired. He had written of the accident, between Naples and Rome, in which one of the horses had reared and fallen, pulling down the carriage, so that a loosened dashboard had ripped Leopold's leg to the bone.

"Yes, yes," he said brusquely, "I am perfectly well, though my rheumatism sometimes pains."

"Your letters were very vivid," Anna offered. "You made us want to be there with you to see all the sights, the balls, the operas - Woferl's above all."

"You would not like it," said Leopold, more vehemently than he intended. He pulled his hand away from hers and then, to cover his reflexive gesture, held his cup to his lips. "No, you would not like Italy at all. The Italians are vulgar and immoral. The rooms are cold in winter and everything is too costly. And one lives rough in lodgings with no comforts whatsoever."

Anna studied him over the tops of her spectacles. "You only just bragged about your luxurious quarters in Milan," she reminded him.

Leopold rejoined dismissively, "Suitable for a pair of bachelors."

Anna sipped her coffee. "In Italy, it is said, many more women are composers than in the German countries," she said. "Should Nannerl perhaps . . . ."

"No, no, no," Leopold interrupted. "The Italians are quite sure that Germans are a benighted race. A German *woman*, well! You must accept it, Anna. Nannerl is finished. She will not thank you if you make her dissatisfied with her life. Is there more coffee?"

As Anna refilled their cups, Leopold thought out loud. "My son breaks down the Italians' foolish prejudice against Germans. He is like quicksilver. He has taken for himself all the lightness and elegance of the Italian style and joined it with our more learned substance. They listen, because they think they hear Italian music, but at its center is the German soul. You can have no idea, Anna." He sighed. Perhaps he must accept that in Salzburg neither he nor his son would ever be truly understood. "The Italians bestowed on him every imaginable honor. The Pope - think of it! - the Pope himself conferred the Order of the Golden Spur on my son. You will find the trunks full of diplomas when you clean them out. The opera was a marvel. I cannot convey the applause, the affection - no, the love - with which it was received. Opera is to them, the Italians, more than meat and drink, and no one could credit that so young a boy . . . . 'Is it possible that one of such tender years . . . ?' He is not like other boys, Anna. You cannot imagine!" Leopold was at a loss for superlatives.

Anna nodded. She was glad to hear how well her son had acquitted himself. But Nannerl was finished, Leopold had said, and he had no sympathy for her blighted hopes. "Nannerl," she mused aloud, "is a grown woman now. There is little I can do to shape her - or make her dissatisfied, for that matter. But Woferl, I hope he has not learned insolence from the Italians. He is perhaps used to too much deference." Why, after all, should her son not help to clean out the trunks he and his father had brought back? It was too much to expect Leopold, who must go to court later in the morning, to turn his hand to the disorder he had brought into their house. But Wolfgang was another matter.

Leopold frowned. He had forgotten how his wife liked to meddle with his son.

Anna raised her hand to her spectacles. "Did you notice?" she asked.

Leopold had already begun to think of the next journey to Milan, to fulfill still another contract for an opera, word of which had reached them in Venice. When his wife brought his attention to her spectacles, which he had not noticed, he suddenly realized the cause of his discontent: while he and his son had been in motion, risking accident, doing great things, his wife and daughter had done nothing but stay in this dreary place, with its small, dark kitchen, battered table, humble clay stove and dented pewter plates set on shelves, concerning themselves with trifles like spectacles. "They do nothing to improve your beauty," he said.

Anna was nettled. "Perhaps not," she said, "but I do see more clearly. I have no doubt, Leopold, that our doings seem insignificant, when seen beside your adventures. But the little journey Nannerl and I took to St. Gilgen was a fine thing for me. We saw inside the house my father built when he was Vice Prefect, and we met everyone from my early days." She could tell that her husband was not interested and forbore the attempt to explain why seeing her name in the parish book had meant so much. She hardly understood it herself.

To Leopold, that Anna could mention St. Gilgen in the same breath as Italy was proof, if proof were needed, that she had no more than the most common understanding. His thoughts turned to the task of persuading the Archbishop to give him and Wolfgang leave to travel once again to Milan.

Wolfgang was delighted to be back again on the familiar streets.

"Was the opera fine?" Nannerl asked her brother wistfully.

"It was," said Wolfgang. "I knew it was, and everyone praised it and gave me presents and bowed when I came into the room. Do you remember our Kingdom of Ruck, Nannie? I was always king when we played that game, and it was like that. I was King of Milan. I love applause and being the center of attention," he admitted.

"Well, you walk as if you are king in Salzburg," Nannerl observed dryly, seeing that her brother strutted beside her.

Wolfgang looked at her quickly, poised to take offense at what sounded like criticism, but seeing her dear face, he laughed. "You are right," he said. "Papa liked me to strut about in Italy, because he was sometimes taken for a tutor to a foreign prince - that was me - and he liked my being mistaken for royalty. But enough about our travels. Tell me what you and Mama did while we were gone."

"I was sad at first, not to be going," Nannerl said. But then Armand d'Ippold told me I need not give up all composition . . . ."

"I should hope not!" exclaimed Wolfgang. "What were you thinking, Nannerl? You are so clever, a better composer than I am. If only . . . ."

"I know," Nannerl said, "if only I were a man, then it would not matter. But I am not." She frowned, as if concentrating on something indigestible that she had eaten. "Armand," her voice grew soft and Wolfgang glanced at her sharply, "finds a thousand parties and balls and little concerts for me and I give him dance suites and songs and that is well enough, though I will never have an opera." She tried to keep the envy from her voice.

"I will ask Papa to take you to Italy next time," said Wolfgang.

"He will not, Woferl," she said. "He has chosen you. He did that long ago."

"Well," said Wolfgang, who knew she spoke the truth and also knew better than to try to change his father's mind about anything, "tell me about Mama's symphony. I had no idea she could compose until we got your letter." He reached out to brush snow that had fallen on her cloak from a branch shaken by the cold wind.

"Mama composed a set of pieces that she put together in a symphony that time we went to Munich and she stayed behind," Nannerl explained. "Do you know, Woferl, we never even asked her what she did while we were gone?"

It seemed to Wolfgang entirely natural not to inquire about one's mother. What could there possibly be to report? "Was it any good?" he asked.

"Yes," said Nannerl. "I had not known it, but Mama said that when she was a girl she meant to be a composer. Sometimes, when she and Papa were courting, he put his name on her compositions so that they could be performed. You know what the Archbishop thinks. Mama told me that Papa said she had real genius."

Wolfgang scowled. His mother had genius? He had to struggle, what with the things people said, in order to remember that his sister had genius. "Could I see Mama's symphony, do you think?"

"I think so," said Nannerl, "perhaps when Papa is at court. Of course, you will be at court, too."

"Not all the time," said Wolfgang. "I am only *konzertmeister*, and not even paid. I can be at home when Papa is away, though of course," he sighed, "he will expect me to do nothing but work."

"Woferl," Nannerl said. "While you were away, I saw something of Mama I had not seen before. She was bold, or free, or something. She bought spectacles and we went to St. Gilgen, and, Woferl, it meant an enormous amount to her to see her name in the parish records. She said it was something she would leave behind, some permanent mark."

Wolfgang shared Nannerl's puzzlement over this information.

"We had really splendid parties. I conducted her symphony and everyone came and you cannot imagine how much praise and speculation there was about the composer. Mama and I laughed about it." Nannerl paused, unsure what to tell him, for fear too much would get to her father. But her brother was her best friend in the world. It would not do to keep secrets from him. "Armand and I . . . ," she said shyly, "We have been spending a good deal of time together."

"Armand is a good fellow," said Wolfgang.

"He is a kind man, Woferl, and full of life - and handsome too."

"Are you going to marry him?"

"He means to ask Papa for my hand," Nannerl confessed. "I have told him I will marry him." She walked along, absorbed for the time in thoughts about Armand, but then changed the subject. "How was it to be so long with Papa alone?" she asked.

Wolfgang sighed again. It was impossible to describe how his father devoted every waking hour to his son's success, how he could not seem to understand that Wolfgang was no longer a child, how he told him the very things that his own eyes could see for themselves. "I am, I do not know, his puppet I suppose," said Wolfgang, "and he speaks for me. He sighed. "It won't do *me* any good to fall in love. Papa will not let me talk with pretty girls, much less court them."

They walked along companionably in silence for awhile. Then Wolfgang said, "I know that you must envy the opportunities Papa arranges for me, Nannerl. But sometimes I envy you."

"Me?" said Nannerl, astounded.

"Yes," said Wolfgang, "because you can go about freely and you can stay here at home with Mama and all our friends. It is nice to see new places and to have people make a fuss. But I like it even better here in homely old Salzburg."

PART
7

39

1771

ON THE SIXTEENTH DAY OF DECEMBER in the year of our Lord 1771, all the bells of Salzburg tolled for the Archbishop Sigmund Christoph, Count Schrattenbach. "It has come, then," said Anna, crossing herself. "May he rest in peace." His death was not unexpected. For a long time Salzburgers had fed on anxious news of their ailing prince. It is no wonder, thought Anna. But the death of an archbishop brought with it great uncertainty. No one could be sure who would be appointed in his place, what his views would be, whom he would honor with preferment, whom he would not.

Leopold and Wolfgang had returned just the night before from Milan, where Wolfgang's dramatic serenata had been performed with signal success during the festivities that celebrated the wedding of the Archduke Ferdinand, son of the Hapsburg Empress, and Princess Beatrice of Modena.

Wolfgang, up early, was telling his mother about Hasse, whose opera had been less well received than his own, despite Hasse's popularity. "He is a kind man. My *serenata* drew much more praise than his opera." Wolfgang preened a little. "But I felt sad when his did not do better." It was at that very moment when all the bells of Salzburg shattered the still, early morning air. Wolfgang's hands flew up to cover his ears. Since childhood, Wolfgang had hated and feared loud, sudden noises.

Nannerl ran up the stairs, flushed from walking Bimperl, the terrier puppy, which Armand had only just given her as a tender of his affection. "I will ask your father for your hand the moment he returns," Armand had promised the day before. "In the meantime, Bimperl will keep you warm at night." The jangle and beating of the bells caused the puppy to cower and quiver in her arms. Now, Nannerl thought unhappily, Armand will have to put off talking with Papa, who will be caught up not only in funeral obsequies but in the jockeying for power and position that is sure to follow. The bells, replacing every other sound, were a bad omen.

Leopold, exhausted and aching from his travels across the wintery mountains, had stayed late abed. Jarred from his sleep by the lamentations of the bells, he hastened to the front room, the creases of his pillow pressed into his face, his hair standing on end. Anna, neatly dressed, as was Nannerl, Wolfgang still in his nightshirt, and a small dog - where had that dog come from? - were caught, speechless in the clamor, amidst all the luggage brought up but not opened the night before. "The Archbishop?" shouted Leopold. Nothing else could account for such an uproar.

Anna nodded and went to her disheveled husband, leaning against him. Salzburg would be desolated after nineteen years of Archbishop Schrattenbach's government. He had been indulgent of Leopold's ambitions for Wolfgang, thought Anna, but had also cruelly locked him up at her husband's behest. Though he had held the reins of government with a fairly light hand, he had deeply mistrusted and feared all women. Still, she thought, there might be worse to come. Better the devil you know. At court, there would be a frenzy of mourning, speculation and edginess. Every officeholder, anticipating the paradise of preferment, fearing the hell of disfavor, would cool his heels in purgatory. No one could jump this way or that with safety. Leopold would be in the middle of it all.

He was a great prince, Leopold thought, feeling the salty tears breech the rims of his eyes. He understood that God had singled Salzburg out for honor when He gave my son to the world. He understood that wherever my son journeyed, he shed glory on his native city. But Leopold's tears gave way to annoyance. What an inopportune time to die! Here he and his son had only just returned, having endured so rough a passage over the hazardous mountain pass between Innsbruck and Salzburg. Though he himself had paid for their travels with the renewed pains of rheumatism, they had brought back with them fresh triumphs from Milan and a *scrittura* for yet another opera, which would magnify their patron. And then to have him die!

As the bells thundered, numbing all senses, Anna mimed eating and led the way to the kitchen, where she and Nannerl set out bread, butter and honeycomb and Anna made coffee with milk. Wolfgang played with the puppy and Nannerl thought of Armand and the upcoming interview, albeit delayed. All at once the bells ceased to ring. The puppy yelped and all four Mozarts laughed.

"Where did you get him?" Wolfgang inquired.

Nannerl, colored and said, shyly, "Armand d'Ippold gave him to me. He . . . he wishes to speak to you, Papa."

Leopold looked up sharply, raising a quizzical eyebrow, while Wolfgang grinned behind his enormous chunk of bread, dripping richly with honeycomb.

Suddenly Leopold gasped, as if in pain. "Oh!" he exclaimed in horror. "The Archbishop held back my salary against my return! Now who will pay the amount owed me?" He exhaled worriedly. "I will have to petition everyone in the Cathedral Chapter and they will all be distracted by the expense of - who knows? Maybe a thousand masses? And mourning will have to be made up for everyone at court and they will have to refurbish the funeral carriage and get black horses and there will be all the dignitaries to house and feed." He had just come from an imperial wedding: a state funeral would, in the same way, engross everyone in Salzburg. He groaned, thinking of the smallness of the amount owed him, a mere 28 florins 30 kreuzer, but it would be an irritation to those who must account for it, particularly at such a time. And then there would be the election and the costs of installing the new archbishop. On the other hand, all occasions would require music and he and his son were on hand to fill the need.

He must begin his petition immediately, the language of which began to fill his head. Whereof his Excellency Count Carl Firmian, in a letter to his brother, no, esteemed brother, the chief Steward, formally requested His Serene Highness of sacred memory to allow me to betake myself, most graciously to betake myself, to Milan with my son . . . . He heard his family's conversation only distantly.

"Tell us more about your *serenata*," Nannerl urged her brother, eager to turn attention away from herself and Armand.

"Well," he said, chewing noisily, grateful that one did not have to eat so daintily at home. "The Archduke applauded first and then everyone could see that they might applaud as well. The Princess, his new wife, stood up and clapped and clapped. The Archduke asked me for a copy of the music to present to his bride. When we first got to Milan, everyone was saying that Ferdinand did not like the Empress's choice of a bride for her son, but I think they were wrong. The Princess is kind and generous, though she is plain. I could only speak to her in Italian, though of course the Archduke's language is German. She whispered to me that the Archduke would give me a position in their court, but he said he could not."

Leopold, who had momentarily forgotten his petition, said indignantly, "The Empress paid for the *serenata*, but you would think she might leave it to her son whom to hire for his court in Milan."

"Could she be still angry," Anna wondered, "because you sent that letter about Signor Affligio to the young Emperor in Vienna three years ago?" She had remonstrated at the time that to burden the Emperor with the ins and outs of his quarrel with Affligio would only anger him. How could a great prince, who reviewed his troops in Hungary one day, concern himself with the petty quarrels of musicians the next?

Leopold said coldly, "I doubt that the Empress has so long a memory or so small a mind."

Anna heard the warning in his voice.

Nannerl, who had been thinking of all the Milanese merriment and music her father and brother had described, asked her brother, "Would you have taken the post if it had been offered?" If Wolfgang were to live in Milan, would Papa and Mama go there too? Once she had married Armand, she could not travel unless he did. She must stay in Salzburg and would never see Italy.

The dog had gone to sleep under the table, his head on Leopold's foot. "Of course he would have taken it," he answered for his son. He drew his foot away from its light burden. "Johann Hasse had the full opera for the occasion, and he is certainly the most popular composer in the Italian style, but your brother's *serenata* outshone Hasse's opera, as I wrote to you. Hasse was good natured, considering. 'Young Mozart will eclipse us all,' he said."

Leopold retired, even before he dressed, to pen his petition, but he had to leave it with crossings out and errors and go off to court, knowing that tardiness would not do on such a day. Wolfgang, looking for some manuscript, found what his father had written on the work table and brought it to his mother. "Why does he *write* like this?" he demanded.

"Like what?" Anna asked.

"Listen. 'Most Reverend, most Highborn Lords; my Lords, Cathedral Provost, Cathedral Dean, entire Sovereign and Worshipful Cathedral Chapter of the Archbishopric of Salzburg, my most gracious and mighty Lords! Your most reverend and most noble Excellencies will not be unaware that' du duh, du duh, du duh," read Wolfgang. "Why does he grovel this way?"

Anna pushed her hand up under her coil of braids to relieve a tight strand that pulled on her scalp.

Nannerl, who was briskly sorting the clothes brought back from Italy into piles for mending and laundering, answered her brother. "Papa knows how things are done, Woferl. It does not become you to complain because he must satisfy his superiors. He is always looking out for you."

"Well, I shall never lower myself like that," said Wolfgang. "I would rather earn my bread piecemeal from merchants than take work in a court that demands such truckling."

"I do not think," said Anna, "that your father much likes subservience either. But he *is* a servant and obeisance is expected." She said this to temper her son's insolence, but in her heart of hearts she thought that Leopold sometimes outdid himself in flattery.

It was not until late in February that Armand d'Ippold was able to find Leopold at enough leisure to ask for his daughter's hand in marriage. Leopold was in an ill humor. The Viennese Emperor meddled in the election of the new archbishop, which was not his place to do. Leopold, distracted by the Emperor's effrontery, could scarcely attend to d'Ippold's suit.

"I am older, I know," admitted Armand, "but I make a good living and your daughter has consented to marry me."

Leopold frowned. Nothing was going right since their return from Milan. First the Archbishop had died, leaving him to petition for withheld wages. Then the Emperor interfered in the affairs of the sovereign court of Salzburg. Now d'Ippold, who was very well in his place, but not a member of the upper nobility, wanted to take Nannerl off his hands. "No," he said flatly. "I do not intend to let Nannerl marry a military man."

"I have risen in the ranks," said Armand courteously, "and have been encouraged to think there is preferment to come. There is much affection between your daughter and me."

"No," said Leopold. "Nannerl has no money. She must marry better than you can offer. As for affection, she can find that at home." Leopold rose. He had more important things to do than argue with this fellow, who presumed too much on his friendship with the family. Friendship was one thing, but one did not marry one's daughter to any mere friend who happened along. Leopold said nothing to Nannerl or Anna about his conversation with d'Ippold. Finally, as she watched Nannerl's anxiety mount, Anna asked her husband whether Armand had not spoken to him.

"He has," said Leopold, pressing his lips together in a thin line.

"And?" Anna asked.

"It cannot be, Anna," said Leopold. "Nannerl can do better than d'Ippold."

Anna felt weariness settle over her. She seemed so often to be in opposition to her husband. In this matter, she must tread warily or risk hardening Leopold's position. "I have observed," she said mildly, "that they are much in love, as we were when we met, my dear. Ours was scarcely an advantageous union for you, as I was penniless and burdened with a mother without resources. Armand helped no end when Nannerl was so dispirited. I think it will be a hard blow to her if you say no."

"You do not understand, Anna," said Leopold.

"What is it I fail to understand?" asked Anna, feeling her temper begin to rise. Be calm, she admonished herself.

"Wolfgang is not like other boys," said Leopold, emphasizing each word. "I have told you that, time and again. There is an aristocracy of genius, my dear, and my son is destined to rise to the top. If his sister marries a mere soldier, will it not be easier for people to say, 'Mozart is a common man, gifted to be sure, but of very ordinary clay.' No, no, Nannerl must do better than d'Ippold."

Anna was stunned. Nannerl, who must sacrifice her musical ambitions so that her father could train his entire attention on their son, must now give up her chosen suitor so that the Mozarts might attempt to pass for minor nobility! She cajoled, argued, raged and stormed, but nothing she could say swayed her husband. She watched Nannerl with pain in her heart.

Upon hearing the news, Nannerl said nothing, but took to her bed with a series of blinding headaches. When at last she arose, she was pale and composed. She felt nothing. "Papa must know best," she said whenever Anna or Wolfgang tried to sympathize.

"Her dog is now her dearest friend," Anna said to Margarethe, whom she could now visit as freely as she had before, Solomon Arnstein's surveillance having softened. Margarethe was as devastated as Anna by the news.

Margarethe knew better than to criticize Leopold. "Is there no hope?" she asked.

"I think not," said Anna slowly. "He is concerned, he thinks, with much greater things. The way the Emperor put pressure on the voting bishops enraged him and made Nannerl's affairs seem small by comparison. But you might think that now that we have a new Prince, Leopold might reconsider."

"It did require an unusual number of ballots to elect the Count of Colloredo to the Archbishop's throne," commented Margarethe. She paid close attention to the politics of Salzburg, though only with Anna did she have opinions on the subject. "I take it the new Prince is little liked?" she said.

"He has such chilly rectitude," said Anna, "and he seems always to look down his nose and wants to reform everything. People say his ambitions have been far too clear. You know, the way he has spent every second winter here for years, giving lavish balls, operas and theatrical performances. Hovering like a vulture, people say."

"Will he let Leopold take Wolfgang to Italy again?" asked Margarethe, who knew of Leopold's wish to travel to the south once again.

"Yes," said Anna. "He says that Wolfgang must honor his *scrittura* for the Carnival opera in Milan. But the Archbishop has made very clear that they must not dilly-dally, and I am sure that Leopold will want to. He is convinced he can find a better post for the boy and perhaps for himself as well. He says that Salzburg is too provincial for Wolfgang."

"But from what I hear," said Margarethe, "Colloredo knows talent and has asked your son to compose a great many pieces for him."

"Yes," said Anna. "Wolfgang composed the small opera to celebrate the Archbishop's accession to the throne and he has asked for all sorts of pieces - symphonies, divertimentos, sonatas, arias, litanies, masses to be finished before Leopold and Wolfgang leave for Italy. He pays for each piece and even gives him a salary to be *konzertmeister*. I think my son would like this Prince if his father were not so dead set against him."

"And I presume," said Margarethe, "that the news about women singing in the opera gladdens your son's heart."

"Oh, it does," said Anna. "Woferl told me he could think of a dozen operas for Salzburg now that women, and not only castrati, can sing. But of course he must first think of his new opera for Milan. I wish," she said, "that Nannerl could go. She needs something to draw her from her melancholy."

40

1773

TODAY IS THE ANNIVERSARY of our wedding day," Leopold wrote from Milan, where he and Wolfgang had gone for the third time. "It was twenty-five years ago, I think, that we had the sensible idea of getting married, one which we had cherished, it is true, for many years. All good things take time!"

Twenty-five years, Anna thought, and so long as I do not oppose my husband in any way, we rub along well enough. Still, she sat alone in the same apartment to which her husband had brought her after the wedding ceremony and which he now scorned as too cramped for his ambition. While he promoted their son's fortunes in Italy, Anna watched her daughter feel her way in the dark. The doors to vocation and affection had been shut equally in her face and Nannerl was learning her prison, an inch at a time, holding herself rigid against new shocks.

"All good things take time," said Leopold, but Anna did not think that time would be good to Nannerl. At twenty-two she was at the height of her beauty. A little taller than her mother, she was a slender, graceful figure, her complexion as fine as a new-blown rose, her eyes gray-blue and steady. Her hair, left to itself, sprang in fine ringlets from her head, but she wore it pulled back, piled over forms and pinned up so that no willful strand escaped. She dressed with both taste and precision, qualities that had once described her performance at the keyboard, and she carried herself proudly. Even so, she refused to give any man so much as the time of day, though she wore at her waist one of the golden watches, elaborately engraved, she had received as a pianistic prodigy on tour in Paris. Although her father kept all the treasure from these journeys locked away, Nannerl had stubbornly insisted that the watch was hers by right. She would not lay claim to any of her earnings other than this watch, by which she might order her day. She had been insistent and her father had yielded.

Anna had expected Nannerl to be angry at her father for refusing Armand's suit, but Nannerl accepted his fiat without argument. When the siege of headaches had lifted, she had dressed herself, asked her mother to do her hair, and had gone about her business. "The world is as it is," she told her mother, rebuffing sympathy, "and Papa knows its ways better than anyone. If, by marrying Armand, I were to harm my brother's prospects, I should never forgive myself." Anna mourned her daughter's loss of good sense. Surely she knew that no one would think less of Wolfgang had Nannerl married Armand. But Nannerl seemed to think that Leopold's reasoning must be accepted entire.

Nannerl did her duty punctiliously. She rose and dressed early, insisting that her mother lace up her stays as tightly as she could, went to early Mass, walked the dog, had her hair done, taught her lessons, saw her friends, helped with housework, walked her dog, went to church again, said her prayers and lay down to sleep. Sometimes of a week's end she played music for gatherings of her friends, composing such dances and ditties as pleased them, accompanying anyone who asked her. Her music was given to the service of others. With some of her earnings, she bought birds in the marketplace - three tomtits and a robin redbreast - and hung their cages next to the canary's. She spent time each day trying to teach them to warble one of her brother's songs. When she saw Armand, which she could not avoid in so small a place as Salzburg, she was polite and distant.

Anna pitied Armand almost as much as her daughter. His striking black hair and mustache had grayed all at once and he walked with less spring in his step. He too was courteous, but he pined more visibly than Nannerl would permit herself.

Nannerl read aloud to her mother her father's letter describing the Christmas festivities in Milan. There were parties every night and Wolfgang performed, being called to entertain the Archduke and his princess. There was torchlight, her father wrote, and the music of bells and carillons, trumpets and drums. Nannerl felt nothing. What was Milan to her? Her mother's birthday passed without notice and the new year came. Nannerl corseted her life with rules that kept her safe: she would not go out at night alone: a friend must stop by to walk with her. She must have company for the opera or she would not go at all. She would walk only on the right side of the street going, but always on the left-hand side coming. She would wear stockings for only three days before washing and drying them by the kitchen stove; she would wash and iron her linen collars and cuffs every day. Dry-eyed and tight-lipped, she went about her business, wishing her mother would not hover, pushing down the rodent nibble of curiosity and yearning that came to her when her brother wrote of composing one quartet after another.

As Anna dusted the instruments one day in early February, she was seized with a plan. Why not, she thought, look for larger quarters? Leopold complained loudly of the smallness of the Getreidegasse apartment each time he returned from his sojourns elsewhere. Perhaps Nannerl would find the search diverting.

Marianna mentioned one day to Anna that Mitzerl Raab was looking for tenants for the *Tanzmeisterhaus*, as her property was known. "It would be just right for you, Anna," said Marianna. She paused, glancing around at Anna's crowded room as if the Archbishop's spies might be hiding in the piles of mending or under the linen goods spread out over the table. "I have heard that Leopold is dissatisfied with his lodging," she said. What she did not say was that Leopold had a growing reputation for dissatisfaction with everything and that many in Salzburg grew tired of his notions, the airs he put on when he returned inflated with Italian successes.

Anna took note that Marianna's hair, once the color of beaten copper, was streaked now with silver. Still it tumbled about her face in rich profusion, however much she braided, coiled or pinned it. Anna's own fair hair was also losing out to gray. "We are growing old, Marianna," she said. "I wonder if we grow wise as well. It is true," she admitted. "Leopold has been spoiled in Italy. With each journey, he is sure that the grass is greener in the next pasture. But the *Tanzmeisterhaus* is across the river."

"True," said Marianna, "but you often walk in the Mirabell Gardens, which is only a hop and a skip from the *Tanzmeisterhaus*."

Anna nodded. "I wonder," she mused thoughtfully, "whether Nannerl might not like a change."

Marianna nodded. "She might indeed," she said, knowing that it was likely a source of pain to Nannerl to see her former suitor as often as she must, living as she did on the busier side of the river.

Anna could not know that Marianna's suggestion had been made at the urging of the Countess Lodron, whose excellent connections had informed her that Leopold Mozart angled in every possible way to find a post elsewhere for himself and his son. The Countess was determined, if she could, to keep young Mozart in Salzburg. In this seventeen year-old boy, she saw the crown jewel of Salzburg's musical establishment. The Countess's father, Felix Arco, was the Archbishop's High Chamberlain, who took an interest in the young Mozart's career. The Countess enlisted her friend, the Countess Lützow, and together they contrived with Mitzerl Raab to offer the *Tanzmeisterhaus* to the Mozarts at a price they would secretly subsidize so that Leopold might be tempted to keep his family in Salzburg. Marianna, though her husband was only a surgeon at court, had been drawn into the plot because she and her daughter were such good friends of the Mozarts and might guide their attention to the Raab apartment.

Nannerl was immediately interested. "Papa always says that this place is too small," she said. "But," she added conscientiously, "is it right to look without him?"

"We can look," said Anna, "though of course your father must make the decision." Or think he does, she told herself.

Off they went, warmly wrapped in fur-lined cloaks, bending against the wind that had frozen the margins of the river, across the bridge and past boat docks to the Hanibalplatz. Fraulein Raab met them there and showed them the rooms of the *Tanzmeisterhaus*, a handsome eight-room apartment on the first floor, above a glover's and a shop that stocked combs and buckles, whalebone and buttons, foreign braid and the like.

"Oh, look, Nannerl," Anna exclaimed. "You can see the theater! How your brother would like that!"

Nannerl looked from left to right. "You cannot see the church from here. The pawnshop blocks it." She liked the reverberation of their voices in the empty rooms, as if they stood inside an instrument not yet strung.

Mitzerl led the way across the empty rooms, with their well-polished, patterned floors, to the back windows. "From here you can look down into the little garden and up to the castle," she pointed out.

I would like this, thought Anna. In summer the garden would be cool and pretty. There was a forest of tree branches and beyond them, church spires, between where they stood and the castle. "Nonnberg," she said with pleasure."

"You can see it in winter," said Mitzerl, "but not in summer."

"So much space!" exclaimed Anna. The thin winter light came in aslant through the front windows on this late afternoon. The Mirabell gardens were close enough to walk Nannerl's dog and Leopold might lodge his carriage at the nearby stables.

Anna put her arm lightly around Nannerl's shoulders, never sure whether her daughter might shrug off such an embrace. "What do you think?" she asked.

Nannerl had, for the moment, forgotten to protect herself from her own feelings. "We would have room for music making and could invite people for dancing," she said, "and Papa could keep his harpsichords and claviers spread about nicely. There would be room for Papa and Wolfgang each to have a writing table, and we could have a pool table and card tables. The stoves are very good and the floors much handsomer than ours."

"The best part," said Mitzerl, grinning broadly, "is the rent." She named a modest sum and quickly, before Anna could inquire why it was so low, changed the subject. "You remember that I rented this apartment to Michael Haydn to use for his wedding feast because he and Magdalena invited so many."

Though Mitzerl clearly thought this the greatest possible selling point, Anna was not impressed. Herr Haydn imbibed more spirits than were good for him, and his wife, a singer, had inclined to religious ranting since the loss of their little daughter. It was, however, true that their wedding had been one of Salzburg's great social occasions some five years earlier.

"Why," asked Nannerl, "is it called *Tanzmeisterhaus*?"

Mitzerl explained. "One of the earliest occupants was a French dancing master who married a Salzburg woman. And then it was sold to Eva Waglhofer, who was wife to another dancing master, as was their son, my cousin, Frantz Spöckner."

"He was one of the witnesses at our wedding," Anna commented.

"When Frantz died," Mitzerl went on, "he left it to me. Now tell me, would not Leopold think it a great bargain?"

"He would, Mama," Nannerl seconded.

"But why is it so cheap?" asked Anna, perplexed.

Mitzerl shrugged, "Because of the love I bear you, my dear," she answered lightly.

Anna mused. "Leopold says we must not sleep like soldiers all lined up in a barracks, now Wolfgang is so grown up. But we must be sure that Leopold sees it as his idea to move here. It will never do for us to want it, Nannerl."

Nannerl nodded. "Well, we heard about it from Frau Gilowsky. Perhaps Herr Gilowsky would tell Papa that the *Tanzmeisterhaus* is empty and for a very low price. We can act surprised and say, 'Oh, no. It is sure to be too costly . . . .' "

" ' . . . .and too far across the river, too far from the shops,' " Anna chimed in. They could persuade Leopold he had made a great find entirely by himself. They could provide just the right amount of opposition to pique his determination.

Leopold and Wolfgang returned to Salzburg in March. Leopold had lingered as long as he might, pleading a disabling attack of rheumatism. "You must spread the word that I am unwell," he wrote, "but it is not true. Cut off this strip of paper so that it will not fall into hostile hands," he instructed, though Anna neglected to do so, putting his letter with the others she carefully saved at his behest. Leopold had delayed, first because the opera must be copied, then because he hoped for word from Florence or Milan that a position had become available in one of these courts and finally because he feared avalanches in the Tyrol. Finally, though, they were home and Wolfgang was immediately commissioned to compose a divertimento for the first anniversary of the Archbishop's enthronement.

"Listen to what Gilowsky had to say," Leopold confided to Anna and Nannerl, not long after their return. "The *Tansmeisterhaus* is available to rent."

"Really!" Anna exclaimed. She felt like a fisherman with a tug on her line. "But surely it would cost far too much! I should not think you would like to be so far from where we are now so comfortable." She caught, in Nannerl's haste to find a stitch she had dropped in her knitting, a wicked glint of the eye and had to turn away, to busy herself with a piece of lint on her skirt, to keep from laughing aloud.

So it was that Leopold Mozart signed an agreement to move his family not to an Italian city as he had hoped, but across the Salzach to the spacious and sunny house in which generations of dancing masters had lived. He thought their good friend Mitzerl Raab foolish to let the apartment go for so little money, never suspecting that there were generous forces with ulterior motives subsidizing the move.

Leopold decided that he and Wolfgang would go to Vienna, where Leopold was determined to secure an appointment.

"Why now, in midsummer?" Anna wondered. "Wolfgang has no commission, and the nobility will be away from the city." Anna was puzzled by her husband's apparently impulsive decision to take Wolfgang to Vienna. Wolfgang was also puzzled. "I am in the middle of half a dozen things," he complained, "and Vienna is so hot in summer. Would it not be better to wait . . . ."

Leopold would brook no objections. He could not wait to be away from Salzburg, which was too small to contain him and his comet, which must streak across some larger sky. "We cannot stay here," he said coldly to Wolfgang. "We have been insulted and may not remain like docile beasts."

"Insulted how?" Anna inquired.

"My son ought to have been appointed *kapellmeister* when Lolli retired," he said, spitting out his words. He glared at her. How could Anna not see what was so obvious?

"Papa," remonstrated Wolfgang. "I could not do justice to such a position. It was good of you to ask for it, of course," he added hastily, "but so many older musicians would never listen to me."

"Indeed!" cried Leopold in exasperation. "Which one of the old musicians has won such acclaim! It is the Italians, always the Italians, who come between us and the recognition we are due."

"I thought you were besotted with Italians," said Anna unkindly.

"They are overweening and ambitious," complained Leopold, "and cannot see what is under their very eyes. I have it in mind," he began, but did not finish what he had begun. His wife would surely object if she knew that he planned to lay siege to the Emperor in Vienna. The court composer had been ill for some time, and Leopold thought it would be wise to have Wolfgang on hand when his death occurred.

"Then take us, Nannerl and me," said Anna. "We have many acquaintances in Vienna."

But Leopold did not want his wife on hand to criticize him. Nor did he want the burden of Nannerl, who was no longer an asset to an impresario.

"Impossible," he said. "If all the Mozarts were to leave, everyone would speculate that we mean to pull up roots. And think," he added reflexively, "of the expense."

Anna was disinclined to argue. Vienna was indeed, as Wolfgang had said, hot in the summer. She would begin to sort their possessions, with an eye to moving to the new house. She and Nannerl would enjoy the cool breezes that blew from snow-topped mountains even in midsummer.

After only nine weeks, Leopold and Wolfgang returned without success.

"We did not see the Emperor even once," Leopold complained. "He had no time for the likes of me. The Empress was civil, but very cool. Herr Mesmer says she took against the boy when the opera went amiss six years ago. Can you imagine holding a grudge for so long a time?"

Anna felt no pleasure in the vindication of her guess that the Empress had been displeased when Leopold had petitioned the Emperor to take sides against Affligio, his own manager of entertainments. Anna had heard gossip, all the way from the imperial capital, that it was the Empress herself who had advised her son, Ferdinand of Milan, not to offer a position to either of the Mozarts.

It happened that the Empress and Salzburg's Archbishop Colloredo, in Vienna for several weeks, had held a brief conversation about the Mozarts. "If you give them an inch, they will take an ell," the Archbishop had said.

"The boy is very able," said the Empress, "but the father is never satisfied."

"Both are able," the Archbishop conceded, "the boy, extraordinary. But the father cannot let well enough alone. I am at pains to let him know which one of us is master."

While Anna could know nothing of such counsels, she feared that her husband, who on the one hand advanced his son's fortunes, might also stand in his way.

41

1774

AS INSTRUCTED BY LETTER FROM MUNICH, Anna searched for and found the music Leopold asked her to send, his own Litany in D major and Wolfgang's Great Litany. Here were the triplets he had mentioned for second violin at the Agnus Dei. She sang through her husband's litany in her head, now the soprano part, now the tenor, now the violins, violas, flutes and trumpets. Wolfgang's Great Litany - not in a blue cover, as Leopold had said it would be, but covered in snuff-brown paper - was, she could tell as she went through it, orchestra and chorus resonating in her mind, far superior to his father's. The soaring and then sorrowing voices set down in her son's hand sounded as clearly as if she sat in church, enfolded by the familiar service that spoke of and to God. Ah, she thought, with sudden understanding. What her husband did not have within himself he must possess in his son. She felt a welling of pity for her husband, who had lately so angered her.

Leopold needed the litanies at once, his letter said. Anna wrapped them up securely and took them out to post, while Nannerl sat by the stove to dry her hair.

"Mama!" Nannerl wailed as her mother returned to a room unusually warm. Anna had earlier brought up extra fuel so that Nannerl's dripping hair might dry before nightfall. "My hair will never dry and I will be a perfect fright!"

Anna hung up her cloak and felt Nannerl's hair, which cascaded - the color of ripe wheat - halfway down her back. "Almost dry," she comforted.

She had been irritated all day that her daughter should undertake such a project in the dead of winter, but it was no good objecting. If she was fair, Anna knew that it was not Nannerl's washing her hair that bothered her, but that Nannerl would travel to Munich for her brother's comic opera, *La finta giardiniera,* while Anna must stay at home.

Nannerl shook the heavy burden of her hair back and went to the mirror. On the nearby table lay her comb, a scatter of hairpins, a large cone-shaped linen pad stuffed with flax, a hairpiece of curls that matched her own, a jar of the orange-blossom-scented pomade her father had brought her from Vienna, and lengths of the wide satin ribbon she would use to finish off the great tower of hair and hide the pins that held it together. She brushed until her hair gave off sparks, then gathered it all into an immense tail, which slithered down the moment she tried to push the pad into place. "Oh!" she moaned. "What shall I do?"

Anna had busied herself folding the underskirts Nannerl would take on her journey. She nearly laughed to see her daughter, now twenty-three and taller than her mother, so entirely baffled. "Let me help," she offered.

"But how will I do it in Munich without you? Papa says I must learn to do it myself."

For someone whose mastery of the keyboard was nearly unrivaled, thought Anna, her daughter was strangely undone by her own hair. She made more pother about her *coiffure* than she ever had about performing before the most august of crowned heads. "Well," she said with asperity. "I could go along with you and do your hair, as I have done these many years, were it not that your Papa is convinced that I alone can walk your dog and clean the birds' cages. And prepare to move, if that should ever come to pass." She shuddered to think of the argument she and Leopold had had, which had left her still feeling bruised and frightened.

"Divide the front hair from the back and let all the hair in front fall down over your face, Nannerl," Anna instructed.

Nannerl, close to tears, ran the edge of her wooden comb over the crown of her head from one ear to the other, and held the shining fall of fine, curling hair aloft as she tried, with her other hand, to place the enormous pad where it must be fastened. "Get the pad pinned up securely - here, like this." She guided Nannerl's hands so that they could feel the way the pad should sit and how the pins should go in through the edges. "Now comb it up again, and carry it back and over, like this." She was not sure Nannerl *could* do her hair by herself, since she insisted on such towering height.

Nannerl flung down the pad and collapsed onto the small red sofa, her hair raining down on every side and covering her face. She tossed it back angrily. "I *cannot* get it right. I shall stay at home and go about my business here. I am not meant for gadding about."

Anna rued the day Nannerl had decided she must dress and do her hair like the greatest noblewomen of France, until now it was second nature for her to wear her hair on such a scaffolding as seemed to Anna a form of torture. She smoothed the topmost of the underskirts, a fashionably short cherry-colored taffeta, trimmed with a braid of blue and gold, to be worn under a wine-colored velvet overskirt and striped bodice, the whole showing off Nannerl's fine stockings and dainty shoes. Anna straightened and put her hands in the small of her back. "Nonsense," she said. "Of course you will go. Your father has found very suitable lodging for you with the Widow von Durst. She will know of a good hairdresser if you find you cannot manage. I can do your hair for you just before you get in the carriage. If I use pomade and plenty of pins and you put your negligée cap on very carefully at night, it will do for a while."

Nannerl sniffled. "I wonder that you do not mind sending me into a house where the lady is sought after by a man who lives apart from his wife."

"Oh, Nannerl!" Anna laughed. "You know very well you want to go. I am not *sending* you anywhere. Here, let me try your hair another way that will be easier for you to do." Anna spent nearly an hour coiling and braiding, pinning up the thick, luxuriant curls, brushing strands into fat ringlets around her finger. Finally she discovered just the right combination of height, the fall of negligent curls along Nannerl's swanlike neck, and ease of construction. After several tries, Nannerl was able to do it to perfection herself.

Nannerl was contrite. "I have been cross as a bear," she apologized. "Now I must rush off to teach little Katharina her lesson." She kissed her mother's cheek. "Thank you for the hair, Mama. And for the clothes and packing and . . . ."

"Go on," said Anna, giving her a little push. "Go with God. You must not keep Katharina waiting."

Nannerl finally went off to Munich, her hair beautifully coifed, her trunks well supplied with elegant dresses. She was both fashionably and warmly dressed, as Leopold had advised. She went with the Mozarts' friends, Frau von Robinig and her daughter Louisa.

"Oh, how I wanted to go with her!" Anna confessed to Margarethe, having kissed and waved her daughter off on her journey.

"And Leopold said no," said Margarethe. It was not a question.

"He did," said Anna. "We had such an argument as I cannot bear to think on." She shivered, remembering.

"This time," Anna had said firmly to him, "I wish to go with you."

Leopold had offered the familiar excuses: she would not like the weather or the bustle of crowds, it would be too costly for her to come along, her leaving Salzburg would be fodder for gossip, someone must prepare the new house for their tenancy, Nannerl's dog and her birds must be tended.

Anna had answered his objections: there was harsh enough weather in Salzburg and she was used to crowds; if she came, she could provide their meals and save money; there would be talk no matter what; and surely the servant could care for the house and animals.

"No," said Leopold. "It is my wish that you remain here. Why not send Nannerl to Munich," he said, seeking a sweetener for his edict. "It would cheer her up to hear her brother's opera, and you remember how taken she was with the Nymphenburg Palace. Many of our friends have said they would come to hear the opera, and they will be company for her."

Anna took a deep breath. "It would be a fine thing for Nannerl to travel to Munich, but I want to go as well. If our friends can travel to Munich, why should not *I*?"

"No," Leopold repeated, "it will not do, my dear." He repeated all his reasons.

"I have answered you," said Anna. "Your reasons are but excuses. You very simply do not want me with you, yet I am your wife and Wolfgangerl's mother, and I have said I wish to join you."

"Do not oppose me, Anna," said Leopold, his voice like iron.

"I *will* oppose you," she answered. "Too often I have not, and see what has happened? Every hope our daughter has had lies in ruins. Despite her genius, there is no prospect for her as a musician."

"I did not make the world, Anna," said Leopold furiously, "but I must live in it. And so must you. *And* my daughter."

There was truth to what Leopold said, Anna knew. Nevertheless, she was too full of feeling for the fragile dam of civility to hold the torrent of her anger and disappointment back any longer. She felt she spoke to a perfect stranger, though she had married him twenty-seven years before. "Not only," she said furiously, "have you deprived her of her music. Now you have refused her the man of her heart, who wished to marry her, give her children and make her happy. And now I fear you will destroy the boy . . . ."

"Enough!" Leopold roared. "I will hear no such slanders from the lips of a woman!"

Anna felt as if ice pierced her heart. She feared she had said too much, that Leopold would find some way to divorce her, mew her up in an asylum or parade her through the town wearing a scold's bridle, that all should see her disgrace. He was within his rights to punish her. Even so, she could not stop. "What I say is not slander," she said furiously, "but the truth. I fear you will destroy our son. You encourage his arrogance and pride and you feed off him like a parasite."

Every atom of Leopold's being shifted. Never, except for his mother, had anyone hurled words at him like weapons. He felt his very structure of bones and tissue sag and crumble. What a hateful woman this was, this termagant who turned on him and struck at his vitals! When he looked at her, he saw his mother, upright, cold, judgmental, pointing at the door with the claw of her hand. He felt tears start in his eyes and cursed his wife that she could thus reduce him. "You understand little. You have not lived and traveled with Wolfgang as I have," he said, mastering his voice. "You have not seen him triumph in competitions, in tests, in the great salons. You have not seen how he is adored in Italy. You have no right to speak in this way to me."

"I have every right," Anna answered. "Wolfgang is my son as well as yours. I have seen him in the courts and salons of Paris and London. I have seen how he is fawned over one minute and dropped the very next. And I have seen how you have interfered with the Viennese Emperor, who is now set against him, and how your discontent with our Archbishop . . . ."

"If petty minds cannot understand . . . ," Leopold sputtered. "I have given my heart and soul to the boy. I have never done anything but advance his prospects. I must endure such fools as you could never imagine, pay court to ignoramuses, give up my own claims so that his may thrive. And yet you carp and criticize. You are cruel." He turned away from her, feeling that he could hardly breathe.

"And have you never been cruel?" Anna said. She knew they would both pay dearly for this quarrel, but it was too late to retreat. Feeling that she walked on glass, bleeding and drawing blood, she lowered her voice, took a moment for her passions to cool and breathed deeply before she spoke. "You once admired what you were pleased to call my genius, Leopold," she said. "That was when you wanted me to marry you. You put your name on the pieces I composed. But then, once I was with child, there was no room in this household for my genius. And then there was Nannerl and her genius. Our daughter may earn some money with her gifts, but she will never be able to venture as far as her soul may go. Now in your eyes, only our son has genius, and him you must make a puppet, whose lines it pleases you to speak. You are only a father, Leopold, not a god." Anna gasped. She had never even known she thought such thoughts.

"I never once," Leopold denied hotly, "thought you possessed of genius. You have made that up. You are full of an unnatural jealousy." There was bitterness in his voice. "Like all women, you are fair on the outside, but on the inside rotten, laying snares for men and then destroying them. I do not wish to discuss this further," said Leopold, folding his arms across his chest. He felt flayed; his very organs might drop out of their case, leaving an empty carcass behind.

Anna paid no attention. "You complain, Leopold. Everyone wrongs you. I have listened and listened. But you wrong me, as well . . . ."

"When I have been away," Leopold interrupted, "I have imagined you as you were when I met you - a beautiful girl, so slim and lovely, so kind, so agreeable. I have seen you thus in my dreams, standing and smiling by a bowl of perfect fruit, which you hold out to me. And then when I see you, I find you old and ugly, sagging and gray, nothing like what I married. You are truly Eve's offspring, holding out apples to lure me away from obedience to God's will. While I exhaust myself to support you in your idleness, you have nothing better to do than to name my faults. What is it *you* do to keep the body and soul of this family together?"

Though she was hurt, Anna felt a spasm of laughter sweep through her frame. "I?" she asked, "Why, I do Nannerl's hair everyday!"

"How can you laugh?" Leopold demanded. "You but prove the truth of what men say, that woman is a frivolous creature, very changeable and not suited to higher thoughts."

Anna was suddenly as tired as she had been furious. "Oh, Leopold," she said, sighing. "We should not be enemies, but here we are, like two cocks in the ring, anointed and spurred and stabbing one another to the death. I am not a great lady, Leopold, nor a famous beauty. I know that."

But Leopold turned from her, mewed himself up with his books and papers, hardly able to bear the few days until he and his son should mount into their carriage and be away for Munich.

"It was truly a dreadful battle," Anna sighed. "It all went through my mind just now. I fear I have been poor company while I remembered."

"I could tell you were caught up in memory," Margarethe said gently. "But here you are, back with me again."

"I said harsh things," said Anna. "And so did he. I am grateful Nannerl and Woferl were both out of the house. They surely must have guessed that something was amiss, for both of us walked around in a stupor. I was fearful, Margarethe, of what he might do, for no one would question his right to punish me for my temerity. But he did nothing other than sulk. Now that he is in Munich, his letters are just like all his other letters. Of course, he wants them saved as a record and would not wish for such a contretemps to be written down."

"Why," Margarethe asked, "do you think he does not want you with him on his journeys?"

Anna considered. "He thinks I would interfere with his control of our son. And indeed I would. My husband cannot see - and it seems so abundantly clear to me - that Woferl will, at some point, have to make his own way. I called my husband a parasite when we argued, and I was ashamed later. It was a hurtful thing to say. But it is true, Margarethe. He *feeds* on our son, *battens* on him. He will never let go, I fear." Anna did not say so to Margarethe, but she thought that she and her husband had inflicted mortal wounds on that bond that held them together. And yet, what choice did they have but to act as if there were amity between them? Perhaps, by acting so, some vital tissue would regenerate. Her husband, she realized, did not act from malice but from love misshapen by need. She imagined him as a bird with an injured wing, who could not but flap around in a circle rather than soar on two good wings. Out of pity, she resolved to be kind to him, if he would let her.

While he remained in Salzburg, Leopold had been disinclined to make peace with his wife. She had committed an unforgivable breach. Nevertheless, he felt uneasy with himself. A man needed a wife, and even though she was unpleasantly inclined to interfere and criticize, he had never found anyone who might suit him better. He must resign himself. Sometimes he dreamed that he was widowed. In his dream, he had to make the necessary rounds, to tell his friends that his wife had died. He was surprised at the strength of his bereavement. He thought it was because she kept the house in such good order, packed up their trunks for travel with such completeness, supplying everything he and his son needed to dress well and to attend to illness or injury.

Perhaps, he thought, when he returned from Munich, they would move to the new house promptly and he would hire some artist to paint her portrait to go with the others. She could sit for Loronzoni or some other painter in her rose-colored gown, but not at the harpsichord nor surrounded by any of the implements of composition. No, she could hold up a length of lace and he would even - without regard for the cost - pay the artist for two hands.

42

1775-1777

PAPA COULD NOT DECIDE whether to be pleased or furious when our Prince Archbishop turned up in Munich," Wolfgang explained to Anna. At nineteen and just home from his success in the Bavarian court, it seemed to Wolfgang that he understood all the workings of court politics. He understood his father as one who plotted and schemed for advancement, wetting his finger and holding it in the wind. "The Archbishop could not hear my opera for himself," Wolfgang told his mother, "because there were too many entertainments for him to attend and that made Papa fume. But he was pleased that the Archbishop heard people - especially the Elector and his family - praise my work. Privately Papa told me he hoped His Grace would be embarrassed because he had not made me *kapellmeister* back here in Salzburg. But Mama, even I, dunce that I am, know that he could not do that. I am too young to tell all those older musicians what to do and how to do it."

"I would not think it wise to embarrass the Archbishop, who is not only our Prince," said Anna, "but the man who pays your wages and your father's."

"I do not think it possible to embarrass a prince," opined Wolfgang. "They are always right, so someone else must always be at fault." He lowered his voice, as he had learned to do with his father, and spoke conspiratorially. "The Archbishop received us at last. He was very haughty. 'It is my wish, Mozart, that musicians in my pay will make their mark in *my* court rather than another prince's.' " Wolfgang sucked in his cheeks and peered down a long nose, speaking in a pinched and reedy voice.

Anna could not help but laugh. Wolfgang had the Archbishop to perfection. "Be careful," she warned him.

"I know, I know," said Wolfgang, "and really, he is very good to me. But he has such a pompous way. I do not like to bow and scrape. I am as good as any prince, Mama, and it galls me . . . ."

Anna put her finger to her lips. "Republican talk, even in private, is not a good idea, Woferl," she cautioned gently. Lately her son had been much interested to hear news from the English colonies in America. But that was different, thought Anna, for in the colonies a person might stand in the woods and shout all manner of sentiments and no one would hear nor take offense.

"But the Prince himself talks of reform, and the Emperor in Vienna, too," Wolfgang retorted.

"Princes may speak differently from their servants," Anna said. "I know, I know," she said, putting her hands up to forestall a barrage of protest, "you do not feel like a servant, but your Prince does not consider you his equal."

"Well, someday," said Wolfgang grandly, looking around him, "they will call this place the *Tanzmeister und Mozarthaus*. " He laughed at himself for his own pretension. "I am glad your picture is on the wall, now, Mama, with the others, though it does not do you justice. You are much nicer looking than your portrait."

The quartet of portraits that now hung on the wall of the spacious music room attested to Leopold's standing. He was no mere artisan, but a man of substance who could afford to have his family's portraits painted. He was uneasily aware that many of his friends could afford better artists and might judge him miserly when they came to make music, play cards or shoot airguns at gaily decorated targets with arch mottoes.

Ever since they had moved into the new house, Anna felt she breathed more deeply of a clearer air. She found herself even thanking the Archbishop for his refusal to let her husband and her son leave Salzburg. It was nearly two years that the four had lived at home together, the first such placid time since the children were small. Anna found herself singing as she worked companionably about the house with the servant girl. Her voice, though no longer young nor supple, set the canary singing in his cage.

Ever since his travel to and return from Munich, Leopold had seemed to Anna to have shrunk in some way, like someone purged from a long illness, holding himself as though he expected any motion to hurt. He had never been more exacting in his service to his Prince. He was, his colleagues thought, too punctilious in his courtesy; he spoke with a deference so extreme that it was almost parody; he bowed a shade too deeply. He believed Anna could not possibly understand how he had been condemned to Salzburg, now a prison to him.

Anna watched with helpless concern as Nannerl's severe habits multiplied. She laced herself into ever tighter corsets, had her hair more splendidly constructed, studied the fashion dolls that came from Paris and designed only the most complicated costumes to wear. She did her duty without complaint. She devoted herself to her father and did everything to help her brother, with an almost Protestant fervor. She insisted, against all evidence, that she would teach her tomtits and robin to sing as she desired; when they drooped in their cages, she scolded them. Anna suggested she let the poor things go, but Nannerl would not give them their freedom.

Wolfgang, like his mother, was entirely happy. The Archbishop - though his father had grown to detest him and called him "mufti," as if he were a Turkish potentate - required serenatas, concertos and music for the shorter masses he favored. When the Archduke Maximilian visited Salzburg, Wolfgang was required to provide the music for a dozen entertainments. He thought he could persuade the Prince Archbishop to let him compose the opera for Carnival. He meant to ask for it himself, rather than let his father do so. Wolfgang had friends in every street and alley, from nobleman to dustman. There were plenty of good-looking girls to flirt with and young men he had known since his childhood, with whom he could attend the theater and roister in the taverns. The strut and swagger he had brought home with him from Italy gave way to his usual rapid, bobbing walk. "There goes Wolfgangerl Mozart," everyone said, as he rushed about both business and pleasure in high good spirits. Every great house was open to him, and when he was not composing for court, he could compose for his friends' name days and weddings and other happy occasions. The *Tanzmeisterhaus* was just right for him, with plenty of space for both work and play. So long as he could compose operas, he would be glad to go on this way forever - or at least until he married and moved into his own house.

But one September day, when he had reached the age of twenty-one, Wolfgang pounded up the stairs. His face was white, though there were red spots high on his cheeks, as if he had been slapped. His hair had flown out of its ribbon, which lay unnoticed on the bridge, trampled under passing feet and hooves.

"What is it, Woferl?" Nannerl asked, dismayed by her brother's wild mien. Anna held out her arms, for he seemed about to faint.

Wolfgang put out his hand to ward her off. "I must leave Salzburg!" he exclaimed, running his hand distractedly through his hair, so that it stood about his head. He had run so fast with the dreadful news that he could scarcely talk for panting. "The theater," he gestured across the Hannibalplatz. "The Archbishop means to tear it down."

"Oh, no!" exclaimed both Anna and Nannerl, almost in unison.

"How can that be?" asked Anna. She knew that the brightest beacon in Wolfgang's life was his intention to follow his smaller operatic works for the Archbishop with major operas, both *buffa* and *seria*, in Salzburg.

Wolfgang took a drink of water from the ladle that hung in the crock, splashing some on his hands, with which he cooled his face. "Our Prince," he said angrily, suddenly understanding his father's hostility to the prelate, "means to replace the theater with a new Ballhaus. And it will be used entirely for visiting companies. We *Salzburgers*," he said bitterly, "are not *good* enough for *His Royal Highness*!"

"Wolfgang," cautioned Anna, though they were securely indoors.

"Well, it is true. I will have to leave Salzburg now. Papa has asked for leave to travel and has been ignored. The Archbishop himself told me I had nothing to hope for here and said I should go for more learning to Naples. Oh, and the University Theater is also to be closed." He strode angrily to the window and looked out on the glorious display of leaves, early yellow and red after the hot summer and recent frosty nights. "Because the man can fiddle a little, he thinks he knows music and can meddle with everything. He does not want instrumental music in church. He shortens the mass and even concerts. He ruins everything he touches."

"And what of your father?" Anna ventured. She tried to imagine her husband's state of mind at news that would tell him that the Archbishop did not respect her son's dramatic compositions.

Wolfgang rolled his eyes and gestured at pulling his hair out in clumps. Anna laughed in spite of herself. Her son, however distressed, had that antic bone in his body that nearly always found fun. Since childhood he had been an apt mimic.

In the nearly four years since they had moved to the *Tanzmeisterhaus*, Wolfgang had crossed to the window first thing every morning, in any weather, to look across the square at the theater. It was the true north of his soul's compass. The Archbishop's intention to tear it down sounded a death knell to Wolfgang. He would leave Salzburg as soon as it could be arranged, travel the world if need be, to find a city where he could compose operas. "Mama," he said, then remembered to include his sister, "Nannerl, I do not need a post in a court. Indeed, I would rather not truckle to some prince or other," the way my father does, he added in his head. "Why," he wondered, "can I not earn my bread by giving concerts and lessons and writing operas in some city where the court would want some things, the nobles others and the merchants and bankers still others? I do not wish to be governed by someone - anyone - who claims to own me, body and soul."

Anna pondered the matter. "It is what you do here," she mused. "But what would your father think?"

"You must ask Papa," Nannerl said at the same moment, so that Wolfgang had a moment's inspiration: two voices could sing at one time, even though two could not speak at once, and the music would make their separate, overlapping thoughts intelligible.

Wolfgang grimaced. "My father has said he would write - that is, I must sign my name - to Padre Martini to see if he cannot find something in Bologne. But I tell you, I would rather live in some German city than in Italy. I wish it were here," he added, longingly. He pulled himself up. "It seems, however, that I cannot stay, however much I wish to."

Leopold was cold with fury when he returned that afternoon. "The Archbishop, in his pride, will kill the goose that lays the golden eggs." He rubbed his hands together worriedly. "But it is partly Wolfgang's fault, Anna. He *will* attempt novelties and it is precisely such departures from what the boy has been taught that the Archbishop does not like. What is the use of all my son's learning if he does just what *he* pleases, but pleases no one else? Think of the E flat concerto. The piano enters too soon and everything is too complicated. And the Andante is too gloomy by half. It pleases no one," he repeated.

"It pleases me," Anna asserted confidently. "I think he must explore this new voice, my dear, perhaps even apart from some court that controls him entirely."

"Nonsense, Anna." Leopold dismissed her without hearing what she said. Ever since their quarrel before the journey to Munich, Leopold had turned a deaf ear to his wife. She had confirmed to him the slightness of her intellect, the flaws in her reason. She was, he had concluded, unable to accord him the respect to which he was entitled as her husband. Even so, he talked to her, for to no one else could he speak openly. "I have searched everywhere for a post," he said, "- in Milan, in Bologna, in Florence, in Vienna, in Munich - so that we can remove from Salzburg. I have had no success. Everywhere there are petty minds, foolish jealousies, unreasonable prejudices. And my son, the wretch, will not submit himself, as someone of his station must." He sighed. "I am an old man now, Anna, and I have given up everything for the boy. I have nothing to hope for now for myself."

Poor Leopold, thought Anna, noting how discouragement and discontent had settled into his face.

"There is a letter in the mails to Padre Martini," Leopold went on, "Perhaps he will . . . ."

Leopold had enclosed the motet *Misericordias Domini*, which Wolfgang had written in Munich at the Elector's request. Wolfgang did not like the letter, which complained bitterly of the deficiencies of Salzburg's music and of the Archbishop's unkindness to his father. There was a whining note to it that was not at all to the young man's taste. He did not want to put his name to it, but Nannerl scolded him roundly.

"After all Papa has done for you, Wolfgang. You should be ashamed. He knows the world better than you do and has sacrificed everything on your behalf."

"But Nannerl, I think he is not right in this matter. Padre Martini will not want a mewling baby on his hands, and that is how Papa makes me sound. And Nannie, if Papa knows the world so well, why has he not been able to find a post?" He drew himself up. "I am a man myself now and know a thing or two."

"You must trust Papa," Nannerl repeated urgently. "He knows what is right to do."

Padre Martini's reply did not come until January, one of the coldest Anna could remember. Wolfgang brought in the post, closely followed by his father. Anna and Nannerl dropped their needlework to hear the long-awaited letter read out.

"It is in Italian," said Wolfgang, his eyes skimming the letter, "So, hmmm. 'I received the Motet . . . . in all sincerity . . . singularly pleased with it, finding in it all that is required by Modern Music: good harmony, mature modulation, a moderate pace in the violins, a natural connection of parts and good taste.' So far, so good," Wolfgang continued, skimming as fast as he might. " 'I am delighted', um, 'rejoice,' um 'you have made great strides in composition, which must be pursued ever more by practice, for Music is of such a nature as to call for great exercise and study as long as one lives.' Oh, and he wants my portrait and my father's . . . ." Wolfgang turned the paper around, studying its front as well as its back. Well," he said, "he says nothing about a post in Bologna."

"Let me see it," said Leopold, snatching and rereading the letter, looking in margins and under blots for something additional that would give him hope. "He offers nothing," he said, his voice bleak.

All through the long, cold and snowy winter, Wolfgang worked dutifully for the Archbishop and with gaiety for the friends and patrons who generously engaged his services. In June, Leopold once against petitioned the Archbishop for leave. He was refused once again, and Wolfgang was ordered to remain in Salzburg to assist in the entertainment of the visiting Viennese Emperor.

Finally in August, when the Emperor had come, been suitably entertained, and gone, Leopold composed one more petition to his employer. He did not show it either to his son - fearing his resistance to its pathos - nor to Anna, who was sure to urge him to leave out the reminder to the Archbishop that the Gospel taught mankind to profit from its talents.

The answer fell like a blow. His Highness' decree was that "father and son shall have permission to seek their fortune elsewhere, according to the Gospel." The Archbishop had added the last phrase himself, in his own hand, displeased that his servant should see fit to instruct him in religious matters.

Though Leopold crossed the river several times every day between his home and the court, he made the journey this day with leaden feet, the parchment he carried weighing him down. With tremulous voice, he read out the Archbishop's words to his wife and children.

There was utter silence when he finished. Far off, in the cool September silence, a dog barked.

Nannerl swayed in her chair, on her face, from which all color had fled, an expression of horror. "We will have to beg in the streets," she said thinly. Her pupils would desert her, once the Archbishop's displeasure was known. Leopold's face was ashen, his hands trembling. Anna wondered whether to fetch a physician to attend him.

Wolfgang stood up. "It is not right," he declared, "that my father should suffer insult on my account. I will tell the Archbishop I will stay and kiss his royal ass all he likes."

For all his bravado, Anna could see that her son was close to tears.

Leopold could not think for the ringing in his ears. "No, no," he said feebly. "You must escape this . . . prison. Perhaps we should all leave. Surely we can find posts in another court."

"But," said Anna, "you have tried. It is not so easy." While her husband continued to compose, his best efforts had long since been in the promotion of his son. It would be easier for younger, cheaper men to find positions.

The same thoughts as went through his wife's head went through Leopold's. He had found no interest in Italy, even among those amazed at his son's precocity. "I must," he swallowed, hesitated, and swallowed again, though his mouth was dry, "grovel and make my peace with His Grace. But you, my son, must go. The Prince is not a forgiving man."

"Alone?" said Nannerl, aghast.

"Alone?" asked Wolfgang, hopefully.

"My brother lives in Augsburg," Leopold said at last, feebly, "and my friend Franz von Heufeld is in Mannheim, where musicians are held in high esteem. Perhaps in Mannheim, the Elector Karl Theodor will recognize the treasure he might have and then, when your position is secure, you can find a place for your father." He broke down, head in hands and wept.

Anna had been silent until now. She knew that Leopold would be in agony if he knew his son were left to his own devices in foreign cities. In some ways, her husband had undermined his son's competence with his own. The boy would have to learn to manage his own affairs. But it also occurred to her that this was Wolfgang's chance to get away, on his own, to establish himself as a man, which he might not do so long as he grew in his father's long shadow. She shivered. Surely what she was thinking was impossible.

"I will," she said slowly, feeling the world revolve around her, "go with him."

PART 8

43

1777

VERYONE FROZE, DUMBSTRUCK by Anna's announcement. She was herself speechless, horrified by what she had just said.

"Mama?"

"Mama?"

"Anna!"

Three voices finally spoke as one. Wolfgang thought again that he could make wonderful in opera what was only cacophony when people spoke.

"Impossible," Leopold said, running the tips of his long fingers along his thumbs. "You do not know the right people." His voice was thin, uncertain.

"Then," said Anna firmly - quite sure that he was right and that she could never act the impresario as he did - "you will teach me who I must know and how to get their ear - ears," she amended, tickled by a sudden vision of a town populated by important and powerful ears.

"But Mama . . . ." Nannerl protested, her voice wavering. She did not know precisely what it was that troubled her. If Mama and Wolfgang went and Papa stayed, what of her? Papa would expect her to cook and clean and do all that Mama did.

Since Wolfgang had heard the dreadful news of the theater's closing, he had entertained thoughts of being gloriously on his own, perhaps in Munich, where he knew everyone, perhaps in Mannheim, where the musical establishment was unrivaled in the German-speaking world. He would escape from the tyranny of his childhood, which it seemed would never end. He was a man now and sure that, left to his own devices, he could find a way to make his living in some great musical city without enslaving himself to a single master. If Mama came, she might stand in the way of his own ideas and pleasures. Of course he could not say so.

Leopold was reeling. In the first place, there was the Archbishop's ingratitude. How could he cut two such faithful servants adrift, when they had provided his court with nothing but splendor? Everyone would know of Leopold's disgrace before long. It took no time for news to travel in Salzburg. He realized drearily that he would have to go to his disagreeable master, bend his knee and tug at his forelock like a stable hand. He would no doubt be taken back into service, but would bear the shame of his dismissal like the mark of Cain, a blazing brand for all to see and for the Italians to snigger over. But worse, how could he let Wolfgang go? While he had at first thought that the boy must get away, he could not bear the loss of him. No, Wolfgang must stay in Salzburg, opera house or no, for without his father's guidance, anything might happen. Wolfgang was not wise to the world. Any charlatan or trickster might have his way with the boy. And Anna! The idea was ludicrous. What did she know? Still, if he provided the letters and relied on his acquaintance . . . . If Wolfgang were to go as far as Paris, there was the Baron von Grimm to rely on, a man of the world who could not be better connected. Anna might be able to keep Wolfgang from running off to join some troupe of mendicant minstrels and mountebanks. There was no telling what outlandish tricks Wolfgang, left to his own devices, might get up to. Leopold shook his head to clear it. His thoughts crawled over themselves like maggots in bad meat.

Anna went to him. "My dear," she said, knowing that his mind must be a turmoil of hurt and astonishment. "Woferl - Wolfgang," she corrected herself, "is a man now, experienced in the ways of the world, and I have traveled as well. I will follow your directions." Anna knew very well that she deceived Leopold, of whose smaller deceptions she had so often disapproved. She would hear her husband's advice and appear to take it, but she meant to do everything in her power to help her son break free of his father's grip on him. Otherwise she would lose her son, she realized, as her thoughts raced. She had already lost Nannerl, who had finally gone into the cage that the world, her father and she herself had constructed, and that needed no lock or key to keep her in. But if Wolfgang did not break free, he would be lost to her in the same way as was Nannerl. It was possible to teach caged birds to sing human songs, but those melodies were never as splendid as the songs they sang on their own in the grasses and trees.

Leopold, burning with the sense of suffering from manifold wrongs, fell ill with fever and a heavy catarrh, and kept to his bed while Anna made most of the preparations for her departure with her son. Weakly, in a strained voice, Leopold instructed Wolfgang over and over. "You must - listen to me, Wolfgang - find a post for yourself in a place where your sister and I can also earn a decent penny. Then we can join you and be happy together again. And you must look out for your mother, who is not a young woman any more. Here. I have, despite my illness, written letters for you. You must not make yourself cheap. Be careful whom you are seen with, for . . . ."

Wolfgang hardly heard him, though he looked as earnest as he could and nodded assiduously. He could hardly wait to leave while fair September weather prevailed. He felt like the poor miller's son in a fairy tale, setting out to seek his fortune, but instead of traveling with an enchanted cat, his mother would accompany him.

Shortly before she and Wolfgang were to leave, Anna went to see Margarethe with a heavy heart. Margarethe, whose hair had never grown back as long and luxurious as before her father, in his rage, had cut it off, welcomed her apprehensively, for Anna looked worn and haggard.

"What is it Anna?" she queried.

"Are we alone?" Anna asked. When Margarethe nodded, Anna held out to her friend the small sheaf of poems that had lain, along with Anna's compositions, in their hiding place under the best linens. "I must leave, with Wolfgang, on a journey," she said.

Margarethe took the poems and, glancing around to be assured that no one spied on them, folded them into the heavy volume she had been reading. She looked at Anna, hearing the quaver in her friend's voice.

Anna recounted the events that had so changed her family's prospects. "We are topsy-turvy," she said. "I am laying in stores for Nannerl, trying to teach her everything I do. The servant girl may be snippy with her, for Nannerl is the younger. Poor Leopold is so ill and listless, and I know it is more his disappointment and fear than any humor a physician can let out with his blood. Wolfgang is itching to be gone, and that, of course, heightens Leopold's sense of grievance."

After a long pause, she went on, "The worst of it is, Margarethe, that I should not keep your poems at my house while I am gone, for what if -" she crossed herself hastily -"I do not return. They would be discovered . . . . But I give them back with a heavy heart, for I know you are hard-pressed to hide them." She had wakened in the night, unable to return to sleep, thinking of Margarethe's difficulty and trying to find ways to resolve it.

Margarethe reached for Anna's hand. "You must not think of me," she said, though she felt a void open within her. Anna had been not only her best and dearest friend these many years, but because of Anna's words, the rhymes that sprang from the deepest parts of Margarethe's heart did not go entirely unheard. What would she do without Anna? Where might she hide her poems? Who, even if only one person, would savor their meaning? "And you, Anna? I had thought your traveling days were long gone," Margarethe said, repressing her regret.

"I am terrified," Anna admitted. "I cannot possibly do what Leopold does, meet and press the right people into service so that Wolfgang gets this concert and that opera contract. In the first place, I am a woman and cannot move so freely in that world. Nor have I the temperament, the power, the connections with influential men. Leopold has written many letters of introduction, of course. But," Anna confided, "to be quite candid, it is as well that I *cannot* play the impresario. Wolfgang will have to make his own arrangements. He cannot depend on his father all his life and . . . ."

"You want him to break the leading strings," Margarethe nodded, "while Leopold wants you to hold them firmly."

"Quite so," said Anna. "Leopold never wanted the children to creep on the floor when they were small, for fear of encouraging their animal natures. I disobeyed him even then, when he was out of the house, and let them play on the floor. Poor Leopold. He has been humiliated. His friends are shocked and angered on his behalf, but *he* knew that *they* knew he must bend his knee to the Prince. It is Wolfgang's good fortune that his father does not order him too to kiss the royal ring and stay, which would be intolerable without the promise of an opera. So Leopold has no choice but to send me off as nursemaid. If I were to let on what I intend, Leopold would not allow Wolfgang out of his sight. Therefore," she said, exhaling forcefully, "I lie. I smile and kiss whom I mean to betray."

Margarethe nodded. They were both of them traitors to the men upon whom they depended.

"It is wrong," said Anna. "I know it is, but would it not be just as wrong - more so - to preserve my soul at my child's expense?" She was talking to herself now. She had made up her mind what to do, but nonetheless searched for a way that would not blacken her soul.

Margarethe held Anna to her. "Go with God," she said.

"Surely," said Anna, "we will see one another again, but I feel such a premonition . . . ."

The next day, she bade farewell to her husband and daughter. Leopold was disconsolate. His skin was gray. He seemed to Anna as fragile as porcelain. He had arisen from his sickbed and dressed, but without his usual fastidious care. His hair was caught back carelessly with a string and his shirt was unbuttoned, barely tucked into his breeches. His stockings were haphazardly pulled on. He took Anna aside, leaving Wolfgang and Nannerl to say their good-byes alone. "You must watch my son carefully," instructed Leopold. "You know his propensities well enough. He will trust anyone who is good-natured. He can be taken advantage of . . . ."

"I know, I know," said Anna gently. She realized that she felt more pity for her husband than any other sentiment. She was taking away from him his purpose in life. It made her feel like a species of murderer.

"And Anna, you must keep an eagle eye on his affections. He is like to fasten his heart on any girl, so she is pretty. He must not. He must find a position suitable for both of us, you understand?"

"Yes," said Anna faintly. "I understand what you desire," she added carefully. Her son must try his wings. He must, at some point, be a man and find some suitable companion for the life he must craft apart from his father. But she could say no such thing, for he would see her treachery and stop her.

Wolfgang and Nannerl came in, hand in hand.

"Come on, Mama!" insisted Wolfgang. "We must be on our way if we are to reach Wasserburg in good time."

Nannerl's face was red and swollen. The hair around her face hung in ringlets. "I am not well," she murmured, pressing her fingertips to her temples.

Anna felt sick with apprehension. Poor Nannerl must be in a turmoil, Anna thought, once again envying her brother his chance to travel, to win acclaim, to realize his genius as she never would. She must stay in Salzburg and content herself with teaching students who could never rival their mistress' skills. Leopold would require her housewifery, which she must add to her other duties. Quietly Anna gave her daughter her blessing, folding her along with her cloak in her arms.

She looked around at her beloved *Tanzmeisterhaus* - whose rooms, despite the early hour, were expectant with early autumn light. She patted Bimperl and bade good-bye to the canary, who sang in full voice. She did not know when she would see any of them again - her husband, her daughter, her home - or what lay before her and her son. She felt ill suited to such an adventure upon which she was set. I am not a young woman anymore - fifty-seven and three teeth short. I have grown a little stout and lose breath quickly.

Wolfgang sprang gaily into the carriage and gave his mother his hand. Salzburg in the early morning sunlight seemed inexpressibly beautiful to Anna. Every roof and cobble shone from the rain that had fallen during the night. The sky was bright blue, the feathery clouds still touched with pink and gold. The trees, whose leaves shivered in the cool breeze that blew from the mountains, had not yet begun their annual riot of gold and russet. Crickets chimed and thrummed. Everywhere were the sounds of waking. Anna heard a babe cry, followed by a man's laughter and the murmur of voices. There drifted across the river the smell of ovens, newly fired, and the yeasty dough, already risen for hours. Carts, set into motion in the dark, already rolled down the steep Linzergasse, carrying the sleepy farmers with their produce and livestock, freshly slaughtered. The geraniums on windowsills gleamed as brightly as jewels. Nowhere in the world were geraniums so brilliantly red, she thought.

As her eyes misted, Woferl took her hand in his own. What a tender heart he has, she thought, smiling at him gratefully.

"What!" he exclaimed as the carriage creaked to a halt, the horses shifting and snorting, as if they objected to the stop. Wolfgang jumped down and the coachman joined him. Anna could see them vociferating with a rough man, who seemed to command a company of workmen repairing the great iron hinge on which the heavy city gate swung. She could see her son gesticulating excitedly and thought, he will make them angry and obdurate. I should go and speak more softly. No, Anna, she reprimanded herself. If Wolfgang makes them angry, he must suffer the consequence.

When Wolfgang rejoined her, he was smiling broadly. "It seems we must wait a short while for some repairs," he said. "They are good fellows. I gave them enough that they will remember me with a drink in the tavern when their work is done. Mama," he said more soberly. "I had not my father's blessing when we left, did you notice?"

She nodded. "He was very unwell," she said, "but you are never without his blessing."

"I know," he said slowly. "But Mama, what he wants for me is not . . . " he hesitated, " . . . always what I would wish. I have to . . . ." He stopped. "The Prince would have me dance to his tune and would keep me a child forever."

He is not, realized Anna, speaking of the Archbishop at all, but of his father. The deference his Prince exacted from Leopold was exactly what Leopold wanted from Wolfgang.

The city gate swung to and the carriage strained into motion. Anna and Wolfgang were off through the radiant countryside, where the harvest brought out the farmers, their wives, children and servants. Some bent to the sweep of their scythes while others gathered the fragrant grain and rolled it into bales. How calm and purposeful they looked from this distance. Anna thought it likely that they had their squabbles and tensions just as city folk did, but who could see it from afar as they bent their backs in a common task?

Just so, she imagined, the Mozarts, were seen by anyone outside the family. She had heard it herself. "Frau Mozart, I marvel to see you, your husband and your daughter united to promote your son's advancement." "Oh Anna, how is it there is never any trouble amongst you? You never seem to be at odds." And to her son, "How fortunate you are, Herr Mozart, that your father and mother have no thought beyond your success." To Nannerl, "How you must rejoice that your brother's music is so prized by everyone." No, she thought, there could be no society whatever, no family, court or farm without its stresses and contentions, however fair appearances might be. Sometimes it took so little, just a touch, a wrong word or look, to start a train of fatal consequences. She feared what she had already set in motion, the intention to deceive, to betray, however good the reason. She shivered.

"Are you cold, Mama?" Wolfgang inquired.

"No, no," she said, "Just thinking of Papa and Nannerl."

"I wish Nannerl had come," he said. "Mama, just the other day I heard the new Court Composer, Fischietti, say in that heavy way of his, that 'the weaker sex have not, not in the least, the general intellect capable of grasping the intricacies of musical composition.' I have heard Papa say something very like that. But Nannerl composes wonderfully."

Anna smiled at him. "Often," she said, "it seems to me that when many people think something is the case, they cannot see what is under their very noses. Of course Nannerl can compose. It is foolishness to say otherwise, but what is foolish is often taken for wisdom."

Wolfgang settled himself back against the seat. "Poor Nannerl," he said, but then springing forward to look out from the carriage, he exclaimed. "Look, Mama! Look! There, in that herd. There is - there! - the brindled one - a funny-looking cow. It is lopsided. See how it staggers!"

Anna looked where Wolfgang pointed. "My father used to tell my sister and me," she recounted, "that in the mountains, cows had shorter legs on the uphill side and longer on the downhill. He said that sometimes a farmer in his cups started his cows to grazing the wrong way round, with their longer legs uphill and shorter down, and then they all fell down the mountain, churned the cream and their wives milked butter ready-made."

Wolfgang laughed at his mother's tale. Perhaps it will not be so bad to have Mama along, he thought. She tells better stories than Papa.

This may be a pleasant journey after all, thought Anna. I will get to know my son in a new way.

By evening the travelers had reached Wasserburg. Anna, exhausted, was content to leave everything to her son. He found a clean and pleasant room for them at the Stern, and ordered up a good supper. She could see that he rejoiced in his responsibilities.

"We are living like princes, are we not Mama!" Wolfgang exclaimed.

44

1777

WOLFGANG LEANED BACK, drained and entirely happy. He had performed for hours, playing every piece of music he had with him, and then improvising until midnight. Finally the lateness of the hour persuaded the hall full of Munich burghers and even members of the nobility to leave off their applause and stamping of feet, to raise a glass in his honor and then take their way home. Though Herr Albert's fortepiano was very good and the hall had a splendid resonance, Wolfgang was heartily tired of music and wished the Widow von Durst would take her leave. But from the kitchen there came the promising sounds of spoons and kettles and such aromas as could make a man swoon in anticipation. He swung his feet onto the chair opposite and took a deep pull from the tankard of beer Herr Albert had put into his hands.

Frau von Durst nattered on. "Did you see what Hedwig Eibl had on? A perfect fright in that pea green, and she wears it everywhere, as if she had no other rag to put on her back."

Wolfgang thought of what his mother had said. "She is a kind woman with a cruel tongue. It is a defect, Woferl, as if she were halt or had a harelip. And yet she was so good to Nannerl, the time she came to Munich to hear your opera, and now she is good to me."

Franz Albert, the landlord of the Black Eagle, where Wolfgang and Anna had put up, rubbed his large hands together with satisfaction. He had an excellent concert hall and could easily persuade people to fill it. Now that his remaining guests had beer to drink, he announced, "I am quite certain,

Wolfgang, that I can find ten men - men of substance and good taste: I know of eight already - who would pay to keep you here if you would give them a concert like this one every month."

Anna had already, in two weeks, discovered that Herr Albert was not a man to be taken lightly. Though he was only an innkeeper, he moved with the confidence of a man who has made his own way, amassing a comfortable income. He was clearly respected, even by his betters. "If each of these men, whatever their station, were to pledge, say, a ducat every month . . . . And you heard what Count Seeau said, that he will give you a couple of operas each year. There are pupils to be had, and surely you would get some commissions from the nobility, maybe even the merchants." He spread his large hands, palms up, as if he held in them all of Munich. "I have no doubt you can make a living here, Mozart, even without a court appointment." Herr Albert stopped speaking, but his words hung in the exhausted concert hall, like a bell that has just tolled, leaving the air alive with vibrations.

Wolfgang did rapid sums in his head. If Herr Albert was right, he could easily earn 600 gulden in a year. He could live on that. He took another swallow of beer, stood up and crossed restlessly to the fortepiano, whose keys he fingered thoughtfully. "I could do it," he mused, almost to himself, "But could I support Mama? What about Papa and Nannerl?" The weight of his father's charge, however he resisted it, lay heavy on him. Each one of his father's letters brought Papa into his head, into his heart. You must do this. Why did you not do that. After the sacrifices I have made for you, how could you . . . .? Suppose that he should decide to take a wife. The lovely Mademoiselle Kaiser came to mind. Would 600 gulden stretch so far? It must, he thought. I could do it. I can do it. I will do it. He turned from the keyboard, as if to announce his next composition. "In any case," he declared, "I could not bear to wear some prince's livery."

Anna watched her son, discerning the contest in him between the hope of independence and the burden his father had laid on him, that he must support the entire Mozart family. Wolfgang, in his pride, had always hated uniforms and pitied the musicians whose masters insisted on it: for all the humiliations the Archbishop had visited upon her husband, at least he did not require that he wear livery.

Poor Leopold. He had been instructed, once he was well enough to beg his prince's renewed favor, that he was to conduct himself calmly and peaceably. Anna knew very well the injured rectitude with which he went off to court each day. It was not that he and Nannerl took no pleasure: they wrote of shooting for money with the air guns and of music-making. But Anna knew that Leopold carried an air of grievance with him like an illness, which set him both on edge and apart from other men.

She looked about her, taking in all the signs of abandoned merrymaking. Wolfgang must not make his decisions with her in mind, or his father. She hesitated to say so in front of others. But perhaps it would carry more weight with her son if Herr Albert and Sophie von Durst heard what she had to say, stood as witnesses, so to speak. "Woferl, my dear," she said, her heart beating rapidly, "you must *not* think of taking care of me, nor of your father and sister. You are a young man. You must make your *own* way."

Wolfgang spirits shot up through the suddenly-opened roof and flew among the bright stars in the black sky. A soprano soared and looped above the rooftops and church spires. He would stay in Munich, then. He could earn enough and do splendid work. A steady mezzo buoyed him up like the air under his wings. His mother would not mind if he composed for the merchants and ironmongers of Munich, so long as he was happy. Operas, he could have operas! "There is no honor in it," came the baritone, the voice of thunder, pressing him down toward the ground. "Poor Papa," he sighed gently.

Anna's small pronouncement, in clear opposition to her husband, left her depleted. It was odd, she thought, that she was so tired. She did not overly exert herself. Yet she could not walk out of doors without the fear that she might take the wrong turn and end in heaven-knows-what quarter, dissolving into fatigue. She was unaccountably shy. Of all the throngs in Munich she knew only the Alberts and Sophie von Durst, and of course, poor Josef Myslivecek, the Bohemian composer whose face was half rotted away by syphilis. Myslivecek meant to be helpful. He spoke grandly of arranging for Wolfgang to compose operas for the King of Naples. Anna, a sociable woman, was surprised that it required effort to talk to any of them, however good-hearted.

Perhaps her fatigue was due to the division she felt, as if she had left a part of herself behind in Salzburg. She knew Leopold suffered because his son had moved out from his shadow. She knew that if she succeeded and her son freed himself from his father's tyranny, she would increase her husband's pain. That part of her that had remained in Salzburg was itself divided. On one hand, it dwelt in sympathy with her husband and daughter who lived in the *Tanzmeisterhaus*. On the other hand, it skulked about like a spy, determined to foresee and forestall Leopold's mastery over Wolfgang. She often feared she was wrong to want to set her son free. Sometimes Wolfgang seemed very young to her, too tender, foolish and unpracticed to live on his own terms. But Leopold's letters, full of advice, admonition and instruction, bolstered her determination.

"Here," said Herr Albert's fat wife, Hanna, carrying in a triumphal bowl of fragrant liver dumplings bobbing on the clearest imaginable broth. "Your favorite, Maestro." She had taken Wolfgang to her wide bosom and meant to fatten him up. Two mothers were not too many, in her opinion. "And you, Anna, eat, eat." She eyed skinny Sophie von Durst without favor, but could hardly ask her to leave.

"Wolfgang is always hungry after he performs," Frau von Durst explained importantly.

Everybody, thought Anna, tries to *own* my son. Is that what my husband fears?

Sophie licked her lips. "Has there been any word from the Elector about a position?" she asked, her quick eyes darting around the large room, with its disordered chairs and empty tankards. Since Nannerl had stayed with her a year and a half before, she had made it her duty to oversee Anna's affairs, and therefore Wolfgang's. She disliked Frau Albert's proprietary air and was more eager for news than for dumplings. She would see to it that whatever gossip there was got around.

At the first whiff of dumplings, Wolfgang left the fortepiano and held his bowl out so that Frau Albert could ladle the puffy morsels into it. He ate with gusto, making room for his hostess beside him. "Sit here, between me and my mother," he said, his mouth full. "And you, Herr Albert. You," he said to Frau Albert, who watched his face, "are an angel. Or at least you cook like one." He finished his first bowl and served himself more. "Oh, I love liver dumplings above everything!" he exclaimed. He basked in contentment. How good Frau Albert was, to have hurried to the kitchen as he took the applause, to shape and simmer these delightful delicacies, when she had spent a full day cooking for her other guests. How excellent everything was!

Hanna Albert's face, already rosy, turned a deeper red and she consented to let the young man fill up her bowl again.

I am a happy man, Wolfgang thought. I will stay. Even if Papa does not like it. He turned politely to Frau von Durst. "The Bishop of Chiemsee has spoken to the Elector. But the Elector said," Wolfgang struggled to keep the edge out of his voice, "that I should go to Italy to make a name for myself and then, perhaps . . . ." He gobbled some more dumplings and followed them with a swallow of cool beer. His father would never understand the delight of stretching out this way with his friends, eating plain food with them at leisure. He pictured his father, frowning over a letter he composed by candlelight. The letter was sure to be full of scolding and instructions. Well, he would ignore his father's advice.

Anna sipped at her broth. "Think of the quandary you put the Elector in, Woferl. Were he to offer you a post, it might well seem to our Archbishop an insult, that a neighboring prince would hire someone he had shown the door."

Wolfgang was surprised by his mother's acumen. He had not imagined that the offer of a minor post could be construed as a matter of state, but of course, princes had nothing else to consider, and they all seemed to have skins so thin it was surprising that their organs did not tumble out. But that Mama should know of such matters . . . !

Franz Albert rose and began to tidy up his hall, setting the chairs in order and picking up the tankards and glasses, for the servant had long ago gone off to bed. "Think about it, Wolfgang," he said. "Your Prince could hardly take offense, so long as you did not take a post with another monarch. How could private subscriptions offend him?"

"Hmmm," agreed Wolfgang, "though my father might . . . ." Leopold was sure to think it beneath his son to depend on burghers and lower nobility. The nearness of Salzburg to Munich might be a point in favor of the scheme, since it was only two days' journey. But proximity counted against the idea, too, for Papa would be close enough to come often and he would surely wish to stay in Munich. Wolfgang did not think that his father would so easily find work, and he did not think that he himself could earn enough for everyone.

Sophie von Durst teased, "A little bird tells me it is not so much the *work* as a certain *soprano* that keeps you in Munich."

Wolfgang blushed and applied himself to his dumplings. He was always ravenous after a performance.

Frau von Durst, pleased with the reddening of Wolfgang's neck, would not give up. "Fraulein Kaiser sings like a nightingale," she said in a stage whisper, "but you know, she is only the natural daughter of the Count Postolka and his cook."

Wolfgang looked up from his bowl. "We cannot choose our fathers, Frau von Durst, and Fraulein Kaiser sings admirably. The Count Postolka, whatever his sins - which cannot be held against his daughter - has seen to it that she has had the best teachers."

Anna could see that her son was hot enough to fight a duel over the honor of the dark-haired soprano, whose voice, flexible and true, had excited the admiration of all Munich. "We must not keep these good people up any longer," she said, hastening to pick up the emptied bowls. "Come, Woferl, you must help Herr Albert, and I will help Hanna to clean up before bedtime. Thank you, Sophie, for coming. You are always at my side." It was ambiguous praise, to be sure.

As she lay in bed Anna imagined Leopold's alarm when he heard of the scheme put forth by the Black Eagle's landlord. She could see him pull out his writing desk, see his long fingers test, then sharpen a quill. She knew his reasoning precisely. He would praise Herr Albert for his good intentions, but then fury and suspicion would overtake him. Just who were these men who would pledge a dozen ducats every year? What would they expect in return for their largesse? She could see her husband's lips working as he channeled his passions onto the paper. Count Seeau might not want to commission operas after all, and the others whom Albert would recruit might not keep to their words.

"Do not worry," Anna wrote to her husband. "Everything will come right in the end, when the hooks and eyes have been put on." What did her husband know of hooks and eyes, the finishing touch of any garment, sewed firmly and invisibly in place? She knew he would be impatient with her words - hooks and eyes, indeed! He would wonder why she did not govern her son with a firmer hand.

She almost laughed when his letter came, saying just what she had imagined. No, no, it would never do. "You can live in that way anywhere, but you must not make yourself so cheap and throw yourself away in this manner, for indeed we have not yet come to that." And Nannerl's note to her brother seconded her father. 'It would not do you any credit to stay on in Munich without an appointment. It would do us far more honor if you could succeed in obtaining a post under some other great lord."

"He is wrong, Mama!" Wolfgang exclaimed. "He says I cannot hope to make a farthing here, but the concerts will begin next month. Mama!" he wailed.

Anna took his hand and raised it to her lips. She hoped Wolfgang would resist his father. Then she could go home. "Prince Zeil is going to Salzburg in a day, Woferl. Perhaps he will persuade Papa to your way of thinking."

She knew that Leopold thought the matter settled: his son had been told to leave Munich, to think no more about Herr Albert's harebrained scheme. Leopold understood perfectly that such a plan would free his son. There was nothing he feared more. In her mind's eye, Anna saw that Leopold slept poorly, twisting and turning in the covers until they were wrapped around him every which way. She did not know if Wolfgang had the strength to defy Leopold, and if he did, whether Leopold would come posthaste to Munich, Archbishop or no.

Prince Zeil failed to convince Leopold. "I suppose we have no choice," said Wolfgang disconsolately. He paced about the room they shared. "Papa says we must leave our friends in Munich. It is a shame. I could do it, Mama. I could make my living here. I know I could, without a doubt. Myslivecek might find a position for me in Naples. But," he paused unhappily, "Papa says we must go." He was annoyed with his mother. First, she had told him he must make his own way in the world, and now she did nothing to keep his father at bay. When he pressed her, she simply raised her eyebrows and shook her head.

Anna was disappointed. She did not in the least want to travel on to Augsburg or beyond to Mannheim. The weather had grown suddenly and unseasonably hot, and she must pack up all the gear, the clothes, the medicines, the music, all the oddments people gave her son. Though the windows were wide open, the air was still and humid. She worked in her chemise, which was soaked, and though she tied a rag around her head, sweat ran down her face. "The devil take all traveling," she wrote to Leopold in a temper.

But Wolfgang was not yet ready to break free of his father, and so on a steamy morning, mother and son boarded a carriage bound for Mannheim by way of Augsburg.

45

1777-1778

"THERE!" EXCLAIMED WOLFGANG with satisfaction as he set his end of the trunk down and straightened his legs, which ached from the effort of moving all their possessions. "Take this, my good man," he said grandly, putting a handful of pfennigs into the porter's hand. The porter's face fell. Wolfgang, always careful to treat servants well, drew out another handful of pennies. He was never sure whether he paid too much or too little for such services: Papa had always seen to such things.

"You will be much better here, Mama," said Wolfgang anxiously, for he was aware that he had neglected his mother since their arrival in Mannheim at the end of October. The inn at which they had lodged was both expensive and uncomfortable. For six cold and rainy weeks poor Mama had spent a good deal of her time in bed, under covers, trying to stay warm.

Anna shrugged off her cloak and looked around her with approval. The room was spacious, with two beds and an alcove where Wolfgang could compose. A blue porcelain stove burned merrily and there was an ample supply of firewood. Good quality wax candles with virgin wicks stood ready to be lit in pewter holders. This was the house of Mannheim's Court Treasurer Serrarius, of which Wolfgang had said only "I have found a fine place for us to live, Mama."

"What does it cost?" Anna inquired, dubious whether they could afford such a room.

Wolfgang hung up his mother's cloak with a lordly flourish. "Only lessons for Klara, the Treasurer's daughter. You will have all the candles and firewood you wish, Mama. And you will like Frau Serrarius. She is a very kind woman. She has invited you to spend your evenings in her drawing room." Wolfgang strutted about the room, admiring the clean walls, the inlaid floor and large windows. He, himself, had made the arrangements.

Dear Wolfgang, always so eager to please. It was an endearing trait, thought Anna, but his open nature might also be his downfall. He hated to hurt anyone, not least his father. At some point, surely, he must dig in his heels, stand in one place and declare himself as sovereign. Oh my, she thought, it is all the talk I hear of the Rights of Man: it has addled my brain!

During the miserable weeks past, huddled for hours under her covers and pining for home, she had found it hard to remember that Wolfgang must court and cultivate the men whose influence he needed to approach Karl Theodor, Elector of the Palatine. The cold and ill health had brought about a lowering of spirit and had undermined her resolve, making her forget the purpose in making this journey. Only Leopold's letters - ordering them to move on, first to Augsburg and then to Mannheim, then chiding them for their haste, complaining about the expense of their journey, while interfering with Wolfgang's moneymaking projects - had kept her in mind that Wolfgang must still answer to his father's dictates. Now, opening to the warmth and light of her surroundings, she asked, "Has the Elector made an answer?"

Wolfgang's cheerful countenance changed. "Papa will not be pleased at all," he said dispirited, "but it is not my fault. I have done everything that Papa would have. Herr Cannabich has spoken for me," he said, referring to the Director of Instrumental Music, who had extended himself on Wolfgang's behalf, "as has Count Savioli. I told you I played, and to great applause too, for the Elector and his wife and I have taught the Elector's natural children, as he wished, and presented them with compositions. Everyone says that the Elector expects me to winter in Mannheim. You would think," said Wolfgang with impatience, "the Elector would understand that I cannot stay unless I can earn something. But blast and damn these princes! They have plenty and so they think a gold watch here and there is all a man needs to live. He can . . . not," said Wolfgang, unable to resist the impulse to imitate the halting way the Elector spoke, "make . . . up . . . his . . . mind . . . what . . . to . . . do . . . just . . . yet."

Anna frowned. "The walls have ears, Wolfgang," she cautioned, for neither of them knew the Serrarius household.

"But even so, Mama, even without the Elector, Mannheim is the best place for me," declared Wolfgang, pacing, too excited to sit still. "There is such talk! Everyone knows about science and reads the best books, and one can get news of the colonies in America, which one could never hear, much less talk about in Salzburg. It is said that a whole regiment of English soldiers has been captured by the colonists! Can you imagine? Oh, and the musicians! They are like no others anywhere! Everyone says the Elector has determined to make Mannheim a paradise for all the arts and sciences. The woodwinds, Mama! Oh, you must hear the clarinets, when they play together with the oboes and flutes! The singers! Superb!" He rubbed his hands together. "The best part is, they understand what I do and they like me. I can make a living here, though I will have to work hard. But I have always worked hard, and here, even if the Elector dillies and dallies, they know my worth. Cannabich has arranged for everything, commissions, lessons, this place for you to stay!"

Anna smiled. Once again her son had found what he hoped for, a way to make a living without depending on a prince. Although his encounter with the supercilious Catholic patricians during their brief stay in Augsburg had left him wary of burghers at first, Mannheim was different, she thought. There were not the religious factions here, so far as she could tell, and Mannheim was far enough from Salzburg that surely Leopold's hold on his son would weaken.

"And even better . . . ."

"Even *better*?" Anna asked, teasing, for Wolfgang was all exclamations and superlatives.

Wolfgang nodded. "The women. Never have I seen so many beautiful women. You can have no idea. Rosa Cannabich is very nice, attractive too, and the Weber girls, Aloisha especially. I told you about Herr Weber, Mama, the court copyist? He has done some work for me and has welcomed me into his home, and he is just like Papa. And Frau Weber sets a good table - she gave me a rabbit stew. Not so good as yours," he added loyally. "There is one son, but the four daughters . . . ! There is Aloisha. She has the voice of an angel for one so young. And Constanze is my favorite, very kind and jolly. A good clear soprano, too. Already we are the best of friends. Sophie is the youngest, and Josepha, the eldest is, well, substantial."

"I thought," said Anna with some asperity, "that no woman could rival your cousin." Woferl, much taken with his cousin, Thekla, had romped and played with her in Augsburg as if they were two exuberant puppies. Anna had even feared that, in the excess of his affection, Wolfgang might go too far and sire a bastard. Therefore Anna had been glad to leave Augsburg, even though her cold had worsened to such a catarrh that she had traveled in a daze. However delightful her son had found his cousin, it was an unsuitable match. Augsburg was no place for Wolfgang to settle. And Anna could see in Leopold's brother and his wife no inclination to let their daughter - their only surviving child - go far from Augsburg, though within its precincts she was allowed more latitude to indulge her appetites than Anna thought wise.

"My cousin," said Wolfgang ardently, "is the best of girls. I have written to her many times already, for I love her with all my heart. She is like you, Mama, without pretension, and like Nannerl, for she is very clever, though she has little learning. But her mind is quick. And she is so beautiful! Such beautiful lips and big eyes and such fine skin. But I am here," he said cheerfully, "and she is there."

"I thought, Mama, that perhaps I can do something for the Webers, for poor Herr Weber is woefully underpaid, like Papa, and not honored as he should be. Why Herr Weber is like a father to me."

"I would not tell your Papa *that*," said Anna. But Wolfgang had already written his enthusiasm for the Webers to his father in Salzburg, who was as alarmed by his son's new-found affection as Anna could have predicted.

"Now that you are settled here in Mannheim," said Anna, "and if you are able to live on what you can earn here, perhaps I should return to Salzburg - though I must admit that I am not eager to leave this cozy room in favor of a drafty coach this time of year."

"Well, stay the winter, Mama," said Wolfgang. "Wendling and Raaff have asked me to go with them to Paris during Lent. Surely you would be happier in your own house among your own friends."

Anna nodded. Wolfgang would be in good company to travel to Paris with Johann Wendling, a flutist, and Anton Raaff, a tenor. Neither was a youngster and each assured Wolfgang that there was good money to be made in Paris. They were sound men, so far as Anna could determine, who would check Wolfgang's enthusiasms. She had some concern about Wendling, for everyone said that he had arranged for his daughter, Dorothea, to become the Elector's mistress for a time. Anna was reminded uneasily that Leopold had once thought of giving Nannerl to the Emperor in Vienna. It still made her angry to think on. What was wrong with men, who would trade their daughters for favors?

In no time Anna was settled, sitting in the room she shared with her son by day and in the evening joining the Serrarius family in their drawing room. Even in warmer and more comfortable quarters she did not feel as well as she might. By now, her catarrh having been cured, she should have recovered her vigor. But she found herself constantly under the weather. Nevertheless, she got out and about and was able to understood her son's attachment to Mannheim. There were always concerts, plays and operas; the musicians were, indeed, as good as any she had heard; conversation was rich and interesting, if, she thought, verging on republican. She watched Wolfgang expand with purpose and enthusiasm, composing, teaching and performing. He is at home here, she thought.

As if on cue, Leopold began to fuss. Wolfgang, who had not secured a court appointment, and Anna were a drain on his purse. "Why can you not do as I do?" he wrote, "ingratiate yourself. Why did you have to hurry off to Mannheim?"

"Why, indeed, Mama!" said Wolfgang furiously. "Because my father ordered me to be off! Surely his memory is not so short! And he is not so poor as he makes out," Wolfgang drew himself up and looked his mother squarely in the eye. "I have earned a good deal of money for my father, and yet he always cries poor. I know he has given us funds for this journey, but really, the money he has sent, *I* earned. Nannerl and I," he amended. "He treats me the way the English treat the American colonies," he muttered, "as a good place to levy taxes."

Good for Wolfgang, Anna rejoiced in her heart. "You must choose your own path, my son, whether or not your father approves."

He looked at her steadily. "I know," he said, but he sighed. It was no easy task to resist his father's will, even from a distance.

And then, just when the future looked so clear, with Wolfgang established among his fellow musicians and Anna making plans to return to Salzburg, the Bavarian Elector died of smallpox in Munich. The Palatine Elector in Mannheim was next in the line of succession and left his capital and went to Munich to be sure of its fealty. Meanwhile both capitals were plunged into mourning. There could be no public entertainment of any kind.

All at once, Wolfgang was adrift. "They say that Joseph II plans to establish a German opera in Vienna, Mama," he announced, "and wants a young, German-speaking *kapellmeister*. Why, surely it is just the post for me! I will ask Papa to write at once to everyone we know in Vienna. But here, Mama, put on your bonnet and your cloak. We are expected at the Webers."

The Webers were too many for their shabby apartment and lived rather higgledy-piggledy, Anna thought. She was drawn immediately to Constanze, the plainest of the sisters. After supper, Constanze inquired of Anna, "You are comfortable at the Serrarius house? I fear that you must find Mannheim a very dull place just now." She had an open, frank face, framed in brown waves, and a humorous curve to her lip. Before Anna could answer, Wolfgang, seizing Constanze's hand and said ardently, "Not so dull with you in town, Constanze."

Aloisha, fine-boned and fair, frowned prettily. "Will you not hear me sing, Wolfgang?" she pouted. "The Elector must soon return to Mannheim, and he has said that *I*" - Anna noticed that she preened a bit and lingered on the word - "am to sing at court."

The eldest, Josepha, nearly twenty, and highly-colored like her mother, commanded, "Yes, Herr Mozart. Leave off flirtation and listen to Aloisha."

Herr Weber peered through his spectacles, his sparse reddish hair standing up like little flames all over his head. "Constanze," he said, "perhaps your mother needs some help in clearing up. Herr Mozart, just listen. You have never heard such purity of sound." He put his hand on Wolfgang's shoulder and led him to the clavier, murmuring in his ear as they went.

When Aloisha had sung, Wolfgang accompanying her at the clavier - and truly, thought Anna, her voice was as pure as quicksilver, as radiant as pearl - Wolfgang came to sit beside his mother. "Does she not have a fine voice, Mama?" he asked her.

"She does indeed," acknowledged Anna.

"Herr Weber wants me to go with him - and his daughter, too - to Kirchheim-Bollanden, where the Princess Caroline of Nassau-Weilburg lives - you remember her from The Hague. She is the sister to William of Orange and she was about to give birth when we arrived, and that was why she couldn't wait for Nannerl to recover . . . ."

Anna nodded. "I remember," she said. "But is this wise? To travel together? You will not get as much of a present from the Princess if there are two to reward."

"Mmm," conceded Wolfgang, "but there will be Herr Weber to see to everything, just like Papa, and I will insist that Constanze come too to help Aloisha with her hair and her dress, and you will not worry if I am with friends."

Now Herr Weber stood before her, bowing deeply. He sat beside her on the sofa, which was draped with a worn shawl. He took Anna's hand into his, though she drew it back quickly, offended by his premature familiarity. "Surely you will allow your son to travel with us. You can see, Frau Mozart, what a good effect our children have upon one another. My daughter is at her best when your son is at the clavier. And see how your son shines when he plays for her. We cannot afford a maid," Herr Weber continued, "for the Elector keeps us on a short string, as you can see." He gestured around the faded room with its modest furnishings. "And so one of the other girls will come as *duenna*, Josepha probably."

"Constanze," said Wolfgang. "Constanze would do very well, for surely Josepha is needed at home to help her mother."

"Very well, then, Constanze," said Herr Weber.

All at once it seemed to Anna that the Weber's living room was a stage set and all of them actors. She alone had not rehearsed her lines. Aloisha, dressed in virginal white stood gleaming at the center and all the rest moved at the direction of the copyist. Wolfgang's eyes went most often to Constanze, but Anna noticed that Aloisha watched him carefully and insinuated herself with deft assurance between him and Constanze at every opportunity. Her son did not, Anna thought, need a duplicate of his father, nor should he arrange to sacrifice his prospects to support another family. But she reminded herself: let him go; he must make his own mistakes.

"Woferl says you can knit," said eleven year-old Sophie softly. She had sidled up to Anna and spoke in Anna's ear. All the others had fallen into lively conversation about what to take on their journey.

"I can," said Anna. "Would you like me to teach you?"

"Oh, above everything," said the child. "Mama has needles and wool but she never gets around to showing me how." She ran from the room and came back with an untidy basket full of tangled wool and a handful of mismatched needles.

Anna cast on a row of stitches and showed Sophie how to push the needle up through the loop, wind the yarn around and bring it through to make first one stitch, then the next.

Sophie prattled as she imitated Anna. Anna, who was startled and dismayed when the girl asked, "When do you think they will marry, Wolfgang and Aloisha?"

"Marry?" said Anna.

"Oh yes, once my father has made up his mind," said Sophie, putting her knitting needles with their clumsy web down on her lap, "nothing can stop him."

Herr Weber sounds, Anna thought with dismay, like Leopold. "Why should they marry?" Anna asked.

"Because," said Sophie, giving away the family plot without guile, "Wolfgang has composed operas in Italy, and he knows everyone and can introduce my sister and get her onto the stage."

"Oh," Anna murmured, her heart sinking.

That evening when she and her son had returned to the Serrarius apartment, Anna said, "I do not think that it is a good idea for you to travel to Kircheim-Bollanden, Woferl."

"It *is* a good idea," Wolfgang remonstrated. "Anyway, the die is cast. It is too late now to change anything." But when he returned to Mannheim from Kircheim-Bollanden, he was a little shamefaced. "Papa will not be pleased," he confessed, "for I paid half the expenses and I was only one of four, but I will not do *that* again. When we travel to Italy, I will pay only for my own share."

"When you travel to Italy?" Anna exclaimed, peering at him over her spectacles.

"Yes," he breathed. "We have a wonderful plan, Mama. We will go to Italy so that Aloisha can get some prima donna roles. I will arrange for opera *scritturas* and she will sing in them. You have no idea how much better she sings now that I have had the chance to instruct her, Mama, and her acting is much better too. She is a dear little girl with the most winning ways. I will ask Papa to write to Lugiati in Verona, and I will happily compose for almost nothing. Aloisha is very young, you know, and needs my help, though of course her father will come."

Anna held up her hand to stop the rush of words. "And what of Wendling and Ramm and your trip to Paris?" she asked.

Wolfgang looked at her earnestly. "Oh, I should not like to travel with them," he said in utter sincerity, though only weeks ago, they were the best companions in the world. "You know that Wendling's daughter was, for a time, mistress to the Elector," he said, looking very solemn. "Herr Wendling rarely goes to church, and Ramm is a decent enough fellow, but too libertine for my tastes. I could not be sure of my own soul in the company of such men. But the Webers are good Catholics. Why, every single day in Kirchheim we went to Mass together, and to confession as well."

"It is not so easy," said Anna with great deliberation, "to get a commission for an opera in Italy. Your Papa has tried and tried, as you very well know. Nor can a young girl simply walk up onto the stage and take the prima donna roles from the Italian singers."

"Papa can arrange it," said Wolfgang confidently. "He has always wanted me to return to Italy."

"Yes," said Anna, "but not without certain prospects, and certainly not to support the Webers instead of the Mozarts." Her heart was heavy as she said, "You had best let your Papa know of your plans."

She was well aware that she could count on Leopold to erupt at the mere thought of her son's scheme. But just to make sure, she stealthily opened Wolfgang's letter when he had gone to dinner, breaking the wax seal carefully, and adding her own postscript. "When Wolfgang makes new acquaintances, he immediately wants to give his life and property for them," she wrote. "So you yourself will have to think over what ought to be done." She thought carefully about her words. "I do not consider his journey to Paris with Wendling at all advisable. I would rather accompany him myself."

It cost Anna dearly to write such a sentence. She did not wish to go to Paris. But she had seen how easily the Weber family had converted her son to their purpose. Wolfgang's openness of heart, his desire to please, made him easy prey for the ambitious and unscrupulous. Leopold was right about that.

"I am writing this quite secretly," Anna wrote, "and I shall close, for I do not want to be caught. " She held the broken seal of the letter over the candle's flame just long enough to soften the wax, singeing the paper slightly, and pressed her thumb on it.

"I took your letter to the post," she told Wolfgang when he returned, "when I went out for a walk to clear my head."

Now, having set out to betray her husband, she had betrayed her son to her husband. Whatever she did, she injured someone. If she encouraged her son to grow up and make his own decisions, she took sides against her husband. In earlier days, when she encouraged Nannerl to heed her calling, she had undermined her marriage prospects. Now she had deliberately drawn down her husband's wrath, jeopardizing her son's independence.

When Leopold received Wolfgang's news, he was as distraught as Anna had known he would be, and sent the letter she had both dreaded and invited. It went on for pages. It regaled Wolfgang with tales of his father's hardship, grief, anxiety and determination to take charge. "I shall write to you very fully and tell you what you have to do. *Off with you to Paris*!" he ordered. Then the thunderbolt. "Mama is to go to Paris with you."

Wolfgang was downcast. "We will have to go, Mama. We have no choice."

Wolfgang was sure that his heart was broken. He now loved Aloisha with every fiber of his being. He would be happy to marry her, to live humbly for love, to advance her prospects. But what was he to do? If he defied his father he would be stranded, as the musicians drifted away from Mannheim to Munich. "You really must consider first of all the welfare of your parents, or else your soul will go to the devil," his father wrote.

46

1778

I CANNOT BEAR TO DIE HERE, IN PARIS, this Godforsaken city, Anna thought. She had always expected, when her time came, to lie close by the graves of her five infant children in St. Peter's churchyard. Each one of her joints - more than she had known she possessed - throbbed. So did her teeth and ears. The marrow had been sucked from her bones and replaced by ice, even though it was a hot July. Her *malaise*, as the Baron von Grimm called it, was quite different from the usual cold or ague.

Enough brooding, she told herself. I will get out of doors, go to church, leave this cell. The dark room smelled of mildew and had no view except of the Mayr's courtyard, with broken paving stones, a splintered bench that lay on its side, a bucket with a hole and rags that were turning into dirt. Anna had no occupation but knitting stockings for Wolfgang. Knitting, without conversation or music, was a very dull occupation. Leopold wrote of the disrepair of his stockings and dressing gown. Yet when she bought wool and sent him a package of stockings, the costs both of yarn and postage angered him. It was no good speaking with Frau Mayr, who was both stupid and belligerent. Sitting by herself, once Wolfgang had gone out for the day, Anna felt her fingers grow cold and clumsy. Sometimes she looked down in puzzlement at the work she did. Her thoughts were so disordered that she could not remember whether to slip the needle through the loop first and then wrap the yarn around, or the reverse.

Every day Wolfgang warned her, "You must not go out by yourself, Mama. The crowds will jostle you and knock you off your feet. The streets are filthy. They smell to Heaven and you will be robbed."

Wolfgang himself went out, of course, in search of the fame and fortune that his father demanded. He found some commissions, some lessons, but not as many as he required to meet expenses - certainly not enough to live independently. "Everything here is the court, only the court," he told Anna irritably. Anna remembered that Leopold had made the same complaint all those years before. "It is not like Mannheim nor Munich, where the merchants and manufacturers were willing to pay for their own musicians." Wolfgang made a face. "I do not like Paris. Everyone is conceited and highhanded." He sighed, "Papa says, 'Be guided by the French taste,' but truly, Mama, the French *have* no taste."

Wolfgang's admonitions or no, Anna decided to brave the street and go to church, where she could pray in German to the Jungfrau Maria. She above everyone, would understand Anna's fear about the illness she felt invading her body. And then, sitting in the cool, gray stone interior of the church, with saints on every hand, Anna would give herself leave to think about home. She denied herself this indulgence most often, not wanting to encourage self-pity and a longing she could not satisfy. But today she would not resist. She would allow herself to think of the bright rooms of the *Tanzmeisterhaus*, the clarion crow of the morning's first cock, the choir of church bells, the clop and whuffle of horses from the nearby stables, the manure smells mixed with those of the gingerbread pigs baking in the shop across the way. She thought of Nannerl taking her measured way from church to lesson to market, her trim figure perfectly upright; of Leopold in his shabby dressing gown, writing letters to the travelers by the fatty light of a tallow candle; of Margarethe's dear understanding face and lonely days.

She took her cloak and went downstairs slowly on stiff and painful legs. Frau Mayr, her limp hair straggling down from her wrinkled cap, tried to stop Anna at the front door. "Oh Madame," she said, "you must never go into the streets. The riffraff will cut your throat and take your purse without a thought."

Frau Mayr's husband, a dealer in scrap iron, had agreed to take Anna and Wolfgang in when they arrived in Paris late in March, drenched and shivering after nine days' travel, the last two in the cold wind and rain that drove through the coverings on the carriage windows. At times Anna had felt she would drown. It was hard to take a breath without swallowing the icy rain that stung her face. Her initial gratitude at finding herself indoors had given way, by daylight, to dismay. The Mayr's shabby back room was not meant to sit in. It was piled full of dilapidated furniture. Anna never saw the sun from morning till night, from one day to the next. The meals Frau Mayr sent up were of poor quality, the meat either bloody or charred, full of gristle and hairs.

"I must go to church," Anna told her landlady firmly. "I have nothing about me to steal." Her dress was unadorned, her pockets as empty as her spirit.

"You must not, for your own good," said Frau Mayr thinly.

"Thank you," Anna said, but she stepped quickly out into the street and was assaulted by the strong odors of bread, coffee and wine, decaying offal flung into the street by the butcher and fishmonger, and the night soil, dumped out the windows to flow down the gutters. At least, out in the air, she could be sure she was alive, whereas, indoors, overcome with lassitude and ennui, she felt she had died. As she stood uncertainly, measuring the strength it would take to walk to the corner, turn to the right and walk to the next, a splendidly dressed nobleman and his retinue surged toward her, crowding everyone out of their way. Anna pressed herself against the brick of the Mayr house. The nobleman wore a green taffeta coat, covered in gold lace and braid over a waistcoat of plum-colored brocade. His tricorn hat, adorned with colored plumes, sat atop an immensely curled and powdered wig. He took care to point the toes of his high-heeled and elaborately buckled shoes with each step, so that his silken calves were amply displayed. He flicked his walking stick, his hold on which displayed the jeweled rings that flashed on each finger. The men with him, carefully dressed to flatter by an imitation that stopped just short of rivalry, listened intently as their principal issued a stream of comments in his rapid, slippery tongue. The gentleman's party cut a swath of silence as it passed, but a sullen murmur grew up in its wake. It is just such personages, Anna thought, that my son must wait on every day. How it must gall him! The fishmonger, a thickset man with heavy eyebrows, stared in the direction of the nobleman and shook his fist, snarling words whose import Anna could only imagine. As Anna began her progress along the crowded thoroughfare, an emaciated woman holding a spindly babe on her hip tugged Anna's arm, speaking low and quickly. The child in its dirty cap with frayed strings looked at Anna incuriously. Anna shook her head: she had nothing with her and few enough coins hidden in her dark room.

"What shall I do?" Anna asked the Jungfrau, who sat impassive in her niche, wearing a painted dress and a crown of stars. The Jungfrau held a stolid infant in her arms. Often Anna had found it useful to speak to the Virgin, in whatever church, for, however it came about, she was also a mother.

"What shall I do?" she asked "My health is very low. Something is wrong, some illness. I believe that if my son and I left soon, we could return to Salzburg in time. But then Wolfgang must ingratiate himself again with the Archbishop, who will surely gloat that he made a fruitless journey so far as to Paris. Paris is not a congenial place; it does not suit him in the least. If I die while we remain here . . . ."

She imagined she heard Leopold say sternly, "Do not even think it. Good God, Anna! How would my son manage on his own? He knows nothing of finances and can easily be taken advantage of. If you still feel unwell you must be bled again. You have waited far too long." And with impatience, "Why cannot you do as I would?"

She imagined Nannerl, lacing herself every morning into tight corsets, walking her dog, going to Sallerl or Kathryl so that they could do each other's hair. "Oh dear," Anna lamented. "I failed Nannerl. I so wanted her to answer - to be able to answer - the call I know she heard. How is it, dear Jungfrau, that we are told in Scripture not to hide our talents and then made - even by churchmen - to do so? In Anna's mind, Nannerl smiled her clever smile and said, "I am content, Mama, perfectly content."

Anna shifted. Her knees pained, and she settled back onto the hard seat. If I die here, she thought, then at least Woferl will be far from Salzburg. He will have a chance, anyway. It was wearisome to think on death, not the dying itself but the difficulties that would follow. Wolfgang would have to tell Leopold - no pleasant undertaking - and Leopold would no doubt blame his son, admonishing and hectoring by letters. Nannerl, she thought, had grown so carefully hedged and controlled that perhaps she would not suffer at her mother's death overmuch. But Leopold, she was certain, - despite his discontent with her - would feel the loss. Anna looked to the Jungfrau Maria, the French *Sainte Vierge*, for guidance but saw only a piece of wood, carved and painted. Why had she been so foolish as to think that the French Virgin would care about an ailing German woman?

Anna's modest outing to the church and back revived her briefly, but then she was cut down by fatigue. Just when she had determined to go to bed and sleep, Frau Mayr announced that the Baron von Grimm was below, asking for Anna. "The Baron," she exclaimed, fluttering. "Here is the Baron von Grimm, at my house. Oh please, Madame, to receive him downstairs in our drawing room. This is not . . . ." She looked around critically at the room in which Anna sat day after day.

"No," said Anna, too weary to go down the stairs to the better kept apartment. "Show him in here, Frau Mayr." It was no doubt spiteful to refuse her landlady, but Anna could not bear the thought of walking down and then walking up the stairs. It was all she could do to summon the civility due the Baron.

He kissed her hand and looked around him disapprovingly. This was too dreary a place for his protégé to stay. "My, um, friend, Madame d'Épinay has found a much better apartment for you, Madame Mozart," he announced. "It is on the Rue Gros Chenet, two rooms, very comfortable and clean, looking out onto the street. You will find it pleasanter. Your son will be closer to those who matter, and there is a good stove. I will send my man to assist you."

Anna was touched. Grimm, a Baron of the Holy Roman Empire, was an important and powerful man, who advised kings and mingled with the highest nobility. Madame d'Épinay, his consort, was also powerful. She presided over a grand salon and wielded no small influence on her own account. "I worry," Anna said, "about my son. I cannot do as my husband could to advance his fortunes. And I am not well." Indeed, she felt very ill and wanted nothing but sleep.

"One must have patience, Madame," said Grimm. "Rome was not built in a day." He pulled out a large gold watch on a gleaming thick chain. "Your son will find work. I have taken him on. But he must exert himself, compose what is wanted and take students. He must not loll about with musicians so much. They can do nothing for him. And he must," said the Baron, "take a position in the matter of Piccini and Gluck." Power radiated from this well-kept man, like heat from a stove.

Wolfgang had told Anna that everyone in Paris was divided: were Piccini's operas better, or Gluck's? "You are kind," said Anna, "but . . . ." She felt a drowsy lassitude overtaking her.

The Baron interrupted her grandly with a gesture of his hand, covered in rings. "Your son has won over Le Gros, Gossec and Noverre. These are all influential men at court, Madame, rest assured. Tomorrow I have arranged it that he will go to the Duchesse de Chabot, who can do him some good. Everything is in hand. You must not trouble your head."

"Thank you," Anna said, rousing herself for the effort of speaking. "I am afraid that troubling her head is what a mother does best. My son is grateful for your efforts on his behalf. And I as well." These courtesies took her last ounce of energy. She was glad when, finally, all that remained of him was the wake of perfume he left behind. The pain that lurked, only its yellow eyes gleaming in its lair, ventured out a little farther each day. With the Baron's departure, it roamed freely, snarling and devouring as it rampaged. Walking through the streets to the church and receiving the Baron von Grimm had taken their toll, as did the pain that returned so fiercely. Anna slept all through the night and, without waking, through the next day. She was still slumbering when Wolfgang came in from the Duchesse de Chabot. Wolfgang meant to wake her. It frightened him that she slept so much. "It was dreadful, Mama," he fumed. "You cannot imagine!"

Anna was thick with sleep. She left her painless stupor reluctantly.

"First of all," said Wolfgang dramatically, "I had to cool my heels for half an hour maybe, in a freezing room, no fireplace, no stove. It was not just my heels I cooled! My fingers! Icicles, Mama! I could hardly move them. And then, when the Duchesse finally had the courtesy to invite me into the room where the company were gathered, she said I would have to make the best of the clavier. 'Perhaps we will find a better one in future,' she said." Wolfgang pursed his lips and minced his words in imitation. " 'I will have to warm my fingers up before I can play,' I said. 'Please to take me to a fireplace.' 'Of course,' she said, and straightway turned her back on me and sat down with some gentlemen at a table, while I waited. And waited. All the windows and doors, everything was open. The wind whipped in and it was raining. I thought I would turn to ice. My head started to ache. I hate such fools, who care nothing for music! Finally I sat down at the clavier and played. It was truly a wretched instrument, not good to begin with and in bad repair, but who cared? The chairs and tables paid more attention than the Duchesse and her company. They went right on, drawing and chattering and playing cards and amusing themselves.

"Mmmm," yawned Anna, her tongue still cumbered with sleep. However reluctant she was to awaken, Wolfgang painted a vivid scene.

"So," said Wolfgang, "I stood up - smack in the middle of the Fischer Variations. 'I can hardly play on such a clavier,' said I, though I thought to myself, I must not insult Grimm's friend, but it was all I could do, Mama. Madame le Duchesse, however, would not let me go. 'But *monsieur*,' "she said, " 'you must stay until my husband returns. Really you must. He would be most put out.' So I did, and when he came, he was a good fellow after all and sat with me while I played, and then, of course, I felt much better. But what a thoroughly unpleasant place Paris is!"

Anna tried to sit up. A wave of nausea swept through her and she groaned. Wolfgang was at her side in a moment. "What is it Mama? Here I have gone on and on and you are ill. Oh, me! What to do?" He looked wildly around the dingy room. "I will send the Mayr's servant to the Baron. He will know what to do." It was, however, hours before the Baron's doctor arrived to bleed Anna, who was by then hardly conscious.

When she finally awoke, feeling a little better, it was in the rooms Madame d'Épinay had found for them. Anna could not remember how she had come to be there.

She was bled again and, for a time, she improved. On some days she was able to get out of bed, even go a little into company, observe the Paris fashions, enjoy what gossip she could understand and write letters to Leopold and Nannerl. Wolfgang's friend Raaff came in to see her almost daily and sang to her in his glorious tenor. "Ach," Anna said to him, "you are a tonic, Anton. Perhaps I will live to see my husband and my daughter and dear old Salzburg yet."

"Of course you will," said Raaff, "but you must not let Wolfgang get as far as Salzburg, where he is not appreciated." He lowered his voice as if there were someone to overhear. "Rumor has it that the Palatine Elector has taken all the musicians from Mannheim to Munich, so that is where you must take your son. I have heard that the Weber girl has gone there and has an appointment at court." Raaff continued, "It is no great distance from Munich to Salzburg. I am going to Munich myself and will take you to Salzburg and just say hello to your husband and beautiful daughter while I am about it. Now, here is Heina to keep you company, and his good wife as well."

The horn player, Josef Heina, knowing of Anna's poor health, often brought his wife, Gertrud. "Are you well enough to walk out today?" Gertrud asked.

"Perhaps, yes," Anna answered cautiously.

"You may lean on me, and we will go slowly," said Gertrud, whose broad, good-natured face Anna had come to love.

"Yes," said Anna. "Like an old lady. Who would have thought . . . .?" She walked carefully, as if she were made of glass, guarding herself from any touch or shock, moving hesitantly so as not to awaken the pain that lay in wait, ready to grasp at her at the slightest misstep or exertion.

Gertrud chattered happily, telling Anna about the new-fangled rod that attracted lightening to it, thus protecting the house alongside which it was fastened. Anna listened with only a part of her attention, though she thought she must remember to tell Leopold. He liked inventions, though this one might be against the will of God. It seemed to her she had so little time left. She thought about the letter from Leopold that Wolfgang had handed her without comment. " 'When you make your father's happiness your first consideration, he will continue to think of your welfare and happiness and to stand by you as a loyal friend,' " Wolfgang read. As Anna inched along in the Luxembourg Gardens, leaning on the Heinas, one on each side of her, she thought what a muddle everything was. It all went back to the vow that Leopold had long ago taken in her presence. It was a vow to God, a violation of his own beliefs, and Leopold had made his son a party to it, requiring, in return for the father's devotion, the utter fealty of the son. While Wolfgang had not agreed to any such contract, Leopold held him to its terms. It was too much for her to resist any more.

"I have been offered the post of organist at Versailles," Wolfgang told her, coming in later when the Heinas had settled her gently on the chaise, "but I shall not take it, Mama. France is not for me. I will be lucky to leave here with any taste at all. Papa says I must write in the popular way, but I do not really care if the Parisians like my compositions. *I* like them, and that is enough. I know, I know, Papa would say that I can dine on my own approval, but still . . . ."

To Anna it seemed that Wolfgang spoke from a great distance. She felt herself eddying, like a leaf caught in the slow whirl of water at the river's edge, while beyond, a swift river plunged downward, pulling at her. She knew that she would soon be swept out into its relentless surge. Before the current seized her, she must explain to Wolfgang.

"Listen to me," she said. "It is a long way to Salzburg. Raaff will help you in Munich, as will Herr Albert and all the others. Watch out for . . . ."

Wolfgang stared at her in consternation. He could hardly make out what she said. What was wrong? He had thought, with the attention of Raaff and the Heinas, that her health was amending. She had, after all, walked out only a few hours earlier.

"I have no money," said Anna, struggling to speak, though Wolfgang could make out only a word or two. "Nothing to leave you and Nannerl. I brought nothing more to my marriage than my voice, to which you are welcome, though it has long been silent . . . ." Wolfgang will sing for us all, she thought, but only if he sings for himself.

Wolfgang heard "voice," but did not know what she meant. She is delirious, he thought, and held her hand. "All will be well, Mama," he tried to reassure her, but he felt fear rise to choke him, a whirling apprehension. What should he do? What would he tell Papa if Mama was really ill? What if she should die?

He sent one of the Baron's servants after Frau Heina, who sent first for a German doctor, and then, seeing how truly ill Anna was, a German priest. Anna felt their ministrations as if from a great height. She could not confess her sins. They were too complicated and she too weak. In any case, she knew that her soul was destined for torment. It was not what rites she observed, but what she had intended, and her intention had been to deceive, to undermine, to separate. The pain had gone. She was numb, though she could feel that Wolfgang held her hand in his cool, supple fingers. Anna drifted and felt that she hovered over the *Tanzmeisterhaus* in the clear July sunlight. She smelled the wisteria in the gardens at Mirabell. There was Leopold, coming from court, smaller, older, more frail than she remembered, and there was Nannerl, walking with her dog.

Josef Heina came to sit with Wolfgang, who hardly knew his mother. She seemed to have left her body behind, though the waxen form on the bed still breathed. Wolfgang reached out to touch his mother's hair, which straggled over the pillow, thinking to tidy it up, but she stirred and he pulled his hand away.

Tears prickled at the rims of his eyes and spilled over. "Mama?" he whispered, his lips near her ear. "Oh Mama, please do not leave me."

Anna drifted with the clouds that cast their moving shadows over the gleaned fields below. Occasionally where the sun broke through, the wheat and oats lit up like gold. She saw the Wolfgangsee and the trees that bloomed at the lake's edge. Apricot trees. There was something about apricot blooms . . . .

Anna could no longer hear her son's voice.

AFTERWORD

ANNA LEFT NO LEGACY EXCEPT HER CHILDREN. Although much has been written about Leopold's influence on Wolfgang, his mother has been dismissed by biographers as inconsequential. The record of her life exists as the slenderest, most brittle of threads. This story is much like a darn, which casts new threads over a hole in fabric, then weaves a whole cloth anchored in the original. Fact and fiction are knit together to tell the story of the remarkable and beloved composer's mother, who may have been as remarkable in her way as her son was in his.

All that is known of Anna's first four years is recorded in St. Gilgen's parish records. Anna's mother was the daughter of a Salzburg court musician. Before she married Wolfgang Nicolaus Pertl, who had earned his living as a musician in Salzburg before taking up administrative duties, she had been married to and widowed by a man named Altman. Wolfgang Nicolaus did die when Anna was four, though not necessarily after being thrown from his horse. He left Eva Rosina, Gertrud and Anna impoverished and the Archbishop collected his household goods for the payment of debts. When the Archbishop tried to collect more from his St. Gilgen creditors, they rose up in protest.

That the sisters lived at Nonnberg is entirely fictional. After Wolfgang Nicolaus' death, Eva Rosina and her two young daughters moved to Salzburg, where Gertrud did die at the age of nine, though the cause of her death is unknown. Gertrud and Anna are sent to Nonnberg in this story so that

Anna can plausibly continue to study music and, later on, compose the real Pertl Chamber Symphonies. Nonnberg - or nuns' mountain - is a real Benedictine convent, founded in the eighth century on the rock face under the cliff on which the castle fortress of Salzburg stands. Nonnberg was and continues to be an enclosed convent with habited nuns dedicated to the preservation of the arts.

Some readers have wondered whether the nuns of Nonnberg would have been, historically, as feminist in their views as Sisters Gisella, Emma and the others. There is no way to know about these particular nuns, who are fictional, but convents had always provided smart, gifted and independent women the opportunity to exercise the full range of their talents - a reality that often perturbed church fathers. Convents were also places to park unwanted daughters, widows and the like. The eighteenth century, also called the Age of Enlightenment, went out of its way to repress women and to make the point that Nature had decreed their inferiority. There would not likely have been such ardent declarations of women's inferiority had women not been staking out claims for greater opportunity and recognition.

In 1710, a decade before Anna's birth, the English essayist Richard Steele wrote, "A woman is a daughter, a sister, a wife and a mother, a mere appendage to the human race." This was the view of most of the men who governed Anna's life. Fathers Kramer and Spenger in their *Malleus Malefacorum* had expressed rabid fifteenth-century misogyny as the basis for the persecution of accused witches, which was more virulent in what we now call Austria than anywhere else in Europe. All but one instance of witchcraft mentioned are real: the case in which Wolf Nicolaus involves himself is fiction. Montague Summers, in his *Geography of Witchcraft*, says that the last official witchcraft trial in Germany took place in 1775, just three years before Anna's death.

Catholic hatred of women, however, had been surpassed during the Reformation by the rampaging Protestants, who tore down images of Madonna and Child because it seemed to them improper to show the Son of God under the power of a woman. Enlightenment thinkers, though they endorsed the Rights of Man, were aware that someone had to darn Man's socks and cook his dinner, tasks they thought women were Endowed by their Creator with the unalienable obligation to perform.

There is some evidence that Anna Pertl Mozart was a musician, though it is slight.

On December 14, 1774 Leopold wrote to Anna from Munich. "Please look up the two Litanies *De Venerabili Altaris Sacramento*, which are performed in the Hours. There is one of mine in D major (the score will surely be with it), a recent one which begins with the violin and double bass staccato (you know the one I mean); at the Agnus Dei the second violin has triplet notes the whole time. Then you will find Wolfgang's great Litany. The score is with it, bound in blue paper. Make quite sure that all the parts are there . . . ." Leopold is certain that Anna can read music, which would hardly be the case unless she were a musician.

Most of Anna's and Nannerl's letters were not saved. To some extent, their contents can be inferred from Leopold's and Wolfgang's responses. On October 6, 1770, Leopold wrote from Bologna. "So you have had three concerts?" Wolfgang added, "I hope that I shall soon hear those Pertl chamber symphonies." Pertl was Anna's maiden name. There is no evidence that Anna, if indeed she composed these works, did so while her family were in Munich.

The facts of Leopold's early life are accurate, but amplified by fiction. The reason for Leopold's sudden decision to abandon his academic studies, in which he had so recently excelled, is an invention, as is the letter from his brother remonstrating about Leopold's leaving his university studies. Leopold's views on music come, in part, from his delightful treatise on how to play the violin.

Some of the Mozart friends are historically real: many of Anna's friends are fictional. Marianna and Wenzel Gilowsky were good friends of the Mozarts, and the Gilowsky children, Katharina (Kathryl) and Franz Xaver, were close in age to the Mozart children. Nannerl and Kathryl were fast friends in adulthood. Lorenz Hagenauer was a prosperous merchant who also served as Leopold's banker and sometime financial supporter of the Mozart concert tours. Margarethe Arnstein is fiction, though information about attitudes toward and treatment of Jews is historically accurate. The proscriptions of Jews' purchasing foodstuffs before certain hours were found in *The Encyclopaedia Britannica*, 1941 edition. Peter Clive's *Mozart and His Circle* provides invaluable information about historical characters.

It is true that Leopold petitioned his mother for money and traveled to Augsburg to make arrangements with Lotter to publish the *Violinschule*. Otto Erich Deutsch, in *Mozart: A Documentary Biography*, includes excerpts from four letters from Leopold to Lotter. On October 15, 1755 he wrote, "I hope that your dear wife is meanwhile happily delivered of her burden . . . . My own dear one sends the same sincere wish; about the end of January she has the same task before her." On January 26, 1756 he wrote, "My wife will soon be starting her journey." On February 9, 1756 Leopold wrote to Lotter, " . . . . I must inform [you] that on 27 January, at 8 p.m., my dear wife was happily delivered of a boy; but the placenta had to be removed. She was therefore astonishingly weak. Now, however (God be praised) both child and mother are well. She sends her regards to you both. The boy is called Joannes Chrisostomos Wolfgang Gottlieb." On February 12 he wrote, " . . . . I can assure you, I have so much to do that I sometimes do not know where my head is. Not, to be sure, because of composition, but because of the many pupils and the operas at Court. And you know as well as I do that, when the wife is in childbed, there is always somebody turning up to rob you of time. Things like that cost money and time." Later on, when he was engaged in a campaign of nearly constant reproach during Wolfgang's and Anna's journey to Paris, Leopold complained of the costs of supporting seven children (though five did not live to see their first year) and his mother-in-law.

There is little reliable information about the early years of the Mozart children. Nannerl told some stories to the trumpeter Andreas Schactner - stories which are often repeated in biographies. But Nannerl's accounts may have been part of the joint project with her father to make Wolfgang into a mythic figure, perhaps, in part, justification for the fact that her own artistry, highly praised in reviews during the long European tour, had had to take second place to her brother's. Nannerl's public performance ended when she was eighteen, though she apparently composed, accompanied her father and his music-making friends, and gave piano lessons.

As a child Nannerl did have a music notebook, which is attributed to Leopold, who is said to have been her teacher. Leopold did use the pages of Nannerl's notebook to record his son's early feats of mastery, as well as some of the early compositions attributed to the little boy. Some pages have been torn out: it is presumed that Nannerl as an old woman gave them to some of the Mozart worshippers who visited her as keeper of the shrine. Nannerl's compositions, mentioned in some of the adult correspondence, have not survived.

The story of Leopold's published lampoon and his public punishment is true, though the nature of the scandal is invented. At first glance this event seems out of character, since Leopold was always careful of his reputation. But it is consistent with his extraordinary enthusiasms and his outbursts of nearly hysterical suspicion and blame, as expressed in his revealing correspondence.

When the Mozarts first traveled to Vienna, Leopold began the lavish and fascinating documentation of the many journeys they took in various family combinations. His letters are prolific and interesting. But he was not only biased and partial in both reporting and advising: he also expected his letters to be read by others than the recipients. His letters are as rhetorical as informative, being designed to promote his son's reputation and fortunes. There is frequent evidence in the letters of Leopold's habit of exaggerating, distorting, even lying. Maynard Solomon's *Mozart* does more to elucidate these habits than most of Mozart's biographies.

Pietro Loronzoni is thought to have painted three of the individual portraits of the Mozart family. Ruth Halliwell, author of *Mozart's Family* – an elaborate defense of Leopold's good name – believes that Anna's was painted by Rosa Hagenauer-Barducci, an Italian portrait painter married to Johann Baptist Hagenauer, son of Theresa and Lorenz Hagenauer. The timing of these portraits and the hands painted therein suggest a family drama. A period of ten years intervened between the Loronzoni portraits of Leopold, Wolfgang and Nannerl and the Hagenauer-Barducci portrait of Anna. The first three were painted after the first Vienna trip, in 1765. Anna's picture was painted not long before her doomed journey to Paris. It was customary for artists to charge by the hand, the painting of which was deemed to be difficult. In Nannerl's picture, four of her fingers show; the other hand is off the canvas. Wolfgang is shown with one fist and one finger, the other hand tucked in his waistcoat. The tips of five of Leopold's fingers show over the top of a book. His other hand hides under a clumsily placed cloth. But both of Anna's hands are pictured holding a length of lace, an interesting expense given Leopold's obsession with earning and saving money. Perhaps he was trying to make it up to his wife, whom he would not take to St. Gilgen, let alone Italy or Munich. Since the tools of a figure's trade are often pictured, it might be surmised that Anna was a lace maker. The lavender suit in which Wolfgang is painted was the gift of the Empress Maria Theresa, but Nannerl's body came ready-painted, as was the custom.

A family portrait, painted after Anna's death, shows Leopold with his violin leaning on the top of a harpsichord, while Nannerl and Wolfgang play four hands. Anna is represented by a copy of her earlier portrait hanging in an oval frame over the harpsichord.

Leopold did, at some point, choose Wolfgang as *the* Mozart genius. He pronounced him a miracle sent to the Earth by God. Nicholas Till, in *Mozart and the Enlightenment*, explains the view of Enlightenment thinkers, of whom Leopold was one, that contracts between equal and consenting parties were crucial: it is the view that underlies American political theory, that good government is possible only when the governed consent to it. According to Till, a vow made to a deity, who was not a contracting party, was seen as an illegitimate contract. The vow that Leopold takes in Anna's presence is an invention. It expresses that part of Leopold's personality given to irrational impulses, both enthusiastic and suspicious.

There is evidence that relations between Leopold and his mother were strained. The drama that Anna stirs up with the old lady is invented, and there is no record that Leopold went to see his mother as they returned from their three-year tour of Europe and England, though she did die soon thereafter. Augsburg's Catholics were not eager to hear the Mozart children - nor were they hospitable to Wolfgang in 1777.

Leopold's procedures for attracting attention in each new town are well documented. Most of the facts of the long tour are historically accurate, though they have been fleshed out from Anna's point-of-view.

Nannerl's prospects in Holland, both romantically and musically, are invented. The family was invited by the Count van Weldeeren to visit the Netherlands, and Nannerl did urge their going. She nearly died of typhoid, which prevented her performing. Wolfgang contracted the disease as well, though he was less seriously afflicted.

Leopold wrote to Lorenz Hagenauer on January 23, 1768, "I shall only say that you cannot possibly conceive with what familiarity Her Majesty the Empress conversed with my wife, talking to her partly of my children's smallpox and partly of the events of our grand tour; nor can you imagine how she stroked my wife's cheeks and pressed her hands. Meanwhile His Majesty the Emperor talked to little Wolfgang and to me about music, and many other things too, which often made Nannerl blush." Joseph II's fictitious proposition to Nannerl derives from this comment. Leopold's reaction to a letter from the Salzburg Court, terminating his salary, is based upon his fulminations in a letter to Hagenauer.

Wolfgang composed the Dominicus Mass for his friend, Cajetan Hagenauer, who became Father Dominicus; Joseph von Mölk did pursue Nannerl; and Nannerl did have a fruitless romantic association with Armand d'Ippold, though in fact this romance did not end until after Anna's death.

There is no reason to suppose that Nannerl considered the life of a nun - nor any to suppose that she did not. Her journal shows her as religiously observant in a relentless, almost mechanical way. In fact, her journal suggests a rather dull life of going to church, having her hair done, attending to household tasks, walking the dog and making music.

During Anna's fatal last journey, the correspondence between Leopold and Wolfgang also represent a struggle for control of Wolfgang's life and career. The letters are a battleground as much as they are a source of news.

The church register of St. Eustache in Paris records "On the said day [July 4, 1778] Marie-Anne Pertl, aged 57 years, wife of Leopold Mozart, *maitre de chapelle* at Salzburg, Bavaria, who died yesterday at Rue du Groschenet, has been interred in the cemetery in the presence of Wolfgang Amédée Mozart, her son, and of François Heina, trumpeter in the light cavalry in the Royal Guard, a friend." The entry was signed by Wolfgang, Heina and the vicar.

Wolfgang wrote the news of his mother's death to a family friend, Abbé Bullinger, reporting to his father and sister only that Anna was very ill. He wrote the truth of his mother's death to Leopold and Nannerl a week later. Wolfgang was right to be nervous: Leopold wrote angry letters blaming his son for Anna's death and insisting that the young man return to Salzburg forthwith.

As slowly as he could contrive, Wolfgang traveled toward Salzburg, where he spent two years earning enough money to repay his father what he had spent on his journey. He broke with the Archbishop while with his prince's entourage in Vienna. There he settled beyond his father's reach. He established himself as a free-lance musician in a city bursting with musical excitement, where he was a popular and well paid composer and performer. He married Constanze Weber, Aloisha's sister, over the objections of Leopold. Constanze gave birth to six children, only two of whom survived into adulthood. Wolfgang made several short forays to other cities and one return visit to Salzburg during his lifetime, but he found the intellectual and political ideas of the Enlightenment in Vienna - and the distance from his father - much to his taste.

Leopold, with whom Wolfgang's relations became more and more strained, died in Salzburg on May 28, 1787.

Nannerl disliked Constanze and shared her father's estrangement from - and abounding pride in - her brother, who inherited none of the money he had earned as a child prodigy, nor any of the snuffboxes, rings or other costly trinkets he had been given. Before Leopold died, Nannerl married Johann Baptist zu Sonnenburg, a widower and father of five, who held the same position that Wolfgang Nicolaus Pertl, her maternal grandfather, had held. Thus Nannerl lived in the same house in St. Gilgen that Anna's father had built and in which Anna was born. Nannerl had three children, of whom only the eldest, a boy named Leopold, survived childhood.

There was, near the end of Wolfgang's life, a period of inexplicable poverty, which has become the center of Mozart legend. His fortunes had begun to mend when, on December 5, 1791, he died of kidney failure at the age of 36.

Constanze, who lived until the mid-nineteenth century, made canny use of Mozart's manuscripts, the sale of which supported her and her two sons. She married a Danish diplomat, Georg Nissen, and together they produced one of the early biographies of Wolfgang Mozart.

After her husband's death in 1801, Nannerl moved back to Salzburg, where she earned her living as a piano teacher until she lost her eyesight. Nannerl, the last vestige of Anna's legacy, died on October 29, 1829.

References Consulted

ANDERSON, BONNIE S. AND JUDITH P. ZINSSER. *A History of Their Own: Women in Europe from Prehistory to the Present*, 2 vols. New York: Harper and Row, 1988.

ANDERSON, EMILY, ed. *The Letters of Mozart and His Family*, third edition NY: Norton and Co., 1966.

ARIES, PHILIPPE. *Centuries of Childhood: A Social History of Family Life*, trans. Robert Baldick. New York: Alfred A. Knopf, 1962.

AUSTIN, STANLEY. *The History of Engraving*. London: T. Werner Laurie, no date.

BADINTER, ELISABETH. *Mother Love: Myth and Reality: Motherhood in Modern History*. New York: Macmillan Publishing Co., 1981.

BATTERSBY, CHRISTINE. *Gender and Genius: Towards a Feminist Aesthetics*. Bloomington: Indiana University Press, 1989.

BELENKY, MARY FIELD, ET.AL. *Women's Ways of Knowing: The Development of Self, Voice, and Mind*. New York: Basic Books, Inc. 1986.

BERNIER, OLIVE. *The Eighteenth Century Woman*. Garden City, NY: Doubleday and Co., Inc., 1981.

BLUM, STELLA, ed. *Eighteenth-Century French Fashion Plates in Full Color: 64 Engravings from the "Galerie des Modes," 1778-1787*. New York: Dover Publications, 1982.

BOWERS, JANE AND JUDITH TICK. *Women Making Music: The Western Art Tradition, 1150-1950*. Urbana: University of Illinois Press, 1987.

BRAUNBEHRENS, VOLKMAR. *Mozart in Vienna, 1781-1791*, trans. Timothy Bell. New York, Harper Perennial, 1991.

BRAUDEL, FERNAND. *Civilization and Capitalism: 15th - 18th Century*, 3 vols., trans. Sian Reynolds. New York: Harper and Row, 1979.

BRODZKI, BELLA AND CELESTE SCHENCK, eds. *Life/Lines: Theorizing Women's Autobiography*. Ithaca, NY: Cornell University Press, 1988.

BROWN, LYN MIKEL AND CAROL GILLIGAN. *Meeting at the Crossroads: Women's Psychology and Girls' Development*. Cambridge: Harvard University Press, 1992.

BRUFORD, W.H. *Germany in the Eighteenth Century: The Social Background of the Literary Revival*. Cambridge: Cambridge University Press, 1965.

BUTLER, E.C. *Benedictine Monachism: Studies in Benedictine Life and Rule*. New York: Longmans, Green and Co., 1924.

Cambridge World History of Human Disease, ed. Kenneth F. Kiple. Cambridge: Cambridge University Press, 1993.

CHERUBINI, RALPH. *Leopold Mozart's Violinschule As a Guide to the Performance of W.A. Mozart's Sonatas for Piano and Violin*, Ph.D. Thesis, Case Western Reserve University, August 25, 1976.

CLIVE, PETER. *Mozart and His Circle: A Biographical Dictionary*. New Have, CT: Yale University Press, 1993.

CHODOROW, NANCY. *The Reproduction of Mothering: Psychoanalysis and the Sociology of Gender*. Berkeley: University of California Press, 1978.

COOPER, ROBYN. "Alexander Walker's Trilogy on Women," *Forbidden History: The State, Society, and the Regulation of Sexuality in Modern Europe*, ed. John C. Font. Chicago: Chicago University Press, 1991.

CRAGG, GERALD R. *The Church and the Age of Reason: 1648-1789*. New York: Atheneum, 1961.

CRANKSHAW, EDWARD. *Maria Theresa*. New York: Viking Press, 1969.

DAVIS, NATALIE ZEMON AND ARLETTE FARGE, eds. *A History of Women in the West: Renaissance and Enlightenment Paradoxes*. Cambridge, MA: The Belknap Press of Harvard University Press, 1993.

DAVENPORT, MARCIA. *Mozart*. New York: Charles Scribner's Sons, 1960.

DAVIES, PETER J. *Mozart in Person: His Character and Health*. New York: Greenwood Press, 1989.

DEMAUSE, LLOYD, ed. *The History of Childhood*. New York: Psychohistory Press, 1974.

DEUTSCH, OTTO ERICH. *Mozart: A Documentary Biography*. Stanford: Stanford University Press, 1965.

DUNDES, ALAN. *Life is Like a Chicken Coop Ladder: A Portrait of German Culture Through Folklore*. New York: Columbia University Press, 1984.

DURANT, WILL AND ARIEL. *The Story of Civilization: The Age of Voltaire IX*. New York: Simon and Schuster, 1965.

ECKENSTEIN, LINA. *Woman Under Monasticism*. Cambridge: University Press, 1896.

EINSTEIN, ALFRED. *Mozart: His Character, His Work*. New York: Oxford University Press, 1945.

EISEN, CLIFF, ed. *Mozart Studies*. Oxford; Clarendon Press, 1991.

EISEN, CLIFF. *New Mozart Documents: A Supplement to E.O Deutsch's Documentary Biography*. Stanford: Stanford University Press, 1991.

Encyclopaedia Judaica. Jerusalem: Keter Publishing House, 1972.

ERIKSON, ERIK H. *Childhood and Society*, second edition. New York: W.W. Norton and Co., 1963.

FILDES, VALERIE, ed. *Women as Mothers in Pre-Industrial England*. London: Routledge, 1990.

FLANDRIN, JEAN-LOUIS. *Families in Former Times: Kinship, Household and Sexuality*, trans. Richard Southern. Cambridge: Cambridge University Press, 1979.

FUHRMANN, BRIGITA. *Bobbin Lace: An Illustrated Guide to Traditional and Contemporary Techniques*. New York: Dover Publications, Inc., 1976.

FUX, JOHANN JOSEPH. *The Study of Counterpoint from Gradus ad Parnassum*, trans. and ed., Alfred Mann. New York: W.W. Norton & Co., 1971.

GAMBLE, WILLIAM. *Music Engraving and Printing*. London: Sir Isaac Pitman and Sons, Ltd., 1923.

GEORGE, M. DOROTHY. *London Life in the 18th Century*. New York: Capricorn Books, 1965.

GILLIGAN, CAROL. *In a Different Voice: Psychological Theory and Women's Development*. Cambridge: Harvard University Press, 1982.

GILLIGAN, CAROL, NONA P. LYONS AND TRUDY J. HANMER. *Making Connections*. Cambridge, MA: Harvard University Press, 1990.

GILLIGAN, CAROL AND JANE ATTANUCHI. "Two Moral Orientations: Gender Differences and Similariaties," *Merrill-Palmer Quarterly*, XXXIV, July 1988.

GLASER, JOSEF AND HEINZ GLASER. *A Guide to Schönbrunn*. Oesterreichische Staatdruckerei, 1966.

GOTTLIEB, BEATRICE. *The Family in the Western World from the Black Death to the Industrial Age*. New York: Oxford University Press, 1993.

GOULD, CAROL C., ed. *Beyond Domination*. Totowa, NJ: Rowman and Allenheld, 1983.

HEILBRUN, CAROLYN G. *Hamlet's Mother and Other Women*. New York: Ballentine Books, 1990.

HEILBRUN, CAROLYN G. *Reinventing Womanhood*. New York: W.W. Norton and Co, 1979.

HEILBRUN, CAROLYN G. *Writing a Woman's Life*. New York: Ballentine Books, 1988.

HILDESHEIMER, WOLFGANG. *Mozart*. New York: Vintage Books, 1983.

HILPISCH, STEPHANUS. *History of Benedictine Nuns*. Collegeville, MN: St. John's Abbey Press, 1958.

Holy Bible. Douai-Rheims Trans (1610). Rockford, Ill: Tan Books, 1971.

HUNT, DAVID. *Parents and Children in History: The Psychology of Family Life in Early Modern France*. New York: Basic Books, 1970.

JAGGAR, ALISON. *Feminist Politics and Human Nature*. Totowa, NJ: Rowman and Allanheld, 1983.

JAHN, OTTO. *The Life of Mozart*, 3 vols. New York: Edwin F. Kalmus, 1882.

JOERES, RUTH ELLEN AND MARY JO MAYNES, eds. *German Women in the Eighteenth and Nineteenth Centuries: A Social and Literary History.* Bloomington, IN: Indiana Univeristy Press, 1986.

JONES, VIVIEN, ed. *Women in the Eighteenth Century: Constructions of Femininity*. London: Routledge, 1990.

KELLER, EVELYN FOX. *Reflections on Gender and Science.* New Haven: Yale University Press, 1985.

KEYSLER, JOHN GEORGE. *Travels Through Germany, Hungary, Bohemia, Switzerland, Italy and Lorraine Containing an accurate Description of the Present State and Curiosities of Those Countries.* London: J. Scott, 1758.

KISHLANASKY, MARK, PATRICK GEARY, AND PATRICIA O'BRIEN. *Civilization in the West, Volume II.* New York: Harper Collins Publishers, 1991.

KNAPP, VINCENT J. *Europe in the Era of Social Transformation: 1700-Present.* Englewood Cliffs, NJ: Prentice-Hall, Inc. 1976.

KNEPLER, GEORG. *Wolfgang Amadé Mozart*, trans. J. Bradford Robinson. Cambridge: Cambridge University Press, 1994.

KRUMMEL, D.W. AND STANLEY SADIE, eds. *Music Printing and Publishing* (The Norton/Grove Handbooks in Music). New York: W.W. Norton and Co., 1990.

KÜNG, HANS. *Mozart; Traces of Transcendence.* Grand Rapids, MI: William B. Eerdmans Publishing Company, 1993.

LANDON, H.C. ROBBINS. *Mozart: The Golden Years, 1781-1791.* New York: Schirmer Books, 1989.

LANDON, H.C. ROBBINS. *The Mozart Compendium: A Guide to Mozart's Life and Music.* New York: Schirmer Books, 1990.

LANDON, H.C. ROBBINS. *The Mozart Essays.* New York: Thames & Hudson, 1995.

LANDON, H.C. ROBBINS. *1791: Mozart's Last Year.* New York: Schirmer Books, 1988.

LASLETT, PETER. "Characteristics of the Western Family Considered over Time," *Journal of Family History,* II, Number 2, Summer 1977.

LECHEVALLIER-CHEVIGNARD, EDMOND. *European Costume of the Sixteenth Through Eighteenth Centures.* New York: Dover Publications, Inc. 1995.

LEPPERT, RICHARD AND SUSAN MCCLARY. *Music and Society: The Politics of Composition, Performance and Reception.* Cambridge: Cambridge University Press, 1987.

LEVACK, BRIAN P. *The Witch-Hunt in Early Modern Europe.* London: Longman, 1987.

LINDERMANN, MARY. "Love for Hire: The Regulation of the Wet-Nursing Business in Eighteenth-Century Hamburg," *Journal of Family History,* VI Number 4, 1981.

LINDERMANN, MARY. "Maternal Politics; The Principles and Practice of Maternity Care in Eighteenth-Century Hamburg," *Journal of Family History,* IX, Number 1, Spring, 1984.

LOESSER, ARTHUR. *Men, Women and Pianos: A Social History.* New York: Simon and Schuster, 1954.

LORENCE, BOGNA W., "Parents and Children in Eighteenth-Century Europe," *History of Childhood Quarter: The Journal of Psychohistory,* II, Number 1, Summer 1974.

MACARTNEY, C.A. *Maria Theresa and the House of Austria*. London: The English Universities Press, Ltd., 1969.

MACE, THOMAS. *Musick's Monument.* (Facsimile of 1676 London edition.) New York: Broude Brothers, 1966.

MARSHALL, ROBERT L. "What if Mozart Had Lived a Longer Life?" *The New York Times*, January 26, 1992.

MAY, ROLLO. *The Courage to Create*. New York: W.W. Norton & Co., 1975.

MCCLARY, SUSAN. *Feminine Endings: Music, Gender, and Sexuality*. Minneapolis: University of Minnesota Press, 1991.

MCDONALD, MARGARET READ, ed. *The Folklore of World Holidays*. Detroit: Gale Research Inc, 1991.

MCGILL, JR., WILLIAM. *Maria Theresa*. New York: Twayne Publishers, Inc., 1972.

MCVEIGH, SIMON. *Concert Life in London from Mozart to Haydn*. Cambridge: Cambridge University Press, 1993.

MEDICK, HANS AND DAVID WARREN SABEAN, eds. *Interest and Emotion: Essays on the Study of Family and Kinship*. Cambridge: Cambridge University Press, 1984.

MIEDER, WOLFGANG, ed. *The Prentice-Hall Encyclopedia of World Proverbs*. Englewood Cliffs, NJ: Prentice-Hall, Inc., 1986.

MELLERS, WILFRID. "Little Time to Spare: What More Could Mozart Possibly Have Accomplished?" *The Atlantic*, January 1992.

MILLER, GENEVIEVE. *The Adoption of Inoculation for Smallpox in England and France*. Philadelphia: University of Pennsylvania Press, 1957.

MILLER, JEAN BAKER, ed. *Psychoanalysis and Women.* New York: Penguin Books, 1973.

MILLER, JEAN BAKER. *Toward a New Psychology of Women*, 2nd edition. Boston: Beacon Press, 1986.

MITCHELL, JULIET AND ANN OAKLEY, eds. *What is Feminism: A Re-Examination*. New York: Pantheon Books, 1986.

MITTERAUER, MICHAEL AND REINHARD SIEDER. *The European Family: Patriarchy to Partnership from the Middle Ages to the Present*. Chicago: University of Chicago Press, 1982.

MÖBIUS, HELGA. *Women of the Baroque Age*. Montclair, NJ: Abner Schram, 1984.

MONSON, CRAIG A. *The Crannied Wall: Women, Religion, and the Arts in Early Modern Europe*. Ann Arbor: University of Michigan Press, 1992.

MORROW, MARY SUE. *Concert Life in Haydn's Vienna: Aspects of a Developing Musical and Social Institution*. Stuyvesant, NY: Pendragon Press, 1989.

MOZART, LEOPOLD. *Nannerl Notenbuch*. München: Hermann Rinn, 1956.

MOZART, LEOPOLD. *A Treatise on the Fundamental Principles of Violin Playing*, trans. Editha Knocker. Oxford; Oxford University Press, 1988.

MOZART, LEOPOLD. *Gründliche Violinschule* (facsimile). Augsburg: Jakob Lotter und Sohn, 1787.

NIEMETSCHEK, FRANZ. *Life of Mozart,* trans. Helen Mautner. London: Leonard Hyman, 1956. First published 1798.

NORMAN, MARIE. "Kathe Kollwitz and the Issue of Greatness in Art," unpublished paper, 1987.

OCHSE, R. *Before the Gates of Excellence: The Determinants of Creative Genius*. Cambridge: Cambridge University Press, 1990.

OKIN, SUSAN MOLLER. *Women in Western Political Thought*. Princeton: Princeton University Press, 1979.

OSTWALD, PETER. "Updating Mozart's Medical History," *Halcyon: A Journal of the Humanities*, University of Nevada Press, 1993.

PALMER, R.R. AND JOEL COLTON. *A History of the Modern World*. New York: Alfred A. Knopf, 1965.

PAUMGARTNER, BERNHARD. *Mozart*. Zurich: Atlantic Verlag, 1945.

PENDLE, KARIN, ed. *Women and Music: A History*. Bloomington, IN: Indiana University Press, 1991.

PERRY, RUTH AND MARTINE WATSON BROWNLEY, eds. *Mothering the Mind: Twelve Studies of Writers and Their Silent Partners*. New York: Holmes and Meier, 1984.

RATNER, LEONARD G. *Classical Music: Expression, Form, and Style*. New York: Schirmer Books, 1980.

REITER, RAYNA R., ed., *Toward an Anthropology of Women*. New York: Monthly Review Press, 1975.

RICCI, JAMES V. *The Geneology of Gynaecology*. Philadelphia: The Blakiston Co., 1943.

RICH, ADRIENNE. *Of Woman Born: Motherhood as Experience and Institution*. New York: Bantam Books, 1977.

RILEY, JAMES C. *The Eighteenth Century Campaign to Avoid Disease*. New York: Macmillan Press, Ltd. 1987.

ROCHE, DANIEL. *The People of Paris; An Essay in Popular Culture in the 18th Century*, trans. Marie Evans. Leamington Spa: Berg Publishers Ltd., 1987.

RUDDICK, SARA. *Maternal Thinking: Toward a Politics of Peace*. Boston: Beacon Press, 1989.

RUDDICK, SARA AND PAMELA DANIELS, eds. *Working It Out.* New York: Pantheon, 1977.

SADIE, JULIE ANNE AND RHIAN SAMUEL. *The Norton/Grove Dictionary of Women Composers*. New York: W.W. Norton & Company, 1995.

SADIE, STANLEY, ed. *The New Grove Dictionary of Music and Musicians.* New York: Macmillan, 1980.

SADIE, STANLEY. *The New Grove Mozart.* New York: W.W. Norton and Co., 1982.

SAINT BENEDICT. *The Rule of St. Benedict in English*, ed. Timothy Fry, O.S.B. Collegeville, MN: The Liturgical Press, 1982.

SCHENK, ERICH. *Mozart and His Times*, trans. Richard and Clara Winston. New York: Alfred A. Knopf, 1959.

SCHNEIDER, OTTO. *Mozart-Handbuch.* Vien: Verlag Brüder Hollinek, 1962.

SCHULER, HEINZ. "Wolfgang Amadeus: Ancestors and Relatives," *Genealogie und Landesgeschichte*, Vol. 34. Neustadt/Aisch: Degner, 1980.

SCHWERIN, ERNA. "Anna Marie Mozart: A Profile," *Mozart Society Newsletter*, #3, Fall, 1984.

SCOTT, JOAN WALLACH. *Gender and the Politics of History*. New York: Columbia University Press, 1988.

SHORTER, EDWARD. *A History of Women's Bodies*. New York: Basic Books, Inc. 1982.

SHORTER, EDWARD. *The Making of the Modern Family*. New York: Basic Books, 1975.

SHURKIN, JOEL N. *The Invisible Fire: The Story of Mankind's Victory Over The Ancient Scourge of Smallpox*. New York: G.P. Putnam's Sons, 1979.

SLATER, MIRIAM. *Family Life in the Seventeenth Century: The Verneys of Claydon House*. London: Routledge and Kegan Paul, 1984.

SMITH, J.R. *The Speckled Monster: Smallpox in England, 1670-1970, with Particular Reference to Essex*. Chelmsford: Essex Record Office, 1987.

SOLOMON, MAYNARD. *Mozart: A Life*. New York: Harper Collins, 1995.

SPELMAN, V. ELIZABETH. *Inessential Woman*. Boston: Beacon Press, 1988.

STAFFORD, WILLIAM. *The Mozart Myths: A Critical Reassessment*. Stanford: Stanford University Press, 1991.

STEARNS, PETER. *European Society in Upheaval: Social History Since 1750*. New York: Macmillan, 1975.

STERNBERG, ROBERT J. AND JANET E. DAVIDSON, eds. *Conceptions of Giftedness*. Cambridge: Cambridge University Press, 1986.

STOTT, GERALDINE. *The Bobbin Lace Manual*. New York: Dover Publications, Inc., 1988.

SUMMERS, MONTAGUE. *The Geography of Witchcraft*. Evanston: University Books, 1958.

SUMMERS, MONTAGUE, trans. and ed., *The Malleus Maleficarum of Heinrich Kramer and James Sprenger*. New York: Dover Publications, Inc. 1971.

TANNEN, DEBORAH. *You Just Don't Understand: Women and Men in Conversation*. New York: Ballentine Books, 1990.

THORNE, BARRIE, ed. *Rethinking the Family: Some Feminist Questions.* New York: Longman, 1982.

TILL, NICHOLAS. *Mozart and the Enlightenment; Truth, Virtue and Beauty in Mozart's Operas*. London: Faber and Faber, 1992.

ULRICH, LAUREL THATCHER. *A Midwife's Tale: The Life of Martha Ballard, Based on Her Diary, 1785-1812*. New York: Vintage Books, 1990.

VALENTIN, ERICH. *Mozart and His World.* New York: The Viking Press, 1959.

VAN ZELLER, HUBERT. *The Benedictine Nun*. Baltimore, MD: Helicon, 1965.

WANGERMANN, ERNST. *The Austrian Achievement: 1700-1800*. New York: Harcourt Brace Jovanovich, Inc., 1973.

WALTON, CRAIG. 'Mozart and the 'Madness' of Love," *Halcyon: A Journal of the Humanities*. University of Nevada Press, 1993.

WIESNER, MERRY E. "Nuns, Wives, and Mothers: Women and the Reformation in Germany," *Women in Reformation and Counter-Reformation Europe*, ed. Sherrin Marshall. Bloomington: Indiana University Press, 1989.

WIGNALL, HARRISON JAMES. *In Mozart's Footsteps*. New York: Paragon House, 1991.

WILLETT, C. AND PHYLLIS CUNNINGTON. *The History of Underclothes*. New York: Dover Publications, Inc., 1992.

WOYCKE, JAMES. *Birth Control in Germany: 1871-1933*. London: Routledge, 1988.

WOOLF, VIRGINIA. *A Room of One's Own*. New York: Harcourt, Brace and World, Inc., 1957.

WRIGHT, LAWRENCE. *Clean and Decent: The Fascinating History of the Bathroom and the Water Closet*. New York: Viking Press, 1906.

ZASLAW, NEAL, ed. *The Classical Era: From the 1740s to the End of the Eighteenth Century*. Englewood Cliffs, NJ: Prentiss Hall, 1989.

ZASLAW, NEAL, ed. *The Compleat Mozart: A Guide to the Musical Works of Wolfgang Amadeus Mozart*. New York: Mozart Bicentennial at Lincoln Center and W.W. Norton and Co., 1990.

ZASLAW, NEAL. *Mozart's Symphonies; Context, Performance Practice, Reception*. Oxford: Clarendon Press, 1989.

COLOPHON

This book was composed in
Adobe Caslon Expert and Adobe Caslon Regular
with drop caps in Beckett.

William Caslon released his first typefaces in 1722. Caslon's types were based on seventeenth-century Dutch old style designs, which were then used extensively in England. It was due to their incredible practicality that Caslon's designs met with instant success. Caslon's types became popular througout Europe and the American colonies; printer Benjamin Franklin hardly used any other typeface. The first printings of the American Declaration of Independence and the Constitution were set in Caslon.

Printed and bound by Thomson-Shore, Inc. of Dexter, Michigan
on 60# Glatfelter Writers Offset.

Designed by Todd Sanders

SMOKE AND
MIRRORS PRESS